Floch
st five
Lead
d *The*
cation
ation.

ks by
nrico

's, in

ty
gly

surprises the genre demands.' *Independent on Sunday*

'Jean-François Parot's evocation of eighteenth-century Paris is richly
imagined and full of fascinating historical snippets.' *Financial Times*

'Parot's clever plotting and sharp eye for detail are, as ever, first rate.'

THE
BAKER'S BLOOD

THE
BAKER'S BLOOD

JEAN-FRANÇOIS PAROT

Translated from the French by Howard Curtis

GALLIC BOOKS
London

Ouvrage publié avec le concours du Ministère français chargé de la Culture – Centre National du Livre.

This work is published with support from the French Ministry of Culture/Centre National du Livre.

A Gallic Book

First published in France as *Le sang des farines*
by éditions Jean-Claude Lattès
Copyright © éditions Jean-Claude Lattès 2005

English translation copyright © Gallic Books 2012
First published in Great Britain in 2012
by Gallic Books, 59 Ebury Street, London, SW1W 0NZ

A CIP record for this book is available from the British Library
ISBN 978-1-906040-36-9

Typeset in Fournier MT by Gallic Books
Printed in the UK by CPI (Croydon), CR0 4TD

2 4 6 8 10 9 7 5 3 1

For André and Théia Ross

CONTENTS

DRAMATIS PERSONAE

NICOLAS LE FLOCH: a police commissioner at the Châtelet

LOUIS LE FLOCH: his son, a schoolboy

MONSIEUR DE SARTINE: Secretary of State for the Navy

MONSIEUR LENOIR: Lieutenant General of Police in Paris

MONSIEUR ALBERT: his successor

PIERRE BOURDEAU: a police inspector

MONSIEUR DE SAINT-FLORENTIN, DUC DE LA VRILLIÈRE: Minister of the King's Household

COMTE DE VERGENNES: Minister of Foreign Affairs

BARON DE BRETEUIL: French Ambassador in Vienna

MONSIEUR TESTARD DU LYS: Criminal Lieutenant of Police

ABBÉ GEORGEL: Secretary of the French Embassy in Vienna

CHEVALIER DE LASTIRE: a lieutenant-colonel

JACQUES MOURUT: a master baker

CÉLESTE MOURUT: his wife

EULALIE, known as LA BABINE: their maid

HUGUES PARNAUX: an apprentice

DENIS CAMINET: an apprentice

ANNE FRIOPE: an apprentice

LE PRÉVOT DE BEAUMONT: former secretary to the Clergy of France

MATISSET: a former grain merchant

OLD MARIE: an usher at the Châtelet

TIREPOT: a police spy

RABOUINE: a police spy

AIMÉ DE NOBLECOURT: a former procurator

MARION: his cook

POITEVIN: his servant

CATHERINE GAUSS: a former canteen-keeper, Nicolas Le
  Floch's maid

GUILLAUME SEMACGUS: a navy surgeon

AWA: his cook

COMTE D'ARRANET: Lieutenant General of the Naval Forces

AIMÉE D'ARRANET: his daughter

TRIBORD: their major-domo

MONSIEUR DE GÉVIGLAND: a doctor

THIERRY DE VILLE D'AVRAY: First Groom of the King's
  Bedchamber

MONSIEUR DE LA BORDE: his predecessor, now Farmer
  General

CHARLES HENRI SANSON: the public executioner

NICOLAS RESTIF DE LA BRETONNE: a pamphleteer

MASTER VACHON: a tailor

JACQUES NIVERNAIS: a cobbler

JUSTIN BELHOME: archivist of the French East India Company

LA PAULET: a brothel-keeper

LA GOURDAN: a brothel-keeper

COLETTE: her maid

I

SECRECY

For all that fog now spread before your eyes
blurs your sight and raises thick vapours all around.

VIRGIL

Thursday 2 March 1775

Nicolas looked with astonishment at the accumulation of sarcophagi cluttering the floor of the Capuchin crypt. This grim tableau of metals, some rusty, others still bright, struck him as resembling a shipwreck. Lead, zinc and silver dominated, their blackened hues dappled in places by the blue-green light that came in through narrow openings. Everywhere were ghastly depictions of heads and bones, faded crowns and sceptres, and a damp odour of mildew and cold candles. It was a Capuchin monk, buried deep in his cowl, who had admitted him to the pantheon of the Habsburgs, an obligatory stop for all foreign visitors to Vienna. It was all very different, he thought, from the tomb of the Bourbons at Saint-Denis. Since the death of Louis XV, he had visited it twice, the first time alone, to pay his last respects to his master, and the second time accompanying Madame Adélaïde, who had wished to meditate before the small brick construction that contained her father's coffin. He had wandered down the long hall where the austere coffins of the princes lay decorously on iron trestles. There was a tranquil, domestic atmosphere about that august place, whereas here it was as if you were being observed by figures out of a nightmare, an impression made all the stronger by the haphazard manner in which the remains seemed to have been laid out. Leaning against a pillar, he recalled the events of the past few months. The successful outcome of his last investigation, in which he had extricated the Duc de La Vrillière, Minister of the King's Household, from a difficult situation, had returned him to Monsieur Lenoir's favour. There was now an atmosphere of complete trust and openness between him and the new Lieutenant General of Police.

At the beginning of the year, he had been given the task of accompanying Archduke Maximilian of Austria – who had travelled incognito under the name Count Burgau – from Brussels to Paris. He had not only had to ensure the archduke's safety, but also to make sure that he was received everywhere he went with the military honours due to a brother of the Queen. The young archduke had grown fond of Nicolas, and had requested his company on the various visits he paid while in the capital. It was during one of these that Nicolas had been witness to a scene that still delighted all of Paris. Monsieur de Buffon, receiving the illustrious visitor, had presented him with a volume of his *Histoire Naturelle* which the young man had politely refused, saying that he had no wish to deprive him of it, a piece of naive ignorance that had occasioned much mirth. Her brother's visit had led the Queen into a blunder which earned her the first signs of unpopularity: because of the archduke's incognito status, the princes of royal blood, Orléans, Condé and Conti, had claimed that he owed them the first visit. There was a heated exchange on the subject between the Queen and the Duc d'Orléans, who refused to budge. During the celebrations at Versailles from which they had excluded themselves, the princes elected to go to Paris to show themselves off in public, to much – indeed excessive – acclaim from the common people.

Nicolas had also been required to travel to the Île Sainte-Marguerite to fetch a prisoner named Querelle,[1] a former archer in the constabulary of France, who was to be confined in a padded cell at Bicêtre. Accompanied by two mounted constables, he sped to the south of the kingdom and took delivery of the prisoner. The man's complaints had come to the attention of Monsieur de Vergennes, the Minister for Foreign Affairs. Nicolas discovered that Monsieur de Laurens, provost general at Aix, had been so taken in by the trustworthy appearance of this Querelle, and the apparent genuineness of his words, that he had happily granted him a significant advance in *louis*. When Querelle had tried to play a similar trick on the treasurer of the constabulary, he was curtly informed that, as he had long since abdicated his functions, he should not even still be wearing the uniform. Pursuing his enquiries, Nicolas further discovered that, having already been sentenced seven years earlier in Montpellier, Querelle had also been accused of extracting four hundred *livres* from the King's consul in Parma, an offence that might have resulted in his being hanged. Not content with all this, he had in addition – according to Cardinal de Bernis, the ambassador in Rome – specialised in high-quality forgeries of orders, passports and edicts.

On his return to Paris, Nicolas was surprised to see Monsieur de Sartine at police headquarters. It transpired that, in addition to his duties at the Department of the Navy, Sartine had temporarily taken over the Lieutenancy General of Police, Monsieur Lenoir having been struck down with a skin disease.

At the Noblecourt household in Rue Montmartre, all was calm and steady. At Christmas, father and son had been reunited. Delighted to receive Louis Le Floch, Monsieur de Noblecourt made sure that every possible attention was lavished on the boy during those few days, setting aside a bedroom and study on the top floor for him, and plying him with books and delicacies. The young man did not seem to have suffered too much from the regime at his school, but Nicolas, with all the perceptiveness of a father's love, noted that his son seemed to be brooding about something. However hard Louis tried to allay suspicion and express his joy at their reunion, Nicolas, although in no way doubting his genuine sincerity, sensed that the boy was suffering from some secret wound. He tried as tactfully as possible to make him talk, having first assumed that it was his mother's exile in London that was making him so sad. Louis rejected the suggestion, either because he wished to conceal his deeper feelings on the subject, or because it was something else that preoccupied him. But when Nicolas saw his son having long, friendly conversations with Monsieur de Noblecourt, or responding with delight to the mouthwatering treats prepared for him by Marion and Catherine – treats intended to make him forget, if only for a time, the unappetising gruel he was given at school – he became convinced that he must have been mistaken and decided to cast the matter from his mind.

On the first Sunday in January, he took his son to Versailles for high mass. The boy watched spellbound as the King's cortège passed through the great gallery on its way to the chapel. He felt a sense of pride on seeing the friendly wave the monarch gave his father, and again when the Queen, with a pretty movement of her head, threw him a smile. On the return journey, he bombarded his father with questions, and Nicolas, relieved to see Louis so happy, answered them all without tiring of them. Louis was elated and captivated by the majestic spectacle he had witnessed, and on his return to Rue Montmartre immediately launched into a breathless account, to which the entranced household listened open-mouthed. Everyone noted that his narrative sense and eye for the telling detail resembled his father's. Chess games, fencing and riding lessons and other distractions took up the rest of this interlude. By the time Louis set off back to school, laden with packages, words of advice and a large supply of quince preserve, he seemed quite serene. Although reassured, Nicolas nevertheless vowed to keep a closer eye on him. He would go to Juilly as soon as possible to find out what he could from the Oratorians.

In point of fact, the commissioner's life was dominated by his new-found love, into which he had thrown himself body and soul.

His unusual situation as an aristocrat who was nevertheless close to the common people, the existence of an illegitimate son, and the nature of his position: all these might have encouraged him to exercise discretion. But in fact he was conducting his liaison with Aimée d'Arranet relatively openly, less concerned with the niceties than might have been supposed. At the beginning, admittedly, he had found it hard to drop a certain reserve, anxious more for the young woman's reputation than his own. But when, after some hesitation, he had opened his heart to his mistress, she had laughed and scolded him, covered him with caresses and closed his mouth with a kiss. As for Admiral d'Arranet, busy with his new role at the Department of the Navy, he still received Nicolas with the same paternal benevolence, revealing none of his feelings about what would have seemed obvious even to the most trusting of fathers. Having long ago consented to give free rein to a daughter who tenderly but imperiously imposed her will on him, he had evidently come to terms with the situation. Besides, wasn't Nicolas the son of the Marquis de Ranreuil, and didn't everyone he knew, starting with Sartine, sing his praises? What more could he wish for his daughter? His old heart, which had been through much suffering, melted at the sight of these children who seemed so happy together and surrounded him with their gaiety.

As for the coterie in Rue Montmartre – Noblecourt, Semacgus, Bourdeau and La Borde, who had known her as a child – they had all succumbed to her charm. Whenever she paid a visit, Monsieur de Noblecourt adorned himself with a large Regency wig, leading Semacgus to tease him with the observation that he reminded him of the ageing Louis XIV flirting with the young Duchesse de Bourgogne. She had subjugated animals and people alike, including – and this was a true measure of her success – Marion, Catherine and Poitevin. As for Cyrus and Mouchette, they followed her everywhere and would lie at her feet when she sat down. At one and the same time learned, serious, impish and lively, she always held her own, with an appetite for knowledge and good food that had conquered this all-male society. Secretly, they were all pleased to see this impudent young woman at last erase the baleful memory of Madame de Lastérieux.[2] Even Bourdeau, so touchy about anything concerning Nicolas, had lowered his defences and was increasingly attentive to her. The commissioner was becoming more secure in his happiness. Their reunions in discreet country inns were no less passionate than the encounters that preceded their separations: every stolen moment was relished by the two lovers. Nicolas, aware of how uncertain their future was and unable to envisage anything beyond the present situation, placed himself in the hands of fate, savouring the happiness of possessing a woman he could love and respect wholeheartedly.

Suddenly, he was drawn from this lengthy reflection by a shadow that fell between him and the declining light filtering into the vault through the narrow openings. A thin man in civilian clothes and a powdered wig, holding a hat under his arm, was looking at him with an expression that was at once inquisitive and ironic. Although the man was standing with his back to the light, Nicolas could see his clear eyes, tight, somewhat cruel mouth and air of controlled sadness.

'Monsieur,' he said in slightly accented French,[3] 'you are a foreigner and you seem to find this place inspiring.'

'I am indeed,' replied Nicolas, bowing with the natural courtesy that this polite approach called for. 'It leads one to meditate on the mystery of time and the frailty of human life.'

Somewhat theatrically and with an almost military stiffness, the stranger rose to his full height. 'I see you are a philosopher, which must mean that you are French! What are they saying in Paris about the new Queen?'

'Her subjects are enchanted with her.'

'Enchained, rather, it is said here in Vienna: enchained to the sleds she has been using so often during this harsh winter to get to her Opéra balls and other entertainments.'

'The Queen's sleds are acclaimed by the people, who are grateful to her for her boundless charity.'

'Truly, Monsieur?' the man replied in a somewhat ironic tone. 'I know the French are given to excessive compliments, and just as given to reversals of mood. In your country, any success lasts only as long as the common people see fit to maintain it. Few nations are as changeable as yours. Wasn't your late King called "the well loved"? And yet his convoy was booed and jeered by the populace during his last journey.'

'He was able to count on his loyal followers. They all mourn a good master.'

'Were you one of them, Monsieur?'

'I had the honour to serve him.'

'Does the new monarch benefit from their allegiance?'

'Of course, Monsieur. The French are monarchists through and through. Our loyalty is our honour, you can rest assured of that.'

'Well, Monsieur, far be it from me to offend you. It was just my manner of speaking.'

They stood in silence for a moment, then the man bowed and withdrew. On his way out, Nicolas questioned the Capuchin as to whether he knew the stranger. The monk raised his head, revealing a moth-eaten beard. He understood not a word of French. Nicolas tried Latin, and the monk, startled by the question, bowed and said, '*Imperator, rex romanorum.*'

It was only then that Commissioner Le Floch realised he had been speaking to Marie Antoinette's brother, Emperor Joseph II of Austria. Had it been a chance encounter, or did the Emperor know who Nicolas was? That was highly unlikely. But he was angry with himself for not recognising him. All he had at his disposal was a note from one of Monsieur de Vergennes's clerks indicating that Joseph II exercised power jointly with Maria Theresa, but that, although she consulted him, she did not yield the slightest authority to him. The

Emperor was said to be unhappy with this subordinate position and, in order to shake off a feeling of futility, spent time travelling through his future States. Having little taste for luxury or outward display, he liked to divest himself somewhat of the burden of his regality and appear as a private individual, the guise in which he had presented himself to Nicolas. He was said to be charming in conversation, skilful at encouraging the clash of ideas, from which, in his opinion, there often emerged flashes of truth. But this delight in open debate did not mean that he would tolerate too much familiarity. However much he might wish to act without constraint, the autocrat soon peered through the mask of the honest citizen.

Nicolas walked out into the cold air, still wintry despite the date, but welcome after the crypt. After brushing away the snow, he sat down on the steps of the Donnerbrunnen, a fountain surmounted by the figure of Providence, its pedestal surrounded by putti. An impromptu guide, sensing a foreigner, informed him – after making sure that nobody was eavesdropping – that four statues representing the tributaries of the Danube, considered immodest in their nakedness, had been withdrawn on the orders of the Empress. The stranger was rewarded with a few coins before Nicolas plunged back into his reverie. He was still surprised to be in Vienna, and he recalled the strange combination of circumstances that had led him here ...

*

It had all happened very quickly, starting two weeks earlier, when Monsieur de Sartine had summoned him. In his coach, on the way to the Ministry of Foreign Affairs, the former Lieutenant General of Police had been silent and lost in thought. The minister, Vergennes, had received them immediately. With his long face, blotchy cheeks and eyes glittering with an amused irony, he had greeted Nicolas formally: they were old acquaintances. Opening the session, Sartine recalled that the commissioner had long been privy to the late King's secret affairs of State, and repeated what he had told Nicolas the previous autumn. Abbé Georgel, secretary to Prince Louis de Rohan, the ambassador in Vienna, had discovered that secret French correspondence was being intercepted by the Austrians. A mysterious masked intermediary had provided him with striking confirmation of this, in the form of indisputable material proof, thus corroborating what was already known at Versailles about the Austrians' spying network, which was spreading its web beyond the Habsburgs' patrimonial States to the innumerable principalities of the empire. Every staging post sheltered agents who were diabolically skilful at penetrating the most ingenious of systems. Unfortunately, the new ambassador in Vienna, the Baron de Breteuil, had been unable to obtain from Abbé Georgel any further information on the masked renegade.

Vergennes had now taken up the story. 'I must admit, Monsieur,' he said, addressing Nicolas, 'that this damned priest's logic escapes me. He bombards me with contradictory dispatches, and says he has the trust of Prince von Kaunitz.[4] As if trust meant anything in such affairs! Kaunitz is supposedly profuse with his confidences. I know from experience what such outpourings are worth, coming from men in power. It is their way of winning the hearts of the innocent and making coarse grass seem like hay.'

He had risen and was now pacing about the room with small, nervous steps.

'What can I do? The gentleman's sensitivity is aroused whenever I demand further clarification of his activities and his secret connections. That's why, Monsieur, I would be grateful to you if you could provide me with a report on our abbé's mysterious interlocutor. We can no longer be certain that the correspondence that reaches us is genuine ...' He sighed. 'Alas, nothing can be taken for granted, for men are corruptible ... I'd also like you to put together, with the help of Breteuil, a memorandum on the recent additions to the empire, especially in Moldavia: its limits, the number and nature of the troops stationed there and other details of that kind, for which I would gladly acknowledge your diligence, but which it would have been perfectly within the abbé's capacity to obtain for himself if he had not considered them irrelevant to his personal glory.'

Vergennes turned to Sartine.

'It will be up to you to work out the details of all this with the commissioner, who will travel, on this occasion, as the Marquis de Ranreuil. I'll also leave it to you to tell him what we've decided. Unlimited credit is available from my offices. Passports will need to be taken care of ...'

Back in Paris, the two men had set to work without delay. Sartine, who had always been cautious whenever he himself became involved in the details of a case, revealed to Nicolas the pretext that had been agreed on to serve as cover for the mission. The Baron de Breteuil, on taking up his post in Vienna, had been unable to take with him in his diplomatic baggage a Sèvres bust of the Queen intended for her mother, as it had not yet been finished at the factory. Nicolas would be given the task of transporting it and handing it over to its august consignee. To give the mission even more glamour and credibility, an officer would be attached to it, a lieutenant-colonel named the Chevalier de Lastire. They would have a berlin at their disposal, and would take Rabouine with them as groom and bodyguard. Nicolas suggested taking Bourdeau, but Sartine would not hear of it: he had only just found his feet again in the Lieutenancy General while still being required to deal with problems at the Department of the Navy. Inspector Bourdeau's experience and the total confidence he had in him made him an essential resource when Nicolas was away.

Nicolas raised the question of language. As English was the only foreign tongue he knew, his investigation could well be severely hampered. Given this, he proposed that Dr Semacgus take part in the expedition.

An outstanding botanist, Semacgus had often expressed a wish to visit Emperor Francis I's botanical gardens at Schönbrunn and meet Nikolaus von Jacquin, a pupil of the Jussieus, famed for his travels in the West Indies and Colombia. The plants brought back from this expedition adorned the imperial gardens. With his usual spirit of contradiction, Sartine objected that this journey was not being undertaken in the interests of science, but changed his mind on learning that the former navy surgeon spoke perfect German. Moreover, he knew him to be a man of good counsel, and, if the need arose, a useful helper. Last but not least, Sartine gave Nicolas a large sum in *louis* and some bills of exchange to be redeemed from a bank in the Austrian capital.

The following day Nicolas had attended the Queen's toilet. As usual, Her Majesty was pleased to see him, and clapped her hands with delight on learning that her rider from Compiègne would be taking her bust to her dear mamma. The Austrian ambassador, Mercy-Argenteau, who was present at the interview, assured him of his support, offered his services and promised letters of recommendation, which Nicolas would receive that very evening. He had known the commissioner since the Archduke Maximilian's visit to France. The Queen scribbled a note for Maria Theresa, which she gave to Nicolas, asking him, with a little laugh, to tell the Empress that it was indeed from her hand. As Nicolas resolved to elucidate this mystery, the ambassador stopped him on the staircase and informed him, breathlessly, that Her Majesty had been trying for some time now to make her handwriting less childish.

There was much surprise in the Noblecourt household at this new venture, as well as a touch of anxiety. Bourdeau, torn between concern that he would not be accompanying Nicolas and his satisfaction at the knowledge that Sartine considered him indispensable, finally convinced himself that this resounding endorsement was ample compensation for any disappointment. Rabouine jumped for joy and hastened to acquire the livery appropriate to his temporary functions. As for Semacgus, as soon as he heard about the expedition, he turned red and ordered his trunk to be made ready. Nicolas made a quick visit to Versailles to see Mademoiselle d'Arranet, who begged him to take her with him, and he had to reason with her and convince her of the unseemliness of such an idea. The preparations took their course. Nicolas thought about what to take, particularly his clothes, which not only had to be suitable for the journey, but adaptable to the most diverse situations. With the help of Inspector Bourdeau, he also acquired a parallel wardrobe, a judiciously chosen collection of disparate costumes appropriate for disguises. The cooks in Rue Montmartre, Marion and Catherine, joined forces with Semacgus's cook, Awa, to provide the travellers with an abundance of transportable provisions along with bottles of drink to wash them down. Terrines, pork cuts, various *andouilles*, biscuits and sweets and a myriad of clay pots containing jellies and jams were carefully placed in a wicker trunk. Rabouine had hired an almost new berlin drawn by six horses, with a coachman and a postilion. The Queen's bust, neatly wrapped in thick twill, was put inside a solid wooden crate filled with straw.

*

Early on the freezing morning of Wednesday 15 February, they all met outside the Noblecourt house. Rabouine, his amaranthine livery with its silver edging half concealed beneath his ratine coat, perched next to the coachman, while the postilion, wearing thick boots, sat astride one of the horses. The Chevalier de Lastire was a man of indeterminate age in a brownish-red cavalry cloak, his hair drawn back and plaited, and immediately gave the impression of being a good companion. Dr Semacgus was wrapped against the cold in a cape with an otterskin collar, his face almost hidden beneath a hat of the same fur. Nicolas was wearing for the first time a creation by his tailor, Master Vachon, an ample cloak with a sable collar endowed with many pockets. He had tied around his neck a cashmere shawl given to him by Aimée d'Arranet, who had made him promise never to take it off. With delight, he breathed in its delicate scent of verbena.

The money provided by Vergennes and Sartine would certainly come in useful. There were fifty-nine staging posts between Paris and Strasbourg and, with a carriage of that size, the cost, simply within the borders of the kingdom, would amount to several hundred *livres*. The usual route went through Chalons, Saint-Dizier, Bar-le-Duc, Nancy, Lunéville, Phalsbourg and Saverne, to name only the most important French stages. The guide produced by the Messageries Royales indicated in addition that if they reached Strasbourg after the gates were closed, they would have to pay the master of the staging post ten *sols* per horse in addition to the road toll. And when they finally got to Vienna, they would need to hire a carriage locally, in order to move about the congested streets.

Their conversations regarding the material conditions of the journey broke the ice with the Chevalier de Lastire. He revealed himself to be quite an expert on currencies and distributed to them little handbooks on square pieces of paper detailing rates of exchange. He explained learnedly that an Austrian *kronthaler* was the equivalent of eighty *livres*, in other words a *louis d'or*, that a *livre* comprised twenty *sols*, a *sol* four *liards* and that consequently a *liard* was worth one *pfennig*, and finally that all this resulted in ... At this point, he seemed to get lost in his own reasoning, bringing up *kreutzers* where florins would have been more appropriate. He ended up trying to convert *pfennigs* into *anas* from the Indies, and Semacgus, who had sailed the seven seas, had to help him out. The company, joined now by Rabouine, who was frozen to the marrow, grew livelier, and the surgeon took advantage of the mood to extract from under the seat little wooden cases lined with sheet metal and filled with embers. These foot warmers were greeted with much enthusiasm, and the gaiety increased when he displayed a travelling chamber pot, in its morocco-leather casket, with a gilded rim that was unanimously praised. He brought their enthusiasm to a peak by opening a little wooden case from the West Indies, containing glasses and four knives with mother-of-pearl handles and two folding blades, one serving as a fork and the other for cutting. They decided to start immediately on their provisions, and the afternoon was spent in an after-lunch nap.

The days passed, punctuated by the small incidents of the journey: an unshoed horse, their bracing walks up the slopes to lighten the load on the vehicle, the constant bitter arguments at the staging posts to obtain the best horses, the filthy inns and the nightly invasions of cockroaches. Semacgus had distributed among his companions little pots of fragrant pomade of his own making, in which camphor dominated, among other substances the identity of which he jealously guarded. Dinner followed lunch, and lunch dinner, all more or less acceptable. The most memorable meal was a feast at the Lion d'Or inn in Vitry-le-François. Grilled *andouillettes* from Troyes, glistening with fat, had whetted their appetites for a rabbit pâté, the pieces of which, the hostess explained, she marinated in red wine and plum brandy for several days. Its fragrant aroma derived from the fact that it was not at all deboned. The whole was cooked for a long time in a pastry casing made of lard, in the centre of which was a navel, as she called it, through which the cooking smells escaped. A pork brawn terrine complemented this treat, followed by a local cheese coated in wood ash and a delightfully cool Champagne wine. The cheese was wonderfully full-bodied, and they tried to discover the secret of its manufacture, but in vain. All that the hostess would tell them was that it was washed thoroughly with a brush before being served, which only made it all the more mysterious.

To crown the feast, they were brought a plate of *roussettes*, light and puffy lozenges of fried and sweetened dough. Semacgus declared that they would be the perfect accompaniment to an omelette made by himself. He rushed to the hearth, seized some twenty eggs – a reasonable amount for four healthy appetites, he asserted – and, with a wink, broke them and separated the yolks from the whites. The former were sprinkled with sugar and stirred with a fork, and the latter whisked, then both were put together and poured, extremely carefully, into a huge frying pan sizzling with pale-coloured butter. Under the effect of the heat, and to the astonished eyes of the audience, the eggs thus prepared swelled prodigiously. Semacgus added copious amounts of sugar, then, taking a bottle of old rum from inside his coat, poured most of it into a saucepan to heat it. He slid the omelette onto a dish, and a smell of foaming caramel rose from it. Then he poured the rum over the omelette and set fire to the whole with a lighted twig. Blue flames flared up, illuminating the joyful faces of the guests. The crustiness of the *roussettes* combined harmoniously with the smoothness of the omelette, a smoothness enhanced by the rum. For a long while, the only sounds were the sighs of pleasure emitted by the four travellers.

Winter persisted, and the cold clung so determinedly to the buildings, even the most impervious to draughts, that the biggest and most skilfully stoked fire could not warm them. Nicolas noted the grim faces of the peasants they came across at the staging posts. The autumn had been harsh enough, and a prodigious quantity of fine fruits had been lost. Now there was a fear that this severe winter would expose them to the double scourge of starvation and ruin. Frost would remain on the ground until midday, when the sun would make the air milder and melt the snow and black ice. When night came, the north wind would start blowing again, bringing clouds laden with snow, and everything would freeze again until the next day.

When they reached Strasbourg, Nicolas was surprised by the city's beauty and wealth, and delighted by the pink cathedral towering over the sloping roofs, which recalled those evenings in the servants' pantry when Catherine Gauss spoke of her birthplace. They stocked up with salted meat, bacon and smoked shoulders, to which Semacgus added a few pots of horseradish, a particular favourite of his. Nicolas had a surprise in store for them. Having heard Monsieur Lenoir mention the Maréchal de Contades's pâté de foie gras, he had talked about it with Lenoir's cook, who had revealed that the secret was jealously guarded by the maréchal's cook, Close, a Norman like him. This bond had done the job, and now they were able to take delight in this quintessential dish, surrounded by a *douillette* of finely chopped veal and covered with a thin coating of golden pastry. A smooth Trottacker from Ribeauvillé was the perfect accompaniment, making for a long, merry evening.

The journey resumed, its monotony made all the worse by fatigue and the lack of exercise. They were rarely even able to look out at the unknown landscapes through which they passed, as these were all too often shrouded in fog and flurries of snow. Fortunately, the Chevalier de Lastire, revealing a new talent every day, enlivened the party with his carefree humour. A frequent guest at Parisian salons, he had adopted many of their pastimes. He would, for example, cut pieces out of sheets of paper to make chains of jumping jacks. He was so good at this, and did it so often, that after a while Semacgus, who had let him use his letter paper, had to stop him, pointing out that the mail was weighed and taxed at a higher rate the further they got from Paris, which made it necessary to use paper sparingly and even to write in as small and cramped a hand as possible. Somewhat put out by this, the chevalier plunged morosely into another pastime popular with men in fashionable circles, and began embroidering his coat of arms on a piece of fabric stretched over a hoop. Once his good mood had returned, he diverted them with accounts of his campaigns. He seemed slightly bitter, and confessed to them that he hoped that this mission to Vienna would bring him the reward for his services for which he had long wished. In his opinion, one ought to be esteemed, above all, for one's prowess on the battlefield. Alas, the price at which one was valued was all too often based on intrigue and unfounded claims. Favour and privilege dominated in those other battlefields: the Court and – sometimes – the bedroom. All too often, those who had barely heard the sound of cannon fire were the most rewarded. They strove to console this man, already of mature years, who saw honours drifting away from him, and Semacgus opened a bottle to toast his future success.

Late on the morning of Wednesday 1 March, after stops in Salzburg and Linz, their carriage, covered in snow and led by two horses that were no more than spectral white shadows, passed through the old perimeter of ramparts, towers and bastions and entered Vienna. Confined within its walls, the city seemed like a small town surrounded by a large sheet of ice on which suburbs were beginning to take shape. Lastire told them that these fortifications had been erected on the ruins left by the last Turkish siege in 1683. Their first impression quickly yielded to admiration at the number and splendour of the palaces, churches and monuments. Luxury and opulence were apparent in the outward aspect of the houses with their carved and decorated façades and in the sumptuousness of the shops. Nevertheless, they could not help seeing this imperial capital through jaded Parisian eyes and judging it somewhat provincial – to such an extent that Semacgus mocked their comments and urged them to avoid this failing, which was common among the French. One had, he said, to change one's tune when one came to a foreign land and consider it without prejudice and without making comparisons.

Nicolas, as ever a collector of people, looked out avidly at strange figures whose clothes reflected the diversity of the nations composing the empire and the proximity of its territories to those of the Turks. The Golden Bull, a hotel recommended by the Austrian ambassador, situated in Seilergasse in the very heart of the city, surprised them with its luxury and cleanliness. It seemed to Nicolas that it could rival the best establishments in Paris: the Hôtel du Parc Royal in Rue Colombier and the Hôtel de Luynes in Faubourg Saint-Germain.

The next day, desiring a little time alone, they dispersed, each according to his preference. Nicolas hurried to attend mass at St Stephen's Cathedral while Semacgus, in spite of the snow, immediately proceeded to Schönbrunn to visit the gardens and greenhouses. Monsieur de Lastire preferred to sprawl beneath a feathered eiderdown, smoking a pipe and staring dreamily up at the joists of the ceiling. Last but not least, Rabouine occupied himself in finding a carriage to hire. Nicolas had wandered the city for the rest of the day until he had been drawn to the modest entrance to the tomb of the Capuchins ...

Night was falling over the square, and the cold was becoming more intense. He walked back to the hotel, which was only a few streets away. His companions all seemed exhausted, as if the accumulated fatigue of the journey had suddenly overwhelmed them. They had a dinner of pea soup and a plate of cold meats accompanied by strongly flavoured black bread and amber beer, then silently retired to their rooms without further ado.

Friday 3 March 1775
Early in the morning, Nicolas left the Golden Bull and proceeded to the residence of the King's ambassador to Vienna. His carriage was a fine one, and Rabouine stood proudly at the back in full livery. The majesty of the building reflected the luxury that had been a hallmark of Prince Louis's tenure as ambassador. Nicolas was immediately admitted to the Baron de Breteuil's presence, in a vast office hung with red damask. In the midst of gilded furniture and lacquers and vases from China, a man in a russet coat and a large, old-fashioned wig was awaiting him. He was of medium height and corpulent, with a firm, energetic face, big, alert eyes, a strong nose, and a thin mouth curiously turned up at the sides and ending in two deep furrows.

Nicolas was aware that his easy-going air was deceptive. They had met some years earlier, in the presence of the late King, and he had gained a strong idea of the man's character. Time had done its work, and Breteuil seemed to have aged considerably. No sooner had they exchanged ceremonial bows than the ambassador put one finger to his mouth to intimate silence. Taking Nicolas by the arm, he led him through a concealed door into a small, dark corridor. They passed through several more doors, each of which Breteuil locked carefully behind him, before finally coming to what appeared to Nicolas to be a small wardrobe room, without any other furniture than a worn Spanish leather chair, a stool and a silver fountain. The ambassador sat down and motioned to his guest to do the same. There was a half-smile on his stern face.

'Forgive this welcome, Marquis. I know it's strange, to say the least, but one can never be too careful. In my current situation, I can be sure of neither the servants my predecessor left me nor those I strive to recruit myself. My people talk, and I can do nothing about it. Let us speak of your mission, about which I have been well informed. We can converse safely here; I've made sure there are no prying ears. Did I not meet you once during a dinner in the King's apartments?'

'Indeed you did, Ambassador. We spoke about your collection of *chinoiseries* with Monsieur de La Borde.'

Breteuil smiled, which made him look younger. Nicolas was reminded of Sartine.

'The late King was fond of you,' said the ambassador, with a sigh, and paused. 'Our secrets, as you know, are intercepted, and have been for months. Although our new master seems quite reluctant to resume communications ...' Another moment's silence. 'What do you know of Abbé Georgel?'

In measured terms, Nicolas summarised what Vergennes had told him.

'That will do for the broad strokes; you still need to know the

31

details. As soon as I arrived I handed the abbé – assuring him, of course, of my goodwill – a letter from the minister urging him to reveal to me the identity of his informant. Immediately, he raised objections. This intermediary would not confide in me, he said, it was an affair of honour. It was as if I had asked him to break the seal of the confessional!'

'I assume that such was not your design?'

'Certainly not! I had no intention of consulting the man in question! Why should I, Breteuil, have any dealings with such a rascal? But it was the duty of Georgel, as a servant of the King, to do nothing to conceal from me, the new ambassador, either his name or the means of communication that had been established with him. It was no use. All I got from Georgel was quibbling and weak excuses. He claimed not to know the man's true identity, the channels through which he had first been approached by him no longer existed, and God knows what else! After all my entreaties, he finally said that he would soon be in a position to arrange things so that all could be revealed to me. I let some days pass, but when I reminded him of his promise he asked for more time.'

'Did you grant it?'

'Certainly not! I assume that, like me, you consider his conduct intolerable. I confess I would never have believed it could occur to a man employed by the King to think that he has a right to keep silent about an aspect of his service when he has been commanded to speak up. Such obstinacy is suspicious, to say the least.'

'How do you explain this reticence?'

'The man has neither honour nor principles. The little pedant was thrown very young into a perverse world. That hostess to philosophers, Madame Geoffrin, undertook his upbringing. It's from his time in her house that he derives that artful self-confidence that can only be acquired at Court or–' he smiled again and looked straight at Nicolas – 'by birth. Since the departure of Prince Louis ...'

A scornful, almost hate-filled grimace crossed Breteuil's face. Nicolas recalled that the ambassadorship in Vienna had previously escaped his grasp on the fall of Choiseul and that d'Aiguillon had appointed Rohan instead.

'… he has considered himself to be influential and has let himself be swayed by self-delusion. He's convinced that he's the man best suited for the task. The Emperor and Kaunitz support this claim, but the man's pretensions do not impress me. I've dismissed him: he's leaving in a few days, on the seventh or eighth. I don't know if that gives you sufficient time to get to the bottom of this affair. I have to say, though, that I've tried everything, yes, everything to convince him!'

The tone persuaded Nicolas that Breteuil had used all his authority, and more. But he knew from experience that neither cajoling nor threats, nor an appeal to the duty of State, had any effect on people like that when their passions had to be satisfied. Clearly, Georgel was driven by other interests: as a Jesuit, he might even be working for the greater glory of his order. Things had taken a nasty turn, and Breteuil's dismissal of Georgel would not make them any easier. There was nothing and nobody to fall back on, and yet, as Monsieur de Noblecourt often said, it was precisely at moments like these that exceptional assistance was most needed.

'Do you wish to stay here with me, Marquis? Along with your … entourage, of course. By the way, have you brought the Sèvres bust for the Empress?'

'Yes, and it's an excellent likeness of its illustrious model. I am also the bearer of a letter from Her Majesty to her august mother.'

Breteuil's face lit up and he put his hands together in a theatrical gesture of adoration, as if in gratitude to fate. 'So, thanks to your zeal and savoir-faire, we will have another audience at the palace. Have you been presented to the Queen?'

'Yes, when she arrived in France in 1770 and I accompanied the King and the Dauphin to Compiègne.'

That was all Breteuil would learn: Nicolas deliberately refrained from adding any further details. When dealing with members of the Court, he had learnt to keep an air of mystery about him. Intriguing his interlocutor with his terseness and never replying to unasked questions had often served him as a shield. He modestly lowered his eyes, inwardly laughing at his own mischievousness. He had scored a point, and against a clever sparring partner. As Monsieur de Breteuil was savouring all this good news open-mouthed, Nicolas thought it a good moment to tackle the other aspect of his mission to Vienna.

'May I count, Ambassador, on your help in drawing up a report for Monsieur de Vergennes on the extensions to the empire, which he hopes to receive through a less exposed channel?'

Breteuil gave him a stern look: the question encroached on a territory of which he considered himself the master. 'Apart from what the minister is demanding, we are already preparing a dispatch on Moldavia and another on the unrest in Bohemia, news of which has reached Vienna. There remains the problem of getting them back to France without the risk of interception. A simple letter will be of no use. These people have no hesitation in opening and searching bags, or in confiscating them. We protest, and Prince von Kaunitz casually blames the tactlessness of his agents. Not that he's one to ever apologise profusely, according to the ministers of the other foreign courts. In the meantime, the damage has been done! How do you plan to proceed?'

'Allow me to keep silent on that matter.'

'The papers will be in code, but we know, alas, what happens to our codes.'

Suddenly, he rushed to the door facing the one through which they had entered and pulled it open. There was a lively exchange of words, and when the ambassador came back into the room he was red in the face.

'What did I tell you? You see how I'm surrounded by spies. That scoundrel of a valet was trying to eavesdrop. Dismiss him, I hear you say. Alas, the next one would only be worse! Fortunately, the door is padded. Prince Louis used to receive his mistresses here disguised as priests ... And for whose benefit is all this? Rohan, d'Aiguillon and their entourage, without any doubt, as well as the Austrian cabinet and perhaps even the spies of Frederick II.'

He paused to catch his breath.

'Marquis, I'm counting on your zeal. You reputation augurs well for the success of our endeavour. I shall immediately request an audience with Her Imperial Majesty, and as soon as I know the day and hour I shall inform you. By the way, you won't have far to go to find Georgel. Having arrogantly rejected my offer to house him, he's staying at the Golden Bull.'

They retraced their steps through the maze of corridors to the ambassador's office. From there, Breteuil walked him ceremoniously to the staircase, declaiming in a loud voice on the latest gossip about the actresses of Paris and the rigours of the winter.

Once in his carriage, Nicolas considered the results of this interview. It was quite a success, he thought, to have mollified Breteuil, who was known to be unapproachable. He nevertheless suspected, beneath the diplomat's honeyed words, an ill-concealed desire to impose his will. Nicolas was useful, and even necessary, to him, the commissioner's contacts being of such a nature as not to be carelessly disdained. Now he would have to listen to Abbé Georgel, the second instrument in this discordant duo. The task had been made easier for him: he knew where to find the abbé. He foresaw a somewhat more awkward encounter with a man who was willing to risk the disfavour of both the ambassador and the minister. As a servant of the King himself, he found that quite shocking, but he understood that Georgel felt sustained by the reputation of his order and assured of the support of the powerful Rohan family, with all that that entailed.

Once back at the Golden Bull, finding Abbé Georgel was child's play. He was enjoying cakes and chocolate in one of the drawing rooms. Thanks to a mirror that covered one whole wall, Nicolas was able to observe him at his leisure before approaching him. He was short, with curly powdered hair, and wore an elegant black coat with a discreet collar that was more reminiscent of a cravat than the adornment of a priest. Clear eyes, a thin mouth between two asymmetrical furrows and a curious involuntary shrug of the shoulders made for a distinctive, if joyless, appearance.

'May I disturb your collation, Father?' said Nicolas, approaching. 'Allow me to introduce myself—'

The man looked at him coldly, his shoulder moving up and down. 'You are the Marquis de Ranreuil, better known, I think, as Police Commissioner Le Floch of the Châtelet.'

He was clearly in no way put out by this unexpected encounter, as well as already informed of everything.

Nicolas felt a kind of threat hovering in the air. 'Come now,' he said. 'You do not think, you know! That simplifies my task.'

A thin, tense smile played over the abbé's lips. 'Take a seat, Marquis. The chocolate here is perfectly whipped – will you take a cup?'

'One could hardly resist such a gracious invitation,' Nicolas said, sitting down.

He had chosen the lightest of tones, but would that suffice to allay the abbé's very obvious mistrust? Georgel had fallen silent. Nicolas needed to find out how much he knew, but as nothing was forthcoming, he forced the issue. 'I assume you know why I am in Vienna?'

'You assume correctly. I understand you are to hand over a Sèvres bust to the Empress, a present from our Queen, not forgetting that little billet-doux from daughter to mother.'

Nicolas appreciated neither the tone nor the content, which he considered intolerable, but he restrained himself. 'You are well informed.'

He remembered the scene at Versailles, when, apart from himself and the Queen, the ambassador Mercy-Argenteau and a few ladies-in-waiting had been present. There had been every opportunity for the thing to get out. Presumably, Georgel had his information from the Rohans.

'So, Abbé, there is no need for me to waste time on the real aim of my mission: to meet you, and enquire of you, at the behest of Monsieur de Vergennes, the reasons behind your refusal to inform your ambassador about a certain grave matter.'

Now was not the time to beat about the bush. He had the impression that the blow had struck home.

'Monsieur,' Georgel replied, 'how can I possibly believe in your impartiality? You have just come from the French embassy. No doubt its present incumbent has been singing my praises. How could I rival that grandee, whose glitter reminds me of a stone that has no value despite its sheen? Will you believe me? Will you listen to me? Will you lend me a benevolent ear after all you have heard about my good faith?'

'You are judging me very harshly, Monsieur.'

'Let me tell you this: I had hoped to be treated differently, given my position, but I regret my hopes have been dashed. Despite the amenities I have enjoyed in Vienna, I desire nothing more at the moment than to revert to my original state. A diplomatic career had no other attraction for me than the satisfaction of fulfilling my duty. I was not drawn to it by inclination. But is that any reason to be treated like a paid lackey?'

'I understand what you're saying, but the Baron de Breteuil is upset with your lack of openness towards him.'

'Quite unfairly! I did all that my duty demanded to prepare for his entry at Court, suffering every possible snub along the way! I shan't even mention the visits I made to ministers and other influential people. I told him everything: my sources, my channels of communication, details of the monarchs' characters and affections, their prejudices for or against us, and so on and so forth. I instructed him in depth on the secret liaisons of the ministers of Russia, England and Prussia, their tortuous schemes to diminish our influence, and the progress of all private negotiations relating to our interests. What more do you want?'

'And what came of all that? Did he not show you any appreciation or gratitude for such zeal?'

'At first, he appeared to respond in the proper manner. But then he ordered me to reveal the methods I had used so successfully to obtain for His Majesty the secrets of the Austrian cabinet. I couldn't. His arrival had dried up the source, and how could I possibly have tracked down a masked man glimpsed at night who had warned me that any attempt to identify him and hand him over would not only be futile but would also put me in danger?'

'What I don't understand is the reason for this reticence now, when everything seemed to work so well under Prince Louis.'

'The ambassador became extremely angry about that, forgetting himself and lashing out at his predecessor, claiming that I had espoused his cause and assuring me that he would one day take his revenge, that he would be Rohan's minister and make him feel the weight of his authority. I replied, without going beyond the bounds of the respect I owe him, that I would inform Versailles of his conduct. Would you believe it? After that scene, thinking that I could still be useful to him, he dared to return to the attack.'

'So,' commented Nicolas, 'you now consider that you owe him nothing, neither your respect nor your savoir-faire, qualities which, up until now, have allowed our Court to keep the machinations of the Austrian cabinet in check. The fact remains, Abbé, that you should consent to help me, coming as I do in good faith from your minister. It goes without saying that, under these conditions, I would be your most devoted advocate at Versailles.'

The unfortunate word had escaped him, and he immediately regretted it. The abbé gave a start and threw his spoon into a bowl of whipped cream, spattering his coat in the process.

'Advocate? Advocate? Did I hear correctly? Am I on trial, then, that I need to be defended? Get it into your heads, you and the others, that nothing will emerge from my mouth, that I have nothing to reveal. In four days, I shall take the coach and leave this den of iniquity for ever.' He raised his eyes to heaven. 'Thank God! At least our Austrian friends have expressed their sorrow at my departure. The Emperor Joseph granted me a farewell audience! Yes, a farewell audience!' He rose to his full height, almost drunk with pride. 'As if I were the ambassador himself! As for Prince von Kaunitz, he lavished on me attentions of all kinds!'

'At least indicate to me how you and your informant proceeded.'

'There is hardly any mystery about it. I'm happy to repeat it for the thousandth time. There would be an anonymous note in neat handwriting. At midnight, a masked man would hand me a bundle comprising dispatches deciphered from our King's secret communications as well as those of the King of Prussia. This would happen twice a week. A former secretary would copy them, and then I would give them back. With that, Monsieur, draw up your statement for the defence. Your humble servant!'

He walked stiffly out of the drawing room, his head held high. It seemed to Nicolas that his efforts had been in vain. They would get nothing from the abbé, at least not with his consent. Hatred combined with wounded vanity always led men of that kind to guilty denials. The confrontation between Prince Louis and Breteuil, with Choiseul lurking in the background, d'Aiguillon outraged by the insults of the Court, and the powerful Rohan family lying in wait: all this had led to ignominious intrigues that threatened the throne and the kingdom. He decided to go for a walk through the city to think about what steps to take.

Once outside, he felt pleased that he had swapped his ceremonial shoes for a solid pair of boots freshly waxed by Rabouine. The melted snow that spurted at every step would have soiled his white stockings beyond repair. He wandered somewhat aimlessly until he reached the Hofburg, the Empress's Viennese palace, which struck him as simple, even austere. It was guarded by a small detachment whose oriental uniform intrigued him. He noted that the houses were regularly numbered. Sartine had planned something similar for Paris, but had not been able to bring his plans to fruition. His steps next led him to a large square called Graben. Surrounded by richly decorated houses, this broad rectangle had at its centre a curiously carved kind of tower, adorned with the symbols of the Holy Trinity. Two ornamental ponds surrounded by wrought-iron grilles placed at either end of the square added to the splendour of the place. He was struck by the gutters jutting out from the roofs of the houses, their ends representing the heads of griffons, and spewing the overflow from the thaw. Shops abounded on the perimeter, with wooden canopies to shield them from the winter weather, but also doubtless from the heat of the sun. There was a great deal of bustle everywhere, with carriages, carts, wheelbarrows and a very varied crowd. It did not take him long to discover that, despite the Empress's professed desire to banish prostitution from her fair city, Graben was swarming with indiscreet courtesans and their customers. At one end of the square, he stopped to gaze at a fresco painted on a blank façade, depicting a caparisoned elephant mounted by a rider holding a hook and wearing a curious conical hat which reminded Nicolas of those worn by the pagans of Asia, as seen in images sent to him by his friend Pigneau de Behaine, now a missionary in the Indies.

At a small stand made of reeds, he bought a piece of breadcrumbed carp in a fragment of music score. This delicacy was covered in a red powder, spicy to the taste, which he much appreciated. Further on, he entered an establishment shiny with brass to have coffee while observing the customers. It was at this point that he became aware that he had been followed by two men who had not been skilful enough to escape an eye as alert as his. Indeed, so conspicuous had they been that even a child would have noticed them. Nicolas was not surprised by this occurrence. In Paris, Monsieur de Sartine had taken this practice to extremes, and the surveillance of foreigners, particularly in time of war, had attained a kind of perfection. As one of the exits from the café led to an arcade, Nicolas rushed to it as soon as he had paid his bill, then suddenly changed direction and came face to face with the two spies. Both were unwashed, and the stench coming off them was highly noticeable. Nicolas resumed his stroll, paying no further heed to the two men. He spent the rest of the afternoon visiting churches until, weary and chilled to the bone, he decided to return to the fold.

Each of his companions had a tale to tell, except for Rabouine, who had already begun paying court to a maid in the service of a lady of quality staying at the Golden Bull. After making sure there were no eavesdroppers, Nicolas gathered the group in his room and summarised the situation. They still had four days to unmask the abbé's informant. It was to be supposed that, whatever Georgel had said, he would make contact with him one last time. They had to discover his identity once and for all. Monsieur de Lastire, although he had joined this war council – Nicolas having been reassured by Sartine that he could be trusted – appeared uninterested in the subject of their conversation and was singing in a low voice. Somewhat irritated by his attitude, Nicolas asked for his opinion.

'I think you'd do better to thank me for going out in this cold weather to buy tickets for the first performance of Haydn's oratorio *The Return of Tobias* at the Kärntnertor theatre.' He performed a little entrechat. 'Just think! Christian Specht, bass, Carl Friberth, tenor, and Magdalena Friberth, soprano, in the role of Sara! A rare treat, I promise you. And in addition' – he mimed an instrumentalist scraping his bow – 'Luigi Tomassini on violin and Franz Xaver Hammer on cello, who will each play a concerto between the two parts of the work. I add, gentlemen, that the libretto is from the pen of Giovanni

Gastone Boccherini, the composer's brother! *La la la … la la … la …*'

'What date is this performance?' asked Semacgus.

'The second of April.'

'What? Do you imagine we'll still be here then?'

'Oh,' said Lastire, 'I'm counting on it. We're waiting for an audience with the Empress, and she's quite likely to take her time. And with that, gentlemen, I leave you, for I fear that my skills are of no use to you – I don't see any charge forthcoming! *Et vivat Maria Teresa!*'

They quickly made arrangements for that evening. Each of them had become aware that he had been followed. They would have to thwart this surveillance, or it might lead to the failure of their mission. It was decided that Nicolas would go out, wearing Rabouine's clothes, on the arms of the lady's maid, who would be softened up with a few florins. He would use the servants' door, which was less conspicuous. Rabouine, in Nicolas's cloak, would divert the spies, as would Semacgus. Lastire would remain in the hotel, keeping an eye on Abbé Georgel's door, and would raise the alarm by lifting a candle at his window to warn Nicolas, who would be concealed in a doorway near the hotel. But the evening passed without incident, and although they kept watch for a good part of the night, they had to admit their failure.

Saturday 4 March 1775

It was quite late in the morning by the time they gathered at table. The Chevalier de Lastire was not among them. Rabouine went upstairs to wake him. After a time, he reappeared, pale-faced.

'Monsieur de Lastire has disappeared. His effects are all gone. His room is empty!'

II

THE TWO-HEADED EAGLE

From childhood, politics trains kings to dissimulate.

MACHIAVELLI

They were so surprised that they all fell silent. Semacgus raised his cup to his lips, put it down, wiped his mouth and only then spoke up.

'Let me abuse the privilege of age and tell you what I think. There are two possible hypotheses, since I immediately rule out the third, which is that of a lack of courage when faced with danger. Either our companion has been abducted, or, for a reason as urgent as it is mysterious, he wished to disappear. But what do we do about it? It is for you, Nicolas, to decide. For my part, I believe that the only reasonable reaction is to ignore the incident. Let us pretend, if not that we arranged it ourselves, at least that we knew of it. And if we are the cause, who could we complain to? Our ambassador? He's new to the post, so this is hardly the moment. The Austrians? If they are responsible for this abduction, they won't be surprised by our silence. If it was a voluntary act on the part of the chevalier, it is not for us to report a departure of which we do not know the true cause. Let us remain calm and keep up appearances.'

Nicolas was listening attentively, but seemed to be thinking a long way beyond the present discussion.

'If he'd been abducted,' ventured Rabouine, 'he would have defended himself. He may love embroidery, but he's a strapping fellow, and there can be no doubting how ardent he would be in a fight. But none of us heard any noise last night, even though we can hear everything …' He went slightly red, although there was also an element of boasting. 'I hardly slept last night. My room's above his. I can assure you there was no noise coming from it.'

Nicolas at last emerged from his thoughts. 'Question the grooms. It's possible he had his luggage removed while we were out. I have no memory of him telling us how he spent the day yesterday.'

Rabouine was already on his way out.

'Wait, one more thing. See if, by any chance, the tickets for the Haydn oratorio were collected by a messenger. That's all. Anything else would exceed the limits of reason.'

He grabbed a little round roll covered in cumin and started mechanically crumbling it. Silence again fell between the two friends until Rabouine returned.

'Well?' Nicolas asked impatiently.

'No messengers, but I did learn one curious thing. Monsieur de Lastire's baggage was never taken up to his room.'

'Now that I come to think of it,' said Semacgus, 'I was struck by the fact that he hadn't changed his clothes since our arrival. So he'd been preparing his departure for some time. We were all so tired when we arrived that none of us noticed.'

'He waited until he knew our plan of action before decamping. If that is what he's done …'

'As for the theatre tickets,' added Rabouine, 'the hotel took care of those itself. They just gave them to me. And there are four of them!' He waved four small squares of ivory paper.

Nicolas shook his head, as if faced with an insurmountable obstacle.

'That seems to plead in favour of one of my hypotheses,' said Semacgus, looking relieved. 'Could it be that by including himself as one of the spectators he was trying to tell us something?'

'But what? To me, that merely adds to the mystery. What are we to tell the Baron de Breteuil?'

'Nothing, unless he asks.'

'The problem is that the chevalier is supposed to be escorting the bust of the Queen and that his presence has been announced.'

'The audience with the Empress hasn't yet been granted.'

They were interrupted by Abbé Georgel, who graciously bowed to all of them, then walked up to Nicolas.

'Good day to you, Marquis. May I dare to hope that you don't hold my vehemence yesterday against me. It was that of an honest heart.'

Nicolas rose, determined not to give too much away. Semacgus stood aside discreetly, taking Rabouine with him.

'Not at all. I appreciated the fact that you said what you meant.'

'I have come to bring you an invitation to dinner from Prince von Kaunitz, *geheimer Hof- und Staatskanzler*, the chancellor of the empire and the Nestor of European ministers. Having learnt through myself of your presence in Vienna he asks you to be his guest, in my company. There is one condition. He wishes to know if you are in good health.'

'I think so,' replied Nicolas, with a laugh. 'Your question intrigues me.'

'He means no harm by it. It is just that he is of fragile health. Even when he was quite young, it was feared that he would die. He does everything he can to avoid chills. When he was ambassador at Versailles in 1751, he dreaded nothing more than draughts, which, as you know, are common there. He has often had to withdraw from affairs in order to receive treatment. He is terrified of epidemics. He suffers from a number of chronic ailments. The slightest breath of wind makes him faint and excessive heat overwhelms him. And you should see his diet! Most peculiar.'

'My carriage will be at your disposal, Abbé.'

'Then we shall go in a convoy,' said Georgel, in a sardonic tone. 'I trust you are aware, Monsieur, what an honour it is to be invited by this great talent, who is so skilled at applying the lessons of the past to the present. His fondness for the manners and customs of the French make him the strongest supporter of an alliance which was partly his work.'

Nicolas bowed.

'Ah, I must also point out to you that the great man has some peculiarities and strange obsessions. He has no objection to time passing but hates being constantly reminded of it. He therefore has no clocks or watches about him and never calculates how long anything will take him. He goes to bed very late and gets up late. Once he has performed his toilet, he has lunch at four, five or six, after work and entertainment. We will therefore be there at four in the afternoon. Be prepared to wait.' He looked pointedly at Nicolas's travelling clothes. 'Full Court dress, of course, with sword and wig. I shall come for you at three thirty.'

He disappeared in a cloud of powder and the smell of bergamot.

Nicolas shut himself in his room for the rest of the day to reflect on why he felt so dissatisfied with himself. First of all, he was angry with himself for not having foreseen the Chevalier de Lastire's apparent defection. He had trusted him, and now he felt responsible and betrayed. This anguish made him think of his son, and he recalled the unhappy look on the boy's face when he had returned from Juilly for Christmas. He still had no idea what had transformed a carefree young man into that vision of sadness. The fact that his gaiety had so quickly returned did not reassure Nicolas. What had happened? He found it hard to fathom and feared that he had missed something vital and had let Louis down. He vowed once more to keep a closer eye on him.

Echoing this commitment, another scruple arose from deep in his heart, prompted by his sense of moral unease. In view of his son's situation, was he not giving too much of himself to Aimée d'Arranet? Of course, his reflection had nothing to do with commonly observed behaviour. In the society around him, he saw children handled like toys or treated like miniature adults. Parents kept their distance, and affection was artificial and ostentatious. It was quite otherwise among the common people. Bourdeau and his five children were a perfect example of a loving and united family. Even Sanson, the public executioner, devoted an exclusive affection to his offspring which compensated for the forced solitude of a family marked out by society.

His heart told him that this was the path to follow, even though the combined affections of Canon Le Floch and the Marquis de Ranreuil – not yet revealed as his father – however reserved their expression, had surrounded him with love. He began again to examine himself, just as in the old days when he had taken confession with the Jesuits in Vannes. What object was worth such passion? Could the risk be weighed up, however hard it was to define: a blind, heedless pursuit, a forgetting of others within the fortress of two bodies and two intoxicated souls? What was his son, compared with such agony? He rebuked himself. Was he not falling back, at his age, into old habits by indulging in such futile splitting of hairs? It was certain that he would suffer many more setbacks before passion waned and reason prevailed: that at least was the opinion of Monsieur de Noblecourt, who was so good at seeing beyond appearances. Perhaps all he had to do was take a deep breath, dismiss the heaviness that weighed on him, and stop himself from brooding too much and instinctively following his own bent. These common-sense thoughts relieved him and he began calmly devoting himself to his toilet.

A mouse-grey coat embroidered with silver thread seemed appropriate. He thought tenderly of the late King, who had been fond of that colour. The King and his father combined in his memory as he kissed the hilt of the Marquis de Ranreuil's ceremonial sword and buckled it on. After adjusting his wig, he looked at himself critically in the cheval glass. It seemed to him that he had grown both thinner and younger. His regular presence at royal hunts had provided the necessary exercise. Love, too, was making him take better care of his appearance. He put on his cloak.

The abbé was waiting for him at the appointed time, wearing beneath his cape a silk moiré coat in a dark-purple shade, which gave him an episcopal air. Arriving at the chancellor's palace, they were greeted in front of the peristyle by a host of lackeys carrying torches: the sky had grown darker and snow was on the way. In the light-filled rooms, the guests were waiting. Georgel took it upon himself to introduce Nicolas to a crowd which included some of the greatest names of the empire. The abbé himself was greeted with great, indeed excessive enthusiasm. He moved with ease, bowing to one, replying to the other and joking with all. His affinity with this world was clear to see, the result of his long sojourn in Vienna. His savoir-faire, his wit and his robe all contributed to his skill in flattering these ironic, haughty people. Prince Louis was much asked about, being still remembered as a man of fashion with whom this society had become besotted. It struck Nicolas that the new ambassador would have to work long and hard before he erased that image and prevailed over this nostalgia for past splendours.

Time passed, and still Prince von Kaunitz had not appeared. Everyone sat down at the gaming tables and began playing animatedly. Nicolas wondered if, in Vienna as in Paris, the income from cards helped to pay the expense of great houses. Every family had its set of hangers-on on whom the maintenance of its way of life depended. To invite people and to divest them of their money was part of the same impulse. There were also gilded rascals here, leaning on the tables, hoping to familiarise themselves with the aristocracy and enrich themselves by cheating at faro.

It struck Nicolas that all courts resembled one another, in their gestures as in their customs. The same solemn bows, the same greetings revealing a panoply of attitudes ranging all the way from disdain to adulation and from flattery to mockery. Georgel had continued to move from group to group like a fly gathering pollen. Breteuil's fears were justified. He was alone and isolated, the butt of slanderous jibes from his servant, and his only hope was to see the abbé leave Vienna as soon as possible. Nicolas overheard a number of exchanges. The road to hell was paved with fine words which concealed others that were less affable, and Georgel's words, circumspect as they were, nevertheless echoed with double meanings for an attentive ear. Whenever he was asked anything about the new ambassador, he immediately claimed to know little about his chief, but his very silence was clearly disparaging. His smooth, measured words seemed to say more than was actually expressed. Alternatively, he poured out a flood of exaggerated epithets that everyone received with cruel, knowing smiles. This indirect manner aroused laughter so insulting that Nicolas had to restrain himself from showing his irritation, for it was the King who was being insulted in the person of his representative. The abbé kept introducing him, exaggerating his qualities and importance. He found himself so overwhelmed with invitations that he gave up declining them: after all, he had no intention of following up on them.

From time to time, he lost sight of his guide as the latter weaved his way from one group to another. His short stature did not make it any easier to keep an eye on him. At a certain moment, Nicolas thought he glimpsed an exchange of words between the abbé and a valet bearing a tray of barley syrup. Georgel had half turned and inclined his ear to listen to the man, who was talking to him with his head bowed. However, there was nothing to indicate that they were discussing anything important. His observation was interrupted by the noise of a cane hitting the flagstones. A double door opened, and the crowd, in a flurry of silk and satin, rose to greet the prince.

As Kaunitz looked around the room, everyone bowed. Nicolas discovered, framed by an extravagant wig, the thin, spiritual face of a man on the verge of old age. The prince offered his arm to one of the ladies, and the guests walked in procession to the room where a huge table had been laid. Georgel, drawing Nicolas with him, had unhesitatingly slipped in behind Kaunitz. They all took their seats and Nicolas, sitting almost opposite the chancellor, was able to observe at his leisure that cold, stern countenance, occasionally animated by a penetrating glance. He first addressed the ladies who surrounded him, clearly knowing how to give the greatest value to even the slightest word. The food was more abundant than choice, and a valet stood behind each guest to serve the dishes that were required. Behind the master of the house stood a small sideboard, on which were vegetables, chicken breasts and fruits for his personal use. He stared for a long time at Nicolas, before finally addressing him in his slightly nasal voice.

'I'm glad, Marquis, that our friend has given us the satisfaction of your presence at this table.'

Nicolas bowed.

'I know, Monsieur,' Kaunitz went on, 'that you are close to Monsieur de Sartine. Not long ago, I submitted a mystery to him. We were interested in discovering the whereabouts of a man with whom we were having trouble and who, unless he was restrained, might well have caused us great embarrassment. He was said to have gone to ground in Paris, where he was living under a false name. His description was supplied to the Lieutenant General of Police with a request to spare no effort in finding him.'

The whole table had fallen silent, spellbound by the prince's words.

'After three months, only a very fleeting trace of him had been discovered.'

'Thanks to testimony from his landlady in La Courtille, Monseigneur,' said Nicolas.

'I think, Monsieur, that we owe you a great deal,' remarked the prince, his face betraying not a flicker of surprise. 'I was also informed that the person in question had embarked for Egypt. But we were not convinced. In fact, we were sure that the man was still hiding in Paris. I did not conceal from your chargé d'affaires ...'

Georgel bowed to all and sundry.

'… my opinion that, despite its reputation, the Paris police force was no better than any other.'

'Monsieur de Sartine, as I can testify, was greatly upset at this judgement by one of the greatest ministers in Europe.'

Georgel was blissfully nodding approval of the commissioner's words.

Kaunitz smiled. 'But eventually he was able to meet our demands. He informed me soon afterwards that the man was in a suburb of Vienna called Leopoldstadt, at a Turkish merchant's, disguised as an Oriental with a black patch over his left eye. All of which proved accurate: the man was found and arrested. I sent Sartine the Empress's thanks. As for me, I was left in justified admiration at the workings of such a wonderful machine. The men who set it in motion could only be geniuses!'

He raised his glass, which was filled with water, then turned to another guest. One by one he paid each of those present the tribute of his exquisite politeness. Finally, he began to hold forth. Broadly speaking, his words were more concerned with past events than with the present. After a few reflections on the misfortune of inexperience and the passion of youth, he bemoaned the all too real situation in which a man mature in both years and experience was unable to contribute his wisdom and force of character.

'I think we can decipher these words,' Georgel said to Nicolas in a low voice. 'Is there a more tactful way of intimating that Joseph II does not pay him sufficient attention?'

As the prince was disinclined to linger, the meal was soon over. Before he rose, he laid out before him on the table a little pocket mirror, a box of toothpicks, a small silver-gilt basin and a tumbler filled with an emerald-green liquid. He cleaned his teeth at some length, rinsed his mouth, spat twice, and carefully wiped himself.

'Even when he visits the Empress,' said Georgel, with a chuckle, 'he doesn't stand on ceremony. Flouting the propriety customary before his monarch, he shamelessly observes this unsavoury practice. And when she invites him to dinner and he's late, she indulges him, waiting for him to arrive before she begins.'

Once the prince had gone up to his apartments, the crowd of guests dispersed. Nicolas and the abbé had to wait for some time for their carriage, surrounded by grooms turning in all directions and unconcernedly dripping wax from their torches. As Nicolas climbed into the carriage, he felt someone brush against him: it was a woman, her face covered with a black mantilla. She slipped a small square sheet of paper into his hand and moved away before he could make a gesture to detain her. Without saying a word to Georgel, he slipped the note inside his glove. He assumed it was an invitation to an amorous rendezvous with one of the women present at the reception, seduced by his looks and the fact that he was a foreign aristocrat. During the journey, the abbé prattled on, congratulating him on his success with Kaunitz. On reaching the Golden Bull, they bade each other a ceremonious farewell and Georgel went back to his room.

Nicolas moved a candle closer, made sure that he was alone, and unfolded the paper. It bore, in capital letters, the enigmatic sentence: TIMOR METUS MALI APPROPINQUANTIS. He was about to call on his Latin when he noticed that there was another sentence, written diagonally across the page: MAXIMAS IN CASTRIS EFFECISSE TURBAS DICITUR. At that moment, Semacgus and Rabouine appeared, looking like good-natured conspirators, and he put the translation off until later. Their demeanour was one that Nicolas knew well, that of people bursting to reveal something. When he tried to speak to them, they put their fingers to their lips.

'We have discovered a pleasant tavern,' Semacgus said, 'where I've ordered a little dinner of local dishes. We'll be at ease there. You may just have to sit and watch us, of course, since I assume you've already eaten. We have things to tell you ...' His large nose creased with irony.

'You're quite mistaken,' replied Nicolas. 'I'm dying of hunger. The gathering from which I've come was the kind where talking prevails over eating. That said, you seem to have forgotten about the abbé. The fact that he's returned doesn't mean he might not go out again!'

'Pah!' cried Semacgus. 'Your argument doesn't hold water. Rabouine here has thought of everything. We have our spies and informers, all in the right places. A plentiful supply of florins opens mouths. Don't worry about a thing.'

They soon found themselves in a narrow room with polished wooden walls on the first floor of a dark little tavern. Nicolas looked around the room, which seemed to hang out over the poorly lit street visible through the naive designs of the stained-glass windows. Rabouine had all the food brought in at once, and arranged it on a sideboard, together with bottles of white wine. That way, they would not be disturbed. Like an inspired priest, Semacgus joyfully chanted the praises of the dinner.

'Egg soup enhanced with caraway and accompanied by quenelles of calves' liver–' he pointed to a bulbous earthenware pot – 'pâté of grouse *en croûte*, a little pan containing saffron sauce which needs to be moistened as soon as the lid is lifted ... roast goose with potatoes and *nudlen* ...'

'What are *nudlen*?' asked Nicolas.

'Something similar to Italian pasta, much used in this part of Europe, coated in sauce which transmits its aromas to them.'

They immediately sat down at the table, surprised by the savoury odour of the soup and the softness of the quenelles.

'If soup,' said Semacgus, 'is, as they claim, to lunch what a portico is to a building, this can only serve as a peristyle to a dinner of tall trees!'

'I'd prefer a salted capon in Paris,' said Rabouine, 'to these grim morsels where brown sugar prevails and the seeds have a strange stench. Even the mustard here doesn't taste like mustard – it's sweet!'

'Those seeds, as you put it, Rabouine, are the divine caraway, philistine!'

For the moment, Semacgus refrained from explaining to Rabouine that grouse was what capercaillie was called here and that it was a difficult bird to hunt, although the mating season made things easier, as it then threw caution to the wind. Once they had appeased their initial craving, and before they tackled the goose, Nicolas asked them what it was they wanted to tell him.

'Gentlemen,' he said, suddenly serious, 'I'm listening.'

Rabouine bowed his head like a guilty child.

'I foresee the worst,' Nicolas went on. 'When Rabouine gets that look on his face, disasters are never far away. He's like a cat spitting on coals, as Catherine puts it.'

'She puts it a little more crudely,' Semacgus said.

'But we're in decent company here.'

Rabouine looked beseechingly at Semacgus, who took a swig of wine and plunged in.

'All right then, Commissioner. Left to our own devices, we decided to enjoy ourselves. As Rabouine wanted to keep his hand in, he made the bird sing.'

'What am I to make of that? What bird are we talking about here?'

'Not the grouse. We said to each other: Well, the coast is clear. Nicolas has taken Georgel away. They won't be back soon. Let's take advantage.'

'I see. And what did you do?'

'I shall evoke a bird whose organ, when well greased, creeps and releases, I speak of the picklock otherwise known as the "nightingale", which opens the most recalcitrant locks and makes them sing if skilfully manipulated.'

Nicolas laughed. 'I give up.'

'Then I shall confess. We paid a visit to Abbé Georgel's room.' And as if to distract Nicolas, he pulled towards him a wing of the goose along with a crisp strip of the breast.

'Master Semacgus,' said Nicolas, a twinkle in his eye, 'I wonder, I really wonder. Did I do the right thing fourteen years ago, saving you from the Bastille? Well, what's done is done. Let's not beat about the bush. What did you find?'

Rabouine sighed happily and drew from his jerkin a sheet of paper on which the blackened fragments of a document seemed to be glued. He handed it to Nicolas.

> *ing openly. They say that*
> *to make Choiseu da   the*
>   *their   It   ing for us*
>   *at Reim   ollowers   wo*
>   *Turgo   at all   face   this*
>   *coalit   light a spar   di order*
>   *and   ating   astle   by th   caused*
>   *dra*
>   *the*
>   *mob*
>   *by   horrible acts.*
>   *Corpora   merch   grain tra*
>   *iguillon   arlement*

'That,' said Rabouine, 'is a reconstruction of fragments found in the fireplace of the abbé's room. We can define the nature of the document: without doubt a letter from France, read then destroyed. But our man was too trusting of the fire: the wood was green and the amount of smoke deceived him as to how destructive it was.'

Nicolas was surprised and impressed to hear such a speech from

Rabouine's mouth. 'This is all very imprudent, but, I must admit, very useful. What do you deduce from it?'

'Rabouine and I,' replied Semacgus, 'have tried to elucidate its mystery. At first sight, it doesn't appear to be a coded message. There are words that are easy to reconstruct: *Choiseul, Reims, followers, Turgot, light a spark, disorder, castle, mob, horrible acts, corporations, merchants, grain trade, d'Aiguillon, Parlement.* The rest is difficult to guess at. Does it refer to some kind of plot? If so, what is Georgel's role?'

'Gentlemen,' said Nicolas, taking out the note he had been given by the mystery woman outside the chancellery, 'look at this. Here's something else that might arouse your natural curiosity. Guillaume, would you like to translate these sentences?'

Semacgus put on his spectacles and carefully examined the paper. 'The writer of this note is well read. I think I recognise Cicero. TIMOR METUS MALI APPROPINQUANTIS. You go first!'

'I would say,' ventured Nicolas, 'something like "If we feel fear, it is because misfortune is coming." I've always translated off the top of my head. The fathers at Vannes often reprimanded me for that. By using my imagination, I was able to guess a great deal. Of course, I was often wrong ...'

'Your arrow has fallen not far short of the target. I would refine your effort in this way: "Fear is the apprehension of approaching misfortune." There remains the other sentence, which is difficult to render. MAXIMAS IN CASTRIS EFFECISSE TURBAS DICITUR. I suggest: "It is reported that he brings about the greatest troubles in the camp."'

'I think I can improve on that,' cried Nicolas. '"They say he caused the gravest disorders to break out in the camp."'

'Disorder again,' said Rabouine, 'just like in that burnt paper.'

'"Castris" could also be castle,' observed Semacgus. 'Another word that appears in that other text.'

'You're right,' said Nicolas, 'both are possible. I was clearly wrong in my first supposition. This note was not from a woman seeking an amorous intrigue. Do these enigmatic sentences give an extra resonance to the limited information on the Georgel document? Especially as only the whims of fate and your initiative have made it possible to bring together two things that would seem to have nothing to do with one another.'

'This strikes me,' continued Semacgus, 'as a curious coincidence. The unknown woman's note announces a present or future danger, in Vienna presumably, but also "in the castle".'

'Could that mean Versailles?' ventured Rabouine.

'As for the other text, which was never intended for our eyes, it suggests the same danger in France. The two sources confirm one another even though we were not supposed to see both of them.'

'That's true,' said Semacgus. 'And why did your mysterious correspondent not choose a more direct formulation than these ambiguous phrases in Latin?'

'This person,' suggested Rabouine, becoming increasingly animated, 'knows Monsieur Nicolas. Firstly, he assumes that he knows Latin. Secondly, sentences in Latin don't arouse suspicion, whereas a more common style would not have failed to do so.'

The dinner continued, and the roast goose was soon reduced to a heap of bones picked perfectly clean. It was very late by the time they got back to their rooms, leaving only Rabouine to preside over their plan of attack. Nicolas found it hard to get to sleep. It was never good to think too much in bed, and in addition, the dinner lay on his stomach: in the excitement of the conversation he had eaten too much too quickly.

Sunday 5 March 1775
The door had opened with a creak then, after a pause, slammed shut. He struck a light, lit a candle, and walked to the door in his nightshirt. Carefully opening the heavy leaf, he discovered, to his astonishment,

instead of the landing, a huge stone staircase descending towards extensive grounds. He saw gardeners pulling stumps or large roots from the ground and striking them as if trying to crush them. Further on, two men were attempting to force open a coffin with crowbars. The dull sounds of their hammering echoed painfully in Nicolas's head. He put his hands over his ears, the blood beating in his temples. Everything tipped over, and he found himself back in the comfort and tranquillity of his room: someone was knocking at his door. Rising unsteadily, and vowing to avoid treacherous foreign wines in future, he asked in a hoarse voice who was there.

'Monsieur Nicolas! It's Rabouine! A footman has just come from the Baron de Breteuil to say that the ambassador will come to fetch you at eleven o'clock. You have an audience at midday with Empress Maria Theresa.'

Nicolas opened the door. 'What time is it?'

'A quarter past ten.'

Just my luck! thought Nicolas. He had only three-quarters of an hour to get ready. He asked Rabouine to help him. He went down half naked into the snow-covered courtyard and had a few pails of icy water thrown over his body. If he could get through this, he would be able to face all the courts in the world. He hurried back upstairs to shave, put on his wig, and again don his grey coat. Just before eleven, he was at the door of the hotel, while the servants looked on admiringly. Rabouine had been given his instructions in case Georgel took advantage of his absence to leave the hotel. The ambassador's coach appeared at the appointed time. The crate containing the Queen's bust was solidly secured to the vehicle, and two valets would keep an eye on it while it was being transported. It struck Nicolas, sitting down next to the ambassador, that he would never have done with wigs. He recalled the mockery he had overheard at Prince von Kaunitz's house: with his old-fashioned wigs, the baron was a laughing stock. For this imperial audience, he sported a brown Regency-style wig which would not have been disavowed by either Monsieur de Noblecourt, loyal to the customs and fashions of his youth, or Monsieur de Sartine, with his tastes as a collector. The ambassador looked flushed and feverish. Beating the floor with his cane, he suddenly began questioning Nicolas on the fact that Monsieur de Lastire was missing.

'What is the reason for this unspeakable absence? What am I saying? A desertion, Monsieur, yes, a desertion! You should be able to hold on to your men. Can you tell me without further ado what is behind this intolerable lapse, which will come as a great surprise to the Empress's household?'

Nicolas did not think that now was the moment for too honest or specific an answer. This angry manifestation of authority had no effect on him. He chose to humour Breteuil, while taking a more conciliatory tone.

'No one could be more upset than I, Monseigneur. Monsieur de Lastire is still young. No doubt the temptations of Vienna have detained him longer than is reasonable. I shall pass on to him your displeasure, you can rest assured of that. Let us think of it no longer. I am here with the bust, not to mention the Queen's letter to her august mother.'

This timely reminder calmed the baron, whose face lit up at the thought of these happy prospects, although for form's sake he spent a few more moments in angry rebuke. Nicolas remembered a piece of advice from Sartine: never upset influential people. It was necessary, said Sartine, to wrap them in assurances and soothing certainties. This preamble over, the ambassador undertook to initiate Nicolas into the subtleties of Viennese Court ceremonial, since any lapse might provoke a real drama. He discoursed at length on the subject, recalling that the respect for rank had in 1725, here in Vienna, pitted the Duc de Richelieu against the Duke of Rifferda, Philip V's ambassador. The conflict had centred on the precedence always granted to the representative of the King of Spain.

'The matter was only settled by the Spaniard's recall. In any case, Rifferda was a traitor who went to Morocco and became a Mohammedan under the name Osman Pasha.[1] A complete account of the disputes between our people and foreign ministers would fill volumes. And,' Breteuil added, full of pride, 'that's very good for the reputation of the King at foreign courts.'

Nicolas refrained from mentioning his conversation with Georgel or his dinner at the house of Prince von Kaunitz: the subject would occur to the baron soon enough. In order to maintain his good humour, as well as out of natural curiosity, he questioned him on the subtleties of the Empress's audience at Schönbrunn. Having passed through the ramparts, the coach was now leaving the old city and entering a flat landscape, covered with snow as far as the eye could see. Here and there were new constructions, although work on them seemed to have been interrupted by the cold. The straight road had been swept and cleaned, and great pyramids of snow stood beside it at regular intervals, bearing witness to the daily efforts of the city authorities. Breteuil, his mind on the audience to come, was silent, one hand keeping the collar of his pelisse closed, the other waving his cane in an irregular rhythm.

'Make sure, Marquis,' he resumed, 'that you keep a close eye on what I do and how I behave and copy me. That way everything will go according to the rules. In any case, everything is calculated in advance: the number of steps, the bows, the choice of seat, the length of the interview. As the representative of our master the King, I will be entitled, according to custom, to a chair with armrests. You will remain standing, except in exceptional circumstances. The Empress is kindly, but nothing escapes her, a fact of which Monsieur de Rohan was all too well aware. By the way, what about Georgel?'

Pretending not to hear the question, Nicolas hastened to ask, 'Who will be there to welcome us?'

'The person in overall charge is the grand master of the Court, the *Obersthofmeister*. His deputy, the great chamberlain, the *Oberstkämmerer* organises the audiences, so his influence is the most marked. But in fact we will be dealing with the *Oberstmarschall*, who will welcome us.'

All this was reeled off while his face quivered avidly. Much to Nicolas's satisfaction, the baron forgot all about his obsession with the abbé and fell back into a state of nervous expectation. Nicolas looked out at the gently undulating landscape, with the outlines of steeper slopes visible in the distance. After passing through a neat little village currently being expanded, they came to a large gate. Admitted by the guards, they were then saluted by soldiers bearing arms with the French fleur-de-lis. Low buildings joined to the main body by stone arches surrounded a vast square in which were two fountains surmounted by statues. Nicolas leant out of the lowered window. In the cold sunlight filtering through the clouds, the ochre-yellow palace of Schönbrunn appeared. At first sight, it looked like a smaller-scale version of Versailles.

'Remember my advice,' murmured Breteuil through clenched teeth, taking off his pelisse.

After some capricious movements by the horses, the carriage at last pulled up in front of the central entrance to the main building. Greeted by an officer, they were directed towards a richly coloured figure who bowed to them ceremoniously. He was introduced to the commissioner, then took the ambassador aside for a moment and spoke to him, before inviting them both to follow him. Nicolas assumed that this man was the grand marshal of the palace. A long walk awaited them. After climbing the grand staircase, they passed through an infinite series of rooms, in which Nicolas was surprised to note the regular presence of porcelain stoves. The warmth spread by these stoves was much more pleasant than that dispensed by the huge fireplaces of Versailles. They were finally admitted, without the excessive formality predicted by the ambassador, into the Empress's study. Admittedly, the room was so small that it would have been difficult to perform all the regulation bows and steps. The Baron de Breteuil was invited to take his seat in an armchair. Nicolas remained standing while two grooms carefully placed at his feet the case containing the precious object of his mission to Vienna.

'Ambassador, your presence gives me great joy,' said the Empress, in French with a slight Germanic accent.

'May I be allowed to present to Your Majesty the Marquis de Ranreuil, entrusted by my master with the task of conveying the precious consignment she is expecting.'

Maria Theresa looked insistently at Nicolas, who, half bowed, did not flinch from her gaze, but bore this examination with the detachment of someone long accustomed to the company of monarchs. Only the late King, who was still such a strong presence in his memory, had once filled him with awe, although his veneration for the man had always overcome his fear and timidity. In exceptional circumstances, the feeling of being his own spectator prevailed over any other reaction.

Those small, deep-set blue eyes continued to peer at him inquisitively, belying the apparently easy-going nature of the countenance. The Empress had sparse hair, sticking up gracelessly and barely concealed beneath a black mantilla. Her huge, shapeless body seemed slumped in the chair, although supported by silk cushions. In the muffled silence of the study, her breathing, coming in short, whistling gasps, was painful to hear. The lower half of her face, which was very red, displayed a smile close to a grin. On several occasions, her face tightened with pain or was shaken by involuntary movements. She tried to sit up, revealing as she did so feet wrapped in cloth and stuffed into misshapen slippers. Nicolas recalled the legs of La Paulet and felt a sudden sense of compassion, encompassing both the monarch and the brothel-keeper. Respecting the conventions, he waited to be addressed. He took advantage of this wait to look around the room, which was adorned with mouldings in blue painted wood imitating porcelain, with patterns of flowers, fruit, and Chinese umbrellas. Hundreds of blue wash drawings and a few framed portraits completed this cluttered but charming whole. The study was suffused with the mingled scents of perfumes and medicinal balms, accentuated by the heat of a room sealed against draughts.

'I am delighted, Monsieur, to receive from your hands and –' she looked at Breteuil – 'those of the King's ambassador, an object so long coveted by a mother's heart.' These words were spoken without any excessive sentimentality. 'Did the Queen receive you before your departure?'

It was merely a polite question, thought Nicolas. Her ambassador, Mercy-Argenteau, had been present at Versailles and must surely have informed her.

'The Queen was good enough to grant me an audience, at which she entrusted me, not only with the task of conveying this bust, but also that of delivering this letter to Your Majesty.'

Maria Theresa held out a podgy hand that was even redder than her face. Nicolas handed over the letter, which promptly disappeared into the depths of a sleeve.

'Let us take advantage of your presence,' the Empress said with a little laugh, 'to have the latest news from France.'

Breteuil was shifting in his chair, not daring to speak. This did not escape the Empress, who was clearly amused.

'But before that, Monsieur, do place the long-awaited bust on this writing desk.'

She pointed with an imperious finger to a small cylindrical desk. It was only necessary to pull out a few wooden pegs and the case was quickly and easily opened. Once the lid had been raised, Nicolas carefully removed the straw, untied the lace that held the thick twill wrapping in place, lifted the bust of Marie Antoinette like a monstrance and placed it on the shelf of the desk.

The Empress put her hands together. 'My God, how she has changed! How beautiful she has become! I no longer recognise my little girl! I'm very much obliged to you for the trouble you have taken. Although that is only to be expected from a man famous for his loyalty to the late King. It is said that he died in your arms. Is that true?'

It was another elegant but direct way of informing him that they knew everything about him.

'I was present, but he died in the arms of Monsieur de La Borde.'

She did not pursue this, since only the question really concerned her, not the answer.

'Is this bust a good likeness?'

'Even the most delicate art and the finest bisque would be unable to render the full perfection of the reality.'

With a sigh of emotion, Monsieur de Breteuil approved this delicate courtier's phrase.

'Yes,' she said, 'we can understand that. By the way, Ambassador, when will we have a double portrait of the King and my daughter?'

'Your Majesty,' he replied, delighted that he was at last able to speak, 'there is currently no original from which a copy could be made. Despite our entreaties it has not yet been possible to persuade Her Majesty to grant a few sittings in succession to the painter Duplessis, who was chosen for the task. But as soon as he has finished the King's portrait, I hope he will begin the Queen's.'

'It's true that my dear daughter writes to me that painters drive her to despair, that some have tried, but that their attempts have produced such a poor likeness that she has given up the idea of sending them to me. By the way, Monsieur, I am assured that she has become the arbiter of elegance, and that thanks to her the fashion for tall hairstyles has grown into a taste for plumage effects. Is that correct?'

'The Queen has no need of tricks to enhance her beauty and, while it is true that the use of feathers as decoration leads to all kinds of excesses, she sets a reasonable tone. The practice has become widespread and gives a great deal of work to Parisian artisans and apprentices. But, as Your Majesty knows, fashion is ephemeral and one vogue quickly gives way to another.'

'I know what you mean, of course. It would seem, though, that these excesses have become well established, that one can no longer walk through a doorway without bending one's knees, that, seen from the balcony, the auditorium of a theatre is a sea of feathers, and that such hairstyles block the view of the stage. It is even said that some elegant women sport mountains, flowering meadows, silvery streams, English gardens and Lord knows what else in their hair!'

It was clear to Nicolas that the Empress liked to keep abreast of what was happening.

'Your Majesty is well informed, but all that is part and parcel of the taste for exaggeration. At the Opéra, I have also seen horns of plenty filled with fruit, which are intended as symbols of the expectations of the new reign.'

'You reassure me. Distance, alas, leads to one receiving a distorted impression. My subjects are better informed than I by all the correspondence that passes so easily between Paris and Vienna. As a mother, I was most upset to hear about a sled accident …'

Monsieur de Breteuil began coughing.

'Your Majesty,' said Nicolas, 'nothing has been more exaggerated than that minor accident. I can speak with some authority, as I was in the sled behind the Queen's. The flag that adorned it scared the horse. It bolted and the driver was thrown backwards. With admirable presence of mind, the Queen seized one of the reins and steered the sled towards a hedge, which broke its course. Her Majesty has since declared that more such accidents might occur, given how unfamiliar the French are with sleds. It seems to me that she has lately been turning away from this kind of amusement.'

The Empress appeared satisfied, either because this account

reassured her or because it confirmed what she already knew. 'Marquis, you are a wonderful storyteller! I will therefore continue to take advantage of your indulgence. Does the Queen ride?'

'She does take a little exercise, always on animals of a certain age that have been well trained, and always on safe ground, without hurdles.'

He had the impression that this prudent reply did not satisfy her entirely and was not received with the same openness.

'Once mourning ended at Court, I understand that balls resumed.'

'Her Majesty was anxious for the Court to gather around her, as was only right, and no longer around Mesdames.[2] Masked balls have indeed been given during this carnival period, the last just before I left Paris. The King appeared in a costume from the time of Henri IV.'

'All of which ends late in the morning ...'

'Late at night, rather ...'

'And does the King take pleasure in these things?'

'His Majesty is not overly inclined towards such festivities. But as the Queen has such a taste for them, he is happy for them to go ahead and takes whatever pleasure he can find in them.'

Tirelessly, Maria Theresa pursued her enquiries. There ensued a curious game, to which Monsieur de Breteuil was merely the overwhelmed spectator. To the Empress's ever more specific questions, Nicolas responded with a feigned enthusiasm that was beyond reproach. Each object of the Empress's curiosity was gradually drained of its reality, reduced to a sham, and dismissed with a charming smile which ensured it would never regain its capacity for harm. As a spellbound onlooker, the ambassador could not help but admire this verbal tennis game, giving points both to the monarch's gentle obstinacy and the Marquis de Ranreuil's polite resistance. Occasionally the Empress's irritation became apparent in the way she gripped her mantilla or the trembling of her leg. Nothing troubled Nicolas, who imperturbably defended his Queen by giving little away.

'Well,' concluded Maria Theresa, 'I shan't take any further advantage of you. Clearly, the Marquis has been well schooled ...'

She did not finish her sentence.

'Ambassador, how has Vienna been receiving you?'

'I have found here, Your Majesty, a reception befitting the closeness of our alliance.'

She touched on several other points before tackling the question of Poland.

'I know,' she said, 'that the division of that unhappy kingdom has been a great blemish on my reign. But circumstances overcame my principles. In order to counter the immoderate ambitions of the Russians and the Prussians, I made demands so exorbitant that I hoped they would be unacceptable and would lead to a breakdown in negotiations. Imagine my surprise and sorrow when the King of Prussia and the Tsarina agreed to everything. Prince von Kaunitz was extremely upset, being utterly opposed to this cruel arrangement and aware of the regrettable pall it casts over his ministry. Let us hope we can limit the damage!'

She sighed and dabbed her eyes with her handkerchief. Then she rummaged in her sleeve and took from it a box encrusted with diamonds, which she handed to Breteuil, and a diamond ring, which she gave to Nicolas.

'Please accept these mementoes, gentlemen, as further proof of my gratitude for the Queen's kindness.'

In the carriage, Monsieur de Breteuil seemed to be mentally preparing his dispatch to Monsieur de Vergennes. His lips moved silently, as if formulating some incisive turns of phrase and rhetorical flourishes. These thoughts led him to question Nicolas again as to how he intended to transmit to Versailles a detailed report on the disturbances in Bohemia, a subject on which first-hand information was available. He received the same answer as previously. Although disappointed, he congratulated Nicolas on his familiarity with Court protocol and the skill of his answers.

However conscious he was of the failings of a man who was often tetchy and difficult, Nicolas nevertheless respected a servant of the King who was so concerned with the service of the State and the reputation of France at foreign courts. He admired the fact that the ambassador was entirely devoted to its representation and glory, and ready to sacrifice a great deal to achieve it. The baron was honouring the name Breteuil in this constantly renewed struggle, just as much as if he were brandishing his standard and his arms on a field of battle. Even though he had only known him a short time, Nicolas was happy to defer to him, as if in tribute to a shared sense of morality and loyalty, which might already belong to another time.

He accepted the baron's suggestion that he follow him to the embassy in order to examine the official and confidential papers that needed to be conveyed to France. Once in the ambassador's office, Breteuil installed him in a little study and brought him an armful of numbered sheets. He had written these dispatches himself, he explained – reviving the rheumatism in his arm in the process – in order to avoid any risks, given his uncertainty about the loyalty of his staff. He left Nicolas alone, asking him only to join him as soon as he was finished. Three hours later, Nicolas handed the papers back to Breteuil and assured him that all the essential points would reach Monsieur de Vergennes. He refused to say more, which greatly aroused the ambassador's curiosity. All he would show him was a small sheet of paper covered with various series of figures. This unsolved mystery reminded Breteuil of Georgel, and he again questioned Nicolas on the subject. Nicolas replied evasively that 'the great work was under way and that the arcana would soon be revealed'. With this alchemical formula, he bowed and set off back to the Golden Bull.

He found his companions on a war footing: Abbé Georgel had ordered a carriage for seven in the evening. Rabouine, now fully in cahoots with the servants at the hotel, had been informed immediately.

He had gleaned other details that were just as interesting and filled out the picture: the abbé had ordered his boots to be waxed, from which it was easy to deduce that this would be no indoor meeting but that he was expecting to trudge through the snow and mud – a detail that was all the more intriguing as darkness had long since fallen.

This new situation had to be dealt with urgently and the necessary arrangements made. The first plan of action they had sketched out had been rendered out of date by Monsieur de Lastire's defection. A new version was now constructed. Just before seven, Semacgus would take their carriage, lie in wait at one end of Seilergasse, and follow Georgel if he went in that direction. Nicolas and Rabouine would again swap clothes. Rabouine would also leave the hotel a few moments before the fateful hour, making a great show of being cautious, which would arouse the suspicions of the Austrian police and distract their attention. Meanwhile, Nicolas, disguised as Rabouine, would go out the back way arm in arm with a chambermaid paid for her help. He would proceed to the other end of the street, where a few carriages for hire were always parked, and would thus be in a position to follow Georgel. In his room, he took off his fine grey coat and donned Rabouine's livery and ratine cloak, while Rabouine himself, having put on wig and tricorn, wrapped himself in his chief's fur-collared cloak. They looked at themselves in the cheval glass: the light was dim enough to make it possible to confuse them. Their plan fell down on one delicate point: they would have to rely on the discretion of coachmen who could only be persuaded to obey the curious instructions of a foreign customer if a handful of silver *thalers* were flashed at them.

Without encountering any opposition, the operation got under way at seven o'clock when Georgel, clearly nervous, walked out into the street and, after a few steps and a suspicious glance around at the surroundings, climbed into his carriage. A few moments earlier, Nicolas, Rabouine and Semacgus had applied the instructions to the letter. As luck would have it, the abbé headed for the end of the street where Nicolas was waiting. At a reasonable distance, the commissioner's carriage, all lights extinguished, set off in pursuit.

He was not yet familiar enough with the city to have a clear idea of the route they were taking, although he did recognise a few monuments. Snow began falling again and he was afraid he would lose the trail, especially as Vienna did not have the same quality of public lighting as Paris. They were advancing now through a less populated area. He realised that they were approaching the ramparts of the old city. He made out massive shapes covered in snow, doubtless the bastions and curtain walls they had briefly glimpsed on their arrival in the Austrian capital. They stopped, and he leant out of the window. The coachman pointed to the abbé getting out of his carriage some two hundred yards ahead. Fortunately, that carriage was brilliantly lit. Nicolas advanced cautiously in the darkness. Having gone some distance, he heard a brief whistle and realised from the noise that followed that his own carriage had made an about-turn. He should never have paid the coachman in advance. He consoled himself with the thought that without that money the man would have refused to participate in such a risky enterprise in the first place. The fact remained that the noise of that incautious departure risked alerting Georgel and putting him on his guard. He decided to continue, still guided by the lights of Georgel's carriage, sure that he was invisible in the darkness. For a moment he stopped, his heart pounding: it had seemed to him that he could hear wet footsteps behind him. He turned, but was unable to make out anything because his eyes were dazzled by an approaching light. The wind had risen in gusts and the snow was falling in increasingly thick flakes: he was simultaneously blinded and deafened.

Suddenly, he was aware of the sound of lights being struck. He found himself surrounded by four or five strangers with lighted lanterns at their feet. Then the abbé loomed up in front of him, taller than usual and somehow unrecognisable. As in a dream, he saw him take off his cape and brandish a sword. He took stock of the situation: men behind him, and Georgel, doubtless accompanied by other hired assassins, facing him. It took him only a moment to understand how dangerous was this trap into which he had fallen. He had to keep a cool head. He calmly took off his cape, rolled it around his left arm and nimbly unsheathed his sword. He soon realised that the only direction in which he could escape was towards the rampart. He recalled the height of the fortifications. He could not jump off them into the void: he would break his legs. He would have to confront these men with his back to the parapet. He did not rate his chances at the end of such an unequal fight. But if they were to slaughter him, he intended to make them pay a high price for the satisfaction. Screaming like a man possessed, he thrust his sword at the nearest of his attackers, who, in stumbling back, knocked over his lantern and extinguished it. That's a good thing, thought Nicolas, for it showed him the course to follow. He thought of the Horatii, of old Corneille, and his famous 'Let him die! Or let a fine despair take him!' Capable of irony in the midst of the greatest danger, he mocked himself for mixing theatre and reality. This was a matter of life and death, and he was betting all he had on an unequal match.

He could hear Georgel, but was it really the abbé who was giving these angry, guttural orders? He assumed that his attackers were Austrians. A second thrust on his part was crowned with the same success: he even hit the lantern himself and knocked it over. He heard a sudden sharp crack and at that instant something lashed his legs and wrapped around them, and he fell. The abbé's coachman had used his whip. He lay for a moment with his ankles hobbled. Barely had he freed himself and risen than four strapping fellows swooped on him, their swords held high. He fell to his knees, still crossing swords with the men, but in this position his situation was becoming untenable. He had just managed to get to his feet again when the braided epaulette of his livery was pierced by a blade. At the same time, his own sword hit something, bending slightly, and went in. He heard a stifled cry and the sound of a body collapsing in the mud.

The fact remained that the number of his assailants seemed constantly to be increasing: doubtless, reinforcements had come running. He could not resist much longer. He felt that he was on the point of being overwhelmed. Jumping off the ramparts was still his last chance, whatever the risk. Just as he was about to yield to this suicidal temptation, he heard what sounded like a rumble of thunder. Even the attackers appeared to hesitate. He realised that a carriage and horses were heading towards them at a fast trot. The attackers scattered, lashed by a whip as they did so. He saw two horses rear up in front of him. A voice yelled at him to get in. He seized the door handle, and placed his foot on the step. He almost fell when the carriage tilted onto its side wheels, but was then thrown against the bodywork. The horses broke into a gallop. He clung on and finally managed to get inside and collapse on the seat, panting with exhaustion. A hail of bullets, some of which hit the carriage, greeted his retreat.

III

STORMS

I love peasants: they are not learned enough
to think crookedly.

MONTESQUIEU

Nicolas was getting his breath back. He touched his shoulder: the gilded braid of his epaulette hung wretchedly down his arm. A few inches more, and his chest would have been run through. A thousand questions were jostling in his head. What an incredible sequence of events! How to make sense of such a confused situation? Had he followed Georgel or his simulacrum? Their operation had been meticulously organised, so what exactly had gone wrong? Clearly their own stratagem had been turned against him and his companions. That could only mean that the adversary had known their plan. Who had he got it from? What was the reason for such a patent and determined attempt to kill him? Last but not least, who was the mysterious coachman who had materialised out of nowhere like a ghost, and what had motivated him to save Nicolas's life? He had mislaid his sword in the course of the rescue. He sighed, pleased that it was not his father's: he would not have forgiven himself for that loss. The carriage had at last slowed down and eventually came to a halt. He was still on his guard: anything could yet happen. The door opened and, there, divested of his coachman's uniform, stood the figure of Monsieur de Lastire, with a finger on his lips and a glint in his eye.

'Not a word, Marquis. Get out of the carriage and walk back to the Golden Bull without stopping: it's not far from here. In a quarter of an hour, I'll join you with my luggage.'

Nicolas tried to speak, but in vain: Lastire was already leaping onto his seat, whip in hand. He knew his way now and, once back at the hotel, went straight up to his room. He hastened to change and waited for the return of Rabouine and Semacgus. He was curious to hear the chevalier's explanations. He was reflecting on his surprising reappearance when the man himself, now in his everyday clothes, opened the door and, with a great sigh, collapsed into an armchair and smiled roguishly at Nicolas.

'Monsieur,' Nicolas said, 'rest assured that I am indebted to you. I owe you my life and will be for ever grateful. But for heaven's sake tell me how you manage to disappear and appear like the gods in a Rameau opera! We were worried about you and couldn't stop speculating about your fate!'

Lastire laughed and stamped on the floor with his boots. 'It's true I owe you an explanation. The most crucial fact is this: you mustn't think that Monsieur de Sartine let you go without a second thought. Good Lord, no! He cares too much about you. Part of him is still in the Châtelet, especially now that he's standing in for Monsieur Lenoir. He was worried about how you would fare in distant climes. My basic role was not to escort a porcelain effigy and embroider knick-knacks. It was to be your bodyguard, but I had a free hand as to how I was to exercise that function.'

It was Nicolas's turn to smile. But immediately his mood turned serious again. 'That's as may be, but I have to say that your logic is not mine; in fact it's even beyond me. What would you have said – and been justified in saying – if I had left you out and concealed our plan of action? Without upsetting your sensitivity, I would have appreciated more honesty from you on the true nature of your activities. I realise that you were probably not in a position to be so honest, and that you did not think it of great importance.'

'If it had been up to me alone, I would have granted you what you ask, but I had my orders. Be that as it may, Marquis, I dare to hope that our relations will continue as amicably as they began. And I observe with relief that your duel with the Grim Reaper, far from diminishing you, has made you all the more animated!'

Nicolas held out his hand. 'Forgive the passion with which I express myself, Chevalier. It is due to the shock caused to our friendship, and the anxiety we felt as to your fate. But perhaps some explanation now would—'

'In that case, I will make an effort to justify my conduct. I concede that it may have seemed strange to you. I belong to a phalanx recently created by Monsieur de Sartine, whose task it is to thwart the machinations of foreign courts both within our kingdom and outside ...'

'The minister told me something about its origins a few months ago.'[1]

'Using police methods without being part of the police, this phalanx is also concerned with keeping an eye on the factions at Court, who, as you know, are often exploited by our enemies. Its work must, however, be carried out in the most absolute secrecy, without disturbing any of the intimacy that exists between the Crowns. It was extremely important that such be the case with Austria, which is supposed to be our ally. I therefore had to disappear, without compromising myself, the better to protect you. There was a very delicate balance to be struck in this affair.'

'May I venture a question?'

'In so far as it is possible, I will gladly answer it.'

'Apart from your decisive appearance on the scene tonight, like a genie in an opera, did you previously try to warn me of imminent danger?'

'I sense that you were much taken with the charms of that masked lady.'

'So that was you?'

'Indeed it was! Forgive the stratagem, but what better way to approach you without being found out than such a disguise?'

'And what of the message? Why was it in Latin?'

'I knew that you had a Jesuit education. And it wasn't vulgar Latin. It was Cicero!'

So Semacgus had been right, thought Nicolas. 'What significance did you attach to the double message – double in every sense of the word?'

'I knew your reputation for fearlessness, so I hoped it would convince you to exercise the greatest caution. Alas, I bet on the wrong card!'

'It wasn't the easiest message to understand. Why make it so obscure?'

'Monsieur, you must stop all this quibbling, which can only be excused by this evening's events … Imagine what would have happened if the note had fallen, been picked up by one of those spies so common in this country, and then been examined by hostile eyes? Where would we be then, you and I, with your clarity and your words of condemnation?'

By now, he was stamping his boots wildly on the floor.

'I enjoy quibbling,' replied Nicolas, 'and I shan't abandon my tendency to be curious, even if it does try your patience. I understood the first message well enough, but couldn't make head or tail of the second. It seemed to be about disturbances at the castle …'

'It was about the supposed link between our abbé and those at Court and in the kingdom who are stirring up the factions against those in power. It's something that Monsieur de Sartine is well aware of and is following closely.'

It was no great surprise to Nicolas that Monsieur de Sartine, whose nostalgia for the days of Choiseul was a barely concealed secret, was well informed of whatever was being plotted against Turgot, the comptroller general of finances, and the spirit of reform. Having, in addition, great plans for his department, which he regarded as vital to the security of the country, he found it hard to bear Turgot's endless objections to his constant requests for credit. But the opposition to Turgot was much wider than that. For the moment, concerned as Nicolas was to calm the chevalier's visible irritation, he revealed the result of the search in Georgel's room.

'What did I say?' exclaimed Lastire after a moment's reflection. 'The hare has come out into the open. For all his attempts to play hide and seek with us, he has been unmasked! It's the clique of the Rohans, the Choiseuls and the Marsans. It's all becoming clear.'

That was not how Nicolas would have described the situation, which seemed to him increasingly confused. He realised suddenly that Lastire was still taking the false Georgel for the true.

'Your prey covered his tracks well,' he said, with a little smile. 'It was not the abbé who was thrusting and parrying in that shadow theatre. You were deceived by appearances, as I was.'

Lastire was unable to conceal his surprise. 'Really? Then you have lost the trail, and as he's leaving Vienna soon ... And yet ... He definitely left the hotel! I was right behind him and there's no question I saw him.'

'Then it must have been his brother! Because I can assure you that the man who attacked me wasn't Georgel. But Semacgus may have recognised and followed the right one. That's our last chance.'

'What are you saying, Marquis?'

Nicolas realised, not without a degree of satisfaction, that the chevalier was still thinking of the plan they had decided upon before he disappeared. He now revealed the inner workings of their last strategy.

For a time, Lastire was pensive. 'Then all we can do,' he said at last, 'is wait for our friends to return.'

Silence fell, and for a while both men were lost in thought. Lastire took out his pipe, put his legs up on a stool, and with his head back, started forming wreaths of smoke. Nicolas felt ill at ease, both physically and, above all, emotionally. His confused mood found an outlet in endless reflections, one thought leading to another with implacable logic. Each question gave rise to a series of propositions which invariably took him back to his starting point. This inability to move forward led to further questions and the same mental process was repeated, made all the worse by the fatigue he felt after the evening's events.

It went without saying that if the chevalier belonged to this secret phalanx, discretion must be his first and most absolute obligation. The commissioner was part of the family, and yet … He recalled that Sartine was well accustomed to keeping information to himself. He liked to conceal part of what he knew, even from those closest to him, including Nicolas. He always preserved an element of secrecy which he could use at the right moment, not only to his own advantage but also to the advantage of the case in progress.

As for the conversation he had just had with Lastire, he was surprised that it had taken on something of the feel of a duel, a verbal one certainly, but one in which the man's changeable personality – which involved an element of contained violence – had been given free rein. Beneath the idle officer doing his embroidery, Nicolas had caught a glimpse of a man of action and decision with an almost volatile temperament: the speed and suddenness with which he had rescued him bore witness to that. He finally realised that this uncertainty as to the chevalier's true nature must reflect his own disappointment at not having discerned his character from the start, of having been completely deceived by appearances. He had always prided himself on his instinctive insight into other human beings, and yet in this instance he had failed to perceive the truth. He still believed that the first impression was often the right one, but the fact remained that Lastire had, from the start, deliberately contrived to appear pleasant and even somewhat foolish because that was the image he wished to present of himself.

It was nearly midnight when Rabouine reappeared, his mission to divert the Austrian spies complete. With a consummate skill born of long experience, he had led them a merry dance, at last bringing them back full circle to the Golden Bull. He seemed eager now to rest from his labours with some comely chambermaid from the top floor. He had reckoned without Nicolas, who asked him to stay with them to wait for Semacgus and draw the first lessons from this eventful night. He gave an account of it to an astonished Rabouine.

As time went by, and Semacgus had still not returned, Nicolas began to worry, already blaming himself for having dragged his friend into this affair. The night slowly passed. At about half past three, the door burst open and an unsteady and beaming Semacgus made his entrance and collapsed into an armchair, making the wood creak alarmingly. Nicolas's immediate fear was that his friend had fallen into his old ways: when he had first met him, fourteen years earlier, Semacgus had been leading, if not a dissolute life, at least a very licentious one, which age and the beneficial influence of Awa, his black cook, had somehow brought under control. But nothing that Nicolas surmised was turning out to be correct tonight.

'Come now,' said Semacgus, looking at them sardonically, 'don't hide your joy at seeing me again. Good Lord, you look like a flock of blue penitents.'

'What does that mean?' asked Nicolas, stiffly. 'What have penitents got to do with anything, let alone blue ones?'

'Oh, I see my first impression is confirmed. Nobody is in the mood for humour. We are forbidden any extravagance. Nevertheless, at the risk of breaking the mood, I'm going to tell you who these penitents are …'

Nicolas knew that, in this state, nothing would stop Semacgus and he would have to be patient.

'A long time ago, putting in at Marseilles, I felt the desire to give my surgical knife a little practice, and so I went in search of some corpse or other to cut up. It was then that I stumbled upon a confraternity of charitable persons whose mission consisted of giving the tortured the consolations of a Christian end and a plot for burial. The common people call them the monks of death. No need to tell you how they greeted my approaches! You remind me of them. Don't look at me like that. Yes, I did drink a lot of brandy, but it was all in a good cause!'

'There we have it!' said Nicolas, relieved. 'Before we go any further, let me tell you what happened tonight—'

'But now I come to think of it,' Semacgus cut in, 'I think there are four of us.' He rose and made an unsteady bow in Lastire's direction. 'A thousand pardons, Monsieur. The fumes of alcohol made all the faces blur into one, so to speak, and—'

'Precisely,' interrupted Nicolas, 'you are entitled to an explanation.'

'Before that, Rabouine, go and fetch me a tankard of cold beer. There is nothing more effective in clearing the head.'

Without waiting, Nicolas launched for the second time into an account of that evening's adventures.

'Pah!' said Semacgus. 'Failure all down the line! Well, it leaves me cold, because I had the real Georgel in my sights!'

'How do you know it was the real one?'

'The same way you know you followed the false one!' roared Semacgus, before knocking back the contents of the emblazoned tankard that Rabouine had just handed him.

What a remarkable fellow Rabouine was, thought Nicolas. Where on earth had he found beer at three in the morning?

'Go on, laugh! Yes, I did have the right one, and he led me a merry dance all over Vienna for hours – in the dark, to boot.'

He rose to his feet.

'Flee, star of the day, let the shadows prevail
Night, it is time to spread your sombre veil!
Now that all is still, let the games begin.'[2]

'Well?' said Nicolas, laughing despite himself at that remarkably accurate bass voice. 'Whom did Georgel meet? Huascar, Zaïre, Ali or Adario?'[3]

'Pah! A much commoner character. Gross features, broad back, big feet and a hemp wig which even our friend Gabriel the sailor wouldn't want. They conversed for a long time in the shadow of a church portal. Papers were exchanged, and gold too. Then Georgel left, and I abandoned him.'

'Why?' asked Lastire, who had been silent thus far.

'What would I have gained in trailing him? The beast was returning to the fold.'

'You didn't know that. What if he had had another appointment?'

'Commissioner Le Floch will teach you, Chevalier, that one sometimes has to choose the lesser of two evils. It seemed to me more useful to discover the nature of the individual in question.'

'I have no doubt, Monsieur, that you succeeded in that task.'

'Of course, Monsieur, beyond anything I could have imagined! He, too, took a carriage, and I followed in mine. Snow is such a godsend, it both deafens and blinds ... He got out at Graben and walked down an alley until he came to a low tavern. I walked just behind him. Unlike Georgel, of course, he didn't know me. He met a man in a black coat. I drank a lot.'

'Why so?'

'Actually, I pretended to drink a lot while drinking a little ... A drunkard doesn't arouse suspicion. I could teach you a thing or two about that ... There were wooden booths. I was back to back with these fellows, half lying on the bench. You know how well wood transmits sounds. I could hear their conversation as if I was among them. Now let me tell you what I heard and the conclusions I drew from it.'

They all moved closer to Semacgus, who had noticeably lowered his voice.

'What were they saying to each other? They were lamenting the fact that the little abbé was leaving, because he'd been so useful to them, and so innocent. The truth was that these two had been providing him with material, for money of course. They had managed to persuade him, with their regular deliveries, on the one hand that all the secrets of the French had long been known, and on the other hand that, thanks to them, he was obtaining authentic Austrian documents.'

'I understand,' said Nicolas. 'We have seen the result.'

'Yes, the result is that the late King's secret network has been rendered useless. It should already have been completely reorganised, but that would have taken months, and only the King was in a position to decide that. But he died and his successor does not seem eager to remedy the situation. Thus, in return for a few small revelations of their own secrets, the Austrians have persuaded us to abandon a system that was useful to our diplomatic service.'

'And what is Georgel's role in all this?'

'The abbé, who is anything but innocent, may be playing at appearing so. He smells a rat, which might explain his reluctance to unmask his informer. It is never an honourable thing to be the foolish object of a deception. Another hypothesis, which does not contradict the first, is that these documents are for him a means to ingratiate himself with those who are manipulating him – as we now know – from Paris. In short, what we have is a man who has been deceived, consciously or not, and who has contributed to the destruction of a whole system. I doubt we'll ever know the full story of this imbroglio … I will add, to close my account, that abandoning my intermediary – a thousand regrets, Chevalier – I followed the man in black all the way to his destination.'

'Which was …?' asked Lastire.

'The offices of the *Statthalter bei der Regierung für Niederösterreich*, which he entered with a key.'

'What does that mean?'

'The offices of His Excellency the Governor of Lower Austria, who controls the police in Vienna, their lieutenant general, as it were. So Georgel, who claimed to be thwarting the actions of the cabinet in Vienna, was merely serving as a screen for an offensive by the Austrians. They read our secrets and hand over their most hackneyed ones to us, all the better to paralyse us. A master stroke, I think you'll agree! And with that, gentlemen, I'm going to bed.'

He got heavily to his feet and walked out of the room, leaving his audience dismayed at these revelations.

Nicolas sighed. 'I shall soon have to go and inform the ambassador of this sad conclusion to our investigation. I doubt he will be best pleased.'

'Nevertheless,' said Lastire, 'it does help to remove a thorn from his flesh. Now that everything has become clear, he knows what he's dealing with. At least he'll be rid of Georgel. It's up to him now to wipe out the memory of Prince Louis, if he can!'

Lastire having pronounced the moral of the story, they went their separate ways.

Monday 6 March 1775

Apart from the tensing of his facial muscles, Monsieur de Breteuil's first reaction did him great honour as the King's representative. He had listened unflinchingly to Nicolas's report, which was presented without flourishes. He immediately deplored the offence done to France and took full stock of the consequences. Then, as if to convince himself of what he had just learnt, he went through all the elements again. That an attempt had been made on the life of an envoy of the Court was of no account: it was one of the risks of the game.

'So, if I understand correctly, the Austrians know all our secrets. Through the intermediary of a supposed renegade, they have used this rascal of a priest to bring about our misfortune. What's more, they have included as bait, and to make the thing more convincing, a few genuine papers of no great political consequence, or long out of date, combined with a lot of others that are forged and full of lies. Is that it?'

He began laughing nervously and twisting his cambric cravat.

'The worst thing about this whole affair is that Georgel thought he could put a spoke in my wheel by keeping me out of his little commerce. The fact is that he has done me a service. I am indebted to you, Marquis, for having enlightened me so effectively. My debt will be all the greater if, when you make your report to Versailles, you insist on the singular disloyalty and unfathomable stupidity of that wretched priest.'

His anger next led Monsieur de Breteuil to express his hatred for Prince Louis, whom he accused of having unthinkingly fallen into the trap laid by the Austrians. Nicolas rode out the storm, although it grew all the more violent when he revealed to the ambassador the gist of the half-burnt paper found in the abbé's room. There followed a bitter diatribe which ended in a sarcastic laugh. This would all be laid at Rohan's door. The Empress had never supported him and the Queen had espoused her mother's antipathy towards a debauched prelate who, to make matters worse, had been an accredited courtier to Madame du Barry. One of these days, he, Breteuil, would be in a position to make him regret his past actions.

'The case seems to be settled,' said Nicolas, 'which means, Ambassador, that there is no reason for us to stay in Vienna any longer. On the contrary, this crucial information, and the fact that your dispatches need to be conveyed, require us to return to the kingdom as soon as possible.'

'Your companions can leave, but not you. And how are we to

convey my dispatches? What are you suggesting? You assured me—'

'It was merely a form of words. What is to be conveyed is the gist.'

'Could you convey that gist to me now?'

'If it's of any reassurance to you …'

Nicolas closed his eyes. He thought for a moment, then began speaking in a monotone, as if he were reading something.

'*There is unrest in Bohemia. A number of villages, discontented with the statute labour they owe to their lords, banded together and proceeded to the town of Königgrätz, hoping to seize it. The raising of the bridges put paid to their plans. The Hussites, a sect who are widespread in Bohemia, seem to be the most roused* … Do you want the beginning of the second dispatch?'

Stunned, Breteuil nodded without a word.

'*The unrest among the peasants is more general and its ill effects greater than I indicated in my first dispatch. As there is an attempt here to conceal most of the disorder, I did not see fit to appear more informed on the matter than the minister desires, let alone to hold forth on the causes of this misfortune which threatens Bohemia and its landed gentry with irreparable losses* …'

Alarmed, Breteuil put his finger on his lips. 'Marquis, this is beyond me. What marvel is this? I demand that you satisfy my curiosity at once.'

'It's quite simple. As a child, I learnt a lot by heart. My Jesuit teachers completed my education in that domain. It is enough for me to know the beginnings of paragraphs. I number them by a method known only to me. After that, everything flows easily.'

'Monsieur, you must teach this! You've solved the problem of secrecy!'

'Provided one isn't subjected to torture,' said Nicolas with a smile.

'The fact remains, alas, that I cannot authorise you to leave Vienna. The Empress wishes to entrust you with a package and a letter for the Queen. We depend upon her satisfaction, which can take time to acquire. I understand there's a medallion that needs to be finished. So you are obliged to remain here until we receive the package. I advise you to take advantage of the city.'

Back at the Golden Bull, Nicolas gathered his companions together and explained the unfortunate situation. Each of them had his opinion as to how best to respond. Semacgus was pleased that he would have a chance to pursue his botanical studies, although he took care not to insist on the fact. Monsieur de Jussieu's recommendations had opened many doors for him and, in a few days, he had enriched his knowledge with a view to his great treatise on tropical plants. Rabouine was happy to place himself at Nicolas's disposal. As for the Chevalier de Lastire, it was his opinion that, now that the Georgel affair had been clarified, there would be no further attacks on the commissioner. The presence of a false abbé proved that the various events of the previous evening were intimately linked. Therefore he proposed, unless Nicolas objected, to leave Vienna. He would entrust his luggage to them and would get back to France as quickly as he could and inform Vergennes and Sartine of their discoveries. He would take with him only personal mail: any other missive would put him at risk if he was intercepted within the hereditary States or the empire. Nobody objected to this proposal. The chevalier planned to leave that very day. Nicolas shut himself in his room to write a few letters: one to his son, one to Aimée, and a short, friendly message to Inspector Bourdeau, who he guessed, despite Sartine's shrewd handling of the situation, was vexed at not having been part of the adventure. At two in the afternoon, Lastire took his leave of them, an opportunity for Nicolas to express once again his gratitude for the man's crucial assistance. They all felt a little sad to see him go: he was a good companion, who had enlivened the monotony of a long journey with his imagination and his shafts of wit. They had also been made aware of the various facets of his personality, how decisive, yet at the same time touchy, this man handpicked by Sartine to combat foreign intrigues against the kingdom could be. Dinner was a gloomy affair. After the action and violence of the previous few days, there was a distinct drop in tension and each man soon took refuge in his room.

From Tuesday 7 March to Monday 10 April 1775
The period that now ensued was pleasant in some ways, but time soon began to weigh heavily on them. Nicolas occupied the first days with a more complete tour of the imperial capital, although the city was not large enough for this pastime to fill all his waking hours. He did not forget those closest to him. He discovered a fine damascened ceremonial sword which he was sure Louis would love. For Aimée, he was attracted by a Corfu coral necklace. He was thoughtful enough also to remember Monsieur de Sartine's hobby. Recalling that, at the minister's urging, Abbé Georgel had sent him a superb curly wig the previous year, he enquired after the best local manufacturer. A unique model ordered by the Magistrato Camerale of the city of Padua,[4] recently deceased, proved to be exactly what he was looking for. He was assured that not even the doge of Venice possessed a longer or thicker one, with such lustrous silver tints. It would undoubtedly be the centrepiece of Sartine's musical wig library.

For Monsieur de Noblecourt, he finally, after constant searching, unearthed an edition of Suetonius's *Lives of the Twelve Caesars* in a text edited by the poet Franciscus Van Gudendorp, bound in full vellum with thick gilded thread as a frame. This superb volume would delight the bibliophile former magistrate and peerless Latinist. Nicolas recalled that he had not long ago parted with a copy of Ovid that was dear to his heart and given it to Louis Le Floch as a present before he left for school at Juilly. A bottle of slivovitz and a snuffbox for Bourdeau, lace handkerchiefs for Marion and Catherine and, last but not least, a fur hat for good old Poitevin, whose head tended to feel the cold, completed his purchases. He had found something for everyone.

The weeks went by, punctuated by a number of unexpected events. The Archduke Maximilian, whom Nicolas had escorted from the border of Flanders to Paris, having learnt of his presence in Vienna and remembering the delight the commissioner's company had given him, invited him to an intimate dinner. He detained him until a late hour, asking him a thousand questions about the Court, those in power, and the use of torture in criminal procedures. It was a practice Maria Theresa was thinking of banning in the hereditary States. In the archduke's opinion, it was not a reliable path to the truth but, rather, a blind method which forced both the guilty and the innocent to accuse themselves. He had an interesting face and a brisk manner that some might have thought abrupt. In that, he resembled the Emperor, although he was less affable and communicative. Coadjutor of the Teutonic Order, he also held the office of Governor of the Low Countries.

Nicolas attended a gala performance of an Italian opera in the presence of the Court at the Burgtheater on Michaelerplatz opposite the Hofburg. He had been struck by the architecture of the building, with its large stained-glass windows and promenade balcony. The multitude and splendour of the immense chandeliers were such that the auditorium seemed to be bathed in sunlight. The three men were dazzled spectators of the premiere of *The Return of Tobias* conducted by Haydn at the Kärntnertor theatre. The whole of Viennese society had turned out to attend this new work by the Kapellmeister of the Esterházys. The oratorio itself and its superb performers were greeted with unanimous applause. Expressiveness and simplicity were so intimately combined that the listeners could not help being moved. As for the choruses, they demonstrated a passion to rival the best of Handel. Nicolas was astonished at the vocal prowess of the soprano, Magdalena Friberth.

At last, a call from Monsieur de Breteuil put an end to their wait. Nicolas hastened to the embassy, where the ambassador handed over, with a great many instructions, the medallion and the letter with the imperial seal intended for the Queen. A few friendly words of farewell, and Nicolas went back to his friends. Preparations for departure did not take long. Only Rabouine pulled a long face, as it would mean bidding a heart-rending farewell to the local girls. Nicolas had virtually to tear him away when they were finally ready to set out on the morning of Tuesday 11 April.

Even though spring should have appeared long before now, the winter continued, as severe as ever, making their return journey especially difficult. The alternation of ice and snow with milder periods of heavy rain transformed the roads into potholes, and several times a day Nicolas and his companions had to get out of their carriage and help the coachman and postilion to get the wheels out of furrows filled with frozen mud. The weather became so bad that for several days they had to stop in Augsburg. Fortunately, the town's inn, the Golden Grapes, took them in while the storm was raging. The innkeeper, an exceedingly affable man named Johann Sigmund Mayr, turned out to be a charming host and a tireless storyteller. At Semacgus's prompting, he regaled them with a thousand anecdotes that enlivened evenings spent around the huge fireplace in the main room. So it was that Nicolas heard again of an adventurer by the name of Casanova who had stayed at this inn, where his good humour and appetite for food, notably for macaroni cheese, had remained legendary. As an apprentice police officer, Nicolas had been present at his arrest in Paris over a question of debt.[5] Thanks to Choiseul's leniency, his forced sojourn at Fort-Lévêque had lasted only a few days.

Between Augsburg and Munich, they were intercepted in open country by a troop of hussars. It was a worrying situation. They were far from anywhere, poorly armed and in no position to put up any resistance. They were forced to get out of the carriage, stand in line and endure an incomprehensible speech from the civilian leader of the detachment, who accused them of being spies. Nicolas showed his *lettre de courrier* bearing the French arms, but this did not seem to impress their interlocutor, who told them they would be searched and their luggage inspected. The letter from the Empress was handled with more circumspection, the ruffian not daring this time to carry out the final outrage: Nicolas had warned him that opening it would be tantamount to a crime of lèse-majesté that would involve the two Crowns. The package that contained the medallion depicting Maria Theresa was treated with less respect. The soldiers looked through their effects, without finding anything untoward, while their leader watched with increasing frustration. At last, without a further word or glance, the troop withdrew, leaving the travellers' things scattered in the snow. It took them more than an hour to get them back into some kind of order. Nicolas noticed that Rabouine was constantly glancing towards the misty slope of a hill. What was it he thought he could see there? When questioned, he remained silent.

Night was coming by the time they set off again. It was freezing cold and the falling snow immediately turned to ice. What had those hussars been looking for? Their leader had examined everything, even Semacgus's chamber pot. Nicolas was pleased that he had used a stratagem to convey the ambassador's dispatches. He had even memorised the list of numbers that gave him the beginning of each paragraph: the key to his system. Even if it had been written down and they had found it, they would have struggled to understand it – except that its discovery would doubtless have made things worse, prolonged the search and justified an arrest. In any case, the episode was just one more in the sequence of extraordinary events that had befallen them since their arrival in Vienna.

Their return to France coincided with a worsening of the travel conditions. It became harder and harder to use the roads, and the masters of the staging posts were increasingly reluctant to risk their horses. The storm was so fierce that at times they were unable to move even at a walking pace. The terrible winter showed no sign of relaxing its grip. Outside the towns, snow accumulated in the depressions, forming great edifices that soon turned to ice before collapsing. From time to time, they all had to join in the hard labour of shovelling away the ice and snow. In places, the freezing rain covered the soil with a sheet of ice three inches thick, which, added to the previous layers, constituted a treacherous expanse on which it was impossible to place your feet and which creaked in a sinister fashion beneath the wheels of the carriage. When the thaw came, the ground was transformed into a muddy tide.

At the staging posts, where they stopped, exhausted, Nicolas had to use all his authority to obtain the best horses. Rumour was rife, and the grim-faced drinkers at the tables lowered their voices at their approach. Several, when questioned, replied reluctantly that this year was likely to be a disastrous one for them. The harshness of the autumn and winter combined, and the fact that there was still so much snow and ice in March and April, hampered the natural cycle of agricultural toil. The earth was sick, and nothing emerged from it. How could wheat grow in such conditions? The superstitious fears that had been aroused did not help. Northern lights had been observed, at night the cracking of the ice awoke the countryside as if the earth had trembled, there had been storms of bloody hailstones, and the sky would blaze like a fire at night and grow dark during the day. To sensitive minds, these all seemed like grim omens, harbingers of calamities still to come. The almanacs distributed by pedlars throughout the kingdom announced to the panic-stricken population that there would be several eclipses in the year 1775, which added still further to the widely felt sense of terror.

The closer they got to Paris, the more overwhelmed they were by contradictory and threatening news. During a halt near Chalons, an anxious Nicolas dispatched Rabouine to take a look at a gathering of hostile peasants. His complicity with the common people would facilitate contact. He returned just as their carriage was about to tip over. Nicolas noted his air of consternation.

'The people are angry,' he said. 'They're talking again about a famine pact, just like under the late King. They weren't very inclined to talk to me, but they finally opened their hearts and told me everything. In a nearby village, there has been a rising against a rich miller—'

'That's curious,' remarked Semacgus. 'I've never heard of a poor miller. It's one of the most privileged positions in these times of ours!'

'And quite rightly so! This one was accused of being the person behind the increase in the price of grain. Informed of this riot, the police arrived, but their threats fell on deaf ears and they were forced to withdraw under a hail of stones. In less than an hour, the mill and its outbuildings were razed to the ground. So great was the people's anger that some even started to dismember the poultry alive.[6] Coaches found in a shed were smashed with lead bars.'

'The villains!' cried Nicolas. 'And was there no reaction from the authorities?'

'Indeed there was. A detachment of gunners arrived, and more than two hundred rioters were arrested. The Criminal Lieutenant of Chalons has announced that there will be grave repercussions. But there is worse yet. Along with the unrest there is a great deal of fear. Old wives' tales are being relayed from village to village, spreading panic among the people.'

'Come now!' said Semacgus. 'Don't tell me it's all the fault of the beast of Gévaudan! That was slaughtered a long time ago.'

'You may laugh, Monsieur, but this is just as bad. They say that in the surrounding forests a woman with a serpent's head has been seen, howling at the moon. It's claimed that her return coincides with events that are disastrous for the kingdom. Her first appearance is said to date from 1740.'

'Is that so?' said Nicolas. 'Why 1740?'

'A young man's remark,' retorted Semacgus. 'That was a terrible year, the worst of the century. The winter would never end, just like this one. In May, the wheat barely covered the fields. People resorted to public prayer and processions of relics. The heat and drought were terrible. Tens of thousands died. The memory of that time lives on.'

'Everyone's of the belief,' said Rabouine, 'that every seven years since 1740, terrible things have happened.'

'Let's see,' said Nicolas counting on his fingers. 'In 1747?'

'The beginning of the War of the Austrian Succession,' said Semacgus.

'And 1754?'

'Take your pick: the birth of Louis XVI, the exile of the archbishop of Paris.'

'No, it doesn't really work for that year! What about 1761?'

'Choiseul went to war and … Nicolas Le Floch was made commissioner!'

They all laughed.

'And 1768?'

'A new mistress for the King: Madame du Barry!'

'And 1775 is this year. If I've understood correctly, we'll have to be careful in 1782 and 1789!'

'As for your woman with a serpent's head,' said Semacgus, 'I'm reminded of an old story. Lusignan, in the Poitou, was famous for the periodic apparition of the fairy Mélusine, whose body ended in a dragon's tail. She would appear at night and let out three mysterious cries. This happened every seven years, whenever France was on the verge of a disaster. No doubt your serpent woman is the granddaughter of that fairy. The story has spread from the Poitou to Champagne and has changed, depending on individual imagination and ancestral fears.'

As they approached Paris, they passed groups of peasants and others walking by the sides of the road. Some had their heads bowed, others threw glances full of hatred at their fine carriage, laden as it was with luggage. During one of their halts, Rabouine had learnt that the disturbances were spreading. They had reached Meaux, where disorder and banditry were rife and merchants and millers were being forced by raging bands to give up their stocks below the current price. Unrest and pillaging were gaining ground, overwhelming the mounted constabulary. The authorities had tried being honest and reasonable but nothing seemed to appease the people's anger.

Worried by this news, Nicolas and his companions entered Paris on the afternoon of Sunday 30 April through Faubourg Saint-Martin. This marshy district was not the pleasantest approach to the capital of the kingdom, remarked Nicolas. They were stopped at the tollgate. He introduced himself to the official and their luggage was immediately allowed in. Their carriage had to make its way through the crowd of innkeepers who always stood there making fantastic promises to entice foreigners and provincials to their 'palaces': a vulgar ploy in which the representatives of reputable hotels, sure of their reputation and the effectiveness of the travellers' guides, did not indulge. These sinister-looking individuals all swore on their consciences that one could not find better fare anywhere else and that their competitors were merely rogues, without honour or integrity, who sought only to fleece any innocent customer who might lend an ear to their fallacious descriptions. Under the impassive gaze of Louis XIV, depicted as Hercules on the monumental gate, a few cracks of the whip dispersed the noisy crowd and the carriage proceeded through the insalubrious streets.

The bells of Saint-Eustache were tolling three o'clock by the time they reached the Noblecourt house in Rue Montmartre. Nicolas's luggage was taken down and Semacgus kept the carriage, impatient to get back to Vaugirard and see Awa again. The commissioner was struck by the sense of lethargy that enveloped the house: it seemed to have been abandoned. There was no fire in the oven in the servants' pantry, and no sign of Marion, Catherine or Poitevin. What grave event could have upset their habits? He climbed the stairs four by four and discovered Monsieur de Noblecourt writing at the rosewood desk in the drawing room, with a sad, intent look on his face. Cyrus and Mouchette, huddled under his armchair, made no noise, but merely turned to look anxiously at Nicolas, with none of the joy they usually showed on seeing him again, although the dog did wag his tail slowly while the cat let out a weak groan. To break this terrifying silence, Nicolas cleared his throat.

Monsieur de Noblecourt raised his head. With a gesture that did not escape Nicolas, he folded the piece of paper on which he had been writing and covered it with his hand. He sighed, and a weak smile crossed his lined face.

'God be praised, there you are!' He put down his pen. 'We were waiting for you.'

'What's happened? I suspect some sad occurrence.'

'How could we ever hope to hide anything from you? You must keep a cool head when you hear what I'm about to tell you.'

Nicolas felt a kind of icy wave go through his body. 'Is it something to do with my son?'

'Don't be too alarmed, there's nothing irreparable. The superior at Juilly informed me that Louis was missing. The likeliest supposition is that he ran away from school.'

'The likeliest ...'

The coldness was followed by a wave of heat and a pain that cut him in half and took his breath away.

Monsieur de Noblecourt stood up in great haste and made Nicolas sit down in a *bergère*. As quickly as he could, he walked towards a sideboard and took out a glass and a decanter.

'Here, drink this. You've often mentioned that cordial dispensed by Old Marie at the Châtelet. This liqueur from Arquebuse is of the same kind. It's a well-known antidote for an emotion of this nature.'

He sat down and waved the paper on which he had been working when Nicolas arrived. 'Don't think that we merely lamented without doing anything. Let me tell you all that has so far been accomplished.'

Nicolas stood up. 'I'm leaving for Juilly immediately.'

'Out of the question,' Monsieur de Noblecourt said firmly. 'Just listen to me. As soon as I was told what had happened, I informed Monsieur Lenoir.'

'Monsieur Lenoir?'

'Yes, Monsieur Lenoir. He has recovered from his illness and resumed his functions as Lieutenant General of Police. I also referred the case to Monsieur de Sartine. They conferred and decided to dispatch Bourdeau to Juilly to investigate. Who better could they have chosen than our friend? He is due back today, and I have no doubt he will be in possession of some useful information. Wait for him, and rest until he comes. You will decide together on what needs to be done. You trust him, quite rightly, and I am sure he will have acted just as you would have done yourself. There is no point debating the matter until we have more of the facts. I was just writing a letter to the Criminal Lieutenant to inform him of this disappearance. It is surely just a childish escapade ... You don't seem convinced.'

'It's just that when he was here at Christmas I found him in a strange mood, as if there was something upsetting him. You should also know that during my mission to Vienna, there was an attempt on my life, from which I only narrowly escaped ...'

'Again!'

'... and I wonder if Louis's disappearance might not have some connection with that.'

Monsieur de Noblecourt was thinking hard, with his chin on his hand. 'Try to keep calm. I know, that's an easy thing to say to a father. We all make many mistakes before we catch up with reason. Reason runs away from us because it thinks it is worth being run after. It does everything it can to test us. You will laugh one day about this trial.'

Nicolas did not feel in a fit state to appreciate the wisdom of the comment. Wounded deep in his soul, he also felt his anguish physically, as a painful knot in his stomach.

'Needless to say, Lenoir has given instructions for the road to London to be carefully watched, as well as the embarkation points for boats to England in the Channel ports. It's quite possible that, on a whim, Louis decided to go and see his mother.'

'That is indeed a useful precaution.'

'Did he have any money with him?'

'None at all. The annual fee for Juilly is nine hundred *livres* and I paid it when he started there. It covers almost everything. In addition I also gave him a small sum to buy any little things he needed and to pay for his return trips to Paris. Not much, to be honest. Certainly not enough for a journey to England.'

There came the sound of hurried footsteps ascending the stairs. Bourdeau appeared, wearing a brown frock coat and riding boots. He was out of breath and his face was flushed. He glanced anxiously at Nicolas, who was still seated, and had to stop himself from taking him in his arms. He turned towards Monsieur de Noblecourt, who, anticipating his question, nodded.

'I'm sorry. Who could have expected such a thing?'

'I could,' said Nicolas, 'since Christmas. I noticed certain things which should not have deceived a father ...'

'What is bound to happen, happens,' remarked Noblecourt. 'There are strange inevitabilities which drive a person to act according to his own nature and the pressing demands of the moment.'

'We will have to clarify all this eventually. Bourdeau, I'm pleased to see you again, I missed you ...'

The inspector's eyes lit up. That Nicolas should think of saying that to him at such a moment filled him with unparalleled joy. He had to make an effort to recover his self-control.

'I met the principal, the teachers, the servants, and his schoolfriends. They all praise your son's intelligence, politeness and loyalty. True, his results had been slightly less good since Christmas. Something was preying on his mind. There was a quarrel with an arrogant classmate, followed by a kind of childish duel, with compasses, in the attic of the school. They were soon separated. The reason for the quarrel? Silence on the matter. No one wanted to speak about it. Louis ran away, leaving all his things except for his seal and the copy of Ovid's *Metamorphoses* that Monsieur de Noblecourt gave him as a gift.'

Moved by this, the old magistrate turned away and went and pressed his forehead against the window pane. Cyrus was moaning softly and scratching at his master's leg.

'He had distributed his Cotignac, or at least what remained of it, among his closest friends.'

'Is that all?'

'There's no trace of him. You know as well as I do the disastrous state of the roads. I questioned the neighbours, the people at the staging posts, the local peasants. Nothing! Nobody saw him. Worse still, the principal told me an extremely disturbing fact. Two days before his ... his departure, a man came to the school and asked to see Louis in order to give him a letter from you ...'

'From me? Impossible!'

'The principal had no reason to object.'

'Or to consent!'

'Louis recognised your handwriting. He and the stranger conversed alone. The next day, he seemed even more sombre than before.'

'Did he describe this mysterious character?'

'He was a Capuchin monk.'

'Another Capuchin! I really can't get on with Capuchins. We have already had dealings with them on some bloody occasions. One in particular. A shadow in a dark cloak! Remember the past ...'[7]

'It's true that a monk's cowl is the best way to conceal an identity.'

'I fear an abduction, somehow connected with what happened in Austria. That was my first thought.'

Bourdeau gave a start. 'You were in danger. I knew it!'

'I'll tell you all about it later. For now—'

'I can't believe,' interrupted Noblecourt, turning to them with red eyes, 'that Louis wouldn't have come and told his father the reasons for his conduct. I don't think he's in hiding, and I trust him completely.'

Nicolas stood up and held out his hands to his old friend. 'The day I entered this house, I discovered what wisdom and goodness are.'

'Now,' said Noblecourt, 'let us indeed be wise. Patience is the main thing. I'm sure Bourdeau has put our police, the envy of all Europe, on a war footing. We just have to wait for information, which should soon come flooding in.'

Bourdeau nodded.

'Monsieur Lenoir, Monsieur de Sartine and Monsieur de Vergennes all asked to see you as soon as you returned. It's said the Queen enquired after you three times.'

Noblecourt rummaged in his desk and took out two letters, which he handed to Nicolas. 'These came a few days ago. This business has got me so muddled, I almost forgot them.'

Nicolas recognised Aimée d'Arranet's usual square sea-green paper and untidy handwriting. In his helpless state, the sight of it warmed his heart. The other letter intrigued him: he did not recognise either the handwriting on the envelope, with its heavy downstrokes, or the red, almost black, seal. He put Aimée's letter in his pocket. Having asked his friends to excuse him, he broke the strange seal, a religious one if he was not mistaken. This envelope contained a message which was itself sealed. The sight of the arms and the handwriting made his heart miss a beat, and for the second time he had to sit down. Worried, Noblecourt and Bourdeau ran to him.

'Bad news?'

'The past is knocking at my door. I have no idea what fate has in store for me.'

IV

DISTURBANCES

His eyes staring into the distance, Nicolas sighed.

'It's a letter from my sister Isabelle de Ranreuil. You can imagine my emotion ... I'm going upstairs to change. Then I'll go and see Monsieur Lenoir and tomorrow I'll leave early for Versailles. Pierre, I'd like you to accompany me to Rue Neuve-Saint-Augustin. Find us a carriage.'

'Will you dine with us?' asked Monsieur de Noblecourt. 'And you too, Bourdeau? Monsieur de La Borde is already invited. You'll be among friends. It'll do you good. The servants have gone to Saint-Eustache for vespers, to pray for ... But don't worry, everything will be ready in time – you know Catherine!'

'It would be ungracious of me to refuse.'

By the time he reached his room, he felt nauseous and short of breath. He sat down on his bed, opened Isabelle's letter and began reading.

> *Ranreuil, 3 April 1775*
> *My dear brother,*
> *It pleases me that for the first time I can give you that name, which unites us for ever. By the time you receive this letter, I will have taken the*

veil. It is with a clear head that I have made the decision to withdraw to the royal abbey of Fontevrault. The great age of our house and the inheritance of my aunt Madame de Guenouel allow me this final proud impulse. The mother superior, who was born a Pardailhan d'Antin, is a cousin of this aunt. I shall lay a large dowry at the feet of the divine bridegroom.

That is why I wish our father's inheritance to revert to you entirely. Friends I still have at Court inform me that you are known there as 'young Ranreuil'. I am not unaware that you once refused the King's suggestion that you take the title which was yours by right and which your services have made ever more illustrious. You will accept it from your sister, thus offering your son the chance of a future which will open great positions to him. You will not thereby lose your office as commissioner. Have no compunction about being the Marquis de Ranreuil. Fulfil the wishes of our father who would have desired you to be so had he lived. Alas! Nothing, of course, obliges you to make such a legitimate act public knowledge. As for our house, it is yours. Our steward, Guillard, will henceforth be accountable to you. Accept all this simply, coming as it does from someone who is descending alive into the tomb, as once you received our father's ring and sword.

Whatever you decide, I will respect your feelings, unless you refuse what I am humbly offering. You have no more loyal friend than I. Fifteen years ago you obliged me to be so. I will say it to you now more freely than I could then, knowing that my words will seem to you to be uttered in better faith now and that you will have no reason to doubt that, with all my soul, I remain, even at the foot of the altar, your loyal and loving sister.

Isabelle Marie Sophie Angélique de Ranreuil
In religion, Sister Agnès de la Miséricorde

This letter, which took him back so abruptly to his younger days, moved him more than he could have imagined. It touched him to the quick, at the very moment when he was most vulnerable. It was as if his moral foundation had been swept away from beneath his feet. In a flash, he imagined that lovely face, and the scissors cutting into her hair, and an existence that henceforth would be one of renunciation and ashes. He tried to get a grip on himself. He could not help smiling at the thought that Isabelle was still writing in the bombastic style inspired in her by the works of the last century. Sincere as her words might be, they still had a touch of the theatrical. As for the content, he was troubled by much graver concerns at the moment and had no desire to add to them. He opened Aimée d'Arranet's letter, certain that he would find comfort in it.

Versailles, 26 April 1775
Monsieur,
Are you mocking me? My suspicions should have been aroused when you assured me of your fidelity. Almost two months have passed since your departure. What is keeping you in Vienna? What is there to keep me in Versailles?
Aimée d'Arranet

At the very moment when the past had come flooding back, must his present abandon him? First his son and now his mistress. Anger rose in him: why hadn't the Chevalier de Lastire given her his letter? Wasn't it more than a month since he had left them to return to France?

He went back downstairs, his arms laden with the gifts he had chosen in Vienna. Noblecourt went into ecstasies over the beauty of the copy of Suetonius. Bourdeau turned first white, then red, on receiving the brandy and the snuffbox. Marie and Catherine, who had just returned from Saint-Eustache, both burst into tears, not only at the beauty of the lace handkerchiefs, but also at the thought of Louis and his father's anxiety. Last but not least, old Poitevin immediately put on his fur hat and ran to light the stove.

Bourdeau went to find a cab, and they set off. In a few sentences, Nicolas summarised for his friend the gist of what he should know about the Austrian expedition, underlining the most significant and disturbing aspects. This brief conversation did not stop the commissioner from noting that here and there crowds had gathered outside bakeries. All the way to Rue Neuve-Saint-Augustin, he felt happy to be plunging back into that close and uncomplicated complicity. It did him the world of good. As soon as they arrived at police headquarters, the old major-domo hastened to inform Monsieur Lenoir, who immediately summoned them, appearing himself in the doorway of his office to greet them. The initial lack of understanding between Lenoir and Nicolas had long since faded. The Lieutenant General's good-natured face lit up with a smile when he saw the commissioner and his worthy associate.

'Marquis, I give thanks to the Empress of Austria for at last restoring Commissioner Le Floch to us!'

'I am more pleased than I can say, Monseigneur, to find you again in such rude health.'

'My illness has indeed almost gone. Just a few moments of tiredness, which the concerns of my office soon put paid to. Now, then, let's take things one at a time. What of your mission?'

'The official part went very well. I saw the Emperor unwittingly, saw the Empress all too wittingly, and both saw and heard Prince von Kaunitz.'

'Did all go well with Monsieur de Breteuil? He's not always the easiest person to get on with.'

'We got on perfectly! The King's ambassador may have his faults, but everything he does is in the service of His Majesty. We were in complete agreement on the most important things.'

'I'm delighted to hear it; he's not a man to be ignored at a time when good and faithful servants of the King are becoming rare specimens. What of the more confidential part of your mission?'

'It yielded the results of which the Chevalier de Lastire must have informed you. Georgel—'

'Lastire? What do you mean? He hasn't shown his face here at all. I thought he'd just come back with you.'

'What?' exclaimed Nicolas, surprised. 'He left Vienna nearly a month ago with my report. We were detained at the request of the Empress, who wished to entrust me with a letter and a medallion for the Queen. What could have happened to him? Something must have prevented him ... That's very worrying, especially after what happened to me.'

He summarised everything to Lenoir, especially what they had discovered about Georgel.

'You should be aware,' he said in conclusion, 'that without Lastire's boldness and courage, I would not be alive now.'

'If Lastire has been intercepted, which seems quite likely, then our ambassador's dispatches, alas, are in the hands of the cabinet in Vienna.'

'Fortunately not,' said Nicolas, tapping his forehead. 'They're all in here.'

Once again, he explained his system. This discovery delighted Lenoir, convincing him that a major part of the mission had been successful. Nicolas took advantage of this good mood to inform the Lieutenant General of what he had been able to observe on the return journey: the gatherings, the unrest among the peasants and the recurring incidents in the towns and villages they had passed, particularly on the outskirts of Paris.

Lenoir's face clouded over. 'What you've just told me confirms what I've been hearing on all sides. The people have been restless ever since Turgot published his edicts on the free trade in grain. There's great anxiety at the fact that the police have been told not to interfere in the movement of these essential supplies. The harvest of 1774 was extremely disappointing, this year's is highly dubious. The state of the roads makes transportation nigh impossible. How are we to bridge this gap? Feelings are running high. Since 15 April, believing that a four-pound loaf would now be sold at thirteen *sols*, people have been surrounding the bakeries.'

'They still are, as I witnessed coming here.'

'Even on a Sunday! There are rumours flying that the people are facing starvation and that the government is speculating on wheat to pay off the late King's debts! The same old mischief, intended to make people believe in a famine pact. Four days ago, on 26 April, the price of bread went up again. At the central market, an angry crowd formed around a steward from a noble house who had paid seventy-two *livres*[1] for a litre of new peas. They threw his litre in his face and screamed that if his ass of a master could afford to spend three *louis* on peas, there was no reason he couldn't give the people bread. The matter was immediately reported to me.'

'I fear,' observed Nicolas, 'that this movement is growing ever larger and angrier.'

'You're quite right. At markets in the provinces, in Versailles and in Paris, an unusually large number of peasants, or people claiming to be peasants, have been seen, some coming from fifteen to twenty leagues away. These people, who are unknown to the local inhabitants, are spreading anxiety, saying things likely to inflame the less enlightened minds. What are we to think? There is every indication that the two movements seem to be merging. One spontaneous, born out of the genuine concerns of the populace, and the other more concerted, organised by persons unknown. I think we are going to need you. But first, go straight to Versailles. The King, Vergennes and Sartine are all waiting for you, as is the Queen.'

'That was my intention, Monseigneur, but I wanted to report to you first.'

Lenoir went up to Nicolas and put a hand on his shoulder. 'I'm very touched. Get your orders from the Court, by all means, but I've already told the relevant circles that I intend to give you complete authority in this business. There are obscure aspects to it which threaten the safety of the King. We are entering difficult territory. Only a man of your experience will be able to tell false from true and suggest the right measures to take. I repeat that my trust in you is absolute. You can rest assured, too, that I am doing all I can in the private matter that most concerns you, and will leave no stone unturned nor hesitate to appeal to the highest authorities.'

'Monseigneur, I am doubly your servant. Alas, I fear this disappearance may have some connection with what happened in Vienna.'

'My God!' said Lenoir. 'Let's avoid contemplating the worst.'

'For the moment,' said Bourdeau, 'all we can do is wait for any information that may indicate the path to follow.'

Back in Rue Montmartre, Nicolas felt reassured by Monsieur Lenoir's openness and support. He found in this benevolent man a combination of qualities, including common sense, which made him, different as he was, a worthy successor to Monsieur de Sartine, and he vowed to be as loyal to the one as he had been to the other. It was seven o'clock by the time they got back to the Noblecourt house. An angry-looking crowd had gathered near Passage de la Reine de Hongrie. They were conversing in low voices and staring at the bakery on the ground floor of the building.

The servants' pantry, once more a busy hive, was echoing to Catherine's commentary. She immediately chased them out, muttering that she did not want men under her feet when she had a dinner to prepare and that, when she was a canteen-keeper for the King's armies, she would never have allowed a soldier near her cooking pot. She made no attempt, any more than did Marion, to conceal her pleasure at seeing Nicolas again. On the first floor, Monsieur de Noblecourt was chatting calmly with Monsieur de La Borde. Nicolas was moved and delighted to see his old friend, the former First Groom of the King's Bedchamber, now a farmer general. He enquired about the health of La Borde's wife. She was gradually recovering from an attack of moral consumption that had somewhat overshadowed their early days as a married couple. Marion appeared, to announce that it was time to move to the library where the table had been laid as usual. Nicolas noticed that Monsieur de Noblecourt was watching him out of the corner of his eye. He vowed to put on a good show and not cast a pall over a reunion among friends which, he suspected, was precisely intended to distract him from his anxieties. He was immediately questioned about Vienna and his journey. He replied with that flair for description so much admired by the late King, humorously cataloguing all the incidents he could possibly tell.

'Now it's my turn,' he said, 'to ask about what's been happening at Court and in the city in my absence.'

'Oh!' cried La Borde. 'Lekain, our great actor, fell seriously ill.'

'Yes,' said Bourdeau, 'of a disease now known as "cauchois", since he caught it off a girl from the Pays de Caux!'

'On 23 February, your friend Caron gave his *Barber of Seville*. The play was authorised at last, but disappointed the public. Only a week later, though, this semi-failure was transformed into a true triumph, a—'

Noblecourt interrupted La Borde. 'And the leaders of the applause worked a miracle! You just have to know how to organise the audience!'

'And the claque!'

'To be fair, the play's a good one, especially after the changes the author made. Reduced to four acts, not as long as before, and to some people, of whom I am not one, not as boring.'

'You speak as if you were there!'

'I was! On Monsieur de La Borde's arm, in a box that was extremely well placed to ogle the beauties on stage and in the auditorium.'

'I see,' said Nicolas with a laugh. 'Our friend has kept a few contacts in the theatre!'

'The marriage has been announced,' La Borde went on, 'between Madame Clotilde, the King's sister, and the Prince of Piedmont.

You've met her, you know how fat she is. This song has been doing the rounds in Paris:

> *'The good prince wants his just reward*
> *He wants it pressed into his hand.*
> *What he gets is Madame Clotilde*
> *Now he's living off the fat of the land.'*

They were interrupted by Catherine, who brought in, with all the gravity befitting the task, a long silver dish containing what she proudly proclaimed was a 'turbot *à la Sainte-Menehould*'. It was presented to the master of the house, who breathed in the aroma and eyed the dish longingly. Much to everyone's surprise, he served his guests but not himself.

'Oh, yes, gentlemen!' he said, with a martyred air. 'I abstain, I deprive myself, torture myself. Please note that I do so of my own free will, in the absence of Dr Semacgus. I want this gesture to be reported back to him. I hope it will make him a little more lenient towards me: a few days without sage or prunes ...'

'There's no point pretending to behave yourself,' said Catherine with a knowing air. 'You know perfectly well that you have a special dish. A pigeon with new peas. And it's still much too delicious for you, if you want my opinion!'

'A dish fit for a king!' cried Nicolas. 'In the present situation, the kind to cause panic in the central market. Madame Catherine, you seem quite spendthrift and little concerned with the interests of this noble house.'

'Mock away, Monsieur. You're quite wrong. It was brought by Monsieur de La Borde here.'

'Yes,' admitted La Borde modestly, 'I've also kept a few contacts at the King's kitchen garden at Versailles. They offer me the first fruits of everything that grows. They wanted to give me asparagus, but in my opinion it's quite harmful and likely to bring on attacks of gout. I preferred, for the sake of our friend's health, to make him a tribute of peas.'

'So light, though!' said Noblecourt, much to everyone's approval.

Catherine uncovered the sautéd pigeon, surrounded by tender green vegetables, and carefully removed the golden-brown rasher of bacon, much to Noblecourt's regret.

'This turbot has such delicate flesh!' remarked Nicolas. 'Firm and yet tender at the same time.'

'We must, as always,' said La Borde, 'double the pleasure of the meal. So tell us how you made it, Catherine.'

'Keep mocking and I'll take it away faster than you can breathe! The main thing is to cook it half in milk half in water. For the flesh to stay white, the stock has to simmer separately for a good quarter of an hour. The back of the fish is then rubbed with lemon and cooked to a turn, but above all without boiling. You remove the fillets once the whole thing has got cold again. Heat a fairly thick bechamel sauce, put the pieces of fish in it, and slip it in a slow oven for a short time to brown.'

'That reminds me,' said Noblecourt, applauding, 'of a story I heard when I was young. The old Duc d'Escars was always complaining about the fact that he had served slices of chicken breast in cream for more than twenty years before young Béchameil was even born and yet he'd never been fortunate enough to give his name to a sauce!'

He was tackling a little wing, sucking it so voluptuously that it was a pleasure just to watch him. Their feast was washed down with the usual Irancy.

'On 10 March,' La Borde resumed, 'the Queen attended an English-style horse race on the Sablons plain, organised by the Comte d'Artois. The horses, all very frisky, were ridden by the princes' grooms. The Duc de Lauzun won the day.'

'Was he competing as a horse?' asked Nicolas casually.

His question was greeted with roars of laughter.

'No, as an owner. It's said that the King was not greatly pleased with the event, the royal family having been somewhat jostled by the crowd.'

'Does he follow his mentor's advice?' asked Noblecourt. 'It appears – you know how well informed I am – that at one of the last balls at Versailles before Lent, the King was also jostled and left without a seat. Maurepas did not hesitate to point out that the monarch should never forget his dignity and never appear without being announced and without his captain of the guards. "We are not accustomed in France," he's said to have added, "to have our King so little regarded in public."'

Bourdeau now also entered the lists. 'On 29 March, the new marshals of France were announced. The beneficiaries have been compared to the seven deadly sins.'

'How so?' asked Nicolas.

'Harcourt, sloth. Noailles, avarice. Nicolaï, gluttony. Fitz-James, envy. The other Noailles, the comte, pride. De Muy, wrath, and Duras lust.'

'On 30 April,' La Borde resumed, 'the King, who was clearly in a bad mood, ordered the pavilion on the Sablons plain to be demolished. At the same time, a pamphlet full of historical and anecdotal remarks concerning the Bastille was distributed in Paris, the intention being to warn "patriotic" citizens that their zeal could land them there. It was immediately seized, although it is still not clear which clandestine printing press produced it.'

'Now there's a useful treatise,' said Bourdeau, 'which ought to give pause for thought to the supporters of an outmoded despotism.'

'What do you mean?' asked Noblecourt. 'Do you wish to undermine the order you serve?'

'No … But I maintain that this order should correspond to natural law and enlightened modern ideas. For example, *lettres de cachet* without trial have no foundation.'

'We are all evolving,' Nicolas intervened, anxious to moderate the argument before it started. 'The Emperor's brother told me that torture is soon to be abolished in Austria.'

Catherine came in to clear the table. La Borde once again filled the glasses. A second dish, roulades of ox tongue, appeared, announced by Marion, who had created it. As they were serving, she told them her recipe in her shrill little voice. The meat had to be left to soak, then cooked with a tasty piece of beef, to ensure its flavour and avoid the stock taking it all away. When it was soft enough, the tongue was taken from the pot to be skinned and allowed to cool. Only then was it cut up into thin slices, each of which was garnished with a little stuffing.

'What kind of stuffing?' asked La Borde.

'That's a secret, Monsieur, which I'm happy to reveal if it entices you even more. I take a pound of cushion of veal or, better still, calf's leg, from which I remove the nerves and gristle. I coat this meat in ox fat, a pound too, plus parsley, salt and pepper, and spices according to taste. At the same time, I add eggs one by one until the mixture is smooth. I used to soften the whole thing with a little water, but Catherine recommended schnapps, which gives it a delicious flavour. In fact, you shouldn't use eggs for stuffing, unless you're using it as a garnish in a stew. Without them, the stuffing would completely melt. But tongue is fragile and the egg helps to hold it all together.'

'This is a real Arabian Nights tale,' said La Borde. 'No sooner do we finish one episode than another begins. Continue, lovely Scheherazade!'

Marion resumed her account. Every slice of tongue was filled with stuffing over which she passed a knife dipped in the egg to bind it all. She rolled the slices one by one, wrapped them in rashers of bacon and put them on skewers. Then she threw a few dried breadcrumbs on the roulades to give them a good colour, cooked them for a short time, and served them with a piquant sauce.

'I'm going to anticipate your question and give you the recipe for my sauce, too. I fry a carrot, two onions and a sliced parsnip in butter until they're brown. Then I add a good pinch of flour, some stock, half a glass of vinegar and, of course, seasoning: mixed herbs, spices, garlic, pepper and grated nutmeg. The whole thing has to simmer slowly until it's the right consistency, not too liquid, not too solid. And with that, gentlemen, if my master allows, I'm going to rest my old legs.'

Nicolas rose and kissed Marion, who was moved to tears by this. Cyrus barked happily while Mouchette rolled on her back and gave little moaning sounds.

'What a delight,' said Bourdeau, 'this dish is as good as a *géline* from my part of the world!' He proceeded carefully to cut a slice of the roulade, revealing the layers of tongue and stuffing and releasing a fragrant odour. 'This crusty bread in this sauce!'

'Talking of bread,' said Nicolas, 'have you noticed that crowd of people just opposite the house?'

'Of course,' said Noblecourt, 'I've been watching them from my armchair. What can we do? The price of bread is rising and people are angry. It isn't the first time this century that such a thing has happened and it won't be the last. When I was still in the first flush of youth, on 14 July 1725, there was a riot and all the bakeries in Faubourg Saint-Antoine were looted.'

'I hear there've been some violent gatherings on the outskirts of Paris,' Nicolas went on, 'mainly directed against rich millers.'

'... *Thieving miller,*
Stealing the corn,
Stealing the flour,
That's why he was born ...'

sang Bourdeau.

'They sing a different song in Brittany, but the meaning's the same:

> *'Na pa rafe ar vilin nemet eun dro krenn*
> *Ar miliner'ʒo sur d'oc'h le grampoeʒ enn.*

'Which means:

> *'The miller's wheel turned only once*
> *But the miller's certain he'll get his crust.'*

Everyone laughed, except La Borde, who shook his head gravely. 'We're up against petty crooks driven by Lord knows what, but clearly with the worst intentions. The comptroller general has forgotten that it's unwise to interfere with our age-old machine, however creaky it may be. Suddenly imposing a free trade in grain leads to fear and disorder and gives rise to excesses and the activities of monopolists.'

'Actually,' said Noblecourt, 'what Turgot is attempting, Abbé Terray achieved by abolishing the tax on wheat and replacing it with State control. How better to obtain the equal distribution of grain than by guaranteeing the surplus from the richer regions to the struggling provinces. It was an excellent method for establishing an equitable balance in the price of bread throughout the kingdom.' As he spoke, he ate his peas one by one and eyed the roulades.

'It so happens, my friends,' said La Borde, with an air of mystery, 'that I have a particular knowledge of all this. You all know how fascinated I am by China, its traditions, its curios ...'

'What do Confucius and monkeys have to do with these millers' tales?'

'Listen and find out. Sharing the same passion, I became very friendly with Monsieur Bertin, whose department of State deals with agriculture. The late King, my master, had entrusted him with the task of corresponding with the French Jesuits in Peking. This passion launched the vogue for all things Chinese. He began collecting art objects, fabrics, prints and drawings.² That was what brought us together.'

'The Marquise de Pompadour greatly appreciated him, especially when he was Lieutenant General of Police. It was through him that she knew everything about everyone!'

'He was also comptroller general and tried to find new ways of financing war. But the Parlement opposed them, and Choiseul said it was impossible to deal any longer with Bertin. A few days ago, I invited him to dinner. He opened his heart to me, with great honesty. He's really bitter at the state of the reforms and the ideas behind them.'

'But isn't Monsieur Turgot considered to have been successful when he was Intendant of the Limousin?'

'Our host is right, at least that's what those in his sect say, those economists who are so convinced that their doctrine is the right one. They sing his praises, whereas in fact what the great man did in the Limousin was a matter of trial and error.'

'He abolished statute labour, which meant a lot to the people concerned! It's a measure that should be extended to the whole of the kingdom.'

'That may be so, Bourdeau, but the man wasn't at all happy, given the poverty of the region. He stood up to the monopolists. He tried to replace wheat with potatoes and to thwart their speculating by selling abroad. What's more, he sacrificed part of his own fortune to relieve the neediest. His promotion to comptroller general delighted his followers. Up until now, they expressed themselves as philosophers, orators and moralists, now they can make decisions as legislators and have the ear of the King. They bring out a host of pamphlets, especially against the financiers. And what is the result? These powerful people, whose support is vital to Monsieur Turgot, conspire against him and try to block his reforms.'

'So,' asked Noblecourt, 'what does Bertin say? Above all, what's his opinion of the man who's governing us, of his character? That's the basis of everything. Any act is merely a reflection of the person performing it. A legislator is never so powerless as when his temperament isn't compatible with his ambitions. Those with the most logical minds aren't always the fairest.'

'Bertin's first observation is that the comptroller is insanely proud, even claiming to be descended from a king of Denmark, Thor, which would make him related to the god Thor! Next, that we should never forget that he was educated at the seminary of Saint-Sulpice and that he was the Abbé de Brucourt. That although he was influenced by the new ideas when he entered the Parlement, his original education has left him with a taste for controversy, made worse by a ponderous way of speaking, which quickly turns tiresome and full of digressions.'

'My usual informant[3] says that he suffers from poor health, and is prone to bouts of hereditary gout. Early deaths are common in his family: his brother died at the age of forty-nine and he himself is already forty-eight ...'

'I believe, in fact,' La Borde went on, 'that this fear has a major influence on his actions. He's frequently confined to his bed, and is often slow and sluggish in his daily work. As if to make up for this, he's all too inclined to rush things through without due care and attention. He has done nothing to prepare public opinion, which, while calling for reform, is not always willing to suffer the consequences.'

'It should never be forgotten,' said Noblecourt sententiously, 'that time is the best ally of a politician and that, without it, there is no decisive or lasting victory.'

'Bertin is extremely worried. There is opposition to Turgot within the council itself. With his lack of shrewdness and dexterity, the comptroller's qualities and virtues are often turned against him. For example, when Madame de Brionne presented him with a fairly insignificant petition, the best answer he could find was that she should understand that the reign of women had passed.'

'And did the good lady accept that?'

'Not at all; she retorted, as if returning a tennis ball: "Yes, I see that, but not the reign of the impertinent."'

Turning suddenly serious, La Borde took a piece of paper from his pocket.

'Bertin showed me a letter from Abbé Galiani,[4] to Madame d'Épinay, dated 17 September 1774. I was so struck by its contents that he allowed me to make a copy. Listen to this: "There will be too little time to carry out his system. He will punish a few rogues, he will get angry and curse, will try to do the right thing, and will encounter difficulties and opposition everywhere. There will be less credit, he will be hated, they will say that he is not up to the task, and enthusiasm will fade and die. We will recover, once and for all, from the error of giving a position like that, in a monarchy like ours, to such a virtuous and philosophical man. The free export of wheat will break him. We are seeing the first signs."'

'Didn't that antiquarian[5] abbé unearth the Roman ruins in Naples? It seems that he's started interpreting omens, like an ancient augur! But there's a real danger that what he's saying is true.'

'Gentlemen,' said La Borde, 'I bow down – and I use the words advisedly – before our host's Mirandolesque knowledge. Galiani is one of the first to have discovered the ruins of Herculanium, buried since the eruption of Vesuvius as recounted by Pliny the Younger.'

'Not only is he lacking in respect for my white hair, or what remains of it, but in addition takes me for an idiot, by expressing amazement at my meagre knowledge. That's surely worth a glass of Irancy.'

He nimbly seized the bottle, filled his glass and emptied it in a single gulp.

'It makes a change from sage! To get back to my ... correspondent, he tells me that, in this difficult period, the King spends his time looking through his telescope, proclaiming and declaiming, idling away his days in weakness and indecision ...'

'He's very young,' Nicolas cut in, remembering that Louis XVI was only a few years older than Louis, five at the most. 'He still has to prove himself.'

'Of course! We shall see, as his great-grandfather said, in whose reign, my young dandies, I had the honour of coming into this thankless world.'

Catherine brought in a plate of sugar cakes.

'Fritters made with fresh cheese,' she announced, anticipating their questions, 'like those sold at the Saint-Denis fair.'

The dinner came to an end in great gaiety, everyone making an effort to distract Nicolas, who, in return, put on a brave face. He walked La Borde to his carriage. The latter, determined to use the savoir-faire he had acquired as a servant of the late King, offered his services. As he returned to his room, Nicolas found Monsieur de Noblecourt waiting for him at the foot of the stairs.

'My friend, let me commend you on your courage. You made sure nothing came up that might disturb this friendly reunion. Physical courage is a gift of nature, but courage of the spirit is a much rarer thing. I thank you for the self-discipline you exercised. I know you did it out of respect for myself and those who love you.'

'I owe you a debt of gratitude, Monsieur, for having organised this evening which, although I could not forget my anxieties, allowed me to keep them under control.'

Back in his apartment, Nicolas sighed with emotion, thinking how lucky he had been to meet the former procurator. He embodied all that, previously, had been represented by Canon Le Floch and his father as examples of rectitude, steadfastness and loyalty. He would have liked the Marquis de Ranreuil to see him in action, but he hoped that, from where he was, he approved his conduct. Still the child from Guérande, he said his prayers, asking the Virgin Mary and St Anne to protect his son. He fell into a deep sleep, lulled by Mouchette's purring.

Monday 1 May 1775

He awoke with a start. Distant, muffled noises reached his ears. He thought he could hear cries. He waited for a moment, struck a light and lit a candle. Mouchette was spitting, her tail as stiff as a brush. He became aware of a heavy tread on the stairs. There was a knock at the door. He asked whoever it was to wait a moment, and put on stockings and breeches, waistcoat and shoes. After tying his hair with a ribbon, he opened up and discovered Poitevin, half dressed, out of breath, looking shaken. He felt a pang in his heart. Either something had happened to Monsieur de Noblecourt or there was bad news about Louis. In a flash, he foresaw every possible misfortune. He admitted Poitevin, who was unable to recover his breath and could barely speak. Nicolas sat him down and brought him a glass of water.

'Oh, Monsieur,' he said at last. 'What a terrible thing!'

Out of habit, Nicolas checked his watch. It was four fifteen. He made an effort to contain his anxiety. 'What's happened?'

'What a horrible death, Monsieur! The poor man!'

A shiver ran down the commissioner's spine.

'I think you have to go downstairs.'

Another voice rose, equally breathless.

'How steep these stairs are … Stop scaring Nicolas … my good old Poitevin … I know him and … I can just imagine him … pale and wide-eyed … doing me the honour of thinking I'm dead.'

Monsieur de Noblecourt entered in majesty, wrapped in a damask dressing gown, his head covered with his favourite madras. He walked to the bed and collapsed heavily onto it beside Poitevin.

'What a climb! Let me get my breath back … Just imagine! Master Mourut, my tenant and baker, has been found dead in his kneading trough.'

'A fit of apoplexy?' asked Nicolas, who recalled the man's ruddy face.

Noblecourt looked dubious. 'I find that hard to believe. It's something else. That's why we woke you. I went downstairs to take a look. I'm sure you'll be as astonished by the scene as I was. I fear we need an experienced police commissioner and perhaps even the insight of a former procurator. This death is extremely suspicious.'

Nicolas rummaged in his desk and took out the little black book in which he noted everything while working on a case. 'Before I go down,' he said, 'I'd like to hear your account of what happened.'

'All right. A few minutes after four … I know it was four, because my Minerva clock had just struck. At my age, I spend part of the night reading … Anyway, I was reading the magnificent Suetonius you gave me as a gift. Tiberius in Capri … I digress. I heard cries and lots of strange noise, although it was still dark. Just as I was about to go down, Poitevin appeared. You know he sleeps in the room above the stable. He said … but perhaps he could tell you what he told me?'

'Monsieur, I was asleep. I was woken by cries. Then there was loud knocking on the door to the little staircase that leads to my lodgings. I put on what I could and went down. There I found Parnaux, the baker's boy, and Friope, the apprentice, in a panic. They had just gone into the bakehouse and had found Master Mourut unconscious. He was—'

'Don't say another word. I'd like to see things for myself, with an open mind. What happened next?'

'They were terrified, and refused to go back down. At that point, Catherine took matters in hand. She led them into the servants' pantry and asked them to wait there. I came upstairs to find Monsieur. He went down with me and together we verified that the baker was dead.'

'I shan't describe anything to you, Nicolas, but I will mention one important detail. The baker's boys gave me the key to the bakehouse. As for the communicating door between that room and—'

'What?' said Nicolas, surprised. 'What door? I had no idea there was such a thing, as often happens when you have something right in front of you every day.'

'When, twenty years ago, I let the ground floor of my house, I didn't want to be separated from the outhouses in the courtyard. Master Mourut took a lease on the house next door. In agreement with me and the other owner, he was granted permission to make an opening between the two houses, at his own expense. He and his wife live there with an apprentice.'

'One of the two you mentioned?'

'No, they live in town.'

'That could make things complicated.'

'We left Catherine in the bakehouse to make sure that nothing is disturbed and nobody enters. She's not bothered by the sight of death. She's seen much worse things on the battlefield.'

'One more question. Do you think the baker died a natural death?'

'I prefer not to express an opinion. I leave that to the Grand Châtelet.'

The three men walked downstairs. Nicolas glanced for a moment at the two baker's boys sitting on stools, their arms dangling. They seemed stunned. As they knew him, they rose to greet him. Outside the service door to the bakery stood the solid figure of Catherine, like a sentry following orders. Without a word, but with an evasive pout, she handed him a large key. They descended a few steps. By the light of two candles – Nicolas noticed that they had barely been started – a scene at once strange and grotesque presented itself. The light, flickering in the draught from the small windows that looked out onto the street, illumined, in the middle of the room, a body leaning forward, of which only the feet, legs and the bottom part of the trunk were visible from the door, the rest being submerged in the kneading trough. This figure was like a collapsed puppet or a launderer cleaning linen in a washtub. Nicolas asked his companions to stop where they were. He himself cautiously advanced into the bakehouse on tiptoe, looking down at the floor. He had forced himself to give the corpse only a cursory glance, but now at last he looked at him for a long time.

The first thing that struck him was that he had never seen Master Mourut dressed as he was now, in a coat of a thick brown, almost red material, flecked grey breeches, black stockings, a shirt with lace cuffs, and shoes with polished – though mud-caked – brass buckles: the attire of a Parisian in his Sunday best. For the moment, Nicolas drew no conclusion from this. The body had not yet stiffened. Of the head, all that could be seen was a thin strip of the back of the neck and the back of the horsehair wig. The whole of his face was stuck in the risen dough of the morning's first batch. Nicolas noted that the pockets were half turned out, as if someone had tried to search them without taking care to rearrange them. He crouched and found a double *louis*, which must have rolled under the kneading trough, and a small tube of thin paper, which he unrolled. It read: *Eulalie, at La G's, Rue des Deux-Portes-Saint-Sauveur*, which surprised him greatly, for various reasons. He put his find between the pages of his notebook. It now occurred to him to touch the body. Why had the Grim Reaper, his old companion, pursued him even here, to this haven of peace, this dwelling so dear to his heart? He drew the layout of the place and a crude depiction of the scene. He knew from experience how deceptive and fleeting memory could be. Monsieur de Noblecourt had sat down on a stool and was watching carefully but impassively.

Nicolas asked Catherine to come and help him. He first had a chair brought close, seized the body by the epaulettes of the coat and slowly pulled it towards him. It was the hands that slid out first, the arms falling vertically. Then the body rose, and the head dropped forwards, drawing with it strips and ribbons of dough stuck to the face and wig. The corpse was now slumped, with its chin on its chest. Nicolas lifted it and noticed that the eyes were open and hardly blurred. The mouth was tightly closed. He removed the dough and flour with a cloth he found hanging from a nail. The ashen face did not bear – and this was the only observation he allowed himself – any trace of asphyxia, or any wound, nor was there anything to indicate an apoplectic fit, even though his memories of Monsieur Mourut when he was alive – a ruddy-faced, short-necked man in his fifties – might well have supported such a supposition. So what had caused him to fall head first into his kneading trough?

He thought for a moment. The most sensible thing would be to have the body taken to the Grand Châtelet and summon Sanson and Semacgus, the only people he trusted, for the usual examination in the Basse-Geôle. Before doing that, he had to determine the exact circumstances of this suspicious death as precisely as possible, question the witnesses, inform Madame Mourut, and observe her reactions. Nothing was to be left to chance. Experience had taught him that hurry and lack of attention to detail, however small, always resulted in false starts and unfortunate errors. It was also important to inform his colleague, the commissioner for the district, and persuade him to let him, Nicolas, take charge of the case. That would be all the easier to do given that his name and reputation, and the authority he had acquired, supported by the trust of two successive Lieutenants General of Police, would rule out any bias and avoid rebellion or dissension. Things would be easy: Commissioner Fontaine was an old acquaintance. He had already been in that position for a few years and had been the attending officer when Monsieur de Noblecourt had been the victim of an attack outside the house.[6] Catherine, as a woman used to the field of battle, had left the bakehouse, and, anticipating the commissioner's request, soon returned with a blanket which, to judge by the strong smell it gave off, must have come from the stable. She took it upon herself to close the dead man's eyes, then covered the corpse with the blanket. In an instant, the room resumed its normal, innocuous appearance. Nicolas looked about him for a few moments, stopping from time to time to write in his notebook.

'Good. I don't think I've left anything out. I see it's possible to put a bar across the communicating door. We need to do so in order to stop anyone coming in from the house next door.'

Poitevin set about this task.

'Now we're going to go out and close the door. Poitevin, can I ask you to keep guard, on a chair of course, and don't let anyone in.'

'Especially as,' said Monsieur de Noblecourt, 'after a certain attack, a small door was cut into the carriage entrance. Several keys were distributed, both in my house and in the baker's. It's possible that —'

'Bourdeau and I have arranged to meet at six. At that point, we'll sort out the details. By the way, our two frightened birds are in their street clothes. Where do they change? We're going to ask them.'

'No need to!' said Catherine. 'They change in the privy, as far as I know.'

'She's right,' said Noblecourt. 'When I leased out the premises, there wasn't one. You know how architects respect the legal obligations as far as they go but, because of the shape and proximity of the houses, put pipes everywhere at random. Nothing is more surprising to those who visit our beautiful city than to see the ugly accumulation of latrines disfiguring the houses, plumped down next to staircases, doors and kitchens, spreading the most revolting smell. Everything gets clogged up, the tide rises and the house is flooded! But nobody talks about it, Parisian noses are inured!'

'It's highly unhealthy, as is the satisfying of natural needs in the street. Apart from our friend Tirepot and his public convenience, people relieve themselves where they can. Monsieur de Sartine had barrels set up for the purpose at street corners.'

'A useful and noble idea! Unfortunately this humane plan earned him nothing but mockery and immediately fell into disuse.'

As they left the bakehouse, they glanced at the place in question. It was a most sordid example of its type. Nicolas, as a man of his century with a keen interest in hygiene, was shocked.

Gradually, the heat of action had lessened his anxiety, but from time to time it returned with renewed strength. Now, for a brief moment, it hit him like a blow to the chest, taking his breath away. What had happened to his son? Where was Aimée d'Arranet? Five o'clock had just tolled at Saint-Eustache. He asked Monsieur de Noblecourt for permission to question the baker's boys in the servants' pantry, where Catherine was already busy lighting the stove. Something struck him: how was it that the fire hadn't been lit in the bakery? It took time to bake the first batch. This was a worrying detail. Was it normal? He would have to check.

He sat down at the table while Noblecourt went back up to his apartments. The two young men came in, holding hands. He knew them well, but realised that they were so much part of the furniture that he didn't even know their names. How many times had they held his horse's bridle, or carried his portmanteau, or greeted him warmly at the carriage entrance? And yet they remained perfect strangers to him.

'I will question you separately.'

The younger of the two looked imploringly at the older one, who let go of his hand and took a step forward, with a somewhat swaggering air.

'All right,' said Nicolas, 'let's begin with you. Your workmate can wait in the courtyard.'

Glances were again exchanged and the apprentice went out reluctantly. Nicolas noticed the down-at-heel shoes, the light twill trousers – too short for him – the shirt and the threadbare waistcoat, the white face with eyes that seemed to swallow the rest of his features.

'What's your name?'

'Hugues Parnaux, Monsieur Nicolas.'

'How old are you?'

'Eighteen.'

'Who are your parents?'

'My mother died when I was born. My father is a retired soldier. Disabled …'

'How long have you been an apprentice?'

'For three years.'

'Does your father pay your fees?'

'He couldn't, the poor man! He isn't right in the head any more. He's at the Invalides.'

'So who pays for your apprenticeship?'

'The churchwarden of my parish.'

'Why don't you live in your master's house, as most do?'

He recalled his own days as a notary's clerk in Rennes ... The number of times he had drawn up contracts of apprenticeship, always on the same model! He recalled the wording: 'The master promises and undertakes to show and teach him the said profession and everything it involves, to hide nothing from him, to feed him, lodge him, give him light and heating, launder his linen, and provide him with a bed, sheets and clothes suitable to his state ...'

'You know the house, Monsieur Nicolas. It'd be impossible here. We'd have to sleep three in a room and anyway ...'

'Anyway?'

'No, nothing! Not everyone can become a master ... I know what I'm talking about. So I lodge with Friope a few houses down. On the sixth floor, under the roof. The house belongs to the master, who lets furnished rooms there by the week or the month.'

'All right, we'll look into that later. What happened this morning?'

'We'd sifted the flour last night ...'

'Was Master Mourut present?'

He seemed to hesitate. '... Yes, at first. He had to go out. He kept an eye on the work from a distance, because he didn't want to get his clothes dirty. When the dough was ready to rise, he left us, saying he wouldn't be long and that he'd light the oven when he came back. All that was left to do was make the loaves and fill the oven with wood. Once started, we leave them to warm up. Finally we scrape down the oven to get rid of the embers before we put the bread in.'

Nicolas let him speak. He knew how important it was never

to interrupt a witness in full flow: the truth sometimes emerged unexpectedly.

'All right. What happened this morning?'

'We woke up at a quarter to five. There was some coffee left over and, in order not to have it cold, we heated it with the flame from a candle. We ate a crust. When we got to the shop, we opened the door to the courtyard ...'

'Do you have a key?'

Nicolas suddenly realised that he was acting as if it had already been established that Master Mourut had not died a natural death. If he had, these interrogations would be a waste of time. Nevertheless, if his hypothesis proved accurate, he would certainly have gained time! Nothing was more valuable than gathering information in the immediate aftermath of an event, when the participants had not yet had time to go over and over their version and tinker with the details.

'Yes, the key to the little door cut into the big one and another leading to the bakehouse from the courtyard. The bakehouse key I gave to Monsieur de Noblecourt.'

Nicolas took the key, which Parnaux had extracted from deep in his pocket. 'And then?'

'We were surprised to see a light in the bakehouse. We always make sure we turn everything off because of the risk of fire. We're usually the first to arrive, and the master joins us a quarter of an hour later. We went into the bakehouse without changing our clothes and there we saw the master in the kneading trough. We ... we called out and went closer.'

'Didn't you try to fetch help?'

'Friope had a kind of fit. He was choking and rolling the whites of his eyes, and his teeth were chattering.'

'But you did at least make sure that Monsieur Mourut was dead?'

'I went up to him and listened, but he wasn't breathing. I touched his hand, and it was already cold. I wanted to fetch help. But Friope was screaming. I calmed him down ... I even slapped him. He followed me into the courtyard to the stables where we woke Poitevin and—'

'One moment. Did you lock the door again?'

'No, by now we didn't know what we were doing.'

'Are you sure there was no one else in the bakehouse apart from you?'

The boy's face tensed as he thought hard. 'To be honest, no, especially as we didn't open the storeroom. But the carriage entrance was closed.'

'Wait! Where is this storeroom?'

'You have to go into the privy and swivel the cupboard where we keep our work clothes.'

'Is it a large storeroom?'

'It's a huge dry cellar. A good place for keeping flour. The master didn't like talking about it, or rather, he didn't like anyone else talking about it.'

'Why not?'

'Because there was too much flour and he thought there would be a shortage.'

'I find all this rather confusing. You're going to have to explain it a little more clearly.'

'He held on to his flour, because he said there'd soon be a shortage in the city and the price of bread would go up. That was already happening. The customers were grumbling, and he'd received threats.'

'What form did these threats take?'

'Charcoal inscriptions on the walls, which Friope kept having to wash off.'

'What kind of inscriptions?'

'Horrible things! They were going to come and ransack the place ... and hang us ...'

'What kind of man was Master Mourut?'

'Good-natured on the outside, but tough and demanding when it came to work.' He made an ironic face. 'And greedy when it came to money.'

'And what about Madame Mourut?'

'She sold bread in the shop. We were nothing to her. We never ate at her table ...'

'And where's the third apprentice?'

'You'd have to ask him,' the boy said, in a vindictive tone. 'He's allowed to do whatever he likes.'

'Including being late for his day's work?'

'Even that.'

Nicolas went out to look for Friope. He found him sitting on a boundary stone, gnawing at his fists.

'Come on, it's your turn.'

He took him by the shoulders, and felt the frail bone structure beneath his fingers. The boy's body was shaking and he was unsteady on his feet. Parnaux was asked to leave the room, with Nicolas standing between the two boys to prevent them conferring. Friope was even less well dressed than his workmate. The interrogation resumed. Friope was fifteen, and his father was a ploughman in Meaux. Nicolas asked the same questions and received identical answers, except when he asked about the third apprentice and detected a mixture of anger and fear. Nicolas pretended to know more about the subject than he in fact did, and this really opened the floodgates: it was as if the boy were releasing everything he had too long held in.

'He doesn't work, doesn't do anything, and the master doesn't even notice ... If he does anything wrong, he blames us, me or Parnaux. He call us every name under the sun. He's always telling on us to the master ... If he could, he'd even ...'

He was biting his lips. He stopped, wild-eyed. Had he realised that he had said too much, or rather that he was on the verge of admitting something that could not be admitted? Nicolas did not show any outward interest in these confused words and refused to drive home his advantage.

'Where does the flour you work with come from?'

Friope sighed with relief. 'The wheat market takes place twice a week, on Wednesday and Saturday. But the master gets more. It comes in and out …'

'Can you explain that?'

'Flour arrives secretly in carts covered with canvas, which regularly take away the empty sacks. They're full when they arrive. There's a whole system organised by the group of monopolists. When they find out through one of their spies that the corporation is planning to check a bakery, the surplus is moved from shop to shop. The one who hides it receives a share of it as payment for his help. They're bound together by solemn oaths.'

'And is your master one of them?' asked Nicolas, alarmed by what he was hearing.

'That's what I'm telling you! Not only that, but he also trims as much as he can from the dough for each loaf, without pity for the poor. A bit here, a bit there. It's all for his own profit. But the Lord God and the Virgin Mary are watching and sometimes this small amount of dough, yes, Monsieur Nicolas, this small amount of dough rises in the oven and produces the finest, most golden, most fragrant loaves, which makes the master furious.'

He seemed almost ecstatic, then suddenly burst into tears. It struck Nicolas that he was the same age as Louis. He waited until Friope had recovered.

'Are you unhappy? You've always seemed such a bright boy.'

'You've always been good to us, Monsieur Nicolas,' he replied, looking admiringly at the commissioner. 'Monsieur de Noblecourt, too, and the cooks, and Poitevin who always slips us a few tasty morsels.'

He began sobbing again.

'But our situation here isn't very peasant. Always half naked, always in long johns and cap so that we're always ready for work. Never going out, except on Sundays. It's like being in purgatory. My body isn't made of iron. Night doesn't bring any rest. As soon as it starts, we begin our day.'

Suddenly, there was a great noise. The door to the servants' pantry opened and Bourdeau appeared, followed by an auxiliary officer and two soldiers of the watch. He made a sign to Nicolas.

V

THE BAKEHOUSE

When we plunge a blind man into darkness,
he is unaware of it; but the sighted man shudders.

MADAME DE PUISIEUX

Bourdeau drew Nicolas aside.

'Unrest is growing in the city. People are gathering everywhere. No violence for the moment, but a lot of heated debate. On the way here, I passed a detachment of the watch entering Rue Montmartre, where several bakeries appear to be under threat.'

'Is it as bad as that?'

'Worse. All night, information has been coming in to police headquarters, confirming your impressions. There's increasing excitement all around the outskirts of Paris, in Beauvais, Passy, Saint-Germain, Meaux, Saint-Denis. There's said to have been looting. Thousands of men have gathered in Villers-Cotterêts. In Pontoise, everything's been turned upside down, and there's been destruction of property. The whole length of the Oise is in turmoil. At L'Isle-Adam, grain barges have been stripped and the sacks torn open.'

'But for what reason?'

'It's said that mysterious emissaries have convinced the common people that they risk dying of starvation because all the grain is being taken to Paris to be sold abroad at a high price. Remember those old stories of a famine pact? Well, they've come back! The worst thing of all is that order will only be restored by taking measures nobody is prepared to take.'

Nicolas was pleased – although he did not say so – to see Bourdeau go back to being a policeman, for whom disorder was a breach in the regular course of the world.

'Nobody's received any instructions, not the police, not the mounted constabulary, not the army. Those who should be taking command are refusing to do so. I heard that even Monsieur Lenoir is demanding written orders, and is refusing to do anything on his own initiative until he receives them. Meanwhile, the situation is getting worse. But what were you talking to the baker's boys about?'

Nicolas gave him a detailed account of the previous night's events and his initial observations.

'Only an autopsy will be able to confirm or refute your suspicions,' said Bourdeau.

'You know I have to go to Versailles today, so I'm going to leave all this in your hands. Have the body taken to the Basse-Geôle, and summon Semacgus and Sanson. I couldn't bear leaving such an important element to the wretched local doctors, whose incompetence we know well. Before that, we'll need to question the widow and the third baker's boy, if we can find him. Concentrate initially on the neighbourhood, especially the house where those two boys live …'

The boys in question were waiting by the door, heads bowed, for this conversation to end.

'I pass them every day,' Nicolas said, as if thinking aloud. 'I live in the same house and yet I don't know anything about them. I'd like them to be put into solitary confinement until the autopsy's been carried out. Find two preferential cells at the Châtelet. Let them be fed at my expense, well fed, and make sure the gatekeepers look after them. Separate cells, obviously.'

He chose not to tell Bourdeau everything. It was not a question of concealment or lack of trust. It was just that there were things which meant nothing at the moment and would only be of interest if they were indeed dealing with a murder. He wanted to give the inspector the opportunity to bring his own experience to bear on the case – and, hopefully, come to the same conclusions as he had. He would doubtless reach them in other ways, but he was sure they would confirm his own deductions. It was his usual method, and so far it had always paid off. He led Bourdeau over to the two young men.

'Does either of you smoke a pipe?'

They looked at each other, surprised by the question.

'No,' replied Parnaux, while Friope shook his head.

'What about the master?'

'No, he doesn't smoke either. Dough is a delicate thing, it takes on any smells that are around.'

Bourdeau nodded, without fully comprehending.

Nicolas took him by the arm. 'There was a strong smell of tobacco smoke in the bakehouse.'

'Someone might have burnt something in the oven.'

'Impossible! It hadn't been lit.'

'And what do you deduce from that?'

'That Master Mourut may have had a visitor before he stuck his nose in the dough. We need to answer the basic question: death by apoplexy, accidental death, or murder? We also need to take into account the matter of the keys. How could the baker have died a natural death, locked in his bakehouse without keys in his pocket?'

Nicolas walked back to the baker's boys and told them what had been decided. Friope began weeping and wringing his hands. Bourdeau gave orders to the auxiliary officers and the men of the watch to leave as discreetly as possible, in order not to provoke any further reaction outside. Although he knew the question was pointless, Nicolas could not help asking Bourdeau if any news had come in during the night concerning Louis's disappearance. The inspector shook his head. There was every indication that he shared the commissioner's frustration and that he was desperately sorry not to be in a position to bring him any comfort, any glimmer of hope. They walked out into the street. Day was just breaking. For Nicolas, contact with the crowd that had gathered in Rue Montmartre was like a shock to the flesh.

They formed a compact, shapeless mass with, here and there, a torch or lantern carried at arm's length, lighting impassive or distorted faces, inscrutable or staring eyes. You could sense an unknown force in the group, which was subdued for the moment, but might be unleashed by the slightest move, the most harmless word, the most innocent gesture. Their exit from the Noblecourt house provoked a muted murmur. It was like the wind in the trees at the beginning of a storm, when the silence is suddenly shattered, giving free rein to the fury of the elements. Nicolas and Bourdeau took care not to pay the slightest attention to this still slumbering beast. A man cried out, 'Bread for two sous!' The crowd applauded and roared their approval, as if with one voice, then everything calmed down and once again these people resumed their motionless wait.

Nicolas knocked at the door of the neighbouring house. It was opened by a bareheaded woman, the Mouruts' elderly maid, who sometimes worked in the shop and was not noted for her gracious manners. To Nicolas's request to see the baker's wife, she replied sourly that her mistress could not be disturbed before the time when she usually woke. Changing tactic, Nicolas seized the woman by the arm and pushed her inside the house.

'I demand to see your mistress immediately.'

A voice rose from the end of the corridor. 'It's all right, Eulalie, bring Commissioner Le Floch here. He's our neighbour, Monsieur de Noblecourt's lodger. Forgive her stubbornness, Commissioner. Because of her age, she can't even do her job properly. Cantankerous, and that's not the half of it! Leave us, Eulalie.'

All this was uttered in a tone at once contemptuous and irritable. The maid walked away down a dark corridor, muttering insults.

'She imagines she can rule the roost in the house and the shop because she was here when Master Mourut was born.' The baker's wife laughed a trifle sourly, as if her mood were forced. 'I've never got used to that name, which forces you to say and do things ... Mourut, can you imagine?'

Nicolas found her words deeply ambiguous. He had entered a small room which was clearly used as a boudoir. Illumined by a tarnished bull's-eye window, it comprised a hearth, a screen, a sideboard stocked with glasses and a folding chaise-longue, the kind that could be transformed into a bed or an armchair at will. Lying on this, in her morning dishabille, was a woman in her thirties. She had a thin, pink face, on which lines had already appeared. On her head was a tight-fitting nightcap of brocaded gauze with two ribbons. Her shoulders were barely covered by a mantlet of white taffeta trimmed in raw silk. Around her neck, she wore a thin black silk ribbon, more suited to day wear than the casualness of the morning. Below a flood of petticoats, one mule-clad foot swung provocatively. Nicolas stared at it so insistently that she noticed and hid it beneath her petticoats in embarrassment.

'Madame,' said Nicolas, 'it is, I regret to say, not as a neighbour but as a commissioner that I have had to force your door. Do you know where your husband is?'

'My husband is an adult. I have too much respect for him and for myself to impose my authority on whatever he has to do.'

Once again, her words surprised him.

'I quite agree with you. Is he often this late?'

'What do you mean, Monsieur? Surely he's in his bakehouse?'

That, of course, was what she should have answered in the first place.

'Did you see him during the night?'

'At night, I rest. When he goes over to the shop, he has the courtesy not to wake me, and besides ...'

'Besides?'

'We have separate rooms.'

'Let me be more specific, Madame. When did you last see your husband?'

There was not a trace of anxiety on her face. Any other woman, thought Nicolas, would already have suspected that something terrible had happened and started to panic.

'Monsieur Mourut,' she said, with a contemptuous pout, 'ate his soup and stew in my company, of course.'

'Was he planning to go out?'

'It appeared so, from his attire. In fact, he confirmed it.'

'For what purpose?'

'He had an appointment.'

'Did he tell you with whom?'

'You are persistent indeed, Monsieur!' she said, in the same oddly haughty tone. 'I gathered from his words that he was supposed to be meeting someone ...'

Anticipating another question, she bit her lip, revealing as she did so a detail which the semi-darkness of the boudoir had hidden from Nicolas. Madame Mourut had two black taffeta beauty spots, a conspicuous one near the dimple of one cheek, and a more discreet one on her lower lip. A curious choice of nightwear for a respectable woman: intended to set off the whiteness of a lady's complexion, they were a strange and even slightly suspicious sight on a baker's wife who had recently woken, as indeed was the black ribbon he had already noticed. She seemed to become aware of this examination, for it was in a distinctly starchy tone that she continued, 'I don't generally interfere in my husband's activities. I have no idea where he was going or whom he was meeting.'

'And what of yourself, Madame?' Nicolas liked asking such vague questions, which sometimes hit their target.

'What do you mean, Monsieur? What was I to do? I was asleep

until you surprised me … woke me, I mean.'

In his work as an investigator, Nicolas was sensitive to slips of the tongue. Most of the time, they betrayed a witness's nervousness, but occasionally they expressed involuntary feelings.

'Please don't take my question the wrong way, Madame. Truth is like a beauty spot. It may be found in the strangest of places.'

He heard a sharp intake of breath from Bourdeau. Madame Mourut flushed and once again bit her lip.

'Do you have a key to the communicating door between your lodgings and the bakehouse?'

'No. My husband has one, and so does the apprentice who lodges here.'

'What's his name?'

'Denis.'

'And his surname?'

'Caminet. Denis Caminet.'

'Why doesn't he live outside, like his workmates?'

She sighed. 'He's the oldest. He's training to become a master. He's the son of a friend of my husband's who died. My husband treats him like one of the family.'

It seemed to Nicolas that she was speaking now with redoubled caution, in a low, expressionless voice. He thought of Mouchette advancing with great caution along the top of a cornice.

'And where is he now?'

'In the bakehouse, I assume.'

This, of course, suggested that he was not in the house.

'No, Madame, he's not there yet.'

'What am I to make of all this, Monsieur?' she burst out. 'You force my door at the crack of dawn, you have me woken up, you torture me with questions which I find absurd and pointless. What does it all mean? I demand that you explain yourself at once. How dare you treat people so intolerably? Who do you think you are? What have I, a poor woman, done to deserve such abuse? Stop bothering me and go, or else explain!'

He had been expecting an outburst like this for some time. Why had it taken her so long? Now was the time to strike the decisive blow.

'All right, Madame, since you demand it, I shall answer all your requests ... But first, I'd like you to go with me to the communicating door.'

'That means going down into the cellar!' she said with a shiver, folding the end of her mantlet over her shift. 'It's cold down there!'

'It will only take a moment. I'd like to check something with you, and then I'll be happy to supply you with the reason for my visit. Please, we'll follow you.'

Without a word, she held out a candle, which Bourdeau immediately took and lit. In the corridor, a low door opened onto a small stone staircase. Two cats passed between his legs, spitting as they did so. Nicolas understood why they were there when he saw the piles of sacks which, as was clear from the touch, contained, not flour, but grain. Madame Mourut seemed to take no notice of this examination. They reached the communicating door. Bourdeau directed the candlelight at it and turned in surprise.

'The key is in the door.'

In an instant, Nicolas gauged the significance of this observation. The consequences followed one from another in his mind. If it was established that the baker had been murdered, the fact that the bakehouse was closed on all sides would constitute further evidence of murder. If such were not the case – which seemed less likely by the minute – what interest would there be in making the death look like murder? If Mourut had locked himself in before dying with his head in the kneading trough, they would have found the keys, that much was incontrovertible. There was no other way out. All at once, he thought of the shop. Was it possible? Why had he not thought of it earlier? Often, in the jumble of details at the beginning of an investigation, an important point was overlooked.

'Madame, how is the shop closed up? Is there a key?'

'More questions! The shop is closed from the inside with iron bars drawn across it.'

Everything was clear again: two keys, two doors, two ways out. They would have to go over the whole of the shop, the bakehouse and the storeroom with a fine-tooth comb. He took the candle, bent down and began examining the floor. He said a few words to Bourdeau, who quickly withdrew. Nicolas deliberately did not break the silence that had fallen. Madame Mourut was shivering with cold, or something else. After a moment, they heard some muted noises, and she recoiled as if in fright. The communicating door shook, then slowly creaked open and the heavy figure of Bourdeau appeared in the doorway. He passed the candle to Nicolas, who raised it above his head. The flickering flame spread a little light over the bakehouse and revealed the body lying on the floor. The inspector had removed the blanket concealing it. The candle sputtered, throwing the little group back into darkness for a moment.

'My God, who is that?'

Nicolas thought the question ill-chosen. 'Alas, Madame, who could it be? I'm sorry to have to tell you that we found your husband dead in his kneading trough.'

He had the impression that the news came as a relief. She suddenly began laughing nervously and was unable to stop.

'Please forgive me, Monsieur … I'm suffocating …'

Still giggling, she put her hands over her face. Nicolas decided to press home his advantage.

'Who were you expecting to find?'

She straightened up, as if cut to the quick. 'Nobody. Monsieur, you are taking advantage of my grief.' Her tone was stern but unconvincing. She looked him full in the face. 'Monsieur, why would anyone kill my husband?'

'But, Madame, who said anything about a killing? We have merely noted that he is dead. We now have to determine the cause of death, taking account of the circumstances. Were you being threatened in any way?'

'The rabble of Paris have been making a great deal of fuss about the bakeries.'

Once again, he was surprised by her words and tone. There seemed to be a discrepancy between her state and her language.

'Was he ill?'

'The work is hard. The heat, the damp ... Always breathing flour dust.'

She had quickly regained her composure. He thought about the best course to take. Should he have her, too, taken to the Grand Châtelet? He had decided to do so with the two baker's boys because he had sensed in them a weakness and a fear which had to be taken into account and from which he had to protect them. It would, he hoped, be only a temporary measure.

With her, it was different. If she were taken to prison, it would immediately set tongues wagging in the district. Nevertheless, it was vital that she should not be in a position to confer with anyone, especially the third apprentice, who had still not appeared. In such circumstances, it was preferable to confine her to her room and have an officer keep a close watch on her.

'Madame, I'm terribly sorry, but I find that I am obliged to place you in solitary confinement.'

She went red in the face, making him fear an explosion.

'Please stay calm, Madame! I'm not arresting you, I'm merely confining you to your home. One of my officers will be here to make sure that my orders are carried out and that you are not in any discomfort. This decision is, I assure you, intended for your protection in case your husband's death proves to be suspicious.'

She did not say a word but her attitude was eloquent enough, if somewhat forced. Nicolas was not impressed. Although he could not have said exactly why, her pose as a martyr seemed as false to him as the calls used by birdcatchers to attract their prey.

She was conducted back to her room, while Bourdeau went in search of an officer who would make sure that this confinement was correctly carried out. In the corridor, they found the maid sitting on a stool, leaning on her broom. She was eagerly watching all the comings and goings with a wicked smile on her lips. Nicolas chose not to tackle her directly. In vain: as soon as she saw him, she got to her feet and rushed to him, eager to speak.

'What's all this hullabaloo? At my age, it's quite upsetting. All these people bringing mud and filth into the house, which I'm going to have to clean up. What has she done? I hope you treated her as she deserves! She ought to be locked up, and I know what I'm talking about. Where's the master while his house is being searched? Let me tell him.'

Her old lined face with its deep-set eyes was framed by a yellowed linen cap. A shapeless grey smock hung loosely on her. Nicolas noted once again how much the situation of domestic staff could vary from one house to another. He compared the lot of this poor, weary, embittered woman with that of Marion and Catherine, loved and respected members of the Noblecourt household. Was that just a way of salving one's conscience? He imagined for a moment what Bourdeau would have to say on the matter. For the moment, the important thing was to calm her excitement, even though it was not without its interest, revealing a few curious nuggets in the lava flow of her words.

'Wait! What's your name?'

'What? Eulalie, but people call me La Babine. I've been working here since I was a girl. Oh, I know you. A long time ago, you were quite the young dandy. And Marion, and Catherine. They're the lucky ones, those two! I'm nearly seventy and I've been here for fifty years. I was born in Le Mans.'

'Ah!' muttered Bourdeau through clenched teeth. 'Le Mans! How can we not trust her?'

'What have you got against your mistress?'

'You'd be surprised at the things I could tell you, Monsieur. As if I'd feel sorry for her over anything that might happen! To tell the truth, I'm delighted.'

She was making no attempt to hide her feelings. But experience had taught Nicolas to distrust witnesses whose apparent honesty was the most subtle method of concealment.

'To her, I'm no better than this broom I'm holding. In the days when the master was still a boy, I was well treated. And yet, seeing how far she's fallen, she'd do better not to put on airs!'

'How far she's fallen? What do you mean?'

She grinned eagerly. 'It's obvious you don't know anything at all. She may have her nose in the air, that one, but the fact is, she's come down in the world. Her father was an officer, an equerry, who got thrown out of his corps because of gambling debts, and fell among riff-raff. He'd placed his only daughter, the high and mighty Mademoiselle Céleste Julie Émilie Bidard de Granet, as an apprentice to a dressmaker in Rue Tiquetonne …'

She let go of her broom and did a little twirl, holding the corners of her smock and mimicking a curtsy.

'… The master fell head over heels in love with her, having spotted her at Sunday mass. He dragged her out of the gutter where I wager she'd have fallen eventually. The dressmaker decided to part company with her because she was corrupting the customers.'

'The customers?'

'I mean the husbands of the customers she called on to deliver the finished dresses. The master didn't notice a thing, and she lied like the strumpet she's always been. She makes herself out to be something great, but she is what she is, and I know what I know. You're a clever young man, I'd guess, and I'm sure you'll be able to sort out the false from the true. You're not going to let yourself be fooled by appearances. But let's not talk about that, I'm not one of those people who tell tales about their masters.'

What would she have said if she had been, wondered Nicolas.

'That does you honour, and I shan't insist. A few more things: the third of the baker's boys, the one who lodges here ... By the way, what's his name?'

'Oh, him! That arrogant little hanger-on. The master lets him get away with everything. As for the mistress ... His name's Denis, Denis Caminet. If you see powder on his face, you can be sure it's not flour!'

'Let's take things one at a time. Where is he?'

'How should I know? Ask him. Frittering his time away, as usual. From dawn to dusk, he drifts from brothel to brothel, so I've been told.'

'Told by whom?'

'I know what I'm talking about. This city's like a village. Everyone knows everything.'

'Is that the normal conduct of an apprentice baker?'

'I'm not saying a word about that,' she said indulgently. 'The master lets him do what he likes, and he must have his reasons for that. But as far as I'm concerned, Denis is a shameless parasite.'

He had had many sparring partners in his career, but La Babine was clearly a formidable opponent. It was obvious that she knew more than she was willing to say. But he did not want to force her, convinced as he was that such tactics led witnesses to remain silent. What she had told him suggested so many different avenues to explore that, if his intuition about the nature of Master Mourut's death proved correct, these would provide very useful pointers for the investigation.

'You clearly don't like him very much. Who are his parents?'

There was a sudden gleam in her dull eyes. She screwed up her face and grimaced, seemingly reluctant to reply. 'Nobody knows,' she said at last. 'He may not even have any.'

'Yet someone must be paying for his apprenticeship.'

'How should I know? Why are you badgering me? Ask the notary who pays his rent.'

She definitely knew a great deal about the Mourut household, much more than she was prepared to say. Did she know that the baker was dead? So far, there had been nothing to suggest that she did. Why did she imagine the police had come here and questioned Madame Mourut? It was best to continue without insisting. They would find out soon enough. Of course, it was always possible that she had been eavesdropping.

'And the other two, Parnaux and …'

'Friope. Poor devils like me, easily exploited, badly housed, badly fed, badly treated. Caminet bullies them and the mistress treats them with contempt. Mind you, they ask for it … I know what I'm talking about.'

'Eulalie, why do you think we're here this morning? You don't seem too concerned!'

She looked at them with an inscrutable expression on her face. 'I have no idea. Something to do with the mistress, I assume.'

'Is there anything that leads you to assume that?'

She came closer, looked behind her and lowered her voice. 'She runs off at night.'

'What makes you say that?'

She lifted a finger to one eye and continued mysteriously, 'Oh, don't think I don't know what goes on. She's out at all hours, in a cloak and hood.'

'Have you actually seen her?'

'Yes, though not last night.'

'What happened last night?'

'Yesterday was Sunday, when I don't work. I spent the evening with a countrywoman of mine who's a portress in Rue Tire-Boudin, not far from here.'

'So you didn't serve dinner to your masters last night?'

She looked at him, a touch uncertainly. 'Who told you that?'

'Told us what?'

'That I served dinner to my masters last night.'

In Nicolas's opinion, it was not up to her to ask the questions. He said nothing, which was the simplest way to force the witness to continue.

'I couldn't have. I didn't get back until early this morning.'

'What time was that?'

'Half past five, just as the bells were ringing in Saint-Eustache.'

At that point, the baker was already in the bakehouse.

'And presumably your mistress was still asleep?'

'I doubt it! I wager she'd only just got back.'

'And Master Mourut?'

'At that hour, he's already at work, or rather, the two boys are.'

'So you didn't see anything to worry you?'

'What kind of thing? It's been a long time since I last cared about anything in this house. Nothing ever happens to bother me – or make me happy, for that matter. I used to, oh, yes, I used to care a lot, but that's passed with age, fortunately. They don't care about me and I don't care about them!'

'Eulalie, I have to inform you that a dead body was found in the bakehouse this morning.'

Not a single muscle in her face moved. He had drawn near her and was looking hard at her emaciated, unprepossessing face, with its yellow skin and little black spots.

'So,' she said at last, in a low voice, 'they finally made up their minds to do it ... It's the person who fears too much for his own skin who risks it the most ... Threaten the rats too often and they'll get you ... once they're released. It was bound to happen ...'

She was talking to herself, a cruel little smile on her lips. She grabbed hold of his arm, and her hand felt like a claw.

'She knows, does she? She knows. Tell me, for God's sake, does she know?'

'Wait a moment!' said Nicolas, freeing himself. 'Who do you think died?'

'Why, Caminet, of course! They paid him back for his threats. God protect them!'

La Babine's words and attitude strengthened Nicolas in his conviction: this was a house of secrets, a place oozing with crime. The further he went with this preliminary enquiry, the more certain he became that a murder had been committed. Bourdeau's expression was testimony to the fact that he was thinking the same thing. They had known each other for so long that they understood each other without having to exchange a word.

'You're mistaken, I'm afraid. We don't even know where Caminet is. Alas, it is your master, Monsieur Mourut, who has died.'

A dull look came into her eyes and she began trembling. 'What?' She gave a kind of croak, then started weeping silently.

Bourdeau approached the commissioner and whispered in his ear, 'Either she's telling the truth or she's a consummate actress. Either way, if what we're both thinking turns out to be correct, she should be confined to her room like the baker's wife.'

'Inform the officer, Pierre. He'll keep an eye on the house, which is to be closed up until further orders. If Caminet returns, have him taken to the Grand Châtelet with the others. Unfortunately, I have to leave you as I need to get to Versailles as soon as possible, so I'm entrusting you with the rest. Report to me upon my return. The important thing now is the autopsy. All these other measures are intended to preserve the evidence. Make enquiries in Rue Tire-Boudin and at the house where the two boys live. And don't forget to inform Commissioner Fontaine. I shall see you very soon.'

He went back to the Noblecourt house, leaving a stunned La Babine in the hands of the inspector. It took him only a short while to get ready. Ensuring he took both Maria Theresa's letter and the medallion with him, he made his way through a small, hostile crowd and found a cab in front of Saint-Eustache to take him to police headquarters in Rue Neuve-Saint-Augustin, where he intended to find a horse that would get him to Versailles. There was no portmanteau to weigh him down, and whenever he stayed at Court now, he had a room at his disposal at the d'Arranet mansion where he kept his hunting costume, his rifles and his Court attire.

The city was almost unrecognisable. As in Rue Montmartre, silent groups of men and women had gathered, not only outside bakeries, but also at the corners of the streets, where they were being harangued by grim-faced individuals who seemed out of place in this everyday scene. For the moment, however, there was no indication that these gatherings might lead to violence, although the city seemed to be in a mounting fever of expectation.

At police headquarters, he was pleased to find a large dapple-grey mare with high withers, which greeted him with a rippling of the skin and a joyful whinny that indicated that they would get on well. The horse's good mood was also manifested in a few caprioles and croupades, which Nicolas was easily able to control. Rider and mount were clearly made for one another. They were soon passing through the walls of the city to Pont de Sèvres. A light mist hovered like steam over the surface of the river. Through it, boats and barges seemed to be gliding in the air. The first rays of the sun were striking the freshly cut stone pyramids intended for the new constructions from the Pré-aux-Clercs to the Point-du-Jour. Black smoke rose from the furnace on the Île des Cygnes. Everywhere, the eye was refreshed by the tender green of an unusually late spring.

Nicolas let the mare carry him and began meditating. Once again, he was convinced, he was confronting crime and death. He made an effort not to link these dark thoughts to the fate of his son. His powerlessness in such a personal situation drove him to despair. He had to control his over-active imagination in order to avoid exaggerated and baleful speculation. That he should have been affected in what he held dearest seemed like an undeserved punishment. Was his passion for Aimée d'Arranet the cause, he wondered. Had his captive heart overtaken his mind and his reason? He recalled the austere but fatherly figure of Canon Le Floch, who had often pointed out that even God's most perfect creatures were neither inexhaustible nor infinite and could only be possessed occasionally and fleetingly. His sister Isabelle had chosen eternal love, which alone was inexhaustible. He wondered what sin, what remorse she was hoping to expiate by taking the veil.

He had not yet thought about her request. He reflected on what marked him out from others. He knew he had had the soul of a commoner in his early years. What a poor little fellow he had been when, as a notary's clerk, he had pounded the streets of Rennes! Yet he had not at the time considered himself in any way inferior to the nobleman he had been forced to become. Everyone had the same beginning and would meet the same end. When they breathed their last, all men were equal, whether noblemen or commoners. He knew whereof he spoke. He had been present at the last moments of a king,[1] and it had been an edifying experience. The priest praying at the bedside of Louis XV had not called him Majesty but *Anima Christiana*, as he would have done with the humblest of the King's subjects. At this memory, a pious shudder went through him.

Even though he was indifferent to the matter, he would accede to Isabelle's wishes. He would do so not for the title, which everyone gave him anyway without knowing why, but the better to equip his son to face a difficult and dangerous world, and to give him the chance to take his place in the long line from which, whatever the circumstances, he was descended and of which he was at present the last representative. Nicolas was relieved to have settled the question.

Would Louis survive at Court? He himself had somehow done so all these years. He had never accepted the idea of being a clock that had to be constantly rewound[2] at the whim of those who set the tone, ringing when they wanted him to, following like a minute hand the movements of an absolute will turning endlessly round and round. To do so, he would have had to concern himself with trivial matters, be lacking in charity, lavish with promises and compliments, and practised in dissimulation. He would have had to appear uninvolved and ignorant while surreptitiously undermining those who needed to be undermined. In other words, he would have had to cease living his own life and only do what others demanded. Instead of which, his only faith and pride was to serve his King, in the best tradition of the Ranreuils, as he had been taught it – all too long ago, alas – by his father the marquis.

Compared with the city, the road to Versailles seemed deserted. As he passed through the Fausses Reposes woods, he felt a pang in his heart. It was here that he had met Aimée for the first time and clasped her to him ... As his horse took him at a jog down the great drive lined with lime trees, where he had almost lost his life a few months earlier, towards the d'Arranet mansion, his impatience increased. His separation from his mistress, although relatively short, had made him realise how deeply attached to her he was. He dismounted, tied the horse to a ring in the wall, and climbed the front steps, surprised not to be greeted as he usually was by a bustling crowd of servants. He knocked at the door. After a few moments, it opened, and the scarred but friendly face of Tribord, the major-domo, appeared and lit up with joy and surprise. Tribord was not wearing his livery and his wigless head was covered in a woollen cap.

'Good Lord, Monsieur Nicolas! It's been a long time!'

'Are your masters at home?' asked Nicolas, increasingly worried by this welcome.

'No! I'm the only one on board. Mademoiselle Aimée has put in at her cousins' house in Saumur and the admiral is tacking from port to port. At the moment, I think he's in Cherbourg.' He noticed the disappointment his words aroused. 'He told me to do you the honours of the wardroom and the stores if you were here in his absence.'

'It was indeed my intention to spend the night here. I am planning to attend His Majesty's hunt. Right now, I have to go to the palace. It's likely I will be back quite late.'

'Will you have dined?'

'Yes, at Versailles. Please don't put yourself out for me. I have one question, though. I wrote Mademoiselle d'Arranet a letter from Vienna. Do you know if she received it?'

'It certainly arrived. A kind of Turk in a turban brought it yesterday. Riding a fine, lively steed. Gave me the letter and asked me to get it to Mademoiselle as quickly as possible. Actually, I kept it. The time it'd take me to send it to Anjou, she'll probably be back here.'

'How can you be sure it was from me?'

'I recognised the seal with your coat of arms, Monsieur. My eyes may be covered in scars but they're still sharp enough to tell a corvette from a frigate on the horizon!'

Nicolas handed him a few *louis*, which he pocketed with a satisfied nod.

'It's always an honour to serve Monsieur.'

'I'll see you this evening, then.'

When he arrived at the palace, he entrusted his mount to the care of a groom. It energetically demonstrated its displeasure at seeing its rider walk away. The groom, whom Nicolas had known for a long time, told him that, even in Versailles, there was a great deal of excitement among the common people and that an incident could occur at any moment, especially at the following day's market. Nicolas proceeded to the building housing the Department of Foreign Affairs to report on his mission to Monsieur de Vergennes. He was immediately admitted. The minister continued to write as he listened to Nicolas, showing his interest with quick glances and the odd muttered phrase. The name Georgel seemed to upset him and he began hitting the surface of his desk with the flat of his hand.

'The insolent fellow! Just imagine, he had the audacity to ask to see me. I didn't receive him, of course. We shan't be using his services any longer, given that he refuses to recognise our authority, in other words the King's authority, as legitimate. Nevertheless—' he looked at Nicolas with a touch of amusement in his eyes – 'to go from that to making him a plotter, a conspirator, and seeing in his attitude, which may have other causes, something darkly suspicious, suggestive of evil intrigues, well, that's a step I'd rather not take. Your imagination is running away with you. The papers that were seized are merely the remains of a casual correspondence exchanged by some wits who think they're important, even though they have no power. As for the attempt on your life, from which you were so fortunately saved by the Chevalier de Lastire, I think we can safely lay that at the door of the Austrian authorities.'

Monsieur de Vergennes was much more interested in Nicolas's account of his audience with Maria Theresa. Nicolas reported his impressions with that gift for narration that always delighted his listeners. He combined his own memories with Breteuil's judgements and other observations gleaned during his stay in Vienna.

'The Empress clearly deserves the good reputation she enjoys throughout Europe. Nobody is more skilful at winning hearts, or puts such effort into it. She knows how important it is, for it is thanks to that skill that she has earned the love of her subjects, so openly expressed in the trials she has been through.'

'Especially when the King of Prussia made life difficult for her. She got herself out of that situation very shrewdly.'

'Yes. She's so industrious, she even works and reads reports as she takes her stroll. Every day, she grants three or four hours' audience, and admits everyone without exception. She deals with all kinds of matters, gives alms personally, hears complaints, claims, projects … and spies. She asks questions, answers them, gives advice, and arbitrates in disputes. Most matters have been settled by the time the audience is over. I would add, however, to be absolutely honest, that a love of gossip somewhat obscures her finer qualities, and that her determination to bind women to their husbands often produces the opposite effect, since at the mere suggestion that a woman is disposed to flirtatiousness, she gives the husband advice that disrupts more marriages than it saves.'

'And what of her relations with her son?'

'Outwardly good, but she jealously guards her authority. When her husband died, she let it be known that she was planning to retire and leave her son to rule in her place. But her natural taste for being in command soon gained the upper hand and she abandoned a project conceived in the early stages of her grief. She claims to set great store by the alliance with France and sees her daughter's marriage, with which she is extremely pleased, as a new means of ensuring it will last.'

'Excellent! But what I'm most concerned about is our ambassador's secret dispatches. Did you manage to get them out? What method did you use to do so?'

When Nicolas revealed his system, the minister could hardly believe it. He rose and rang a bell. Soon afterwards, a clerk appeared, cut a quill and began writing at top speed to Nicolas's monotone dictation. The whole recital took three-quarters of an hour.

'... *The public accuse the Emperor of having been too hasty in depriving the landowners of the surplus of the taxes they demand from the people, and everyone is agreed that the Empress would like to leave things on the old footing of servitude towards the feudal lords in order to close the public's eyes to the burden of their own servitude to the authority of the monarchy, and even more so perhaps out of a feeling that one should proceed more slowly with innovations, even when they are prompted by a spirit of humanity and justice. Be that as it may, Monsieur, it would be hard to ignore the fact that the least one can expect from the current situation in*

Bohemia is a strong wave of emigration in favour of the King of Prussia. A constant state of war between the peasants and their masters could make this emigration an almost daily occurrence, which would harm Bohemia and be of great advantage to Prussian Silesia. That's it, Monseigneur.'

'Marquis,' said Vergennes, delighted, 'I would never have imagined ... Your system should be widely adopted.'

He quickly seized the transcriptions, went back to his armchair and began studying them without further ado. The audience was over, and Nicolas withdrew.

This second audience left him with a taste of ashes in his mouth. The only thing the minister had taken from his report was what most affected the interests of his own department. But then he rebuked himself. Why should he feel disappointed when he knew, from having observed them over the years, that men in government might be plagued with a thousand concerns, but that the greatest was the concern with self-preservation? Endlessly moving from one matter to another without ever having the chance to go deeply into any of them, they must surely miss the point quite often. Doubtless Vergennes had reacted with all the ignorance of a man who, because of his diplomatic functions, had been too long away from the Court and the city. To such a man, it must be clear that Commissioner Le Floch, however great his reputation, should simply obey orders and not start to think about matters that did not concern him. His judgement, and his ability to disentangle the mysteries of domestic crime, in no way suited him to deal with matters of vital interest to the kingdom. And it was true that the outrageousness of the ideas put forward by those in power were, for Nicolas, a constant source of doubt and scepticism.

He went back to the palace and entered the ministers' wing, where he was planning to see Monsieur de Sartine, who divided his time between the Department of the Navy in the morning and the palace in the afternoon. He was hoping that the former Lieutenant General of Police, who was more familiar than Vergennes with the ins and outs of political intrigue, would be duly impressed by the news he had brought back and more inclined to draw the necessary conclusions from them.

He was about to have himself announced when the door of Sartine's study half opened and an individual with his head covered in an incredible turban came out and held out his hand to him. It took him a moment to recognise the Chevalier de Lastire. It was not until they had exchanged warm greetings that Nicolas realised that the turban in question, which had astonished Tribord, was actually a bandage so skilfully constructed as to deceive a less than observant spectator.

'I'm choked with remorse,' said the Chevalier. 'I didn't keep my promise to deliver your post. It was only yesterday that I handed it over to the Central Post Office, apart from the letter to Mademoiselle d'Arranet, which I delivered on the way to Versailles.'

'But what happened to you?'

'It's a long story, too long to tell in this vestibule. Suffice it to say that the Austrians were reluctant to let me go. May I invite you to dinner this evening? I don't know the town well, so I leave the choice to you.'

'The easiest thing would be to meet at the Hôtel de la Belle-Image at seven. I have often eaten there and the food is perfectly decent.'

They parted company and Nicolas hastened into the room, where Sartine stood waiting for him.

'It's time you learnt to be more punctual, Monsieur! The whole of Versailles has been buzzing with rumours about you: that you decided to enter the service of the Empress, that she fell under your spell and can no longer do without you, that even the Emperor Joseph praised your gift for repartee during a certain macabre encounter.'

Nicolas yielded to his interlocutor's pleasure, while pretending to be surprised. Sartine loved to dazzle others with how much he knew, thanks to his unequalled intelligence service. He was clearly in a good mood, as this affectionate mockery proved.

'Don't tell me you're surprised?'

'From you, Monseigneur, I always expect the unexpected! However, if it had been up to me, I would have returned a long time ago. Sadly, it was not up to me. Allow me, as proof of my gratitude and loyalty, to show you that the time I spent in Vienna wasn't completely wasted.'

He placed an oval-shaped cardboard box on the desk.

In an instant, Sartine reverted to being the child who had once played with a spinning top in the streets of Barcelona. He had immediately recognised what Nicolas had brought him. He picked up the box, raised it to eye level as if it were an offering, put it down, seemed to breathe it in, then, timidly, almost regretfully, lifted the lid and removed the silk paper. He closed his eyes, an expression of pure bliss on his face. Nicolas noticed that he was trembling. Was the taste for collecting a kind of illness? Sartine finally obeyed an inner voice, even though part of him seemed to be resisting. His eyes filling with tears, he at last plunged his hands into the box. As he did so, he let out a sigh. He lifted out a flood of silvery curls that spread like the tentacles of some sea monster. Finally, he could hold out no longer, and plunged his face into it.

'Nicolas,' he managed to say, although his voice was faint, 'I thank heaven that the Empress left you the time to seek out this treasure. What a gem! What a wonder! Look at it shimmer, see how it changes shape, how the reflections dissolve. Where did you find it?'

'At a wigmaker's in Vienna, recommended by Georgel in the days when he was the honest secretary to Prince Louis. It's a unique model, the official headdress of the Magistrato Camerale of the city of Padua.'

'Ah!' cried Sartine. 'I'll bring it out to a melody by Albinoni.[3] The Chevalier de Lastire has told me a great deal ...'

Nicolas did not react to this sudden change of register, being accustomed to it from Sartine.

'I know you've seen Vergennes and that part of your mission had a fortunate outcome, even though it confirmed our failure. That's what happens when priests get ideas above their station and think they're all Alberonis.[4] It produces a curious mixture of pretension and little domestic crises. Breteuil's arrival was the fuse that sparked this particular crisis. Georgel thought he could make himself indispensable, manipulated as he is by those more cunning than him. He forgot that we serve higher interests under which we must restrain our ambitions, share our successes and demonstrate an ability to distance ourselves and attain complete humility.'

Nicolas smiled inwardly. However deep his devotion to Sartine, he remained clear-headed. On many occasions, he had experienced the man's innocent tendency to take the credit for other people's actions and build his own reputation on the successes of his subordinates.

'That old secret network belongs to a bygone time. It only meant something when motivated by the late King ... We mustn't cling to the past, or indulge in impotent nostalgia. We must rebuild our system, overhaul it completely ... That's what I'm doing in my new state. I already mentioned something about it to you. Monsieur de Lastire, Admiral d'Arranet and you yourself are its elements – my chess pieces, so to speak.'

'I agree, Monseigneur, that the Georgel affair can be written off, given that you now know the ins and outs of the situation, but this paper, which Lastire must have mentioned to you, is another matter and even more disturbing.'

He handed over the reconstruction of the paper seized from the hearth in Georgel's room in Vienna. Sartine gave it a somewhat cursory examination, then waved it in the air.

'Nonsense, fit only for the inspectors' weekly report! None of it means a thing. Turgot has given himself a stick to be beaten with. He can't complain now and blame everyone else.'

'So you don't see any indication of unrest or danger in it?'

'Get a grip on yourself, Nicolas. I fear that, out of a legitimate concern for the safety of the State and the King, you have spent too long suspecting everyone and everything. There is no reason for you to feel ashamed, it's what we expect of you and why you are under my authority.'

If any proof had been needed that Sartine, as all Paris claimed, was still running the police through his accomplice, Monsieur Lenoir, this remark would have been enough to convince the most sceptical.

'Then what about that attempt on my life, which was clearly linked to Abbé Georgel's schemes?'

'It continued with the attack on Lastire. Think about it, my friend! The Austrians felt they had been provoked, and were taking their revenge. Not our friend Kaunitz, who's much too sensible. Perhaps the Emperor and the authorities in Vienna, who weren't fooled by the supposed object of the Marquis de Ranreuil's mission.'

So the Chevalier had been attacked, which explained the bandage.

'Nevertheless, Monseigneur—'

'No, Nicolas! And you'd do well to avoid corpses pursuing you even into our friend Noblecourt's house ...'

He really did know everything before anyone else! Now that Monsieur de Saint-Florentin, the Duc de La Vrillière, Minister of the King's Household, was ailing and in disgrace, Sartine had rediscovered his taste for police work while standing in for Monsieur Lenoir during his illness.

'... You persist in scattering dead bodies beneath your feet before delivering them still warm to the indecent experiments of your surgeon friend and the public executioner!'

It was an old refrain of Sartine's. Time for Nicolas to change the subject.

'For someone like myself, Monseigneur, who left France two months ago, the anxiety and unrest among the people is very noticeable. Paris seems to be in a fever. Yet no orders have been given ...'

'Monsieur Turgot has been battering us with his innovations. There are moments when taking action would be weakness and would give the enemy the opportunity to strike. Let's not yield to panic. That would merely lead to the clumsiest and most ill-considered of reactions. Monsieur Turgot wants the State to change its old habits. Well, we shall see which of the two wins out in the long run, Monsieur Turgot or reality.'

'But—'

'No buts, our young rebel. Go to see Their Majesties and receive the praise your mission has earned you. Then go back to Paris and study your mysterious death. Let's hope it's not a murder! A master baker, with all that's going on!'

'Nevertheless, there is violence in the provinces. I myself—'

'That's enough. You're starting to annoy me. Tell it to Turgot. He's the one who's got us into this predicament.'

And Monsieur de Sartine went back to contemplating the new addition to his collection.

Once again, Nicolas left the minister's study with a sense of helplessness. Knowing from experience that one should never answer an unasked question or raise a delicate matter that has not so far been raised, he had abstained from pointing out that Monsieur Lenoir had ordered him to follow the development of the unrest over the price of bread and the free circulation of grain. It was Monsieur Lenoir he had to obey. What would Monsieur de Sartine have said in the old days if he had taken his instructions from the Minister for the Navy? Basically, what Sartine had said was not so very different from what Vergennes had said. But although the latter's attitude was understandable, given his diplomatic concerns, Sartine's seemed wrapped in pretence and prevarication. That was confirmed by his vicious tone when it came to the comptroller general, which left no doubt as to his feelings: Monsieur Turgot's announced reforms deserved the sternest censure. Regretfully, Nicolas, without himself forming an opinion on a matter he had not thought about, suspected a factional stand. It seemed that Sartine, liberated by the death of the late King, had gone back to his old friendships and inclinations. There was also no doubt that, as Minister for the Navy, he felt a long-lasting acrimony towards a comptroller general with whom conflict was inevitable. The department Sartine was running was a constant drain on resources and prone to increasing the treasury's deficit. In addition, the Duc de La Vrillière's decline had led him to hope that, with the Queen's overt support, he would obtain the post of Minister of the King's Household. Everyone was convinced that he would be much more comfortable there than in a department where he still had everything to learn.

The fact remained that this refusal to consider the urgency of the current situation, this ironic flippancy about the coming dangers, left a bitter taste in Nicolas's mouth. There was a strong risk that opportunities would be lost. He had known other times when the glory or downfall of the throne had been in the balance. He had come to wish for a monarchy freed from private contingencies, a monarchy which would express the general interest. In a vague way, being used to service, and having always tried to avoid anything that might make his certainties waver, he placed this hope in the young King. He clung more than ever to the kind of loyalty he had learnt about from the tales of chivalry he had once read by candlelight in Guérande. But he could not help feeling a pang when he realised that Sartine, who knew everything, clearly knew nothing about the fate of Louis, or he would surely have mentioned it.

VI

A TWENTY-YEAR-OLD KING

Royal authority is only ever shaken by the instruments
it believed were intended to strengthen it.

D'ARGENSON

Luck had smiled on him. As he was walking, lost in thought, in the
Hall of Mirrors, trying to find a way of gaining access to the Queen,
he came across the Empress's ambassador to Versailles. Hardly a
day went by that Monsieur de Mercy-Argenteau did not appear at
Court with his friend the Abbé de Vermond, the Queen's reader, for
a private visit. The ambassador immediately poured out a stream
of compliments on the success of a journey of which he seemed to
know every detail. Having asked Nicolas why he was here, he offered
to conduct him into the Queen's presence. He took him by the arm
and led him to the royal apartments. As he did so, he continued his
comments, for it was in his nature to overwhelm his interlocutor
with words, out of the midst of which a specific, insidious question
occasionally emerged.

'My dear Marquis, there has been much talk here about your
Viennese triumphs. I wager – and I'm sure you'll confirm this – that
Monsieur de Breteuil was pleased to have crowned his debut with
the arrival of an envoy such as yourself. It can certainly be called an
unqualified success. And what did Kaunitz say?'

His head spinning from Mercy-Argenteau's superfluous eloquence
and florid style, Nicolas answered his increasingly insistent questions

as simply as he could. The ambassador continued with his extravagant praise until they reached the Queen's antechambers, where an usher placed them in the hands of one of the ladies-in-waiting, who in turn admitted them to the small rooms behind the Queen's bedchamber. These almost bourgeois audiences never failed to surprise those less familiar with Court customs. It was well known that the Queen was weary of the ceremony of the levee, which she considered an imposition. She was gradually abolishing this slavery: once she had done her hair, she would wave goodbye to the audience in her ceremonial chamber then, followed by her servants, disappear into her private rooms. There, she would meet close friends, or sometimes Mademoiselle Bertin, the rising star among dressmakers, who had been introduced into the Queen's entourage at Marly by the Duchesse de Chartres soon after the death of Louis XV. For now, only the Abbé de Vermond was present, reading aloud from Anquetil's *Histoire de France*. The Queen, who had been pensive and bored, was unable now to conceal her joy on seeing the visitors.

'My friends,' she cried, 'come and distract me from this dear abbé, who is saddening me with stories of wars and treaties! My rider from Compiègne! It took you a long time to return …'

It seemed that many people had missed him, except, he thought bitterly, those of whom he was fondest. He immediately excepted the Noblecourt household from this observation.

'… How is my dear mamma?'

'Your Majesty can rest assured that she is in excellent health, as far as I was able to judge, having had the honour of spending more than an hour in her presence.'

She put her hands together in a somewhat forced expression of delight. 'Did she ask many questions about her daughter?'

'The Empress thinks of nothing but the Queen's happiness.'

'I am sure that is so.' She threw Monsieur de Mercy a slightly provocative glance. 'I hope she was not too *grandig*?'[1]

Nicolas was convinced that the ambassador knew every detail of his interview with Maria Theresa. Had he informed the Queen? In broad outline, certainly. He looked at Marie Antoinette's hair, which was so high that you were obliged to look up to see the top of it. Her mother's fears on the subject were well founded. He had heard that one of the reasons for no longer dressing in public was that it was now necessary to step into your clothes rather than putting them on over your head, an exercise that could not decently be carried out in public. He realised that the Queen was waiting for an answer. He surmised the meaning of the German word.

'Her Imperial Majesty showed me the most sustained kindness, and did me the honour of making me her messenger to my Queen.'

She tilted her head and gave him a charming smile. Half bowed, he handed over the package and the letter. She looked at her mother's message with a kind of anxious circumspection, offering an image of indecision as if she feared an expected and much dreaded admonishment. After a moment, she threw the letter on the mantelshelf behind her and opened the package with little sighs of impatience. She gazed at the medallion, then, in a somewhat theatrical gesture, lifted it to her lips. A surreptitious glance in the direction of Mercy caught Nicolas's eye: it seemed to him that she was much more concerned with what the ambassador would report than with the spontaneous expression of filial affection.

'How grateful I am to you, Marquis, for being my dear mamma's messenger. She has declared herself well pleased with your visit, as the ambassador has been telling me. How did you find Vienna?'

'As Your Majesty knows, it was my first visit to the city of the Caesars. Its splendour and riches are a constant marvel to the traveller, as are the embellishments wrought by your mother. I also had the privilege of attending the first performance of Haydn's oratorio *The Return of Tobias*, at the Kärntnertor theatre … and I dined at the Prater and drank Nussberger like a true Viennese!'

The Queen laughed and clapped her hands. A young lady she might be, but she was still a child at heart.

'I thought of you a few days ago ...'

Nicolas bowed.

'... when my brother-in-law introduced an engineer who builds automata. One of them actually drew my portrait. Isn't that remarkable? How is it done? Perhaps like the ones Monsieur de Vaucanson[2] showed us—'

Nicolas raised a finger to his lips.

'Oh, yes, of course, that's a secret between us.'

The glances exchanged by Mercy and Vermond did not escape the Queen's attention.

'Yes, that's right! The marquis and I, gentlemen, have our secrets. I hope my mother did not overwhelm you with too many questions on my clothes?'

'I impressed on Her Imperial Majesty that it was the Queen's duty to be the arbiter of elegance, the ideal on whom the French model their taste.'

The Queen nodded and looked insistently at Mercy. 'Now that's the sort of thing you should be telling my mother. Marquis, I should not like to be deprived of your presence again for too long.'

Realising that the interview had come to an end, Nicolas bowed and withdrew backwards. Once in the antechamber, he felt pleased to have navigated his craft so skilfully in the presence of such treacherous witnesses. Inwardly, he found himself slightly ridiculous, and yet, in using such courtly language, he was merely being polite and not sacrificing the truth. There still remained between the Queen and himself the memory of their first encounter in the forest of Compiègne, an encounter full of surprise and laughter. She was still at heart a shy but impish adolescent girl who recognised him as the young man he had been then. As he descended the stairs, a hand came to rest on his shoulder. It was the Abbé de Vermond.

'Monsieur, I should like to assure you that I am at your service. I am an old friend of Monsieur de Breteuil's. He has written to me in praise of you. Until we meet again!'

And with that, he went back upstairs. What a strange place the Court was, a country with tortuous roads. Apart from the successive strata of names, titles, positions and honours, there was also another hierarchy of hidden powers, family relationships, secret friendships and unofficial influences. These clans and groups, held together by subtle links, plotted their ascendancy, promoted their followers and spun their webs. It was the confrontation between these various influences that determined the balance of power, that balance that caused some to falter and others to rise. Nicolas recalled that the Abbé de Vermond was still friendly with, and indebted to, Choiseul, as were, for different reasons, Breteuil and Sartine. There was no reason to suppose that the snub-nosed former minister, a man of great arrogance, had in any way given up on the idea of returning to office: on the contrary, he seemed to be motivating his troops to organise themselves, extend their sway and recruit new members. You were of little account in this country if you did not belong to one of the opposing factions. Ignoring the risks he ran, Nicolas had only one allegiance, and that was to the King. That others might think he inclined towards their cause was a matter of indifference to him. In this particular case, he knew that the Queen, either out of gratitude to the man who had brought about her marriage or out of a spirit of intrigue, was determined to do everything she could to favour the return of the former minister. There was nothing to suggest that this fiercely held desire corresponded to the wishes of the Empress and Emperor in Vienna. In fact, it was quite likely that they were less inclined than she was to desire the return of a man whose career was considered to have run its course and whose whims no longer suited the present situation.

Wishing to ponder all these things, Nicolas entered the grounds, where he finally sat down at the edge of the Swiss Lake. There he stayed for many hours, until the cold of evening drove him from his refuge. The sun was setting on a landscape still numbed by the excessively long, rough winter. The dark blue-green waters of the Grand Canal appeared devoid of life. It suddenly struck him that one day Versailles, like Athens and Rome, would be reduced to fields of ruins, a vast, nostalgic remnant of faded grandeur.

Fortunately, the need to act always provided the impulse that saved him from melancholy. He walked back to the great stables and retrieved his horse, which was now rested, rubbed down and fed. He rewarded the groom for his skilful care. Picking up that morning's conversation where they had left off, the groom told him the latest news. Things were getting worse. Apparently, the château of the Duchesse de La Rochefoucauld at La Roche-Guyon had been overrun. That great family were known to own most of the flour mills in the Paris area, a monopoly which had already marked them out as being part of the supposed famine pact. An angry mob of about two or three thousand men were said to have threatened the noble lady, leaving her almost overcome with terror. The same mob had later looted a boat transporting wheat whose path they crossed. The plan had then been formed to proceed to Versailles, the thinking being that their sheer numbers would impress everyone, the local people would join them, and they would force bread to be sold at two *sols* a pound. The latest rumour was that the Saint-Germain market had been sacked during the day. At seven o'clock, Nicolas found himself sitting at table with the Chevalier de Lastire in front of a roast lamb and a dish of new beans.

'I have an extraordinary adventure to tell you about,' Lastire began. 'After leaving Vienna, the first part of my journey passed without incident—'

'I'm sorry to interrupt you,' said Nicolas, 'but have I understood correctly? You left a month before us, and yet you've arrived almost at the same time.'

'That's true, alas, and with good reason! Carefree as things were originally, they soon turned into a nightmare. I made good progress at first. It was bitterly cold but at least the ground was hard, even though it treacherously concealed a few deadly patches of black ice. I must confess I prefer that to the muddy potholes we encountered on our outward journey. I was as cautious as I could be, sometimes taking back roads and only approaching a town when I had to change horses. In fact, my route was an extremely tortuous one, convinced as I was that my hurried departure had immediately been reported to the Austrian agencies and that they would try to stop me and check my papers, and perhaps slow me down. It was just as well that I did proceed that way, for in the early stages, everything went as planned. Things became more complicated when I reached the borders of the hereditary States. I found myself in a kind of funnel where roadblocks and patrols were commonplace. Twice, I was almost stopped, and I was only saved by the speed of my horse. The necessity of halting at the staging posts forced me back onto the main roads. In addition, the weather had turned stormy again ...'

'But you managed to escape all these snares and—'

'Not at all! On the road from Linz to Munich, I was trapped by a band of men in black, accompanied by a large troop of hussars. Their threatening demeanour, their weapons aimed at me, the solitude of a place where anything could happen, and the fact that it was getting dark, all led me to exercise caution for the moment. But when I bent over my saddlebags, pretending to look for my passports, I took them by surprise and came out with pistols blazing. I put two of those scoundrels out of commission, gave my horse a good whack and set off at full tilt. My escape was followed by a volley of shots. A bullet tore my horse's ear off, and it bolted. As we sped away, another bullet ripped across the top of my skull. Blood starting pouring down my face and I couldn't see anything. Holding on for dear life, the reins wrapped around my arms, I abandoned myself to that wild flight, soon losing consciousness of what was happening to me. Weeks went by—'

'Weeks?'

'On its last legs, my poor horse sought out a final resting place and rode into an isolated farm, where a peasant found me unconscious. Unconcerned about the reason for my being there, he took devoted care of me. It was not until I woke up that I discovered what had happened. I realised how much time had passed, and also that the man had assumed that my injuries were caused by broken branches, which are a constant hazard for riders. Of course, I didn't disabuse him of that idea. He had religiously kept him hands off my luggage. I thanked my saviour and set off again, painful as it was for me to ride. From this point on, I could not go too long between halts. Thank God, there were no more alarms, apart from – and this seemed to me the last straw – those threatening gatherings on the outskirts of Paris. But you yourself have returned very belatedly. Why is that?'

Nicolas told him why, recounting how he and his companions had also been intercepted.

'We let them get on with it, having nothing compromising on us.'

'That's true, but don't forget that in my case I had letters and an urgent mission to carry out. I almost didn't make it. Here I am with a turban on my head, not for the first time!'

They clinked glasses and set about demolishing the lamb, whose crisp skin concealed some wonderfully tender and flavoursome meat.

'Chevalier, I was very pleased with the journey we took together, even though I am sorry about what happened to you later. Your presence got me out of a tight corner. It's a pity we no longer have a task to accomplish together.'

Lastire joyfully struck the table. 'Don't celebrate too soon. You're wrong, as a matter of fact. Monsieur de Sartine wants me to remain at your side during this period of unrest, especially at a time when family worries are much on your mind.'

'I'm glad to hear that,' said Nicolas. 'But …'

He did not finish the sentence, and a long silence fell, which they filled by devoting themselves to the meal with almost meticulous attention. What was the reason for the irritation that Nicolas felt? Accustomed to examining his own conscience, he realised that, although he was pleased that Lastire would remain at his side, he regretted that Sartine had imposed his presence, using as a pretext a situation he had himself downplayed when his former commissioner had talked of the risk of unrest in Paris. That was all part and parcel of Sartine's tortuous way of doing things. He loved working on several fronts simultaneously, thus justifying his reputation as a 'universal spider'. His webs crossed and intertwined, sometimes becoming so tangled that they snapped. It seemed, too, that poor Monsieur Lenoir was being kept in the dark. Nicolas would just have to accept this state of affairs, even though it rankled with him that Sartine had revealed his personal affairs to a stranger without saying a word to an anxious father. Deciding to carry on regardless, he picked up the threads of the conversation.

He talked of the situation in Rue Montmartre, which was especially troubling in that the dead man was a master baker. Lastire found the details of the investigation fascinating, as if discovering a scene that was new to him. They decided to meet again the following evening at Monsieur de Noblecourt's house, as Nicolas had to take part in the royal hunt. The chevalier was so talkative, and so attentive to his needs, that Nicolas felt his misgivings vanish away. The journey to Vienna had created a bond between these two servants of the King. His one worry was Bourdeau's predictable reaction to such an intrusion into their habitual way of doing things. He decided to think no more about it for the moment: he would sort things out as they went along.

Their conversation continued as they walked in the street. Like the commissioner, Lastire had pondered the reasons for the current unrest. He put the blame firmly on the summary way in which Turgot was pushing through his reforms, particularly the establishment of a free trade in grain. When they reached the main square, he bade farewell to Nicolas without indicating where he himself was lodging: he knew where to reach the commissioner in Paris. At the d'Arranet mansion, Tribord and a stable groom were waiting for Nicolas. He entrusted the mare to them, asking them not to feed her: in harnessing her, he had noticed how fat she was – too many little treats at the royal stables, no doubt. He went up to his room, where he pondered the events of the day, which had left him with mixed feelings. It took him a long time to get to sleep, plagued as he was by dire thoughts of the risks his missing son might be running.

Tuesday 2 May 1775

Truly, people always did as they liked with him! He hated being woken suddenly. The knocking at his door had not stopped. He got up, lit the candle, glanced at his watch, which showed that it was six o'clock, and told whoever was out there to come in. Tribord, fully dressed, grim-faced, launched straight into an unsettling speech.

'It's getting colder, Monsieur. I wager we'll soon have some more rough weather. Gaspard, one of the footmen, who lives over by the Saint-Germain road, has seen increasingly large groups of people on their way to the market. Others coming from Paris have been right past this house. I wanted to warn you. I don't think you'll get to the palace safe and sound wearing a hunting coat. We'd best do something about it.'

Nicolas thought for a moment. He knew only too well how impulsive the common people could be, how they used everything as an excuse for excess. They had no ears, and shouted without listening. Their ideas were a mixture of truth and falsehood, informed by rumours which took on a life of their own and grew as they were repeated. Everything contributed to this agitation: tall stories, posters, inscriptions on walls, the exhortations of impromptu orators in gardens and cafés. Tribord was right: to appear in the midst of this wave of demonstrators in a royal hunting coat would surely be seen as a provocation and could well lead to an unfortunate incident. Nevertheless, in the current situation, he deemed it essential to see the King, and he asked the major-domo to find him some clothes which would make it possible for him to merge into the crowd. Tribord immediately set about his task. Nicolas gazed at his rifles, gifts from the young King, the same rifles which Louis XV had once entrusted to him. He felt a sudden sense of regret. His master having died too soon, the crown had passed to a man who was little more than a child. Times were harsh and history was rushing ahead, urged on by fierce new interests. Even though the coronation had not yet taken place, there seemed to be a growing feeling of dissatisfaction with the young monarch, in whom so much hope had been vested. Nicolas had barely finished washing when Tribord reappeared, his arms laden with old clothes. Worn ratine breeches, an unbleached linen shirt, a brown panne-velvet waistcoat, down-at-heel shoes and an old tricorn: this would certainly have the desired effect. Last but not least, Tribord handed him a dagger, its blade somewhat diminished with use, which he would be able to conceal. He advised Nicolas to plunge his hands in the cold ashes of the hearth and rub his face with them to avoid looking too clean. Still anxious, Tribord also advised him to take care when leaving the avenue leading from the house to the road. It would be better to go through the neighbouring wood, which led straight to the road. He could emerge from the trees pretending to straighten his clothes as if he had just passed water. There was a kind of mounting excitement in the former sailor, doubtless the same that seized him when the fusiliers' drums and the ship's bell called the crew to action stations, and berths and bulkheads came crashing down to make way for the cannons.

Nicolas followed his advice and cautiously came out onto the road to Versailles. It was lit here and there by lanterns, the long stretches of darkness between them gradually lightening as day broke. All around, men and women were walking quickly. Some were carrying torches. Only the pounding of shoes on the road and the occasional cry broke the silence of this advance. He had fallen into step with the others, making sure he remained an equal distance from everyone. The closer the column got to the palace, the larger it grew, swollen by others joining it from side roads. Twice, riders appeared and stopped beside one of the groups. He assumed they were here to pass on orders. At no time did any soldiers or policemen appear. If there were any police present, he knew from experience that it would be in the form of spies hidden among the crowd. He could not stop two men from joining him and hastening to start a conversation with him.

They told him they were from Puteaux and Bougival respectively. Informed that the people were marching on Versailles, they had decided to join in. One was a wigmaker and the other a mason. Nicolas was forced to walk along with them, and as he did so he tried to understand what was driving them. They appeared innocent enough, and genuinely upset at the rise in the price of bread. This foodstuff was, as they kept reminding him, their one means of subsistence.

'The thing is,' said the mason, a strapping fellow of about thirty, 'when you don't have anything any more, only bread saves you. Or else you die, or beg. It mustn't go higher than two sous a pound, and even that's too much!'

'And don't forget,' said the wigmaker, a short, sickly-looking young man with a pointed nose, 'for that price all you get is a brown loaf full of bran. That's pure discrimination. The rich, the aristos, get to eat white bread! But we who work have to be content with the less nutritious kind. Is that fair, eh? What do you say, friend?'

Nicolas remembered how, as a child, he had sunk his little hand into a loaf of black bread. He had loved the acidity of the dough. He did not think that pointing this out would be appropriate in the present situation, so he nodded without replying.

'You have to admit,' said the wigmaker, 'that the Parisian doesn't eat his fill. The roof tiler up there on the tops of houses, the errand boy, those who carry huge loads, they're all at the mercy of the monopolists and crushed like gnats as soon as they try to raise their voices. This lousy bread that doesn't even provide us with the means of subsistence, we earn by the sweat of our brow. So if they take even that out of our mouths ... The young King has to know this. What about you, friend, what are you doing here?'

'I'm a printer's assistant,' said Nicolas, modestly lowering his eyes. 'Out of work, for the moment.'

The man stared at him. Suddenly, a nasty glint came into his eyes, and he grabbed Nicolas's hands and looked at them carefully. After a long examination, he seemed satisfied. Nicolas had thought for a moment that he had been discovered and that they would see him for what he was: a policeman. But luckily, the charcoal had made his nails so black that, in the dim light of early morning, it was easy to make a mistake and confuse the blackness with the indelible stains of printer's ink.

'You're like us. No work and no bread.'

The crowd, which had grown like a river swollen with streams and tributaries, was now moving towards the market in Versailles. Breaking free would have been a risky proposition: it was better to wait and see how the situation developed in order to be able to report on it later at the palace. His companions told him that emissaries had gone around giving the meeting point. So far the march had been, if not orderly, at least calm and peaceful. Everything changed when they reached the royal town and a group of agitators led a few of the more hot-headed to a bakery that had the misfortune to be situated there. In no time at all, it was completely ransacked. When the human tide reached the market, its full fury was unleashed. Nicolas saw his two tranquil companions suddenly come to life and lend their hands to unchecked plunder. Frenzied women tore open sacks of flour from the stalls and put handfuls of it in the hollow of their aprons then turned, with fierce, provocative expressions on their faces, ready to fight tooth and nail to protect the little they had. Nicolas realised that some were actually men in disguise. Peasants could be heard proclaiming with conviction that in acting in this way, they were fulfilling the wishes of the King, a new Henri IV, and that, anyway, their quarrel was with the monopolists who were starving the people. Others, respectably dressed and shod, brandished mouldy bread which, they screamed, was intended to poison the people. Once the word 'poison' had been uttered, it spread, unleashing boos, cries and insults.

False rumours passed from one person to the next, fuelling further waves of rage. A half-naked harpy displayed the contents of her apron, filled with spoilt flour, and proclaimed, wild-eyed, that she wanted to take it to the Queen. The riot looked set to continue when troops appeared, led by the Prince de Beauvau, the captain of the guard. Swiss Guards, French Guards and cavalry advanced on the crowd. There was a first eddy of panic, with people pushing and shoving in different directions. Then some of the demonstrators, bolder than the others, and encouraged by the insults heaped on the prince, started to throw handfuls of flour at him. His horse reared amid a white cloud. Leading these hotheads, Nicolas was surprised to see Monsieur Carré, director of the kitchens to the Comte d'Artois, the King's brother, who was goading the mob in word and gesture. Infuriated beyond measure, one of the French Guards set about him and ran him through with his bayonet. The man collapsed, gushing blood. Beauvau at last managed to rise above the mounting clamour and asked the people what they wanted. The answer was unanimous.

'All right!' he cried. 'Bread at two *sols* a pound.'

This announcement was well received. The rioting stopped and everyone set off for the bakeries to get bread at the agreed rate.

As if by magic, order was restored. Nicolas took advantage of this lull to slip away, anxious to get to the palace as soon as possible. As he did so, he passed more groups of men whom he judged to be onlookers rather than rioters. When he got to the Place d'Armes, he was unable to pass through the gates, which had been hurriedly closed. An official informed him that the King had set off for the hunt but, seeing a highly threatening crowd advancing along the Saint-Germain road, had had his coachman do an about-turn and ordered the gates to be shut. Nicolas had to make a large detour and enter the palace through a door known only to himself, at the corner of Rue de l'Orangerie and Rue de la Surintendance. From there, he walked to the ministers' wing, managed with some difficulty to be admitted by the ushers, and went straight up to the roof, in order to obtain a panoramic view of the situation from the terraces.

From up here, he could see below him the junction of the three great avenues that converged on the palace, Avenue de Saint-Cloud on the left, Avenue de Paris in the middle and Avenue de Sceaux on the right. No particular agitation was noticeable in the last two. Only the Avenue de Saint-Cloud was still filled with people who, from a distance, looked like columns of caterpillars unwinding and slowly changing shape. There were still a few onlookers near the Réservoirs, in Rue de l'Abreuvoir, to the right of the main gate. There was nothing to suggest that the palace itself was under threat. Nicolas went back down to 'the Louvre'.[3] From there, he walked to the marble staircase that would take him to the guardroom and the King's antechamber. On the way, he came across Monsieur Thierry, First Groom of the King's Bedchamber, who burst out laughing at the sight of his face and clothes. Throwing caution to the winds, Nicolas told him that he had to speak to the King immediately. Thierry, who knew and liked him, refrained from asking too many questions and led him through the Bull's Eye salon into the Council chamber. The King was in shirt and breeches, having taken off his hunting coat, and was walking up and down, his head bowed, between this room and the neighbouring bedchamber, where his grandfather had died a year earlier. In the absence of his ministers, most of whom, including Maurepas and Turgot, were in Paris, he was holding a kind of permanent council. There was much bustle around him, but he himself was calm. He stopped pacing and watched as Nicolas approached. It was clear that he did not recognise him, until Thierry whispered in his ear.

'Ranreuil,' he said with a smile, 'we didn't recognise you. Your outfit!'

'Sire, I beg Your Majesty to forgive me for appearing in his presence in this disguise. It was necessary to gain an idea of the degrees of unrest among the people. I've just come from the market and—'

'Ah, at last someone who can inform me. I don't know where my ministers are. Turgot and Maurepas are in Paris, but the others ...' He did not finish the sentence, but instead stared myopically at Nicolas.

'Sire, the market has been turned upside down and a few bakeries looted. The captain of the guard, the Prince de Beauvau, was insulted and covered with flour. It was only when he announced to the crowd that the price of bread was now two *sols* a pound that calm was restored.'

The young King's face turned red. 'What?' he said. 'The prince took that upon himself?'

'Yes, sire.'

At that moment, an officer entered and handed the monarch a message. He put on his spectacles and read it.

'Ranreuil is right. Beauvau informs me that he did indeed take this ridiculous step. He claims there was no middle course between letting them have bread at the price they demanded or forcing them to buy it at the current price at the point of a bayonet. All this is contrary to my orders: all he had to do was restore the peace while totally forbidding my soldiers from using their weapons.'

Something, Nicolas thought, which was much easier said than done.

'I wrote to Turgot this morning that he could count on my standing firm. Now, thanks to this blunder, everyone will think himself justified by a decision that will be attributed to me. Ranreuil, do you have a good hand?'

'I believe so, sire.'

'Then I will dictate a letter, and you can take it to Monsieur de Turgot yourself.'

He indicated the council table.

'Everything is quiet here. The rioters had begun to be quite heated. The troops brought them under control. Monsieur de Beauvau questioned them: most said that they had no bread, that they had come to get bread and showed some poor-quality barley bread, which they said they had bought for two sols and which was the only bread anyone was willing to give them. I am not going out today, not out of fear, but to keep everything calm. The market is over, but for the first time the greatest precautions must be taken to make sure they do not return to lay down the law; tell me what they might be, as all this is very embarrassing.' [4]

The King stopped and looked pensively at Nicolas. He bent his tall frame, took the letter, read it and signed it. Leaning on both fists, he moved his face closer to the commissioner's and murmured, with tears in his eyes, 'We have our good conscience on our side, and that makes us strong. Oh, if only I had the charm and bearing of my brother Provence, I'd speak to the people, and everything would be perfect! But I stammer and that would spoil everything.'

Nicolas had a lump in his throat. He suddenly realised that, for the King, he was an elder, one of the men who had been close to his grandfather when he himself was still a child. He brought his emotions under control, shaking his head like a horse. He would have liked to make a gesture to demonstrate the depth of his devotion, but could not make up his mind to do so. This inner struggle did not escape the King, who smiled. There was a silent exchange between them that Nicolas would never forget. The King pulled himself together and asked him in a low voice to report to him, and nobody else, anything he was able to find out about the current disturbances.

Nicolas quickly left the palace and walked back to the d'Arranet mansion, where he found Tribord nervously waiting for him. His scarred old face betrayed his anxiety.

'Mademoiselle came back ...'

Good news at last, thought Nicolas, although disturbed somewhat by the grim expression with which the announcement had been made.

'... and immediately left again.'

'What do you mean?'

Tribord was shifting from one foot to the other. 'What can I tell you? That's the way it was! When I told her you were here, she immediately gave orders to turn back. Off she went, and don't spare the horses!' Seeing the expression on Nicolas's face, he ventured an explanation.

'Don't distress yourself. It seems to me that when women run away it's because they're only too eager to stay.'

Nicolas shook his hand and went upstairs to change, then retrieved his mount and set off at a gallop back to Paris. He tried during this journey to close his mind to any emotional impulse, convinced that it was not love that should be depicted as blind, but rather pride. He concentrated on the mission he had been given by the King. The letter to Turgot was a sign of his benevolence and good faith. But it also implied a kind of submissiveness on the part of the monarch towards the comptroller general, a slightly unsettling innocence – even though, for now, he was demonstrating great composure, left as he was to face this trial alone in a deserted Versailles. That was something to be thankful for, coming as it did from a shy, awkward adolescent who needed to be brought out of his shell. One thought sustained him. Each man had his own trials to confront: kings, lovers and fathers were all puppets of a providence that drove their passions and interests. Everything seemed calm as he drew near to Paris, although he had learnt not to trust these deceptive lulls. It was certain that the events in Versailles would stimulate further unrest as soon as the news of them had spread, transformed and distorted as they would be by rumour and additions motivated by self-interest. There was never any lack of people ready to exploit a dangerous situation for their own ends.

It was early afternoon by the time he reached the comptroller general's office in Rue Neuve-des-Petits-Champs. Immediately admitted to the study of the minister, whom he had met several times at Court, he found him writing, his bandaged right leg resting on a tapestried cushion. Turgot raised his head and scowled at the newcomer. Nicolas noted his height and corpulence, the fine head with its abundant curly hair, the light-blue eyes, the left one smaller than the right. It was not an unpleasant countenance, but it conveyed a sense of effort that was more moral than physical. Nicolas presented himself and handed over the letter from the King. The comptroller general's naturally white complexion betrayed his feelings as he read, turning red when he proceeded to a second, more attentive reading. When he looked up again, his gaze was both soft and remote, and Nicolas wondered if, like the King, he was short-sighted.

'Monsieur, on whose account were you at Versailles? You're Sartine's man, aren't you?' The tone was both inquisitorial and offensive.

'Monseigneur, I was at Versailles to deliver something from the Empress of Austria to our Queen and to participate in the King's hunt. As luck would have it, I was caught up in the riot and when I finally reached the palace this morning I was able to give His Majesty an account of the events. As for the rest, I am the King's man just as I was the late King's man.'

This answer did not mollify Turgot, who continued to question him in an arrogant tone before dismissing him unceremoniously.

Rue Neuve-Saint-Augustin being very close, he decided to inform

Monsieur Lenoir of the turn of events. He found him overwhelmed with dark presentiments. As soon as he saw Nicolas, he launched into recriminations. He was angry at the false rumours circulating, of which the worst was that the police had advised that the people be supplied with all the bread they wanted at the price they wanted, even if that meant compensating the bakers subsequently. That, as the commissioner pointed out, was an inevitable consequence of the King's supposed promise that bread would be sold at two *sols* a pound. The rumour from Versailles had spread like wildfire. Nicolas informed his chief about his audiences with the King and Turgot and also about the investigation into the events in Rue Montmartre, which might have unfortunate consequences in the current situation.

'I fear some difficult days ahead,' said Lenoir. 'We're being dragged along with no thought for what may happen next. Without restraint, reforms become abuses and those who apply them too quickly are tactless and destructive. There is no more absurd whim than to set oneself up as a reformer! Once the hand is committed, the whole body is drawn in. France is an old machine set in motion a long time ago, still working more or less, but likely to break at the first shock! Just in case, I'm going to have the grain market protected tomorrow. We must avoid a repetition in Paris of the unrest in Versailles. I've asked for dragoons and musketeers to reinforce the watch and the French Guards, but I shall give orders that under no circumstances are they to open fire, even if that means being insulted and manhandled by the rabble. How did you find the King?'

'Both nervous and calm, and leaving everything up to the comptroller general.'

'There's the rub! Monsieur de Sartine thinks we should rouse the King to take a greater interest in affairs of State. Alas, the one area where there's no problem stimulating him is his taste for gossip, scandal and slander. He takes too much pleasure in reading the intercepted correspondence that Monsieur d'Oigny brings him. Obviously, in such cases, nothing is easier than to fabricate or carefully select evidence. And there are so many people involved in intrigue. The postal service does not offer safety or secrecy for families or friends. It is sad, my dear Nicolas, to find the same thing in this monarch as was noted in the late King: a bad opinion of everyone and a general mistrust which, in his case, or so he believes, justifies his standing aloof.'

By the time Nicolas left Monsieur Lenoir, he was extremely worried by his lack of resolution and the many doubts assailing him. Coming from someone in his position, such indecision could lead to the most unfortunate changes in direction when action had to be taken. Perhaps Lenoir had got to the point where he almost unconsciously hoped for more unrest, in order to expose the stupidity of Turgot's draconian initiatives. In Sartine, too, he had sensed an attitude that was even more ambiguous than ever. The difference was that Sartine embellished it with an amused cynicism which Lenoir did not possess. Entrenched in his own friendships and ambitions, Sartine doubtless believed that you needed to be shrewd to appear an honest man, but never so stupid as to actually be one. He had often reproached Nicolas for his innocence. May God help him to keep it! Fifteen years in the police force, working on special investigations, did not allow him any illusions about the way of the world, or the honesty of those in power. Not that this weakened his devotion to his former chief. It was just a matter of not being taken in by him. As for Monsieur Lenoir, he seemed like an honest man caught in a tempest he could not control but reluctant to take extreme measures.

Nicolas returned his mount to the stables at police headquarters and got back to the Grand Châtelet by cab. There he found Bourdeau, Semacgus, and Sanson, the public executioner, debating whether they should proceed with the autopsy on Master Mourut in his absence. His arrival settled the matter. He questioned them about the crowd of people who had gathered at the foot of the grand staircase and were now heading towards the skylights that made it possible to look down at the corpses on display in the Basse-Geôle.

'The object of their curiosity,' said Semacgus, 'is the body of a beautiful young girl whose body was fished out of the Seine.'

'That's hardly an unusual sight,' said Nicolas. 'The bodies of the drowned are brought here every day.'

'It isn't so much the body that's attracting the people, as the supposed miracle of its discovery. The family had placed on the river a wooden begging bowl with a lighted candle and bread consecrated to St Nicolas of Tolentino at the monastery of the Grands Augustins. There is an old belief that the begging bowl will stop where the body is to be found, in this case level with the Jardin de l'Infante at the Louvre.'

'I thought such superstitions were long forgotten,' grunted Bourdeau. 'There's nothing more dangerous. In 1718, a poor old woman looking for the body of her son nearly burnt down the whole city. The candle set light to a boat carrying flour, which continued downstream, spreading terror and setting the houses on the Petit-Pont on fire. A whole district was destroyed.'

By now, they had reached the cellar where they were accustomed to plying what Sartine called 'their macabre trade'. Nicolas enquired after Madame Sanson and the children, much to the delight of the executioner, who was always overjoyed at any personal attention from the commissioner. Dr Semacgus and Sanson were getting ready, and laying out their instruments. For once, Bourdeau did not light his pipe, but ostentatiously took out the Viennese snuffbox given him by Nicolas. He offered Nicolas a pinch, then took one himself. The silence was immediately broken by a long, sonorous series of sneezes. As the two practitioners began examining the corpse, Nicolas took out his little black notebook.

'My dear colleague and I are in agreement,' said Sanson after a while, as ceremonious as ever. 'A superficial examination reveals no lesions and no suspicious marks.'

Semacgus nodded. 'Nevertheless,' he said, 'allow me to temper my approval of your statement. There does appear to be a curious necrotised wound on the palm of the right hand.'

Sanson bent over and examined the body again.

'A scratch left untended, which has become a little swollen ... I would put it down to the change of temperature ...'

'You are no doubt right. Let us at least note the fact.'

The mouth was carefully inspected with the help of a metal instrument.

'Clearly he was not choked by the risen dough,' remarked Semacgus. 'Although ...'

'Although?' asked Nicolas.

'I see what the doctor is saying,' said Sanson. 'The man did not choke to death, although everything suggests that he did.'

Nicolas found this observation somewhat strange.

They now proceeded to open the body. Although Nicolas had often attended similar operations, they always set his nerves on edge. It was not so much that he could not stand the horror of it all, as that the scratching of the instruments on and in the flesh, the cracking of the bones and the noises emitted by the manhandled corpse, as if in protest against this barbaric treatment, filled him with an overwhelming feeling of despondency. He knew, though, that without this attempt, however derisory, to penetrate the secrets of the body, many crimes would remain unpunished. He closed his eyes, and ran through, in his mind, a tune he had learnt from an old teacher at the collegiate church in Guérande. It was a motet played on the organ and accompanied by the Breton instrument the bombard. Words exchanged in a low voice by Semacgus and Sanson drew him out of his daydream. Having restored a semblance of normality to the body and washed their hands and arms in a tub which one of the executioner's assistants had brought in, they turned to the two policemen. Contrary to their well-established procedure, neither said a word.

'Gentlemen,' said Nicolas, 'we await your report.'

Sanson sighed, and raised his hands in a gesture of powerlessness. 'To tell the truth, it seems an idle exercise to try and determine the cause of death and consequently to confirm or invalidate the theory that we are dealing with a murder. I'm sorry to say it would be almost impossible even to attempt to do so.'

Semacgus remained silent.

'I understand,' replied Nicolas. 'However, knowing how careful you always are with words, I note that you used the expression "almost impossible". There's a tiny but real gulf between "impossible" and "almost impossible". The law usually requires something more tangible. I must therefore ask you: what does that "almost" mean?'

Sanson turned to Semacgus, who was still unruffled. 'The fact is,' he resumed, hesitantly, 'we discovered some internal disorders indicating that an attack of something stopped the course of this man's life.'

'Something like death?' sighed Bourdeau, ironically.

'A phenomenon due to an unknown cause, or rather, too many unknown causes. Everything suggests that the observed phenomena are diverse, confusing, contradictory and yet crucial to the *processus mortis*. The heart and vessels have been damaged and the lungs clearly gave out, which may have led to asphyxia or the heart stopping, or both!'

'But can you confirm that the dough is in no way responsible?'

'The dough had nothing to do with it,' said Semacgus, breaking his silence. 'He fell into it, or was pushed into it, but it didn't kill him. I confirm our friend's analysis. There is a mystery here.'

Sanson, anxious to get back to his family, left them immediately, offering an invitation to dinner. Semacgus stood where he was, deep in thought, and motioned them to remain. After a moment, he went to the stairs and listened to make sure that Sanson had indeed gone. All this greatly surprised the two policemen.

'Don't look so astonished. Sanson's friendship means a great deal to me. That's why I wanted to avoid hurting a man of such delicate sensitivity. He has all the qualities of an empiricist, but his medical knowledge is limited. I have the advantage over him of twenty years sailing the seven seas. Now that he's gone, I can express my opinion openly.'

Semacgus's long face radiated a kind of jubilation that continued to surprise them.

'The wound we noted on the hand,' he went on, in an authoritative tone, 'has no particular significance for me, except in so far as it reminds me of something I observed during another autopsy, although I do not recall the exact circumstances at the moment.'

'But what's the connection with Monsieur Mourut? Your words are confusing!'

'I don't know. The fact remains that our man displays all the symptoms of a very terrible death by poisoning. Remember my remarks on the strange wound to the hand. I didn't want to contradict Sanson in front of you, but that necrotised wound continues to haunt me.'

'What could it be?'

'I am still groping in the dark.'

'The wound is indeed intriguing,' said Bourdeau. 'Is it possible that the poison could have been introduced into Monsieur Mourut's organism through it?'

'Extraordinary as it may seem, it's quite possible. At the time of the Borgias, in Florence, there were gloves containing hidden blades. They allowed you to make a cut and then instil poison through it. Everything points to the likelihood that we are dealing with something similar here.'

'I shudder to think of it,' said the inspector.

'How might the poison be identified?' asked Nicolas. 'Are you at least sure that it was poison and nothing else?'

'I'd bet my right hand on it. The curious appearance of the blood, combined with other signs of internal corruption, removed my last doubts.'

'But how can it be proven?'

'We have to find the murderer and discover his method.'

'That would be like putting the cart before the horse,' concluded Bourdeau, 'or catching the serpent by its tail! It won't be easy to convince Monsieur Testard du Lys. Our Criminal Lieutenant would scoff at the idea of a gnat's bite, let alone the poison of the Borgias!'

Semacgus gave the inspector a curious look, almost said something, but then had second thoughts.

'Let's keep this mysterious idea to ourselves,' said Nicolas. 'The best thing would be, I think, to take poisoning with an unknown substance as a point of departure. Monsieur Testard du Lys won't ask for more than that. As for our friend Sanson, I'll accept his dinner invitation soon. I can mention in passing that other discoveries have led us to lean towards the theory of a murder.'

They agreed with Nicolas, although Semacgus was still lost in thought. As they left the Basse-Geôle, Nicolas questioned Bourdeau on what he had found out.

'It seems to be the general opinion that the Mouruts were not a happy couple. The lady is not liked: the customers complain of her arrogance. The husband is said to have been harsh to the poor, shrewd at increasing their debts and ferocious when it came to recovering the interest. He's also said to have been a cuckold, although there is nothing as yet to confirm that. The wife has supposedly been lifting her petticoats for the apprentice, who in turn throws his money away in brothels.'

'And our two baker's boys?'

'Opinions on them are mixed. Some pity them, others vilify them. There's much gossip about their morals and the nature of their friendship. The older one is considered a little too affectionate towards the younger. It wouldn't take much, a word out of place to the authorities, and they'd end up at the stake.'

'There's a world of difference,' said Semacgus, waxing indignant, 'between the unnatural creatures who haunt the terraces of the Tuileries and are hounded by Monsieur Lenoir, and two poor boys crushed by hard work and life in the city who come together for mutual support. It's true they risk the stake. An apprentice was sentenced to it in the 1720s.'

'For practices that are tolerated so openly at Court, where catamites are everywhere to be seen!' said Bourdeau. 'Unfortunately, what is said about these baker's boys rather throws suspicion on them in this case. Fear makes people do bad things. What if they were being threatened by their master with being thrown out on the street?'

'In fact it was the other apprentice who looked down his nose at them. Where the devil is he? Has he returned?'

'There's still no sign of him. All our spies are on the lookout. As for the paper found on Mourut, Rabouine assures us that "La G." refers to La Gourdan, known as La Comtesse, the well-known brothel-keeper, whose new premises are in Rue des Deux-Ponts-Saint-Sauveur.'

'In the old days,' said Semacgus in a ribald tone, 'a distinguished clientele used to be well catered for in her old establishment in Rue Sainte-Anne. There was nothing to find fault with, although of course Venus took her revenge from time to time, if you know what I mean!'

'Don't stir up painful memories,' said Nicolas ironically.

'Not at all, Monsieur. I have all I need at home, a diet without pepper, but quite spicy enough for my taste.'

'I think, Nicolas,' said Bourdeau, 'that before confronting La Comtesse, a preliminary visit to our old Paulet would be useful. She knows that world well, and has its secrets at her fingertips.'

'I'm not very happy at the idea. Why don't you go?'

Nicolas did not have a pleasant memory of their last encounter, when she had blamed him for La Satin's departure for London, making the remorse he had been feeling even worse.

'I'm sure,' insisted Bourdeau, inscrutably, 'that she'll talk more openly to you, having known you for so long. She won't say a word to me.'

'All right, I'll go. Reluctantly. With age, our old friend has become more prickly than ever. I hope she'll at least offer me ratafia! That's always of high quality in her house. And what of Madame Mourut?'

'Still confined to her room.'

'We need to convince her that the confinement will last until she tells the truth. As for the apprentice, issue his description. I want him found at all costs. Gentlemen, it's getting late …'

Bourdeau and Semacgus grinned, both at the same time, much to Nicolas's astonishment.

'We must confess, dear Nicolas,' said Semacgus, 'that we have mounted a plot.'

'Yes, we were planning to help you forget your troubles for a while.'

'Monsieur de La Borde, whose taste for anything relating to the arts you know, has offered us tickets—'

'I don't trust our friend's taste. Where are you taking me? To La Gourdan's?'

'Pierre,' said Semacgus, 'don't you find that his character has soured with time? He sees only the bad in people. Is it right to cast doubt on the intentions of friends like us? What an insult! Come, my dear fellow, let's leave him to his bad mood.'

Laughing quietly to himself, he took Bourdeau by the arm.

'Come now, gentlemen, tell me what you have to say. Don't take my word amiss. Knowing you so well, I may occasionally tease you a little.'

'Thank God for that,' said Bourdeau. 'Here I was being called a libertine. Me, a family man and a model husband!'

'What of me?' said Semacgus. 'A hermit at Vaugirard, a lay brother entirely devoted to botany and the relief of our fellow men, I feel highly offended and almost ready never to say another word to this acerbic and mocking magistrate.'

'Enough! I surrender to your friendship.'

'At last, a reasonable statement. Very well, then. Tonight we're invited to the Opéra for the first performance there of *Céphale et Procris* by Monsieur Grétry, to a libretto by Monsieur Marmontel. A piece that was originally performed at Versailles for the wedding of the Comte d'Artois and Maria Theresa of Savoy.'

'Now Guillaume has turned into Mercury!' said Nicolas.

'There he goes again! Come, Céphale, Procris, Monsieur de La Borde, the Court and the city all await us.'

It struck Nicolas that the house was on fire, and yet the Court and the city were still running to the Opéra. To what purpose? He spruced himself up a little in the duty office, where he kept a spare coat, and then the three men caught a cab to take them along Rue Saint-Honoré. He did not ask Bourdeau if there was any news about Louis: if there had been, it would have been the first thing he would have said on his return from Versailles. There was, however, another delicate question that could not be avoided.

'Pierre, we are going to benefit from some valuable help.'

His tone was unconvincing, but he had been unable to find a more skilful way of broaching the subject.

'What help are you talking about?'

'From the Chevalier de Lastire. Sartine wants him to join us for this case and also as regards the current unrest.'

The reaction was immediate. 'What has Sartine to do with this? Are we helping him to hold the capstan and empty the bilges on his ships?'

'The chevalier's the liveliest companion in the world,' said Semacgus, a statement that could not have come at a worse time. 'Not to mention the fact that he saved Nicolas for us. Without him we'd all be in mourning now.'

'When it comes to that,' said Nicolas, 'Pierre has quite a head start on the chevalier.'

Despite these last words, intended to moderate the inspector's possessiveness, the harm was done and Bourdeau was clearly upset, although he said nothing more. To insist would only make matters worse. The rest of the brief journey was punctuated by various jovial remarks by Semacgus, who could not understand his companions' silence. As usual, they had to force their way through a great throng outside the Opéra. Nothing ever changed, neither the bustle of footmen opening carriage doors, nor the brandished torches dripping wax. They quickly climbed the steps, in a hurry to get in out of the chaos. A surprise awaited Nicolas in a corner of the foyer: Monsieur de Noblecourt, leaning on Monsieur de La Borde's arm and smiling at them. He was wearing a magnificent Regency wig that Sartine himself would have envied, a russet coat with silver trimmings and a cravat of blonde lace from Valenciennes. There ensued a tumult of congratulations.

'Here we have Jupiter supported by Mercury!' cried Semacgus.

'Do I have wings on my shoes?' said La Borde.

'Have I ever released a thunderbolt?' said Noblecourt in the tone of a noble father in a tragedy.

A man in a black coat came up to La Borde and embraced him. 'What an honour, my dear colleague, to know that you are in the audience this evening! I can rest assured that at least one master will hear my work and understand it.'

'Don't trust him, Grétry,' said Noblecourt. 'He's a follower of Gluck!'

The composer's smile changed to a grimace. He was about to reply when a kind of Fury in a robe appeared, hands on hips, and began haranguing him.

'Ah, there you are, you heartless monster, you—'

'What's the meaning of this, Mademoiselle? Go back to your box immediately.'

'Certainly not! You make me laugh with your question. You should know, Monsieur, that a rebellion is brewing in your orchestra!'

'What, Mademoiselle? Rebellion in the orchestra of the Royal Academy of Music? What's the meaning of this? We are all in the King's service and must serve him with zeal.'

'Monsieur, I should like to serve him too, but your orchestra constantly interrupts me and stops me singing.'

'And yet we keep time.'

'Time? What kind of beast is that? You should follow me, Monsieur, and realise that your music should be the humble servant of the performer in the recitatives.'

'When you perform a recitative, I follow you, Mademoiselle, but when you sing an aria in strict time, it's up to you to follow me.' He stamped his foot. 'Now be quiet and go!'

He took a vast scarf from his pocket and mopped his face with it, while the woman withdrew, her face red with passion, in a great rustling of fabric.

'The silly girl wears me out!'

They settled in La Borde's box beside the Queen's. Familiar with the customs of the place, Nicolas looked down at the audience. Maurepas was there, accompanied by his wife, whose guttural voice could be heard throughout the auditorium. The Prince de Conti sat enthroned in his brilliantly lit box. La Borde had seen where his friend was looking.

'The prince is in his element, posing as the arbiter of taste. That's quite risky for the performers, because his opinion is crucial. A word from him can mean the difference between success and failure, and there is no appeal. The work's fate is then sealed at his Monday dinners at the Temple.'

'Nothing too daring tonight, though. Grétry and Marmontel are a perfectly reliable team.'

'Don't believe it. This opera will revive the controversy. Grétry is in the tradition of Rameau, a French overture, recitatives, ballets and entractes.' With a smile, La Borde turned to Noblecourt, who was looking at the auditorium through his opera glasses. 'It's sure to please our friend who clings to old-style opera as he clings to old-style cooking!'

'I shan't respond to your teasing ... If the piece fails, Marmontel will abandon his partner. Remember what he was telling us, before Nicolas arrived, about his first encounter with the composer: "I was asked to hold out my hand to a desperate young man who was about to drown himself if I didn't save him!" He won't hold out his hand twice.'

The performance proceeded, to a reception that was neither one of great enthusiasm nor one of outright rejection. The subject was entirely conventional: Céphale, husband of Procris, expresses his passion to Aurore, who convinces him to chase away his wife. Diane reconciles the spouses, but Procris is accidentally killed by her husband while out hunting. La Borde, as an attentive host, had made sure that everything was as it should be: slices of cold chicken in jelly were brought in, as well as champagne, macaroons and sugared almonds. Semacgus had to intervene to temper Noblecourt's ardour and stop him helping himself greedily to all these sweet things.

The opera ended to polite applause from the audience. On the way out, tongues were already wagging. Most of the connoisseurs declared themselves dissatisfied, asserting that the worst of the composer's comic operas at the Comédie Italienne was better than this attempt at the lyric. The most indulgent praised the ballets, the most pleasing part of the work for their expressiveness and picturesque qualities. Grétry was going from group to group, looking distraught and saying that Gluck had stifled him. Nicolas noticed a tall, beautiful woman holding forth. La Borde nudged him with his elbow.

'That's Sophie Arnould, who sang in *Iphigénie en Aulide*. She's fallen out with Gluck and is on the verge of being replaced by Rosalie

Levasseur, who's ugly but a schemer, as well as the mistress of the Austrian ambassador, Mercy-Argenteau, who's supporting her in her career.'

The singer, who held her head with pride, greeted the Prince de Conti and suddenly raised her voice to pronounce the last word on that evening's entertainment.

'This music by a Belgian is much more French than the words of this opera!'

VII

FEVER

Count, you are called for,
You really must come and see,
The people are at the gates.
That's nothing to do with me,
The Opéra awaits.

ANONYMOUS, 3 May 1774

Wednesday 3 May 1775

Unusually, Monsieur de Noblecourt was up before Nicolas, and was already sipping his morning sage warily. Cyrus and Mouchette sat up and lifted their noses expectantly: the commissioner's arrival usually meant brioches and a few other choice morsels. But only the chocolatière appeared, brought in by Catherine. Mouchette miaowed with disappointment, arched her back and fell asleep, while Cyrus sighed and lowered his hoary muzzle onto his old paws.

'What a bother!' said Monsieur de Noblecourt. 'We'll have to find another baker for the moment, and perhaps even another tenant.'

He did not seem at all affected by his night at the Opéra and hastened to demand a detailed account of the journey to Versailles. Nicolas was only too happy to oblige.

'Our masters seem quite relaxed about all this, from what you're saying. Believe me, Paris won't escape the storm. Everything begins and ends here.' He thought for a moment. 'And what of our case? I say "our case", since crime has had the audacity to pursue me into my retreat and disturb my daily routine.'

'So you also think this was a murder?'

'Oh, appearances are only appearances, which means they are nothing, or rather that they reveal what someone wants us to believe or what we expect ourselves. They are contradictory and yet, thanks to their very obscurity, help to enlighten us. We must swim against the tide. You see, the desire to find the guilty party drives us to subject the accused to the torture of isolation. We mortify them, we weaken them, and we end up with the opposite of what we hoped for ...'

Nicolas was accustomed to these pompous pronouncements, having gradually discovered, to his surprise, that they often concealed a grain of truth.

'I am all the more convinced that, as always, you need to examine the past. But whose past? That is the question. Nothing more, nothing less. We must lift the heavy veil ...'

He suddenly jumped to another subject entirely.

'As for Louis, don't worry, I am certain the conclusion is near. You must never despair. From one minute to the next, we go from misfortune to joy! Have you seen Aimée?'

Noblecourt could read Nicolas like a book.

'To be honest, my long absence has vexed her. For now, she's avoiding me.'

'Oh, have no fear, she'll come back. We complain about women who bewitch us with their charms, enslave us with their favours and ruin us with their whims. Their spells are well known and it is the lover himself who provides them with the weapons to subjugate him. Don't insist – she may have taken offence, but she'll return soon enough! It's a passing sorrow whose insignificance is its only strength.'

With this somewhat cynical philosophy ringing in his ears, Nicolas left Rue Montmartre. He was hoping to catch La Paulet recently risen from her bed, at a time of day when the Dauphin Couronné, liberated from the night's immoral deeds, was waking to be tidied and cleaned, just like an honest house. He had no news of the Chevalier de Lastire, who was doubtless detained by other matters. He would show himself soon enough. His absence was not unwelcome: at least Bourdeau, whose sensitivity worried Nicolas, could not take umbrage. It was starting to rain, and he jumped into a passing cab, sank into the seat, and withdrew into himself.

The city was deceptively calm. Was unrest expected? Accustomed as he was to noticing the slightest details of a scene, he immediately spotted, much to his surprise, the fact that the brothel in Rue du Faubourg-Saint-Honoré was surrounded by a cordon of police spies. He recognised them without much difficulty, even though they pretended to ignore him. What was the reason for this surveillance? Who had given the orders? He would have to look into it, mention it to Bourdeau.

Wrapped in multicoloured cotton, the black girl, whom he had known since she was very young, greeted him warmly. Her saucy, mischievous air led him to assume that the mistress of the house had launched her on a career of prostitution. Madame, she told him, was at her ablutions. She led him to the back part of the house. La Paulet, hearing someone enter her room, did not turn away from the delicate labour that kept her in front of her swing mirror and began inveighing against her supposed visitor.

'Just who I need to see, La Présidente! Oh, how I miss La Satin! With you, everything is going to rack and ruin. I haven't entrusted this house to you only to hear – and not from you – that the two new girls, Adèle and La Mitonnette, started simpering and coming over all prudish last night, not only refusing to go along with the customers' wishes, but actually rebuking them. And these were customers who'd demanded our best specimens. If you, La Présidente, aren't capable of choosing the right girls, well! The first rule is that they meekly accept whatever strange tastes a man might have. If a customer wants to do something with them that they can't tolerate, they're entitled to leave him as long as they immediately give their reasons either to me or you. If their complaint isn't considered admissible, they forfeit three days' pay and have to service only old men for two weeks. What do you have to say to that, eh?'

'My dear Paulet, I'd find it hard to say anything!'

Supporting herself on her white marble dressing table, she turned round with some difficulty, revealing a chubby face covered in fresh ceruse, to which the crimson had not yet given a touch of life.

'Ah, there's the other scoundrel! Show yourself, then, I've been wanting to talk to you for a long time. Those damned informers of yours denounced me again. That bearer of stinking buckets who's been patrolling Rue Saint-Honoré for days ...'

Her huge body was quivering with anger.

'You get a poor girl pregnant, that's a mere trifle to you. You throw her out on the streets with your seed inside her—'

'But—'

'No buts, you're going to hear what I have to say. The child is born and grows up. Remember him now, do you? When by chance you find him again, you chase out his mother and send her into exile, and then imprison the child in a monastery! What do you think he finds there? Insults, kicks, thrashings. He decides to run away and finds himself penniless on the road to Paris, forced to beg in order to survive. He's picked up, warmed and fed while his good-for-nothing of a father spends his time nonchalantly riding back and forth. What do you say to that? I, whom he calls his aunt, I tell it as I see it. I await the few bad reasons you're going to give me.'

Whatever the passion and the insulting nature of La Paulet's words, Nicolas felt a wave of happiness overwhelm him. Louis was here, alive, safe and free. He had to hold back his sobs.

'You're putting words in my mouth, Madame, but I'm prepared to forget that out of consideration for the woman who took my son in. The rest is more complicated than anything your anger could conceive. With that, go and fetch Louis and leave us alone. I will see you afterwards.'

Submissively, she rose with difficulty and went out dragging her feet and muttering indistinctly. It struck Nicolas that she seemed as ill informed as he about the circumstances of Louis's departure from his school. A moment later, Louis entered, with a stubborn look on his face and his eyes lowered. He seemed frozen in an attitude of defensive hostility. This was a long way from the hoped-for joy of their reunion.

'I'm pleased to see you, Louis. Now I'm waiting to hear what you have to say.'

He had expressed himself as affectionately as possible, but his words were met with silence. He would therefore take things in hand.

'You say nothing. In that case, I'll tell you what I really think. Whatever wrongs you believe I have done you, I am not to blame. Only your mother's discretion and honour are the cause. She left it all too late to reveal your existence to me. In these circumstances, I ask for respect and total honesty from you. Open your heart to me and explain your strange disappearance, which I cannot help but think must have been caused by some unusual occurrence. Otherwise, I will be forced to conclude that you behaved in some dishonourable manner, which I find hard to believe of a Ranreuil.'

'You do not know me well, Father, if you can think that. I must tell you that I am not satisfied with your conduct towards me and I consider ...'

What was the reason for this arrogant, self-satisfied tone? Bitter memories came back to Nicolas, memories of his confrontation with his own father at the Château de Ranreuil. Cautious and patient as he usually was, he felt anger rising within him, and only just managed to contain it in time.

'Louis, you forget yourself. Your words are hurtful to me. Please explain yourself without these pointless recriminations. Then we will weigh all this in the balance of our own consciences.'

Louis, who had been breathing hard, now appeared to calm down.

He swallowed. 'All right,' he began, hesitantly. 'Things went too far. I was insulted, humiliated, called the son of a—'

'Be quiet! And never let your mother be insulted.'

'How do you know they were talking about my mother?'

'Because being a foundling myself, I know the kinds of things that can be said in a school.'

The past was returning, painful and bitter.

'It was indeed my mother who was called a—'

Nicolas stepped forward and put his hand over his son's mouth. To his surprise, he found that Louis's face was burning hot. 'Are you ill?'

'I caught a chill on the roads.' He was less tense now. 'I couldn't stand it. There was a fight, a kind of duel.'

'With compasses. I know.'

'We were separated. I was put in solitary confinement. I had been languishing there for several days when your message arrived, brought by a Capuchin monk.'

Nicolas was aching to speak, but decided not to interrupt him.

'He told me you were angry about what had happened and were ordering me to leave the school immediately and join my mother in London. He said you never wanted to see me again.'

'How could you have believed something like that?'

'It was your handwriting, and the envelope bore our seal. How could I have doubted it? Anyway, here is the letter. See for yourself.'

Nicolas took it and was astonished by the accuracy of the forgery. 'And did you really think I was capable of abandoning you like that?'

'No, never … but at the time, yes … I felt desperate.'

'Why was I told you'd run away?'

'The monk – who I see clearly now wasn't sent by you – told me I was to make it look as if I'd run away and then meet him at a crossroads. When I got there, there was no sign of him. I didn't know how to get to a port and sail for England. I came back to Paris in wagons. Given the circumstances, I couldn't just show my face in Rue

Montmartre. My one recourse was the Dauphin Couronné, where my aunt took me in.'

'Your aunt?'

'La Paulet. I always called her my aunt when I was a child.'

He began sobbing. Nicolas opened his arms, and Louis threw himself into them. They embraced for a long time.

'What you need to know,' Nicolas said, 'is that the affairs I am dealing with and the powerful interests concerned lead me to believe that someone was using you to get at me.'

'I can understand that. Father, I don't want to go back to Juilly.'

'Of course not. In any case, I have other plans for you. But I have no desire to impose them on you without knowing where your own wishes lie.'

'I want to serve the King as a soldier.'

'Then my plans are very similar to yours. We will talk further about this. Now go and get ready. I'm taking you back to Rue Montmartre, where, at the very least, a fatted calf will be killed in your honour! Thank your … aunt for her solicitude and tell her I should like to speak with her about another matter.'

Louis left the room with a light step, turning at the door to throw a last, radiant look at his father. La Paulet returned, again dragging her feet. Nicolas remained silent.

'I'm for it now,' she said. 'You're going to tell me off, I can feel it. You'd be right. I prattled away without understanding. The boy enlightened me. This all puts me at a disadvantage with you, although …'

'Although?'

'You shouldn't have sent La Satin to London. I miss her, and I miss the way she ran my house, which was doing so well in her time.'

He did not know which of these regrets was uppermost in La Paulet's heart. No doubt both.

'How sensitive you are!' he said. 'It was she, and she alone, who made that decision. There is one thing I regret, which I'll admit to you: the fact that I reacted so harshly when I saw her keeping shop in the lower gallery of the palace. You have to realise, it's a place where I have official duties to carry out. That's all, although it's already a lot. But let's forget all that, I have a favour to ask of you.'

He remembered the sad look La Satin had given him and his heart contracted with pity. La Paulet was smiling, though: they were getting back on their old footing. She collapsed into a *bergère*, which creaked and groaned beneath her weight, and, supporting her many chins with a swollen hand, she waited, her eyes half closed.

'My good old Paulet …'

'Don't try to convince me with soft words, I know your ways!'

'The way you've treated Louis has strengthened our old bond.'

'More rope to hang yourself with!' she grunted. 'I see what you're after. Very well, let's make peace. You'll have your ratafia. I have a new shipment.'

She got to her feet and opened an elegant rosewood sideboard, took out two engraved glasses, and filled them with an amber liquid. She knocked back the first in one go, clicked her tongue appreciatively, filled it again and held out the other to Nicolas. He was impressed by the fact that she had glasses with gold borders on a background of black varnish, of the kind that the gilder and framer Glomy had made fashionable under the late King.

'Still the same supplier?'

'The son now,' she replied, staring dreamily into space.

Nicolas took a sip: it was soft yet fiery to the taste.

'Good, isn't it?' she said. 'You won't find better than this! I have to like you, Nicolas. God, we've been rubbing along together for quite a time now … And now here we are, back to our old selves.'

'Yes, here we are again, just like before. What can you tell me about La Gourdan?'

She grimaced, and her little eyes, set deep in her fat face, narrowed until they were invisible. 'Now there's a policeman's question! As if you didn't know her!'

'It's not about what I know. I'd like to hear what you think of her.'

'The woman has no morals.'

The word struck Nicolas as strange, coming from La Paulet. His reaction did not escape her.

'Don't think I don't know what you're thinking,' she said, looking straight at him. 'The truth of the matter is, there are limits I'll never cross. I've never made any girl work for me against her will, nor bought a virgin from her family, as others do.' She shook her head knowingly.

'Whereas La Gourdan—'

'The bitch! Not content with having younger and younger girls in her seraglio, girls who've been sold into prostitution by their parents, she's involved in all sorts of other dubious business.'

'Such as?'

'La Gourdan's a usurer. She buys up a whole lot of fabrics, muslin, silk from Tours, taffeta, silk stockings.'

'Where's the usury in that?' asked Nicolas, who could feel the ratafia warming his cheeks.

'When you know that the person who's selling all this stuff is in a hurry to have cash, you'll realise that La Gourdan gets the merchandise at a hundred per cent loss for the seller.'

'What else?'

'Want more, do you? I'll give you more! She corrupts women married to shrivelled-up old men, finding vigorous young stallions to satisfy their appetites. She receives clandestine couples. Her speciality is fleecing the English, who've been coming over in droves since the peace treaty. When she gets hold of a pretty girl, she plays the stern chaperone, the attentive governess, and shows her off, all prim and proper, in the Tuileries. All this to attract customers, who are willing to pay good money for someone they think's a poor orphan. God, the number she's fleeced!'

'Anything else?'

'She works hand in glove with the directors of pleasure gardens and places like that: the Vauxhall, the Saint-Germain fair, the Chinese redoubt. They give complimentary tickets to her girls in order to attract all and sundry to their shows and festivals. What can an honest house do to compete with that?'

She was becoming increasingly heated in her denunciation of her rival. She moved her *bergère* closer to Nicolas until they were almost touching and leant forward, mysteriously.

'And there's something else I'm sure you don't know.'

'How do *you* know all this?'

'I've been in this business a long time! Do you think there's anything I don't know?' She raised her voice. 'A girl I trained who's with her now tells me everything that goes on there. La Gourdan is also involved in political intrigues. Now that's something you should never do. We're tolerated by the Lieutenant General. One foot wrong, as you know, and we're all in a mess. This has been going on for a long time. It all started in Rue Sainte-Anne and is still going on in her new place in Rue des Deux-Ponts-Saint-Sauveur. Her house is a centre for meetings—'

'Of an amorous nature?'

'Not at all, imbecile. Merchants, financiers, the kind of people everyone's talking about these days, who deal in grain and flour. You see what I mean? The kind of upstarts who are controlling the market with their monopoly. Well, the last meeting took place three or four days ago, at night. And they weren't there for an orgy.'

'Do you know what they talk about at their meetings?'

'My God, don't you understand anything? Their business, of course. La Gourdan's house is full of secrets. They enter it without being seen, through the door reserved for dissolute priests. It's connected to the house next door, which is occupied by a picture dealer. Anyone can go in there without causing a scandal. He's in league with the lady in question. There's a passage at the back of a wardrobe which leads to her place.'

'This is quite an intriguing picture you're painting.'

'One last piece of advice. Ask Inspector Marais, who keeps the register of brothels. Now there's someone who knows a lot!'

And with this parting shot, they bade one another farewell, fully reconciled. Nicolas found Louis waiting for him with a package in his hand.

'I brought with me the books I was given by Monsieur de Noblecourt.'

'You could have sold them to provide for your needs.'

'My books! Monsieur de Noblecourt's books! Do you really think I could have done that, Father?'

'Of course not, I was joking. I know you're well aware of how much respect you owe him, and how fond he is of you.'

They were no sooner out in the street than they were approached by a strange figure. Nicolas recognised Tirepot, with his oilcloth and his buckets. With his back to the light, he looked like some fantastic bat.

'Nice to see you, countryman,' said Tirepot. 'Knowing you were here, the others decamped. There've been protests in various districts. This morning, bread was fourteen *sols* for four pounds.'

'Can you tell me why they were all here, around the Dauphin Couronné?'

'Why, to protect your son here! He's been here for several days, with the old lady. Bourdeau's orders.'

So the inspector had known, and so had Noblecourt. They had presumably wanted him to settle matters with Louis himself, while at the same time ensuring that nothing happened to him.

'Tell them there'll be a bonus,' he said, slipping Tirepot a double *louis*.

'As generous as ever.'

'It seems to me your buckets are empty.'

'Oh, yes! I've given up the profession, there are no more customers.'
He began singing, waddling like a performing bear as he did so.

> *'With this long cloak, I wandered here and there,*
> *Carrying two buckets for people to shit in.*
> *But these days people shit everywhere,*
> *So I'm out on my ears, without a pot to spit in!'*

'But you still have all your gear with you!'

'I've always been on good terms with the spies, out of friendship
for you. So now I've joined them full time, and the buckets are a good
excuse for me to be wherever I want to be.'

'I may have need of you. Where can you be found?'

'Bourdeau and Rabouine know where.'

In the cab taking them back to Rue Montmartre, Louis expressed
surprise that everyone spoke to his father in such a familiar manner.
Nicolas explained how sensitive an honest man should be: you had
to be in tune with those who talked to you, especially when they
expressed, as best they could, their friendship for you. When they
reached their destination, he dropped Louis, knowing that everyone
was waiting for him expectantly as the child of the house. At the corner
of the church of Saint-Eustache, he asked the coachman to stop the
carriage, having spotted Bourdeau striding up and down. He opened
the door and the inspector hoisted himself inside. The coachman was
asked to wait.

'I was afraid I'd miss you.'

Nicolas squeezed his hand. 'I'll never forget this, Pierre. I know
what you did. Louis has returned to the fold. I understand everything.
Your sensitivity touches me more than I can say, and my debt to you
is greater then ever.'

Bourdeau blushed and his eyes misted over. He quickly changed the subject. 'I don't know all the whys and wherefores, but alarming news continues to come in to the Châtelet. Threatening groups have entered Paris, led by people who seem to know what they're doing. They've been seen at Porte de la Conférence, Porte Saint-Martin and in Vaugirard.'

'Tirepot told me that at the Dauphin Couronné.'

'It's reported they were using an agreed vocabulary. In Vaugirard one of them asked a booted rider about their destination. The answer was "three points and thirty-one", which was repeated among the group and then passed back along the rows. Apparently, everyone knew which direction to take. The largest group went straight to the corn market. They must have reached it by now.'

'Are the local people following the crowd?'

'They're not actually taking part. Of course, some tag along out of curiosity and take advantage of the looted bread, but they're not really involved in what's going on. Most are closing their doors, opening their windows and looking out, as if watching the Corpus Christi procession pass by. Even most artisans, who might have been thought sympathetic to the movement, have remained calm.'

'And the civil authorities?'

'Complete disorder, uncertainty and incompetence! By an unfortunate coincidence, the garrison's ceremony of blessing the flags was due to take place and the Maréchal de Biron has let it continue. He refused to give the counter-order requested by—'

'Requested? Are we in a situation where we can but request? Whatever happened to orders? This is all beyond me.'

'– by Monsieur de Maurepas, who in any case had merely suggested it. Biron feared that such a measure would have alarmed the people and sparked further unrest. Black musketeers have, it's true, taken up position at the central market.'

'Let us hope their fortitude and determination impress the crowd!'

'Apart from that, there are no orders. We are the only ones running from one place to another with all our spies to get an idea of the advancing tide. Everywhere the same passivity encourages the boldness of the demonstrators. When Turgot returns from Versailles, he'll find a band of hotheads waiting for him outside the comptroller general's office brandishing mouldy bread and claiming that it's an attempt to poison the people. One of our men grabbed a piece. The bread turned out to be stale, but not mouldy. It had been smeared with a kind of green dye. Last but not least, the house of the commissioner of the Maubert district, Monsieur Convers-Désormeaux, was overrun and ransacked. Where are we going?'

'To police headquarters, my dear fellow, trying to avoid the comptroller general's office!'

In Rue Plâtrière, they had to do an about-turn because of a gathering outside a bakery. A small group of men and women were yelling and trying to force open the shop, striking the front with sticks, rods and iron bars. In the end, the only thing that saved the baker was the batch of loaves which he threw to the crowd from the first-floor window. Nicolas noted that some of the participants were wearing aprons made of hide and caps that hid their faces, and carrying sacks and hooks. One of them approached the carriage, his eyes bloodshot.

'To the Bastille!' he screamed. 'We must march on the Bastille and then Bicêtre. We'll force open the dungeons and release the prisoners into the streets.'

'The Bastille!' muttered Bourdeau. 'Let them try. The place is impregnable!'

Some men of the watch were standing by, powerless to act. Insulted and threatened with stoning, they pretended to load their rifles, but their officers ordered them to retreat. Passing the carriage, one of them said through clenched teeth, 'Let them give the order, and we'll open fire on these bastards!'

The carriage set off down Rue Jussienne, where, by way of contrast, everything was perfectly calm. The unrest seemed to be spreading in patches, like a slow flood, leaving most of the city untouched. Nicolas gave orders to the coachman to get them to police headquarters by the shortest route possible. When Bourdeau asked him why they were going there, Nicolas answered with a summary of his conversation with La Paulet.

'Anyway,' he said by way of conclusion, 'we can't do much to help right now, given the lack of orders. But of all the things our old friend told me, the most important one, I'm sure you'll agree, is these clandestine meetings concerning the trade in flour. We must find out–' he hammered the threadbare velvet of the seat with his clenched fists – 'what Master Mourut was doing at La Gourdan's house. Was he there for wenching or was he a participant in these meetings, as suggested by all the grain and flour in his cellars? I'm convinced we're dealing with people who are speculating and controlling the market.'

'So in your opinion this wasn't a domestic crime?'

'One thing doesn't rule out the other.'

'Why, then, are we going to police headquarters?'

'Because that's where we'll find Inspector Marais's office.'

Bourdeau struck his own forehead. 'Why didn't I think of that? He's the man we need. The head of the vice department, who keeps the register of the girls and checks the daily reports from the brothel-keepers. He's a slippery customer, always playing a double game, even a triple one, not easy to find, extremely cautious, involved in all kinds of intrigues, and in possession of a thousand secrets regarding men in high places. He's ripe for a fall.'

'Do we have anything we could use against him? Is he a new Lardin?'[1]

Bourdeau gave a thin smile. 'I just remembered that one of his clerks is in cahoots with La Gourdan.'

'That's normal enough. We can't do without such accommodations. It's a world in which the clerks extort money from the brothel-keepers and the unfortunate girls, exercising an almost tyrannical hold over them. As if the business wasn't already debauched enough! The girls come to the conclusion that the law's not on their side.'

'That does go on, yes, but only within certain limits. This particular man, whose name is Minaud, goes further. He warns La Gourdan of complaints against her that the Lieutenant General isn't in a position to dismiss.'

'You seem well informed, Pierre. How do you know all this?'

'While you're at the top of the heap, I'm still at the bottom. In one leap, at the age of twenty, you bypassed all the stages. That was lucky for you, and for me. It does mean that, even though I may be an old horse, fit only for the knacker's yard, I still have contacts at every level. In this profession, it's the only way to survive. When the name La Gourdan cropped up in our investigation, I looked up some of these old contacts ...'

Bourdeau was incomparable: he always anticipated Nicolas's as yet unexpressed wishes.

'Mere gossip won't get us far. But through one of her girls, who's infatuated with Rabouine, we're in possession of a letter from Minaud to La Gourdan.'

He took out a small piece of paper and began reading.

'*You are in a great deal of trouble, Madame. The police have just received a new complaint against you. I immediately stole it, with the help of you know who. If you come to see me at four o'clock, I'll hand it over to you. That should avoid your having any further difficulties.*

'*I should point out, Madame, that you are not alone in having problems. I've just lost the sum of twenty-five* louis, *which puts me in a difficult position, as I have an IOU to pay tomorrow. Nobody, Madame, is fonder of you than I. I'll expect you at four o'clock. Please be punctual. A paper that has been withheld may just as easily be released ...*'

'The villain! With this, we have Marais, Minaud and La Gourdan! It's priceless!'

'The punishment certainly ought to fit the crime.'

'We should be able to use some persuasive arguments, in case Marais is uncooperative.'

'What's more, it's a double-edged sword, the lady will feel the blade, too.'

Holding the balance of power as they did, their confrontation with Marais proved unpleasant but far from difficult. The man kept rubbing his hands, but had no defence against Nicolas's arguments. After a few pitiful attempts at resistance or distraction, which were soon blocked, he finally consented to tell them what he knew about La Gourdan.

The lady, whose real name was Marguerite Stock, had married a man named Gourdan, a tax collector in Champagne, then director of taxes in Brest. Soon separated from her husband, she had kept a tobacconist's shop. Under the name Darigny, she took up the trade of brothel-keeper, first in Rue Sainte-Anne, then in Rue de la Comtesse-d'Artois, which was why she was known as the little comtesse. There she received the finest people: the Prince de Conti, the Duc de Chartres and the Duc de Lauzun, the Marquis de la Tremoille and the Marquis de Duras. All this confirmed what Nicolas already knew. Marais looked distinctly uncomfortable negotiating this dangerous area, not at all happy that the nature of his relations with the best-known brothel-keeper in Paris had become the subject of close scrutiny.

Nicolas did not use his heavy artillery immediately. Instead, he launched a series of skirmishes, catching Marais so unawares that the man finally came to the point. The situation must be serious, thought Nicolas, and he must be feeling genuinely threatened by it. Why else would such an old hand lower his guard and surrender so totally?

La Gourdan, he revealed, was facing legal proceedings in which her reputation and her future were at stake. A first complaint had been lodged against her by a haberdasher whose wife she had corrupted. When she threatened to appeal to her friends in high places and have the husband locked up if he tried to get his wife back, the complaint had been withdrawn. But more serious, in Marais's opinion, was the prospect of a ruling by the Parlement that could lead to La Gourdan's arrest for corrupting Madame d'Oppy, the wife of the great bailiff of Douai, who had been temporarily incarcerated at Sainte-Pélagie for adultery. Making concessions, La Gourdan had agreed to testify to the police. Despite that, she was still in grave danger of forfeiting her position and fame. The services she had rendered and her association with Marais no longer guaranteed her immunity. She seemed ripe for yielding to Commissioner Le Floch's demands. As for the mysterious meetings held at the house in Rue des Deux-Ponts-Saint-Sauveur, which seemed to have no connection with the trade in lust, Marais had kept regular note of them, again confirming what Nicolas knew. But he had not been curious enough to record the names of the participants, a surprising oversight for such a well-organised man.

On the way back, Bourdeau remarked that Marais must have felt under great pressure to have been so conciliatory. His reasoning could be reconstructed. Clearly the man had judged it useful and timely to cooperate with a commissioner like no other, a marquis to boot, whose renewed influence with Monsieur Lenoir and position at Court – of which he must have heard frequent reports – made him a powerful ally in case he was implicated. Nicolas agreed, impatient now to tackle La Gourdan without delay. They had to move forward, and he was also thinking of the two baker's boys whose confinement he had no wish to prolong.

At the entrance to Rue Montorgueil, which they had reached after a long detour via the banks of the river and Rue Saint-Honoré, a surge of people around them forced them to stop. Nicolas debated the matter with the coachman. Should they turn off into Rue Tiquetonne and venture into a maze of narrow streets to get to Rue Saint-Denis? That might be to risk an incident, and he could not make up his mind to do so. It was therefore decided that they would walk to the Gourdan house. A light rain started to fall. On the corner of Rue Tiquetonne and Rue Saint-Denis, a broad stream covered the crossroads. A boot cleaner had just dragged a bridge on castors from out of a dark alley. Bourdeau and Nicolas watched in amusement as a brave fellow ventured across this unsteady gangplank. He stumbled, fell in the water and got back on his feet, soaked. He ran off quickly, pursued by the boot cleaner yelling that he wanted his three *sols* for the crossing.

'Now there's a lucrative trade for a rainy day!' Bourdeau remarked. 'Provided the customer doesn't run away!'

'Woe to those who slip. You could make it if you jumped, but then you might have your eye out with your umbrella, or someone else's eye!'

'And what happens,' said Bourdeau, amused, 'when two big men come face to face on that rickety bridge?'

'It's a dangerous spot. Even a little shower turns it into a lake! Let's be careful!'

In this narrow street, where most of the houses were new, La Gourdan's looked respectable enough. It was a tall, thin house, bounded on its right by the courtyard of a building set back from the street and on its left by an almost identical construction. A maid in an apron opened the door to them and asked them in a friendly manner if they were the provincials who had reserved two rooms along with their 'favourites'. They disabused her of that notion and asked to see the mistress of the house without further ado. As the maid withdrew to inform La Gourdan, Nicolas remarked to Bourdeau that she would not have looked out of place in an honest house. She returned immediately and asked them to follow her to the first floor. They were requested to wait in a richly furnished drawing room. The walls were entirely covered in purple damask with gilded beading. The furniture consisted of *bergères*, a three-seat ottoman and six cabriolet armchairs covered in crimson velvet. Everywhere there were pier glasses and painted overdoors. There were also two paintings on the walls, one of a reclining Venus and the other a portrait of the late King. The only indication of the nature of this house was the abundance of risqué engravings and prints which drew the attention with their provocative subject matter.

A middle-aged woman entered. She could easily have passed for a pious lady on her way to compline. She wore a monochrome grey dress that reminded Nicolas of the good lady of Choisy.[2] She was slim, with a long face and a pale complexion that owed little to the artifice of ointments. A kind of mantilla covered a blond wig with a bun, slightly out of place so that her natural hair, light brown in colour, peeped through. A Roman nose and a mouth with teeth that were too regular to be true did not detract from the general impression. What did spoil it slightly was the small eyes and lips so thin that only a line of carmine revealed their position. On seeing her, it was easy to understand how, out strolling solemnly, accompanied by one of her girls in modest attire, she had been able to deceive so many gullible souls from across the Channel eager to sow their wild oats with a charming young Parisienne.

'Gentlemen, I've been told you wish to speak to me. I assume you are in search of some refined distraction such as only this vast city can provide. You've made an excellent choice. My house is the finest, most fashionable you could find. The upper crust of the Court and the city frequent it and I assure you I can provide you with—'

It was time to put a stop to this patter.

'I fear,' said Nicolas, 'that you are mistaken about the object of our visit. It is of a somewhat particular nature …'

The lady's smile was halfway between that of a shrewd merchant and the knowing grin of someone who has been close to every possible immoral deed.

'That's perfectly all right, gentlemen. I shan't ask any more questions, I can easily foresee the kind of indulgence you expect of my house. I am determined to satisfy all your desires in terms of

212

imagination and variety. In particular, I have some newly arrived young morsels fit for a king. I was reserving the first taste of them for connoisseurs such as yourselves.'

'You seem still to be labouring under a misunderstanding, Madame,' said Nicolas, eager now to get to the point. 'I am a police commissioner at the Châtelet, and I'm here to question you on the orders of the Lieutenant General of Police. This gentleman is an inspector and is assisting me in this duty. I must inform you that your statement will be taken down.'

He saw La Gourdan's fingers turn white as she gripped the back of the armchair on which she was leaning. Nicolas had not revealed their names. Either she already knew them, even though she had never had dealings with them, or she would do all she could to find out who they were, something she certainly had the means to do.

'Gentlemen, gentlemen,' she resumed in a soft, almost repentant voice, 'forgive me for having mistaken you for provincials in search of the pleasures only available in Paris. My house is highly regarded. My girls are all registered. I inform the police when foreigners pass through and when anything untoward has happened during the night. You may find it more helpful to consult Inspector Marais and others who know what a good person and what a loyal subject of His Majesty I am …'

'The police clerk Minaud, for example?'

'Why deny it? He among others …'

'Whom you supply with money.'

'I see no harm in what your words imply. There are services exchanged between friends, to which, indeed, others may lay claim if they wish.'

'You certainly don't lack nerve! So the recipe is to have friends, debtors even, in the police. And how does one do that? With money, Madame Gourdan.'

A look of commiseration came over her face. 'These are normal practices, Monsieur, and I am surprised that they shock you, unless I am to understand that you wish to benefit from them. But, you see, I have my arrangements with your colleagues and I don't see why I should have to do the same with you.'

What she was saying was all too true: the police could not do without these dubious go-betweens recruited from the world of prostitution.

'I could easily tolerate such arrangements, except when they interfere with the execution of the law and hinder the course of justice, which, may I remind you, is blind to this kind of compromise.'

He was asserting this, but was he so convinced of it himself?'

'I am your humble servant, Monsieur, but it seems that you don't know me. I could tell you things .... Besides, it is wrong to attack an honest woman who has for so long contributed to the well-being of a great many people.'

'That's exactly what I was saying to the inspector before you came in. I was telling him how useful your trade is. Yours is without doubt the most highly regarded, best-known and most frequented house.'

She looked up with a strained smile, thinking she had won the day.

'Nevertheless,' Nicolas went on, spinning his words like a spider its web, 'it is precisely these qualities which commit you to being honest with the Lieutenant General of Police, force you even to remain an example of what is lawful and tolerated.'

'But what have I to fear? These are empty words, idle threats! Take care, what you are attempting is unwise and you will end up sorry that you even conceived the idea, let alone that you failed in it. This is all stuff and nonsense!'

'Madame,' declared Bourdeau, 'vice is a dangerous thing when it is without scruples. Your conduct leaves much to be desired. One does not speak in that tone to a commissioner. What use to you are your relations in high places? You count too much on them. They may, if need be, help you to get out of prison one day, but they certainly won't stop you going in!'

'For heaven's sake,' she cried, suddenly losing her arrogant manner, 'what am I being accused of?'

'Don't worry, we have an embarrassment of choice where that's concerned. I advise you not to pretend ignorance.'

'Monsieur, you are speaking to a lady!'

'Yes,' said Nicolas, 'to La Gourdan, keeper of a tolerated brothel. You have overstepped the mark, Madame, and now you are beginning to try my patience. I will satisfy your curiosity eventually. In the meantime, come down off your high horse and control yourself.'

He opened his little black notebook.

'Firstly, repeated and detailed complaints have been lodged against you for having bought children from their unnatural parents and using them in your trade, and for having corrupted a number of married women.'[3]

'Am I the only person guilty of that? And in any case these complaints have been withdrawn.'

'Including the one pending, which concerns an important lady, the wife of an officer of the crown?'

'I testified against her.'

'Yes, against your will. We shall see what the Parlement decides. To refresh your memory, you may, according to the royal edict of 1734, be branded, whipped and ridden through the streets on a donkey, with your face turned towards the tail, and a straw hat and signs designating you as the keeper of a brothel.'

'I have never seen such obstinacy as yours, Monsieur. What blackmail! If one can't trust the police, who can one trust?'

He had to admire the woman's audacity. He unfolded a small sheet of paper and began reading.

'*You are in a great deal of trouble, Madame. The police have just received …*'

By the time he had finished, she was shaking with fear or anger, it was hard to say which.

'And what have I to do with this gentleman? I don't even know him.'

'How do you know you don't know him? Did I mention his name? You pay him to steal certain documents.'

'I assure you I do not. Nobody does my profession more honour than I. I could name you—'

'That's enough. Inspector, write up the statement. Then take Madame away.'

'To prison?'

'No, better still, to Bicêtre. That'll loosen her tongue.'

He had wagered a great deal on the effect that would produce. He had not been mistaken. The veneer cracked all at once.

'Oh, Monsieur, don't ruin me! Why are you so determined to have me sent to that horrible place, adding infamy to the uncertainty of my state? How could you be so cruel?'

He had to admire her performance. It mattered little that he had lied to her, he had achieved his goal: she seemed on the point of surrendering.

'Madame, I am perfectly happy to hear what you have to tell me, but rest assured that if you make the slightest attempt to deceive me, you will immediately leave Rue des Deux-Ponts-Saint-Sauveur for a grim destination. I advise you not to prevaricate, and to keep to the truth. Then, and only then, will we see what we can do.'

'Do you admit,' said Bourdeau in a monotone voice, 'receiving a suggestion from the police clerk Minaud that for twenty-five *louis*, he would make sure that a complaint against you went missing?'

'Monsieur, I would never dream of … All right, yes, I admit it.'

'Good! That's a first step. Did you get that down, Inspector?'

Bourdeau, who was leaning on the mantelshelf, pretending to write, finished scribbling and continued.

'Secondly, do you admit corrupting married women in your establishment?'

'Certainly not!'

'Falling back into her old ways already,' said Nicolas. 'Never mind, we have wider weapons. I read. *I am, Madame, the unhappiest of women. My husband is a decrepit old man who does not provide me with any pleasure.* Should I continue? Should I remind you of the penalty for this crime?'

'I admit it, I admit it,' said La Gourdan, aghast.

'Good, we're making progress. Now, let's go on to something much more recent. I warn you I shall be even more inflexible in this case. Your answers will be proof of your sincerity and will influence my final decision.'

'Go on, Monsieur,' murmured La Gourdan in a faint voice. She had sat down and was twisting the ruche of her cuffs.

'Madame, on the night of Sunday 30 April to Monday 1 May, a couple, whose clandestine encounters you allow, spent a few hours in this house. Can you tell me any more about that?'

He was fishing blindly, as he had once fished for crabs among the rocks of Le Croisic. One day he had got a nasty bite from a conger eel which simply would not let go: he still bore the marks. La Gourdan seemed to calm down. He knew what she was thinking: if that was all this was about, there was nothing wrong with giving in on this point.

'In this house, you know, that kind of encounter is not uncommon.'

'You didn't seem so sure of that a moment ago.'

She bit her lips again. 'We offer a refuge for love. Obviously, we have to be discreet, so—'

'So you can't go too far. I see. Just tell me about that evening.'

'It was a Sunday night, so there weren't many customers. But a couple did come, the one you're talking about, I suppose. A woman in a veil – about thirty-five, I'd say – and a young man in a tricorn, with a mask over his face.'

'Come now, Madame, this was no masked ball. Don't tell me you open your doors to just anyone. What were their names?'

'A messenger had brought me a note from a Madame Marte.'

Marte, thought Nicolas. Marte, Montmartre, Rue Montmartre. Madame Mourut had not looked very far for her assumed name.

'So,' he said, 'on the basis of that name, a room was reserved?'

'The usual terms: a fire lit in the hearth and a midnight supper.'

'The usual terms?' echoed Bourdeau.

'Yes.' She seemed taken aback: had she said too much?

'Meaning that these encounters were regular?'

She sighed. 'They'd been coming here for about six months.'

'What time did they arrive?' asked Nicolas.

'On the stroke of nine.'

'And leave?'

'That, I don't know. We don't keep an eye on how our customers spend their nights.'

'Let's go back over the details. They arrived together – stop me if I make a mistake – and they came in through the back door, the secret one used by priests. Did they go up to the second floor?'

'The third.'

'Did either of them come down again?'

'… No.'

He had noticed the hesitation and leapt on it. 'Actually, I think the man came down.'

She was looking at him wild-eyed, on the verge of panic. Bourdeau looked at Nicolas, intrigued.

'How do you know that?' said La Gourdan.

'The commissioner,' said the inspector, sententiously, 'has ways of knowing everything, everywhere and at any time. It's obvious that you don't know him. It's also obvious that you are not being entirely honest and that you are breaking our agreement.'

'No, no. If I did so, it was innocently.'

Both Bourdeau and Nicolas were starting to enjoy this game of tennis, in which the advantage was always theirs.

'All right! About eleven, the couple rang for another bottle. The maid didn't go up, either because the bell pull was broken, or because she didn't hear. So the young man came down to the ground floor.'

'Did he meet anyone there apart from the maid?'

'I couldn't tell you that. Anything's possible. There's so much coming and going in this house …'

'Lots of ins and outs, I imagine,' said Bourdeau, completely deadpan.

'Might he have met your other customers?'

'He may well have seen some of my regulars …'

'Even though you said that Sunday isn't a very busy night.'

'That's right. But there are always officers up from the provinces, couples …'

'Meetings?'

'Threesomes and foursomes, quite often.'

'That's not the kind of meeting I'm talking about. I fear, Madame, that my goodwill is fading, thanks to your reluctance to be honest. What do you think, Inspector?'

'I think a dungeon might—'

'Gentlemen, please don't take advantage of a poor woman!'

'Then let's have done with this,' said Nicolas. 'Someone as shrewd as you should have realised by now that we already know a lot, and that what we expect from you is confirmation and details. Was there, yes or no, a meeting in your house on Sunday night? What kind of meeting was it and do you know the names of those who attended?'

La Gourdan's reaction betrayed her surprise at how much the two policemen knew about the activities of her house.

'Commissioner, this place sometimes serves as a meeting place for those who wish to gather discreetly. Such was the case, I admit, on Sunday night. An unliveried footman warns me a week in advance. There are a dozen guests. A very mixed group: courtiers, a priest, merchants …'

'What kind of merchants?'

'Grain merchants, from what I gather.'

'Could one of them have seen the young man in question on Sunday night?'

'I really don't know … anything's possible.'

'Do you know the names of those who meet?'

'No, none of them.'

'They should appear on the nightly report you submit to Inspector Marais. What conclusion are we to draw from this omission?'

'Actually, I did find a piece of paper on the floor of the room where they'd just held their meeting. It must have fallen from someone's pocket. It was all yellow, some kind of old prospectus. There was an address on it: Monsieur Hénéfiance, seed merchant, Aux Armes de Cérès, Rue du Poirier.'

'Better still! Did you keep it?'

'No.'

'That's a pity. Let's try and get a better idea of the timetable that evening. At what hour did the meeting start?'

'About half past ten.'

'And finish?'

'Just after midnight.'

'I'd like to speak to your maid.'

'Gentlemen, there's no need to involve—'

An icy glare from the commissioner quickly cut short this attempt at resistance. La Gourdan rang, and the girl who had admitted them entered.

'On Sunday night,' said Bourdeau, ingratiatingly, 'did you show a couple to the room on the third floor?'

She looked at La Gourdan, who raised her eyes to heaven then signalled to her to answer.

'Yes. A lady in a closed mantle with a hood and a young man in a mask – pale as a wigmaker, he was.'

'How do you know?'

'I saw him in breeches when he came down half dressed to look for a bottle. The lady must have drained him dry.'

She was surprised that her attempt at humour fell flat.

'What time was that?'

'Oh, I couldn't say for certain, but it was after midnight. I can't forget the scene. Those gentlemen were coming out. When he saw one in particular, the young man gave a start and ran back upstairs as if he'd seen the devil.'

She made the sign of the cross.

'Would you be able to recognise that gentleman?'

'Yes, yes, he was next to a torch. He was wearing a nice dark-red coat. Because he had the light in his eyes, he didn't notice a thing.'

'If that's so, then I'm afraid, Madame, that we're going to deprive you of ... of ...?'

'Colette,' said the maid.

'... Colette, for a couple of hours. She's a crucial witness in a criminal case.'

'Monsieur!'

'We thank you for your help, so willingly given. It goes without saying that we shan't forget this favour. And you shouldn't forget Monsieur Minaud. I'm sure the Lieutenant General would appreciate anything you could tell him on that subject!'

They went back to their carriage, which, having made a great detour, was now going up and down the street, the coachman not knowing outside which house to wait for them. They got back to the Grand Châtelet without mishap. There, in the Basse-Geôle, Colette recognised the corpse she was shown as the man from the meeting, let out a scream and fainted. Once again, Old Marie's cordial proved its efficacy.

221

VIII

APPEARANCES

All that follow their noses are led by their eyes
but blind men; and there's not a nose among twenty
but can smell him that's stinking.

SHAKESPEARE

In the inspectors' office, Nicolas was absent-mindedly leafing through the duty register, which recorded the events of the day as reported by the commissioners, spies and guard posts throughout Paris. Whenever a detail or a name caught his attention, he knitted his brows. Suddenly, he slammed the volume shut, making Bourdeau, who had been calmly smoking his pipe, jump in surprise.

'There's no point in waiting, we've waited long enough! Rabouine tells us the worst has passed. That's always the case: the tide recedes just when you finally decide to contain it!'

'It's because Turgot, having returned from Versailles, seems to have taken matters in hand. Our men have been sent out to arrest the insurgents.'

'Doubtless with the usual caution: to refrain from overt force in order to avoid violent reactions.'

'On the quiet, as usual! The spies locate the suspects, and they're arrested either when they separate or when they arrive home! The latest news is that mounted musketeers have been told to clear the streets and disperse what's left of the crowd. The comptroller general didn't have an easy task: the Maréchal de Biron, captain of the guards, wouldn't hear of it. He actually had to be shown orders in the King's handwriting before he would admit that he was wrong!'

Nicolas had already stopped listening, his mind elsewhere. He was wondering, without telling the inspector, where the Chevalier de Lastire, whom Sartine had so offhandedly imposed on him, could possibly be. Had the disturbances made it hard for him to show his face? Or was he following them closely, his mission being to report on them? The man himself had been quite sceptical about the possibility of unrest. This brief reflection led to another, more intriguing one. The presumed murder he was trying to clear up appeared linked in some mysterious way to events in the kingdom, and yet everything seemed to point to the fact that these same events had been long planned. He stood up.

'Pierre, I'm going straight to Rue du Poirier to find out about Hénéfiance. I need to set my mind at rest. I'm convinced that our case has some kind of connection with the meetings at La Gourdan's brothel. I want to drive this Hénéfiance into a corner before all these people go to ground. It will give me a better idea of what we're looking for. In the meantime, find out about Mourut's notary. Remember what La Babine said. We'll meet back here. Whoever's first will wait for the other.'

The commissioner's carriage took a roundabout route to get to Rue du Poirier. Leaving the Grand Châtelet, it went along Rue Saint-Jacques-la-Boucherie and Rue des Arcis as far as Rue du Cloître Saint-Merry. This stretch of the journey allowed him to observe that pockets of unrest remained here and there, but that the conflagration was now sporadic. The police were out in the open now, reinforced by the musketeers. The city nevertheless bore the scars of the mob's anger: many shops, and not only bakeries, had had their windows and doors smashed in. There had clearly been a lot of looting, made all the easier by the incompetence of the authorities.

They turned into Rue Taillepain, then Rue Brisemiche, and finally came out into Rue du Poirier. It was a narrow, muddy, foul-smelling street, which had clearly not changed in centuries. Sartine, a great expert on Paris, had once explained to him why so many of these streets had names connected with bread: it was an allusion to the former bakery in the Saint-Merry cloister and the loaves made there for the canons. It had also long been known as a place of ill repute, a place where you could find the lowest class of prostitutes, decrepit streetwalkers, many just out of prison, who haunted the alleys and tollgates. Getting out of his carriage, he took a few steps and looked curiously at the old, half-timbered buildings, which reminded him of the houses in Auray, back home in Brittany. You could still see the hook from which the iron chain that had closed off the street several centuries earlier had once hung.

An unpleasantly musty smell seized him by the throat. A few steps away, he saw a strange construction, a kind of large box made out of rough-hewn old planks with a sloping roof nailed to it. The whole thing was leaning back against a blind wall and was supported on the right by the gnarled trunk of a Virginia creeper whose still bare branches rose into the sky. On the roof of this intriguing edifice, an old, hairless dog lay asleep, its head on a big flat stone that confirmed how solid the construction was. There was an awning at the front, articulated so that it could snap shut like a trap. Sitting on an old sheepskin was an elderly legless cripple bent over his task. Behind him hung garlands of old shoes, indicating that he was a cobbler. Nicolas approached him politely.

'Good evening, friend! With all the disturbance there's been today, your street's really quiet.'

The man looked him up and down, as if assessing what he might expect from this fine figure. The examination must have been conclusive because, after spitting out the tacks he had in his mouth, he gave Nicolas a toothless smile.

'That's because there's nothing to loot in this poor street. Those loudmouths I saw passing this morning have to learn to be patient.

I swear, on my plank and my stool, that all this is just birdseed for simpletons and that they won't be any better off in the long run. But here I am, chatting away, instead of getting on with my work. Name's Jacques Nivernais, at your service. If your shoes are damaged, which doesn't seem to be the case here, I'm the man to mend them.'

He seized a low-fronted shoe and made ready to polish the heel with a piece of wood.

'What's that?' asked Nicolas.

'A nice hard, smooth piece of boxwood I rub over and over the leather of the heel to make it shiny. You have to rub it in hard, a shoe like this doesn't change all by itself!'

'I'm very interested in old Gothic streets, as it happens. How long have you been living here?'

'Since I came back from the siege of Prague with Monsieur Chevert.'

Nicolas took off his tricorn and saluted. 'A great soldier, my friend.'

'He knew how to talk to his troops. He was a small man, but big-hearted. It was thanks to him that I got enough money on my discharge to open this workshop. So I never fail to have myself rolled ...'

Lifting the sheepskin, he indicated an open crate mounted on castors and with a shaft attached to it for pulling. He noticed the commissioner's puzzled expression.

'It's Fritz, my dog, who pulls it. Yes, I have myself rolled to Saint-Eustache to salute his grave and the fine inscription I've had read to me.'

'My friend,' said Nicolas, touched, 'in Rue Montmartre, at the third house after the cul-de-sac, ask for Catherine Gauss, and say Nicolas sent you. There'll always be a bowl of soup, some bread and stew for you.'

Genuinely moved, the man tugged at his moustache. 'Not everyone talks like that to an old soldier,' he muttered. 'If you tell me what you're looking for, I'm the man to help you find it.'

'Well,' replied Nicolas, casually, 'there are a few things I'm curious about. I need someone who's known the street for a long time.'

'You've found him! I was ill for ages in Bohemia, but then in 1747 I hung up my hat here, and I haven't moved since. I live here, I work here. Let me see your boots, Monsieur, I'll shine them up for you as we talk.' He clicked his tongue. 'They're worth the trouble.'

Nicolas stretched his leg out in front of him. The man smeared a viscous brown paste on the boot.

'You wouldn't by any chance know a grain merchant named Hénéfiance in these parts?'

'Hénéfiance … Hénéfiance? Wait, the name sounds familiar. Oh, yes! Just down there, after the old wall, you'll see a house that's been long abandoned. A nasty story. None of us knows all the ins and outs of it. Old man Hénéfiance was rich, one of those leeches who suck the blood of the people and traffic in grain with other disreputable characters. When he died, his son took over the business. Soon after that, he was arrested without anyone being sure why. One day, the officers came and seized everything. Apparently, he was sentenced to the galleys. There was a rumour that he escaped. Why are you so interested?'

Nicolas ignored the question. 'And since then, the house has been abandoned?'

'To tell the truth, I don't really know, I don't keep an eye on it all the time, but if there had been any movement in it, I'm sure I would have noticed. I'm a kind of permanent porter. Given my position here, nothing escapes me.'

Both boots having now regained an unparalleled sheen, Nicolas rose from the stool where he had been sitting. He generously rewarded the cobbler, who promised he would visit Rue Montmartre. He had the impression he had gained not only a friend, but also an observer in Rue du Poirier who would be sure to inform him if anything unusual happened. A good turn never went amiss, and what you got back was often greater than if you had consciously asked for it. He advanced along the street, which was deserted at this hour of the day. There was nothing opposite the Hénéfiance house apart from an old mansion, itself abandoned, with a peeling façade. The oldest dwellings in the district were gradually being demolished in order to build blocks of apartments, sometimes six or eight storeys high. There was always an interval after the sale and before demolition started. The Hénéfiance house had a stone wall in front of it, with a wooden carriage entrance in the middle, surmounted by a moss-covered capital. This outside wall was joined to the wall of the house itself, a two-storey construction with boarded-up windows. Nicolas tried to open the heavy door, but in vain: a strong lock prevented any movement. He searched in his pocket and took out a picklock and a small box. In the box was tallow, with which he greased the picklock before inserting it. Within a few seconds the bolt had sprung, but the door still would not open. He decided to try a more violent method and gave it a powerful shove with his shoulder. He had to repeat the action before the door finally yielded with a great creaking of its hinges. He went in and carefully closed the door again behind him.

In front of him was a poorly paved courtyard: grass was beginning to grow in the cracks. To his left, the house, with a small flight of steps leading up to the entrance. To the right, and facing him, other buildings, barns or sheds. He decided to conduct a thorough inspection. His picklock allowed him to enter the house quite easily. He took a few cautious steps in the shadows of a bare room that seemed to him to have been the servants' pantry. He advanced some more, and suddenly the floor gave way beneath his weight with a sharp crack and an explosion of dust. He had thrown both hands out in front of him and was able to catch hold of the solid part. His legs dangled in emptiness. He finally managed to get back on his feet on one side of the gaping hole. He struck a light, took a sheet from his notebook and set fire to it to make an improvised torch. Through the hole, he could see a cellar filled with shadows and indistinct objects. He lit some more pages and finally found some pieces of candle next to a passageway. He went back to the hole in the floor and looked carefully at the floorboards that had given way. Kneeling, he checked the places where they had broken. He passed his finger over them, bent further over, and felt the wooden fibres. There was a mystery here: the floorboards were of solid oak and in no way rotten or even perforated by furniture beetles, which in Guérande were known as 'timekeepers of death' because of the regular noise they produced. They certainly should not have given way. On closer inspection, it was clear that the boards had been neatly sawn through – and recently, too.

His mind began working at high speed. If this act was as recent as it seemed, the house, far from being long abandoned, was still receiving visitors. Had a trap been set? Once again, questions crowded into his mind. Either this was a precautionary device intended to protect the place from prowlers – but what was there to preserve in these ruined premises? – or someone had known he would come here, had preceded him and had sawn through the floor. In the first case, an objection arose immediately: the trap had been set only recently; he knew enough about wood to be sure of that without fear of error. In the second hypothesis, had the intention been to kill him, or any other intruder? He leant over towards the hole. The ground was not a long way down. There was a good chance one might survive, although there was an equal chance of being maimed, or even killed if one fell head first onto the stone. It was possible that this was simply the best way of not drawing attention to the cellar. Making any unwanted visitor in the Hénéfiance house fall into it might be a way of saying that it did not contain any incriminating evidence. He knew he was thinking too fast, and tried to slow down, convinced that he would never reach any logical conclusion while his mind was overwhelmed with the emotion of the moment.

Whatever the hidden intention of whoever had planted this trap, he would get nothing for his troubles. Nicolas was not only unscathed, he would now most certainly visit the cellar.

He continued his inspection, cautiously, finding only empty rooms with peeling walls. The furniture must have been confiscated when Hénéfiance was sentenced to the galleys. The living quarters did not contribute anything he could use. He needed to look at the outbuildings. He started with the shed facing the house. As he approached it, he began to hear furtive, hurried noises, followed by prolonged silences. He froze, all his senses on the alert, as if he were at the hunt. The sound of movement was increasing. He put his hand into the wing of his tricorn where he kept the miniature pistol he had been given by Bourdeau – always the final argument in difficult situations. He cocked it and, with his finger on the trigger, opened the door of the shed, holding his breath, his heart pounding. An unexpected sight stopped him dead. Dozens of rabbits, dazzled by the sudden daylight, stared at him, their ears up. He realised that the ground was like a warren, full of holes and burrows. An involuntary movement of his arm provoked general panic. In an instant, the animals rushed into their underground refuges. He noticed a heap of half-eaten cabbages. He smiled. The mystery had definitely deepened. A house long abandoned and boarded up, and yet a human presence who set traps and raised rabbits! Was the same malicious mind behind both things, or was he dealing with two acts performed by two different people? He inclined towards the first of these possibilities. If some local inhabitant had decided to raise rabbits, he would surely have built hutches instead of this improvised warren. He summed up: the house was frequented by a person or persons unknown who, while doing their best to make it seem as though it was indeed abandoned, set traps, raised rabbits, and even fed them cabbage. This last detail struck him as significant. After the winter the kingdom had endured, cabbage was a highly expensive luxury. Why was so much money being spent for such a trivial purpose? He examined the turned-over earth, hoping to detect human traces on the soft soil. All he could see were some curious, even inexplicable prints. He turned to the left, where there was a door leading to another barn. Nothing there drew his attention. It in turn led, through a kind of corridor between two supporting walls, to a room directly adjoining the house.

The door to it was a heavy one. He picked the lock and entered. It slammed as it closed behind him. He opened it again and noted that it was slightly out of kilter, an effect accentuated by pieces of lead nailed to its perimeter. Yet another mystery, on the meaning of which he could only conjecture. Perhaps it was to stop the rabbits from getting into the house. Yet there was no way through. In comparison with the other rooms, this one seemed less dilapidated. It had pine panelling and a hearth with a brazier that had only recently been used. A pervasive smell tickled his nostrils. He lifted his candle for a closer look at the walls of the room. Facing the door, he found the explanation for this strange smell: there, on the panelling he saw, shining in the light, a large coal-black capital K over which a line had been drawn, and a green capital I. He held out his finger: the paint was still fresh! Someone had been here very recently – doubtless the same person whose presence he had already detected – to trace these mysterious signs. He had to find out how this person gained access to the house and, in order to do that, he would have to go through the whole place again. He was about to turn when he noticed some balls on the floor which took him back twenty-five years.

As a child, he would occasionally sleep in an isolated room high in one of the towers of the Château de Ranreuil. Several times, in the early hours of the morning, he had heard a heavy step pounding the floor of the attic above him. This irregular noise, which struck terror into him, suggested the presence of someone staggering and stamping, then silence would fall again, even more oppressive than the preceding manifestations. His nurse, Fine, to whom he had had the unfortunate idea of confiding his terror, had convinced him that a ghost wandered the upper reaches of the château.

'*Doue da bardon an Kraon!*' she had cried. 'God forgive the dead!'

Then, after making sure that Canon Le Floch was not in the vicinity, she suggested to Nicolas that, in case it happened again, he should utter nine times, without taking a breath, the sentence: '*Mar bez Satan, ra'z i pell en an Doue.*' 'Go away in the name of God if you are the devil.' The marquis, informed of this, nobody knew by whom, had lost his temper and, one morning, had taken his godson by the hand. They had gone up to the attic and, as dawn broke, a dark shape had appeared in one of the loopholes and jumped down onto the floor. Forbidden to scream, Nicolas had opened his eyes and recognised an eagle owl, which strutted solemnly before going over to a heap of branches, bones and castings and beginning to tidy it. The lesson had not been forgotten. From that day, the boy convinced himself never to judge by appearances alone. His father had belonged to that class of happy sceptics for whom only one criterion mattered: that based on reason and empirical examination. He dreaded above all those false minds ready to accept anything without analysing it. Quoting the hermit of Ferney,[1] he did not believe that, in order to 'pay court to the Supreme Being', it was necessary to chant, whip yourself, mutilate your flesh, run about stark naked, fast, or perform any one of a thousand other outrageous acts. Reason, for him, had to reject all forms of prejudice, which were obstacles in the way of progress. Only progress held the key to truth, he would tell Nicolas, with a lofty but amused air. That combination of qualities made an honest man. He respected the normal dogmas of religion as long as they went along with the most universally held beliefs. This influence survived in so far as Nicolas, whose simple faith was unshakable and part and parcel of his loyalty to himself, was nevertheless a child of his century, always looking beyond appearances. That this could give rise to contradictions, he knew and took into account.

The problem was that if the castings had come from an owl, of which there were many in the city, what were they doing in this closed room? He examined the hearth. Perhaps the bird had been nesting on the roof and the balls had fallen down the flue. Although not very satisfied with that explanation, he decided to accept it for the moment. All these isolated clues were multiplying and posing questions that were by no means easy to answer. A further tour of the house, from the cellar to the attic, yielded nothing. A persistent, almost sweet odour hovered here and there, which he could not define, but which was nevertheless familiar. Where could he have come across it before? He finally gave up, left the house and decided to place it as quickly as possible under the surveillance of a network of spies.

*

He returned to his carriage and rode back to the Grand Châtelet. On the way, he passed a few detachments of mounted musketeers. Order was being restored and arrests being carried out. Daylight was fading over a city so silent, it seemed to have been struck dumb after the day's events. He climbed the steps of the great staircase four at a time and sighed with delight when he saw that Bourdeau was already there. He immediately recounted his visit to Rue du Poirier. His account left the inspector intrigued, if puzzled.

'We're being deceived,' he said. 'It seems to me that someone is trying to lead our investigation astray.'

'Indeed! It could be that this whole display of clues, meaningless as it seems, is deliberately meant to mislead us and play on our lack of understanding. Its aim is either to draw us to the Hénéfiance house or drive us away from it. I already have an eye on the place, unfortunately a legless one ...'

Bourdeau laughed. 'You are making an enigma out of a mystery!'

'He's a crippled old soldier who has a cobbler's workshop not far from the house.'

232

'And you won this man over into working for us?'

'Dear Pierre, all you have to do is know how to listen. But we also need two spies keeping watch on the house. They can take turns, one by night, the other by day, until further orders.'

On a piece of paper, he drew a map of the street and the position of the Hénéfiance house.

'And you, *quid novi?*'

'La Babine gave me the name of Mourut's notary. She kicked up a bit of a fuss at first, pleading loyalty and discretion, but the animosity she feels towards her mistress and Caminet prevailed.'

'And what happened?'

'I went to see this Master Delamanche in Rue des Prouvaires, on the corner of Rue des Deux-Écus. Without any hesitation, he revealed some hidden aspects of this case that ought to be of great interest to you. Just imagine, the baker paid for Caminet's apprenticeship himself. That's nothing: he could have been doing that in secret for the son of a friend. But his will makes Caminet his sole heir, and in fact recognises him *de jure* as his natural son.'

Nicolas was silent for a moment, as if weighing up the full significance of this revelation. 'Did Caminet know?'

'Hard to say. Even the notary couldn't tell me.'

'Let's not jump to conclusions. This revelation suggests several things, some of which are contradictory. Even if the apprentice knew his origins, he would have to have been informed of the contents of the will and to know that he was the sole heir. Judging by Madame Mourut's misalliance, she came to the marriage with nothing, neither a dowry nor a *donatio propter nuptias*.'

'Mercy!' cried Bourdeau. 'Unlike some, I was never a notary's clerk in Rennes.'

'Forgive me, Pierre. I mean that there was no stipulation in the marriage contract that she could claim part of the inheritance in the event of her husband's death.'

'And therefore?'

'Therefore the lady can expect nothing and will find herself in the street, with no more than she had before. A prospect which, as I'm sure you can imagine, must be intolerable to someone so preoccupied with her standing.'

'But did she know?'

'That's the question! It's quite possible the two of them plotted the husband's death in order to enjoy his estate undisturbed. Is it large, by the way?'

'Larger than you might assume, certainly larger than you might suppose of a Parisian baker. This case is becoming ever more complicated, and now there's this business of the Hénéfiance house, which—'

'Not so fast! Let me stop you there. There's nothing yet to prove that there's a connection between the two things. It remains a subject for further investigation, especially as, if the money passes to the apprentice, the lady is saved.'

'There's another possibility,' said Bourdeau, slyly. 'Perhaps he wanted to kill the husband in the hope the wife would inherit. Judging by what people say about him, he wasn't likely to spend much longer in the bakehouse. He would have squandered his fortune soon enough. He's quite young and the lady's already a bit past it ...'

'All of which makes it an urgent priority to question Madame Mourut again. I was already planning to, and now I shall do so immediately. After which, let's meet back here to organise our entrenchments.'

Bourdeau smiled at this warlike vocabulary. It was not something that Nicolas had picked up as a notary's clerk in Rennes, but rather from his father the Marquis de Ranreuil, a great soldier.

In his carriage, Nicolas pondered this uninterrupted fight against crime that had kept him busy for so many years. The King's service had drawn him into missions that followed closely on each other's heels, some indeed immediately giving rise to others. He had been a frail cockleshell carried along by the waves. No normal everyday life, no rest, and other consequences, too. He thought of Louis, whom he had had the good luck to find, but whose childhood years he had missed completely. He closed his eyes and saw Aimée d'Arranet's face. Where was she?

Should he write to her? Would his message even reach her? A sense of futility overwhelmed him. But then emotion suddenly prevailed over the idea that he should give himself up to fate. Fate was something over which he had no control anyway, whereas happiness was something you could create for yourself day by day. Then, abandoning these thoughts, he returned to his concerns of the moment, reflecting on the best way to deal with Madame Mourut.

She looked up at him with an angry expression when he entered the room. She was dressed in black percale. Pale, without make-up, she looked her age.

'Monsieur, am I to be kept confined to my own home for much longer?'

'That's entirely up to you. If I am convinced that you are telling the truth, this constraint will be lifted immediately. If not ... I therefore advise you to yield and answer the questions I'm going to ask you.'

She looked at him closely, clearly trying to detect some hidden meaning in his words.

'Madame, let me lay my cards on the table, so that you can judge for yourself. I know where you spent the night of Sunday to Monday and who you spent it with. I even know the identity of the young man in question. If you should take it into your head to deny the evidence, I can immediately call a witness who's waiting in my carriage, wrapped in her fichu.'

He had often observed that an abundance of small details strengthened the impact of a statement.

She shrugged. 'What could you do to me?'

'I could arrest you on the spot, take you to the Châtelet and present you to the Criminal Lieutenant.'

'On what grounds, Monsieur?'

'Suspicion of murdering Master Mourut, your husband.'

'Monsieur, the last time I saw him, he was alive and well.'

'Eating his stew, no doubt?'

The blow hit home. She crossed her arms in a display of pride. 'Someone told me they saw him.'

'Who is that, Madame? Are you just telling me another lie?'

'That's all I can say.'

'It's not enough. Could it have been Denis, Denis Caminet, your young lover, who went down to fetch a bottle and came across a group of men, among whom he recognised his master?'

She gave a sharp little laugh. 'You don't understand.'

'You're quite mistaken, I can reconstruct perfectly well what happened. You weren't born to be a baker's wife. You had to get used to it. A young man appeared, he took an interest in you, you liked him. You resisted at first, then yielded. All perfectly ordinary, if immoral. What's a little out of the ordinary is killing the husband. That's going a bit far. Not to mention frequenting the house of someone like La Gourdan! What of decorum, Madame, what of—'

'Who are you talking about? I don't know the woman.'

He had the impression that she was telling the truth.

'What did you think the place where you met Caminet was exactly?'

'An inn, Monsieur. Quite well kept, in fact.'

'I see I shall have to enlighten you. The place is a brothel, run by La Gourdan, and not just any brothel, but the most prestigious in Paris.'

She burst into sobs. 'Denis didn't kill my husband, Commissioner. I'm going to tell you everything. When he went downstairs, he thought Monsieur Mourut recognised him. He came back upstairs in a panic. Then, when nothing happened, he calmed down a bit. He decided to leave Rue Montmartre, where the work was not to his liking. He would find a way to get by in Paris and as soon as things were going

236

better, he would get in touch with me. I gave him the jewels I was wearing that day to tide him over. We waited ...'

He handed her a handkerchief.

'... He decided to leave through the door in Rue des Deux-Ponts-Saint-Sauveur while I would go out the back way. I ran and found a cab and came back to Montmartre.'

'And since then, have you had any news of him?'

'How could I? Confined as I am here, with your henchmen at my door!'

'It's vital that we find him. His absence can only arouse further suspicion.'

He reflected, deliberately prolonging the moment.

'Madame, I'm going to give you back your freedom. On one condition: that you inform me if you hear anything, anything at all, from Caminet. If he shows himself, let me know. Are we agreed?'

'Yes, Commissioner.'

He left her and went to find La Babine. She proved incapable of telling him the exact time her mistress had returned home, having herself been away until the early hours of the morning. Given her animosity towards the baker's wife, he assumed she was telling the truth. He told her she was free to go anywhere she wanted, as long as she did not leave Paris. He found himself back out in the street, suddenly overcome with weariness. He was so tempted to return to the Noblecourt house to rest that he had to take himself in hand. He ran to his carriage in order not to give in to the temptation.

At the Grand Châtelet, a surprise awaited him. Semacgus, who had spent the day at the Jardin du Roi, comparing the collections of the herbarium there with his sketches from Vienna, had arrived eager for news after the events of the day. He had found Bourdeau and they had talked over the situation while waiting for Nicolas. He gave them a rapid account of his visit to Rue Montmartre.

'How was the lady?' asked the inspector.

'Madame Mourut talks a lot, keeps silent when it suits her, loves to argue and sometimes bites.'

'What a fine way to sum up a woman,' said Semacgus with a laugh.

'Do you think she's telling the truth?' said Bourdeau, intrigued.

'By and large, I think she told me something close to the truth. There are still of course some shadowy areas. It's work in progress. I'm not sure if she really knows what happened after her lover left her. I would observe that, by going out through the door leading to Rue des Deux-Ponts, he must have known there was a risk he would run into Mourut ... And if Mourut did recognise his apprentice – who was actually his son – he would surely have tried to wait for him. That's a lot of ifs and maybes ...'

'Master Mourut, said Bourdeau, 'died in his bakehouse. Are we to imagine a long conversation between the two of them, then a return to Rue Montmartre, followed by a poisoning, if that's the theory we are still accepting?'

'Given what we know of it,' said Semacgus, 'the poisoning could have been carried out in the street. But is it likely? It doesn't seem to me to hold up. It would suggest a great deal of preparation, as if it were all premeditated. But everything points to the fact that Caminet was surprised to see his master in La Gourdan's house. I don't think we can state anything for certain at the moment.'

'Guillaume's right,' said Nicolas. 'If that meeting wasn't a chance one, it suggests a logic rare in this kind of tragedy, which is usually much messier. Let's retrace our steps for the moment. Caminet leaves La Gourdan's house and runs straight into Mourut. *De facto*, Mourut doesn't know that the young man has just been with his wife. We assume a chance encounter. If it took place, what happened? If it didn't ...'

'If it didn't, we're in act five, scene three,' said Semacgus. 'We don't know the ending of the play.'

Nicolas fell silent, lost in thought. There were still pieces missing from this puzzle. The elements fitted too neatly, whatever the alternative chosen … Of course, they could force the various hypotheses in one direction rather than another, but there was simply not enough evidence to do so at the moment.

Semacgus had leant forward towards Nicolas's legs, his two hands on his knees.

'Old pains, Guillaume? I didn't know you needed a stick.'

'Not at all! Although it is sometimes hard to keep standing for too long. No, I was admiring the shine on your boots and—'

'What a strange thing to admire! I'm proud to say that it was one of Chevert's glorious soldiers who, out of friendship for me, made them shine so brilliantly as to dazzle you.'

Puffing a little, Semacgus got down on his knees and seized the instep of the commissioner's right boot. He put on his spectacles, which, out of vanity, he rarely used.

'This must be serious,' said Bourdeau sardonically. 'Our man is getting his lenses out!'

'You may laugh,' said Semacgus. 'I need them in my botanical work. You'll see when you're my age, or rather, you won't see anything at all. As a matter of fact, I see very well from a distance.'

He fell silent and collected a small particle that resembled a piece of a human nail.

'Was the work slapdash? Is there still some mud?'

Semacgus did not reply and carefully examined his find.

'Is he going to speak,' cried Bourdeau happily, 'or will we have to tear the words from his mouth? Let's fetch Sanson!'

'I am concentrating on the circumstantial, although as yet unable to extricate myself from the predicament in which I find myself.'

'Good Lord,' continued the inspector, 'Monsieur de Noblecourt has acquired a following! Semacgus is making pronouncements!'

'You may mock,' said Semacgus. 'We shall talk further of this.'

Carefully, he put the fragment inside a huge handkerchief, knotted the four corners and stuffed it deep into one of his coat pockets.

'Just one question, Nicolas, before you leave me free to elucidate this point. Did this soldier of yours really clean your boots?'

'With all the love and care of a job extremely well done. He brushed, scraped, waxed, polished and shone, and finally brushed again. Including the spurs.'

'And then, as Bourdeau here told me, you searched the Hénéfiance house.'

'That's correct, after walking in the street.'

'Thank you, that's all I wanted to know. I won't say anything more today.'

'All of a sudden, he's a man of few words!' said Bourdeau.

'Now then, gentlemen,' said Nicolas. 'Let's take this seriously. I think the time has come to question our two baker's boys. I hope their stay in solitary confinement has worn down their resistance. I remain convinced that they know more than they are willing to admit.'

Bourdeau looked at his watch. 'Let's pay them a visit, after which you will be my guests in our usual tavern.'

Semacgus was the first to accept the offer, which he did eagerly. Nicolas remembered that his son was waiting for him. But the evening was already well advanced and he would be back quite late even if he refused the inspector's offer. In addition, he would still have to take stock after the interrogation. Louis must be exhausted and would fall asleep early. They walked downstairs into the part of the old fortress that served as a prison.

'Let's begin with the younger of the two,' suggested Bourdeau.

He ordered the gaoler to give him a lantern and have them taken to the cells by one of his gatekeepers. Night had fallen and the prison was plunged in total darkness. The gatekeeper went in front of them, his keys clanging against the wall. In a loud, sneering voice, he expressed his surprise that anyone should be paying for these two rascals to be well treated. You had to be mad to throw good money out of the window like that, at a time when the price of bread kept rising. Nicolas told him, curtly, to be quiet and take them to the cells without comment. The man paid no attention and started doing his sums.

'Oh, I know it's easy when you have someone protecting you. They've been here two days already. A room with a bed, that costs five *sols* a day, in other words ten *sols*. And would you believe it, the sheets are changed every three weeks? As for food, you have to reckon with a *livre* and four *sols* a day. That's terrible, when you think that a labourer barely earns a *livre* for a working day. Some people are so lucky, you feel like swapping places with them.'

'If you don't shut your mouth,' cried Bourdeau, 'it's your own place you'll lose. And don't get any ideas about mistreating them, we'd find out immediately.'

The man muttered and fell silent. They had come to the massive door of a ground-floor cell. The key made a scraping sound as it turned in the lock. The gatekeeper kicked the door open, took a step forward and raised his lantern. A ray of dancing light illumined the emptiness and came to rest on the bed. At first, all they could see was an indistinct, huddled shape, motionless beneath the sheets. Nicolas's nostrils were intrigued by an unpleasant smell he knew well, at once sickly and metallic. He suddenly felt a cold sweat break out all over his body. He sensed that something terrible was happening. It was in a dungeon not far from this one that an old soldier had hanged himself. Whatever the horrible crime of which he was guilty, the memory of that man still filled Nicolas with remorse. An anxious silence fell over the group. There was no sound but their breathing.

'The little devil's already asleep,' said the gatekeeper hesitantly.

Semacgus threw a glance at Nicolas, who immediately realised that his anxiety was shared.

'Everyone move back,' he ordered. 'Dr Semacgus will wake the witness.'

The surgeon approached the narrow bed. With delicate gestures he pulled back the blanket, which slid off without resistance. Nicolas moved the lantern closer. The sheet fell and revealed a pitiful sight. Rolled up into a ball and apparently lifeless, Friope lay on the bed, which was covered in blood. Semacgus seized his frail wrist, took a small mirror from his pocket and held it in front of the young man's mouth. This moment seemed like a century to Nicolas, who could see only the surgeon's vast back as he bustled about. He threw behind him some narrow strips of bloodstained cloth. His grave voice rose.

'Gatekeeper, run and fetch the local doctor immediately.'

Next, turning to Nicolas, he shook his head, compassion writ large on his broad face.

'Nicolas, your witness is safe, although much weakened.'

'Did he try to—?'

'No, not at all. It's something more surprising than that: your baker's boy ... What's his name, by the way?'

'Friope, Anne Friope.'

'Anne! All is explained.'

'Guillaume, your words are increasingly confused.'

'The fact is, your baker's boy isn't a boy, but a girl, yes, a girl!'

'A girl?'

'Quite well developed, too! So much so that she was two or three months pregnant. She's just had a miscarriage, but although she's lost a lot of blood, I think she'll pull through. Bourdeau, can you fetch some hot water, bandages and shredded linen, a clean sheet, and a blanket that's warmer than this awful threadbare drugget.'

'That explains a lot of things,' said Nicolas, 'and also complicates them even more.'

A noise was heard. A man entered the cell, led by the gatekeeper, who, tantalised by what had happened, tried to move closer to revel in the spectacle: he was pushed away by the commissioner. Raising his eyes to the newcomer, he recognised the thin face and gentle, ironic eyes of Dr de Gévigland.[2]

'Monsieur, what a surprise to see you here!'

'My dear friend!' cried the doctor. 'You know my field of research. I managed to get a job as a king's doctor at the Châtelet as a supernumerary to Monsieur de la Rivière and Monsieur Le Clerc. They gladly let me take on more than my share, which is why you see me here this evening.'

'You already know Inspector Bourdeau. Let me introduce a friend, Dr Guillaume Semacgus, navy surgeon. We take full advantage of his great experience during our investigations.'

'Doctor is pitching it a little high,' said Semacgus. 'I wouldn't like to justify any unfavourable judgement on the body to which I once belonged.'

'I have the greatest respect for that body. Would you by any chance be the expert on exotic plants, the well-known botanist whose praises are sung by Monsieur de Jussieu?'

'I am indeed he, Monsieur, at your service. But time is passing. What we have here is a miscarriage. In a word, this young woman was passing herself off as a man. Her breasts were bandaged to hold them in and the rest in keeping.'

He gathered the strip of cloth which had intrigued Nicolas. A weak groan was heard. Nicolas and Bourdeau stepped aside to leave the prisoner in the hands of the practitioners. The water and blanket were brought by the gaoler, who was aghast at these events. After a while, Semacgus and Gévigland reappeared.

'From our mutual observations, it appears,' said Gévigland, 'that the prisoner is indeed female. Her weak constitution, her age, and no doubt also the fear and distress she felt at being incarcerated, led to this accident. To protect her unborn child, she should not have indulged in any strong physical activity. Her work at the bakery was fatal to her. She now needs to be kept quiet and rested.'

'Yes,' said Semacgus. 'Light food and liquids, groats, bread soup, and thin drinks. Later, a few glasses of good wine.'

Nicolas was about to speak, but his friend anticipated him.

'Questioning her is out of the question for the moment. Monsieur de Gévigland has offered to keep an eye on the patient tonight in order to avoid any concomitant fever that might endanger her life.'

They still had Parnaux to question. His cell was around the corner of the same gallery. They found him sitting on his bunk, his head in his hands. He started in panic when the three men came in and looked at them anxiously. He was shaking, certainly with cold, but also perhaps with apprehension at what was to follow.

'My friend,' began Nicolas, gently, 'I must tell you that we have made progress with our investigation, and that we are now in possession of information which casts serious doubt on your initial testimony. As a result, Friope and you are suspected of—'

The young man sat up in alarm. 'Friope has nothing to do with any of this. As for me, my conscience is clear. I'm not guilty of anything. All I did was follow Caminet the other night. You must believe me, Monsieur Nicolas.'

He stopped, overwhelmed.

'Now, there's a good reaction we will certainly take into consideration! Let's take a closer look at what you have to say. You claim you followed Caminet. At what time was this?'

'About half past eight in the evening. He went out on foot. I trailed him as far as Rue des Deux-Ponts-Saint-Sauveur. There, he entered a courtyard and disappeared. I waited. Half an hour later, a cab stopped at the end of the street. Madame Mourut got out and followed the same route as Caminet.'

'Good. Did you see any other visitors?'

'Several, arriving in fits and starts. Some officers out for a good time, then a group of men who stopped outside the house in three carriages. They went in through the door giving onto the street.'

'Did you recognise anyone among them?'

'No, the carriages blocked my view.'

'Did you continue waiting?'

'Yes, until half past midnight.'

'How can you be so certain of the time?' asked Bourdeau.

'I have an old watch of my father's. It was taken away from me when I was brought here.'

'Don't worry, you'll get it back. Carry on.'

'The group of men came out again. I recognised the master among them. He didn't get into a carriage. He seemed to hesitate.'

'Master Mourut?'

'Yes, that's right. He stayed there for a long time, alone, without moving. Yes, a full quarter of an hour before the rain ... well, by the time it started raining, everything was over. Just then, when the other one appeared—'

'Who?'

'Caminet! A violent quarrel arose between them. The master tried to drag him away, but the other defended himself tooth and nail. In the end, Caminet fell and his head hit a bollard. He stopped moving and the master put his head in his hand and moaned. He was moving it from side to side, as if saying no. Then a third man intervened. He seemed to know the master. He bent over the body, stood up again and took Mourut by the arm. In spite of his resistance, they left together. In a cab. I heard it moving off. I went back to our lodgings. Friope didn't know anything about it, he was sleeping, the poor thing. I hid it from him.'

'At what hour was all this?'

'Before one o'clock, I think.'

'That's a very detailed account. The fact remains that you didn't think of helping Caminet. Didn't you even go to him?'

He burst into tears, like a child caught doing something naughty. 'I was too afraid. I feared that I would get the blame for it all. There

245

were a lot of reasons why that might have happened. In fact, you're proving that. You think I had something to do with it, don't you?'

'You must admit there are a number of things in your story that might make us think that. What was the meaning of your behaviour? Why were you spying on Caminet? What was your intention?'

He looked from one to another, hugging himself as if trying to keep a secret safe inside him. 'He was threatening us, Friope and me ...'

Nicolas saw fit to help him. 'You're still hiding something from us, the original cause of all this. It's in your own interest, and in Friope's, to trust us. So, still nothing? In that case, I'm going to tell you what the King's police, who do not crush the innocent, but hunt down the guilty, would be entitled to think.'

Parnaux lifted his head and listened to the commissioner with feverish attention. The trap Nicolas had set him was only intended to test his honesty.

'This is what we assume. Friope and you resented Caminet's mockery. And what was the reason for this constant contempt? Did he suspect that the two of you had one of those shameful friendships which, if it had been exposed, could have put you in great danger? So, with your backs to the wall and nowhere to turn, you decided to take action. You knew the master was exasperated by his behaviour. So you collected rumours, gossip. You wanted to be sure, to have proof, to meet blackmail with blackmail. Isn't that it?'

'Yes, Monsieur Nicolas,' replied Parnaux with an eagerness which would have deceived the most hardened of police officers, but in which Nicolas saw nothing but relief. 'I admit all that.'

'Alas, the value of your chivalrous confessions won't gain you any privilege or leniency in the present situation. You're still trying to deceive the law by concealing something basic. Who is Friope?'

'What do you mean? He's my workmate.'

'No! We all know that Anne Friope is a girl and, moreover, pregnant.

She has just lost her child. Yours, I assume? Don't worry, her life isn't in danger. I'm sorry to have to tell you this news so abruptly, but your lack of openness has forced my hand. Deceivers like you always rely on the gullibility of those they exploit. That is to show contempt for the march of truth.'

Head bowed, Parnaux was weeping again.

'I await your explanation.'

'It's true. We took a lot of precautions. But there was always the moment when we changed into our work clothes. Caminet, who was always late, arrived one day without warning and saw Friope. He threatened to expose us, unless ...'

'Unless?'

'... she yielded to him. We resisted as long as we could. Last Saturday, he gave us an ultimatum. It was then that, in my desperation, I decided to follow him. That's God's honest truth!'

'But that doesn't explain why Friope disguised herself as a boy.'

'We had met by chance and it was the only way we could find to be together. The name helped, especially as Anne had no contract ... Master Mourut accepted the idea, it was less expensive for him.'

'And more risky!' said Bourdeau. 'He must have been in good favour with his guild to allow himself such liberties!'

'We weren't harming anyone. Anne did her job as well as anyone else – better than Caminet, for example. Can I see her?'

'Later. She's in good hands and is being well looked after. Is that all you have to tell us?'

'Help us, Monsieur Nicolas!'

'I'd like to. If only you'd asked my advice before! Well, we'll see.'

After the gatekeeper had closed the cell door, they left the prison in silence. Bourdeau and Semacgus waited while Nicolas stopped for a moment to write in his black notebook. Then they walked through the rainy night to the nearby tavern in Rue du Pied-de-Bœuf. The host greeted them joyfully and, without even asking them, brought a pitcher of their favourite wine.

'What do you suggest this evening, countryman?' Bourdeau said.

'Alas, with the day we've had, no customers, no dishes. I've been preparing, though, a steamed shoulder of veal to be served cold in its jelly tomorrow. I'm happy to serve it to you now, nice and hot. It's been cooking with its bones, some strips of bacon, a little tarragon vinegar, carrots, onions and plenty of spices. The clay casserole has been sizzling away in the oven for three hours. I just have to reduce the sauce and it's ready to serve.'

'There's an account that makes the mouth water,' said Semacgus. 'And while we wait for you to reduce the sauce, what is there for us to nibble on?'

'A dish I was keeping for myself, but which I shall give up in your honour and in that of my countryman here.'

'And what is this dish?'

'Soft roe and herring eggs, my own recipe.'

'Good,' said Nicolas. 'Now that we've concluded this important negotiation, I await your counsel, like King Arthur at his table.'

'It's strange,' remarked Semacgus. 'Hardened as I am by the years, Parnaux's statement seemed quite convincing to me.'

'Although Nicolas did have to drive him into a corner. In my opinion, his honesty had to be dragged out of him little by little.'

'Bourdeau's right, but fear is a bad counsellor. We may see it that way because we knew the answers to the questions we were asking. What mattered most to him was protecting Friope. But let's not jump straight in to accepting what he was telling us. There are plenty of details, but the crucial part is still missing ...'

'And,' Bourdeau went on, 'based only on his statement, without any other witness to confirm it, we're asked to accept a quarrel, a struggle, a third man, a flight, a lifeless body. And to crown it all, Caminet nowhere to be found, dead or alive. Plus a baker who died in such strange circumstances that there's nothing to indicate for certain that he was murdered, or if he was, exactly how! Not to mention a false baker's boy, a clandestine couple, a miscarriage, along with a bit of mutual blackmail and what ensued!'

A long silence greeted this vehement speech.

'Our doubts are centuries, our uncertainties are gone in a flash,' murmured Semacgus after a while.

'An investigation is like a ladder, the wise man should stay in the middle,' concluded Nicolas.

Bourdeau was looking at them, dazed.

'It's the homage of your peers to such a fine flight of oratory!'

They all burst out laughing, only to be interrupted by the triumphant arrival of the eggs and the soft roe arranged on slices of toasted bread and topped with a steaming, fragrant sauce. The three men immediately fell on them greedily. The host explained that, to avoid them splitting, especially the eggs, he cooked them in a lot of butter at a carefully calculated heat. Everything depended on the speed: you had to be careful not to sear them or overcook them. You threw in some sliced shallots to give them colour and taste. Next, you had to mix a spoonful of good mustard, a pinch of brown sugar and a squirt of dry white wine in a bowl. Once this was well combined, you had to throw it in the pan as quickly as possible, not stinting on the pepper and parsley.

'And why not poach them first?' asked Semacgus.

'It's all because of the seasoning. It sets better and the difference between the surface and the inside doubles the pleasure.'

'We, too,' said Nicolas, resuming the interrupted discussion, 'must make the various ingredients hang together, as I often say ...' He filled their glasses. 'There are some things we know for certain. Almost all the protagonists in the case were at La Gourdan's, except Friope.'

'There's nothing to prove that she wasn't,' said Bourdeau.

'That's true! As for Caminet, if he was killed on the way out of the brothel, then logically he can't have been involved in his master's murder, if murder it was. Madame Mourut, on the other hand, was at liberty to do whatever she wanted, unchecked, from the time she returned from Rue des Deux-Ponts until her husband's body was discovered. Not to mention La Babine ... But there's no reason for her to bear a grudge against her master and, besides, she has an alibi. The chronology of these events is becoming somewhat confused in my mind. Pierre, this is something you excel at. I'd like you to draw up a chart of the activities of all the suspects, hour by hour, from Sunday evening until the discovery of Monsieur Mourut's body on Monday morning.'

'Yes, I will. It will be very useful to determine any links there may be between the crime or crimes and the intrigues at La Gourdan's on the subject of flour. We mustn't procrastinate. Everything seems to point to the fact that Mourut was involved in the monopoly in some way, and may even have been an active member of a society whose main aim was to control the grain market. What conclusion are we to draw from that?'

The tavern keeper brought in three plates filled to the brim. The veal was so tender that the meat shook like jelly. There was another pause.

'What if,' resumed Semacgus, 'the evidence of domestic dramas within the Mourut house is blinding us? Your investigation may be getting diverted, obscuring the true reason for this tragedy. There are too many deceptive ingredients here, leading us astray. It seems to me, my brave knights, and you, Sir Lancelot, that if we knew more about the way Master Mourut died – and, trust me, I am doing the best I can to discover it – there would no doubt be matter there for new hypotheses.'

'If what you suggest is correct, Guillaume, it means that we can't dissociate the two cases. There may be a connection that escapes us between all this and the unexplained aspects of our trip to Vienna.'

'Not to mention,' said Bourdeau, 'the curious intrigue of which Louis was the innocent victim.'

Semacgus gave them a lift in his carriage, which had come to the narrow Rue du Pied-de-Bœuf at the appointed time. Nicolas found the house silent. He went up to the third floor, where he discovered his son asleep, with Mouchette at his feet. He sat down in an armchair, thought for a moment about the march of time before giving in to exhaustion. In the morning, Louis found his father asleep by his bedside.

IX

VINCENNES

Can anyone be proved innocent,
if it is enough to have accused him?

JULIAN THE APOSTATE

Thursday 4 May 1775

Rested – although his limbs ached from his night in the armchair – washed and shaved, and with his hair brushed, Nicolas went downstairs to Monsieur de Noblecourt's apartment, where he came upon a charming scene. His host, in his usual morning garb of madras and scarves, was talking to Louis, who was sitting opposite him in the place normally occupied by his father during their dawn conversations. The commissioner leant against the doorpost, allowing himself a little respite to listen to what they had to say.

'You have to understand, my boy, that appearance is essential. If the appearance you present to those who observe you does not correspond to polite custom, they will be sure to condemn your shortcomings. The attitude you adopt to avoid the pitfalls and appear harmonious and polite must not seem studied or learnt. It should come naturally from your temperament, the secret spirit that results from your inner union. Do you understand?'

'Of course, Monsieur. But I also need to know what should be avoided, as well as the practical rules that form the basis of an honest man's reputation.'

'Your father and I, and all our friends, are here to show you the way. I think particularly of Monsieur de La Borde, who is so familiar with the ways of the Court. Let's begin at the beginning. Your mind and body should always be in agreement, so that everything develops in harmony. Just as a face is more pleasant when there is a symmetry of the features, always look for balance, above all in the manner of expressing yourself. Aim not for effect, but for the most natural utterance, unmarred by any ostentation, any raising of the voice that would be disturbing to the ear and destructive of the effect of the words. But don't worry, you have that tone as your birthright. You will have to take care not to exaggerate it, which would make you fall into affectation and pedantry.'

'I will make sure, Monsieur, that it is as it should be.'

'Be sure to avoid priggishness! Don't fall into that fashionable malady, mockery. Never think that it's necessary in society to make spiteful remarks or offensive insinuations. Some will tell you that it is in this way that one acquires the wit and language of those circles. But remember, any praise you will attract by taking that path would rebound against you and lead eventually to your being ridiculed in your turn. Never hurt anyone in that manner. That's the behaviour of a coward. Your victim won't always understand your words, but if he does you may find yourself with a duel on your hands. There are enough opportunities to risk your life over serious matters. But then I think you know what I'm saying. Didn't I hear something about compasses?'

Louis bowed his head and smiled. 'Are you mocking me, Monsieur?'

'No,' replied Noblecourt, choking with laughter, 'just using a little affectionate irony! This harmony I advocate should equally be applied to your appearance. Consider your father. From the Marquis de Ranreuil he has inherited that presence that everyone envies him. Keep your head straight, and make sure your limbs are symmetrical. Physical ease is also the mark of an honest, well-tempered soul. Nor is it seemly to put both your hands in your pockets, or behind your back:

it's coarse and would make you look like a porter.'

'These are principles worth pondering,' said Nicolas, abruptly stepping forward.

Louis stood up and yielded his place to him. His father reported to Noblecourt the events and discoveries of the previous day. He leafed through his black notebook with such a pensive air that the former magistrate became anxious.

'To see you, one might say that you have come straight from the lair of Trophonios.'

'Monsieur,' asked Louis, 'who is this Trophonios?'

'Well,' said Noblecourt, delighted with the question, 'the oracle of the Boeotian Trophonios was located in a tomb-like cave. Anyone who ventured to consult him came out burdened by sad thoughts, with gloom in their eyes and unsteady steps.'

Nicolas described the strange inscriptions on the walls of the Hénéfiance house. Somewhat to Noblecourt's annoyance, Louis was stamping his feet with impatience.

'If you'll allow me, Father, it's child's play to understand what was meant. At Juilly, everyone was very familiar with that kind of thing!'

'Good Lord! I didn't think that the education dispensed by the Oratorians was so broad! Go on.'

'Don't take it badly, but your reading is not correct. It isn't about a line through the K and an I painted in green, but … Did you make a drawing of the letters?'

Nicolas showed him his little black book, open on the sketches in question.

'It's as I thought,' said Louis after a moment's examination. 'You need to take it a different way entirely. The K with a line through it is a *K barré*, a *cabaret* or tavern. The green capital I is a *grand I vert*, or Grand Hiver.'

'A tavern called the Grand Hiver!' cried Nicolas in surprise. 'I don't know anywhere of that name.'

'He takes after his grandfather and father,' said Noblecourt to Cyrus, who was wagging his tail under the table.

'And what do those three points or dots you've drawn above it mean?'

Nicolas had somewhat forgotten this detail. 'I think they refer to a watchword I heard in the crowd of rioters on the road from Versailles to Paris.' He thought for a moment. 'No, in fact, it was something reported to me ... by Bourdeau, I think. Something a rider said to the crowd, at Vaugirard. I'm not sure yet what all this means. A watchword there, but in this case? Perhaps a signature, a means of recognising or authenticating the message. I really have no idea.'

'Could it be,' asked Noblecourt, 'that these clues were put there specially for you? Or for someone else, whose identity we don't know?'

'Both hypotheses seem equally uncertain.'

'Louis,' said Noblecourt, much to Nicolas's surprise, 'please leave us, I need to speak to your father.'

After Louis had left the room, Noblecourt paused for a moment, apparently meditating, then took a deep breath and looked Nicolas in the eyes.

'It falls to me to talk to you about Louis's future. Oh, I know I have no right to—'

Nicolas raised his hand in protest.

'No, none at all,' Noblecourt continued, 'except the privilege of age and friendship. Last night I spoke for a long time to Louis. Whatever the circles he was close to in his childhood, it has to be acknowledged that his mother and his own nature have protected him from the worst. Vice has slid off him like water off a duck's back. Good blood cannot lie, and here he is, aspiring to serve the King as a soldier. You suspected that he might, so I'm not teaching you anything. I assume such a wish does not upset you?'

'You assume correctly.'

'We still have to determine how to grant it in the best possible conditions. Late last night, I had an unexpected visit from the Maréchal de Richelieu. You know how he loves to appear unannounced like that. It wasn't me he had come to see. He had received a letter from your sister Isabelle …'

'My sister!' said Nicolas in astonishment.

'Yes, Sister Agnès de la Miséricorde, a nun at Fontevrault. Richelieu was fond of your father the marquis, but then of course he knows everybody! I admire Mademoiselle de Ranreuil's savoir-faire. In her missive she informs the maréchal that she has given up her title and that Nicolas, known as Le Floch, is now the Marquis de Ranreuil and head of the house. She seeks for her nephew Louis a place among the pages in the Grand Stable, who, as you know, are under the authority of the First Gentleman of the Bedchamber and the Grand Equerry. It was as First Gentleman that Richelieu came to question me. You can imagine what I told him.'

'But my birth and my son's birth—'

'A plague on your modesty! I know of course that the school for pages is reserved for those of the highest birth, who come from families ennobled before 1550. But fortunately your sister thinks of everything. She had enclosed with her letter a long statement filled with extracts from the charter of the Ranreuils. Your ancestor Arnaud, it appears, accompanied the constable Du Guesclin on his expedition against Peter the Cruel, King of Aragon. Last but not least – and I have been hesitating as to whether to mention this – it seems that Richelieu is in possession of some mysterious information about your mother, who also, it seems, came from an ancient line!'

A strange emotion seized hold of Nicolas, and yet the face that imposed itself was that of Canon Le Floch. The man who had loved, protected, fed and cared for him. Sensing his disquiet, Noblecourt hastened to continue.

'The maréchal, out of favour and fearing that he would be repulsed, was able, thanks to his old accomplice Maurepas, to approach the King, who, although reluctant at first, agreed to everything when your name was brought up and he found out that you were unaware of these moves. I will only add that the services the pages perform for the King and the aristocracy give them a great boost for their future careers.'

'It's said, though, that, under Monsieur le Grand and Monsieur le Premier, their education is somewhat neglected in favour of horsemanship, the use of arms and the study of social usage.'

'It will be up to us to remedy that. I have already started, as you know.'

'And you give me even more reason to be grateful to you, if that were possible.'

'Let's talk no more about it! As for the fees, they will be much easier for you to bear than those of the school at Juilly. True, it will be up to you to provide the boy with clothes and equipment. The pages of the Grand Stable not only attend the King when he returns from the hunt and lead him to the chapel, but hold his stirrups straight when he mounts his horse. They precede the princesses or carry the tails of their dresses and walk beside their carriages. During the hunt, as you have seen many times, they are present all the way through, changing and loading the rifles, collecting the game killed and keeping count of it. They are used as errand boys and, in times of war, they assist the King's aides-de-camp. Last but not least, any page leaving after three or four years has the right and privilege to choose a second lieutenancy in a corps of the army.'

'Do you think that Louis will submit to the discipline this work demands? The pages' noviciate is harsh and newcomers are ruled with a rod of iron by the older boys. Total obedience is the first of the qualities required.'

'Any choice involves an element of risk. But don't worry, Richelieu assures me that things are not as severe as they used to be and that no page has ever joined a regiment without being well liked by everyone. And as everyone will find out very quickly that the maréchal has his eye on the boy, whom in fact he intends to house in Versailles,[1] nobody will dare to pick a quarrel with your son.'

'But no preferential treatment, please!'

'As for the clothes, it's the King's livery with a blue coat and crimson and white silk braid, then for riding a waistcoat and red breeches with gold braid, and at the hunt a small blue twill waistcoat and hide gaiters. Louis will look magnificent!'

Noblecourt noticed a kind of anxiety on Nicolas's face.

'I know what's troubling you. But look at yourself. Remember what trials and snubs you endured when you first arrived in Paris. The highly honourable prospect facing Louis is an infinitely easier and more favourable entrée than yours was. To be frank, he will either assert himself or fail. There is nothing to guarantee that his birth won't be flung in his face, but, supported as he will be by a famous name, as well as being descended from a family devoted to the King's service, the odds are in his favour. It will not be up to you, Nicolas; his own character will decide. Think about it and give me your answer. Richelieu is waiting. Talk to Louis once your inner court has reached a verdict!'

Nicolas thanked Noblecourt and left Rue Montmartre on foot. His head was whirling, and he forced himself to empty his mind. The Paris he loved so much was bustling around him, offering a thousand distractions to the informed observer. But his anxieties had filled him with gloom, and he saw in this spectacle only what was sad and disturbing. There, outside Saint-Eustache, he pitied the unfortunate women with heavy baskets on their backs, their faces almost blood-red from their efforts, breathing heavily like a blacksmith's bellows. Was it his grim mood? It seemed to him that he passed only filthy, half-naked creatures, debased by poverty and without any sense of who or what they were. There were porters labouring under enormous burdens, and for the first time he saw them differently, struck by their destitution. Their extremities were so distended that all the blood moved into the upper parts of their bodies, causing great bulging varicose veins. The constant forward thrust of the body often caused a twisting of the vertebra and left many of them hunchbacked. The city had returned to normal, its peace secured by the many mounted patrols. Sentries were keeping guard outside the bakeries.

At police headquarters, the old major-domo seemed so overcome with grief that Nicolas could get nothing from him. He discovered Monsieur Lenoir in shirt and breeches, filling trunks with files amid a cloud of dust. He gave a weak smile when he saw Nicolas.

'It's so very much like you to come and pay your respects to a poor wretch in disgrace. Oh, but I see from your expression that you are not aware of the latest news. This morning, I received a package from Monsieur de La Vrillière containing two letters, one from the King, the other from the comptroller general, both informing me of my dismissal!'

'Your dismissal, Monseigneur?'

'My immediate dismissal! Apparently, because of its lack of action, the police contributed to what happened. I was badly served ... We were not up to the demands of the situation ... Turgot doesn't know everything.'

Was it that the police had acted badly, Nicolas wondered, or that Lenoir had been attacked at Court?

'The King's letter was sufficiently curt to remove any remaining illusion. It has left me very disappointed.'

He took from his cuff a small piece of paper, which he began to read in a distressed tone.

'*Monsieur Lenoir, as your way of thinking does not accord with the stand I have chosen, I ask you to send me your resignation ...* That's how it is.[2] Two armies are to be created, one inside Paris, under the command of the Maréchal de Biron, and the other outside, under the

259

Marquis de Poyanne. The troops now have orders to open fire … The provost's court will deal without delay with those who have been arrested. But I still say that there were few popular uprisings in Paris while the old ordinances were observed.'

He had collapsed into an armchair.

'Well, fate certainly teaches us some valuable lessons. When the King died, you were removed from the police force through my unjust prejudice against you. That was my fault then and a source of remorse to me now.'

'Monseigneur, please believe me, I—'

'No, no, it must be admitted, however lenient you are. It does you honour and gives me some comfort. You see me confounded. How is one to harden oneself against such reversals of fortune? The soul may be swayed, but it has to believe that nothing is ever written in stone. In the meantime, take the thing as a kind of relief, the harness at last thrown off. Blessed be he who dismisses you and gives you back to yourself, your family, your friends, among whom I count you …'

'I did not dare say so, Monseigneur.'

'Loyalty like yours is rare these days. Defeat allows us to see such things more clearly. Man is a machine with many motives: self-interest, vanity and a thousand other things. Divine and human philosophies may create some harmony between them. Misfortune disturbs this harmony and submerges our whole being, insulting its misery. Oh, one should remain inured to all that.'

A string of increasingly incoherent remarks followed, then he raised his head with a kind of defiance.

'I have nothing with which to reproach myself, and I'm not even exiled. Besides, being sent to some obscure spot in the country is nothing when you carry the truth in your saddlebags. In this case, I didn't receive any instructions. The important thing was to avoid an explosion and not fire on the people. I've always thought that with absolute moderation, a concern for leniency, a well-reasoned impassivity, the anger of the people faded by itself. The trick is to leave them with just that degree of anger and effrontery that satisfies their nature without their being led into excesses detrimental to authority. I observe that, with a few exceptions who, I fear, will be used as an example for the others, most of those who were arrested last night were from a higher stratum of society. Well-dressed men of all ages, all curled and powdered, who didn't seem to show the effects of poverty. Who, then, had urged them to this adventure?'

'You think that—'

'I fear you have not been sufficiently listened to, and that there is some plot behind these events. My departure is a move in a billiard game: I'm an unimportant ball, but they've touched me in order to hit Sartine, who has never concealed his reservations concerning the free trade in grain. They're going in for the kill now, you'll see. Turgot and his fellow physiocrats will try to move forward and overtake their opponents. I don't claim that reform is impossible, only that it's being imposed in the worst way imaginable. They can't see the wood for the trees. But who cares? The comptroller will serve his term and then we will reappear. The people will soon scorn him. He and his small band of dogmatists think they are winning, but it won't last.'

'Monseigneur, I feel obliged to give you an account of my investigation. You will immediately grasp the interest of it. At the same time, I would like to take advantage of your instruction and counsel.'

'You can count on my counsel. As for instruction, you will have to get that from Albert, my appointed successor.'

'Albert?'

'Yes, another of these extreme economists! Just think, the intendant to the trade having under his control the department dealing with grain! It's a blunder of major proportions. How can one appoint to the police, the day after a riot against the monopoly in grain and the high price of bread, the official responsible for the preservation and circulation of these essential commodities? A tiresome, cantankerous individual, to boot! His study of canon law has made him as pernickety as he is arrogant. In this post, a delicate one, as I know only too well, you will have to serve a tactless, slow, heavy and bad-tempered professor. Your position at Court should protect you from his snubs, but you'll still have to deal with his specious quibbling and splitting of hairs! Now then, where are you with your case?'

Nicolas launched into a detailed account of the ups and downs of his investigation. He tried to show how his enquiries into the presumed murder in Rue Montmartre kept coming up against the question of the trade in grain. Although nothing had yet been firmly established, everything pointed to the likelihood that the baker's death was somehow connected to the mysterious meeting held at La Gourdan's brothel, in which the victim had taken part. Apart from that, Mourut's immediate circle was extremely suspicious and there was nothing to rule out the possibility that the guilty party was to be found there.

His head sunk in his collar, Lenoir seemed to have dropped off to sleep, but his right hand, drumming on the surface of the desk, revealed that he was thinking hard. He was about to speak, changed his mind, then finally motioned Nicolas to come closer. He began speaking in a low voice.

'I'm sure you recall last year's scandalous royal almanac. For the first time, it mentioned a man named Mirlavaud,[3] the King's treasurer for grain.'

'That curious reference persuaded the most credulous that there was a famine pact from which the late King profited in order to meet the expenses of Madame du Barry.'

'Not only Madame du Barry, but many others, it was said. There were even songs written about it. A heinous slander, which made it all the more credible. The rumour started in 1765 when Laverdy, who was then the comptroller general, signed a contract with a rich miller named Malisset. The plan was simple: a certain amount of grain was to be set aside to balance the market and avoid shortages. When the price of grain went above a certain level, the State would sell and replenish the stocks, and Malisset would receive a two per cent commission. It was at this point that a fanatic named Le Prévôt de Beaumont, who was the secretary to the Clergy of France, got the idea into his head that the King was involved in a scheme to control the market. He was preparing to spread so much poison about the King's faithful servants, especially Choiseul, Sartine and myself, that in November 1768, he was sent to the Bastille. He's in solitary confinement, despite which he still manages to get letters passed to the outside world.'

'What?' cried Nicolas, horrified. 'Is he still in the Bastille after seven years, without ever being brought to trial?'

'He's still as mad as ever, and his madness is a danger to the State. He isn't in the Bastille any longer, though: he's been moved to Vincennes, where he continues to proclaim his innocence. Not a month passes without my receiving one of his petitions. I want to help you: it will be, in a way, my legacy to you, the last thing I can do for you while I still have some authority left and Monsieur Albert has not yet taken over.'

The end of this sentence was uttered through pursed lips and in a tone of inexpressible contempt. Lenoir seized a large sheet of paper, a quill which he dipped in an inkpot held by a red, chubby-cheeked cupid, and began writing, stopping briefly from time to time to find the exact word or phrase. He dried the ink with a sprinkling of powder, heated the wax, let a thick drop fall on the paper and pressed it angrily with his seal.

'There, nobody will stand in your way now. I will read it to you. It is addressed to Monsieur de Rougemont, governor of the royal château of Vincennes.

'Monsieur,

Please place yourself at the disposal of my special investigator and give him immediate access to the prisoner of State whom you know. He is authorised to speak to this prisoner, without any witnesses, for as long as he likes. Remember that he is acting in His Majesty's service. Please countersign this note and give it back to my envoy.

Paris police headquarters
4 May 1775
Lenoir

'I am not just advising you to keep this secret, I am demanding it. Rougemont won't say anything if he doesn't know what it's all about. As for you, I repeat, absolute discretion, and I except nobody from that prohibition. This is a matter between you and me, and divulging it, as I'm sure you will understand, would threaten more than our positions, in so far as we still have them.'

'All the same, Monseigneur, aren't you afraid that a prisoner who appears to maintain communication with the outside world might be inclined to let this be known?'

'I trust blindly to your skill to ensure that the man will find it more disadvantageous to talk than to keep silent. He just has to be persuaded that his interests lie in keeping absolutely quiet about your conversation.'

He stood up. Nicolas was distressed to see that there were tears in Lenoir's eyes as he held out his hand.

'Don't forget me! Now go.'

Overcome with emotion, Nicolas left without turning round. Outside, a familiar voice hailed him. It was the Chevalier de Lastire.

'I went to Rue Montmartre to find you,' he said, 'and was told you were probably at the Châtelet. I've just come from there, having obviously been unsuccessful. I decided to try my luck with Lenoir, and God be praised, here you are!'

'How is your wound?' Nicolas had noted that the chevalier was still wearing his turban-shaped bandage.

'It's healing. My head has been through a lot worse than that! I'm terribly sorry, believe me, not to have taken more of a role in the investigation you are currently pursuing. I've been all over the city, after a quick trip to Versailles ... No point in saying any more about that. The popular discontent will be short-lived. No thanks to the authorities, who've handled things so badly. But there will be consequences: there's a rumour that Sartine, and therefore Lenoir, helped to stir things up out of hatred for Turgot. Now there have to be a few executions, as soon as possible, to make an example. That's the only way for order to be restored. Although it seems already to be restored, judging by how quiet the city is. I have to continue my researches, in order to clear Monsieur de Sartine of the accusations which are sure to be made against him. So I don't think I'd be of any use to you in Rue Montmartre. How far have you got with that?'

Nicolas had been sworn to secrecy by Lenoir, and he had no intention of betraying that trust, even to his friend. He kept his answer vague, while observing to himself that the situation was running in his favour. He could not help recalling Bourdeau's misgivings about Lastire. The fact that he could not participate in the investigation was sure to please the inspector, whose happiness mattered to him.

'Suspicion is falling increasingly on the baker's immediate circle, wife and apprentices. We'll get there in the end.'

Lastire offered him a lift in his carriage, an offer Nicolas declined with the excuse that he preferred to return to the Châtelet on foot in order to get a better sense of the atmosphere in the city. The chevalier left in a jovial mood, promising that he would soon buy him dinner in return for the one in Versailles. Nicolas walked to the Châtelet via Place des Victoires, Rue des Petits-Champs and Rue Saint-Honoré. He felt saddened by his interview with Lenoir. He was not taken in by his chief's gentle irony, knowing that it concealed genuine sorrow.

He was reminded of certain periods in his own life, certain dark moments when everything had seemed to collapse about him without any possibility of salvation, when the heart and soul, crushed beneath the burden, seemed powerless to resist. In his opinion, Lenoir was a magistrate who gave every indication of working for the public good. Repaid with ingratitude, he was now concentrating all his efforts on repressing a profound despair instead of using his concern and loyalty, and perhaps more, in the service of the King.

It was necessary to overcome misfortune, and force oneself to become detached. It was that detachment that allowed him to confront the difficulties life kept bringing him, like a river depositing on its banks the flotsam it had collected during its course. He was moving like a sleepwalker, thinking of what men had constantly to confront and their attempts to find a middle way, a way that was balanced. Not to sink under the weight of humiliation was as essential as not to take refuge in the ultimate failing: pride. The way in which one withstood the consequences of a defeat revealed the true nature of a human being. The Marquis de Ranreuil had often remarked that it took less courage to lay siege to a city than to overcome certain vicissitudes in which only the heart and soul played their part. Semacgus accused of a serious offence, Sartine facing disgrace, Madame de Pompadour plagued by the intrigues of her rivals, and the late King, so courageous in his death agony: all of them had taught him, each in his or her own fashion, the supreme quality: nobility of spirit. Now Lenoir had fallen and, more affected than he was willing to reveal, was also confronting it in his own way. All these examples, and his own, confirmed to him that it was better to suffer injustice than remorse. These reflections revived the budding casuist from the Jesuit school in Vannes. The perfect example was where the virtue of humility became a kind of self-regard and ended up as the deadly sin of pride.

Returning to the present, he decided to ask Bourdeau to find out if there was indeed a tavern called the Grand Hiver and to continue searching for Caminet, whose corpse was still nowhere to be found. Why had he disappeared? Had the body been stripped bare by some wandering dealer in second-hand clothes? That was common enough, and when it happened the body was usually hidden. He would have to make enquiries in that direction. Everything was complicated by the fact that they were still not sure how exactly Master Mourut had been killed. He next looked for a pretext that would allow him not to lie to Bourdeau about how he was spending his time. He would say he was paying a visit to Anne Friope, neglecting to add that he would then be going to Vincennes.

Pleased to have found this honest stratagem, he covered the rest of the way with a lively step, avoiding being splashed by passing carriages and jumping over the dirty puddles left by the rain that had fallen in the past few days. Outside the Grand Châtelet, he came across a busy-looking Rabouine, whose face lit up when he saw his chief.

'What good wind brings you here?'

'There has been some movement in Rue du Poirier. A woman entered the ruined mansion opposite the Hénéfiance house. I had Tirepot at hand, so I left him on guard.'

'And what happened?'

'Some time later, the chimney of the Hénéfiance house started smoking.'

'Smoking? That's interesting. Continue the surveillance.'

He found Bourdeau impatient and obviously out of sorts. Nicolas, who knew him well, assumed that Lastire's brief visit to the Châtelet had a lot to do with it, that it had revived a prejudice that dated back to the journey to Vienna and a sense that there was a bond between them from which he felt excluded. But once Nicolas had pointed out that the chevalier was currently otherwise engaged, Bourdeau cheered up and took a great interest in Rabouine's news of the smoking chimney. Nicolas gave him the task of finding the Grand Hiver inn, the discovery of which he owed to Louis's ingenuity. Bourdeau would check the lists of the office of security, where that kind of business was recorded, and, if need be, would pay a visit to the place itself. He would have to devote himself urgently to this task while Nicolas went to see how Anne Friope was now and questioned her if her condition allowed it. At that moment Catherine appeared, out of breath. She had come to inform Bourdeau that a legless cripple, a former soldier of the King, had presented himself in Rue Montmartre on a little wagon mounted on castors and pulled by a dog, citing the commissioner's name. After gorging himself on a copious helping of bacon soup moistened with wine, he had left a message indicating 'that a woman had entered the house'.

'Not much point running all the way here if you already know that!' said Catherine, irritably.

This confirmation of Rabouine's information set them speculating further and allowed Nicolas to conceal his planned visit to Vincennes. After seeing Anne Friope, he ought to go straight to Rue du Poirier to see the situation for himself. He would indeed go there, but on his return from Vincennes.

He found Dr de Gévigland by the prisoner's bedside. She was as well as could be expected, having slept the rest of the night. The doctor asked for permission to go home and get some well-earned rest. He would be back that evening to examine his patient. Nicolas found the young woman dressed in a kind of monk's cowl, her head on a pillow made up of her male clothes. She seemed both scared and embarrassed to see him.

'Mademoiselle,' he said, 'I'm pleased to see that your condition has improved. I must, however, ask you a few questions. Your friend has confessed that he followed Caminet on Sunday night. I know that Caminet was blackmailing you.'

She appeared relieved.

'Parnaux remains one of the suspects – as do you – in the death of Master Mourut, but also in the disappearance of Caminet. I know Caminet was threatening you, and Parnaux was seen near his body.'

He was playing somewhat with the truth, groping his way, stating as certainty what was far from certain. The young woman's reaction was immediate.

'That's all lies, he didn't go anywhere near him.'

He refrained from reacting to this, not wishing to interrupt the spontaneous nature of her words.

'No, he didn't go anywhere near him,' she repeated in a lower tone. 'I can vouch for that.'

'Did he tell you that?'

Her bloodless face turned red and she burst into tears. He felt an immense pity for this lost child overcome with misfortune.

'Yes.'

'In that case, your words do not count as evidence in a criminal investigation, and Parnaux remains one of the suspects.'

She was choking. 'I was … I was there … I followed Parnaux when he went out … I feared the worst, so I pretended to be asleep and then followed him!'

'Didn't he see you?'

'No. On the way back I wasn't able to catch up with him and pass him. It was raining. I got back after he did. He was going mad with worry. I had to admit everything.'

'Did you go and see Mourut?'

She looked at him in alarm. 'Never, Monsieur Nicolas. We went to bed. Then we got up like every morning and went to the bakehouse at the usual hour.'

'Rest assured, Mademoiselle, that all this will be duly checked. I am prepared to believe you until we have proof to the contrary.'

'How is my friend?'

'He's worried about you. Of course, I have informed him of your condition.'

He was in a state of some bewilderment by the time he left her. Each testimony depended on the previous one like the elements in a house of cards. It needed only one of them to be a lie for the whole edifice to come crashing down, calling into question the whole painfully constructed logic. He took a cab, and to throw any possible pursuer off the scent, asked to be driven to Place Royale. He got out and told the coachman to wait for him at the corner of Rue de l'Égout and Rue Saint-Antoine. He slowly strolled twice round the square, turned into Rue de l'Écharpe, entered the church of Sainte-Catherine, came out again through a side door, and got back to his carriage without anything untoward drawing his attention. Once he reached Vincennes, he asked the coachman to wait some distance from the fortress. He did not head straight to the prison, but got to it by a complicated route during which he finally convinced himself that he was not being followed.

He presented himself before the two drawbridges which protected the entrance to the château, a small one for visitors on foot and a wider one for carriages. He had to pass through three doors, the last one of which could not be opened from the inside without help from the outside, nor from the outside without help from the inside. Having shown his credentials to a mistrustful gatekeeper assisted by a guard, he found himself in the middle of the courtyard, from which rose the keep. It reminded him of the tower of Elven, an old Breton fortress whose prodigious bulk had taken him by surprise one day when he was hunting wolves with his father, the marquis, in the nearby forest. A forty-foot moat surrounded the château and made it inaccessible. The keep was five storeys high with four corner towers. There were again three doors at the entrance. He was made to wait in a large room on the ground floor, which a gaoler told him was a torture chamber, while pointing out that it was not used much these days. The governor soon appeared, muttering furiously about having been disturbed just as he was starting his lunch. He peered at Lenoir's letter, examined the seal and looked Nicolas up and down. He finally yielded, having no choice, although he demanded to be present at the interview, as was only fitting when dealing with a prisoner of State being kept in solitary confinement. He was so insistent that Nicolas had to threaten to have him punished if he attempted any further obstruction. Reluctantly, the man gave in.

He was led to the prisoner's dungeon through a succession of dark passageways and staircases. A smell of mildew and saltpetre seized him by the throat, reminding him of what was said of a stay in this prison, 'that it was worth its weight in arsenic'. Again, there were three doors to the dungeon, each equipped with iron bars, two locks and three bolts. It was clear to Nicolas that the precautions at Vincennes were infinitely more stringent than in the Bastille. One door opened from the left, another from the right. Opening them was a whole ceremony of scrapings, creakings and the screeching of hinges.

He saw nothing at first on entering the cell. The weak daylight falling from three iron grilles arranged in such a way that the bars of one blocked the gaps in the other dazzled him after the darkness of the galleries. His eyes gradually became accustomed, and he began making out details. The cell was a vaulted room three times as high as it was wide. Against the far wall, sitting on a wooden bunk containing a drawer, a man was looking at him, wrapped against the cold in a frayed cloak. Above the raised collar appeared the remains of a torn cravat, and above that a pale, emaciated face with wild, inquisitive eyes. He had long hair and a beard, and seemed ageless. His hands were held tight in rings linked to the walls by chains. His right foot was attached in the same way to a square block of stone in the floor. This system allowed the prisoner to move with great difficulty and only within a limited radius.

The two men remained silent while the gatekeeper noisily closed the dungeon doors. Nicolas was quickly thinking about how to begin. He reproached himself for not thinking about it earlier instead of letting his mind wander, as he all too often did. He had no intention of lying, throwing his weight around, or holding out any false hopes.

'Monsieur,' Nicolas began, 'I would understand it if you were surprised by my presence. I'm the Baron d'Herbignac ...'

He was not lying: that was indeed one of his titles, Herbignac being one of the dependencies of the land and domain of Ranreuil.

'... and I have been given the task by the King to visit the prisons and especially those prisoners who have been detained without trial.'

The man looked him up and down sceptically. 'Nice to see the King taking an interest in his prisons after reigning for sixty years! Monsieur, I expect nothing any longer from anyone. I can but listen to you.'

Nicolas realised that the prisoner had been kept in ignorance of the death of Louis XV and the accession of Louis XVI.

'How long have you been living in this prison?'

'Living is pitching it rather high! For six years, Monsieur, after eleven months in the Bastille without ever having discovered the reason why. I'm sure you know it, although I can only speculate. I have my suspicions, though, and far from incriminating me, they do me credit.'

'What is that reason? I'd be grateful to you if you could tell me.'

'In 1768, I unwittingly discovered a terrible pact drawn up by an infernal league, a conspiracy against the King and the whole of France.'

He was gradually becoming heated, raising his arms as much as his chains allowed him and causing them to clank horribly.

'A league! A conspiracy! What are you saying? Are you sure?'

'I wish to God it didn't exist! It's because they want to stop me exposing them that I'm rotting in prison.'

'And who are its instigators?'

Le Prévôt de Beaumont[4] looked at him and motioned him to come closer, tapping with his hand on the wood of his bunk. Nicolas sat down next to him. A stench like that of a trapped animal rose to his nostrils.

'I have to take precautions, they listen to me,' murmured the prisoner, casting an anxious glance around him. 'Let's talk low. I don't know why I'm telling you this when I don't even know you. I suppose you inspire confidence. The perpetrators of this conspiracy are De Laverdy, Sartine, Boutin, Langlois, Choiseul, Lenoir, Cranat du Bourg, Trudaine de Martigny and many others, including some very famous names. Why am I still being kept in prison for denouncing the famine pact if it doesn't exist and no other charge has been laid against me?'

Nicolas found his argument quite logical for a man who was said to be mad.

'Consider, Monsieur, the monstrous abuse of power represented by an arrest for no stated reason. My employment gone, my property seized, my affairs abandoned, my existence wiped out, what a tragedy! Add to that a nocturnal abduction and the loathsome despotism of judges and inquisitors. Oh, I have many grievances, many legitimate causes for complaint! I appeal to His Majesty. Our King cannot remain insensitive to so many iniquities.'

Nicolas, accustomed by now to the half-light of the dungeon, noticed, at the height of a man's eyes, some inscriptions that seemed printed on the walls. Le Prévôt caught his glance.

'Despite the constant torments to which I am subjected by my gaoler, I work, I compose. I copy extracts from the books I read. The Comte de Laleu, who lives in the château and has a library of four thousand volumes, is pleased to let me have some without the governor's knowledge through the good auspices of the turnkey. My God, I've thrown caution to the winds. What are you doing, fool? You revealed a confidence, and now this fellow's going to repeat it!'

'Monsieur, I give you my word of honour that Monsieur de Rougemont won't hear a word of anything you see fit to tell me in the course of our conversation. But in return you must promise not to reveal the subject of our interview to anyone. It is for the King's ears and his alone.'

'As you wish. You're looking at the walls. In all my dungeons, I leave some testimony to my denunciation despite the successive layers of whitewash used to erase them.'

'But where do you find the ink?'

'I use tallow, Monsieur, blackened on a plank held in a candle flame. My pen is made of birch twigs, curved to spread the hot tallow on the wall. As you can imagine, it's a long process: I can barely manage more than fifty letters in an hour. But let us return to the matter that interests us.'

'The famine pact?'

'Yes, Monsieur. The idea, as I'll keep repeating until the day I die, was to lease the supply of grain, renewable every twelve years, to four millionaires. They were to institute regular shortages, constant high prices and, in years when the harvest was poor, general famine in all the provinces of the kingdom, by controlling the market through an exclusive monopoly on wheat and flour. The supervising agent of this operation was a man named Malisset, who had owned a bakery near the church of Saint-Paul. He had become a miller, had gone bankrupt, but was protected by the police. He gave the orders to an army of workers, stewards, buyers, storehouse owners, guards, threshers, winnowers, sifters, controllers, inspectors, tax collectors, clerks, merchants, bakers and so on and so forth! That was what I reported to the Parlement in Rouen, which led to my being snatched from the world of the living.'

'And since then, there has been no change?'

'Oblivion, violence and silence! Even in the lives of the saints and martyrs, Monsieur, there have never been torments so long, tribulations so contrary to nature, as those I've been made to endure for six years in this hellish keep. You see me in this reduced state, on a pallet shaped like a scaffold, in a dungeon, chains on my feet and hands, often naked, always starving, deprived of everything, even though my board and lodgings, as I've discovered, amount to three thousand *livres* paid by the royal treasury. It all goes to Rougemont, who treats me far worse than he has been ordered to, and constantly makes false reports about my conduct. Above him, my abductor, the cruel Sartine, whose hatred and anger grow the more I resist, seems determined to see me die, one way or another.'

Suddenly, and quite unexpectedly, Nicolas looked the prisoner in the eyes and murmured, 'Three points and thirty-one.'

The man moved back. 'Traitor!' he cried. 'You want to make me talk! Are you, too, part of the infernal plot?'

'Monsieur, I assure you I am not. It is simply that this phrase struck my ears at a popular gathering. It was uttered by some suspicious-looking men who seemed to be organising the disturbance. If you are, as you claim, concerned with the interests of the King, the State and the people, explain to me what that formula means to you.'

Le Prévôt de Beaumont hesitated, looking deep into the commissioner's face as if trying to read something in it. 'Monsieur, I don't know why, but everything leads me to take you at your word. By ways and means which I cannot describe in detail, for much was down to chance and I was often the blind tool of fate, I heard about this rallying cry. I sense that the world hasn't stopped and that everything continues as before ... There were at the time a number of secret meetings, and that phrase was the password. You can be sure the *nihil obstat* has changed and may now serve other purposes!'

'But what did it mean? Or was it just an empty phrase?'

'I think these meetings were of the council of plotters. They were held in Paris, in three different places, hence the three points, and had thirty-one participants. That was the first key. A second one, of which I am ignorant, no doubt specified which of the three places was chosen for a particular meeting ... That's what I've always thought.'

'I am very grateful to you. Do you take snuff, Monsieur?'

He held out his open snuffbox and they both took pinches. The resultant explosion of sneezing, as Nicolas had often found, created and strengthened a feeling of mutual trust.

'Monsieur,' Nicolas went on, 'I'd like to venture a few more questions. Does the name Hénéfiance mean anything to you?'

Once again, the prisoner seemed startled by how much Nicolas already knew. 'Monsieur,' he said, 'I reiterate, your knowledge of the matter goes further and deeper than I suspect you yourself realise. I don't think I am risking anything worse by enlightening you, although, to tell the truth, I know little more than you do. The one thing you don't know is that the younger Hénéfiance's attempts to deceive the brotherhood were denounced by a baker in Rue Montmartre, whose name I don't know. This man hoped to increase not his trade, but his share of the monopoly, by destroying a rival and competitor. Hénéfiance, who had never even met the man who denounced him, was destroyed as if by a thunderbolt sent down from heaven.'

'One thing. When exactly did you learn the details of this affair?'

'Not long before I was abducted by Sartine's henchmen.'

'Monsieur,' said Nicolas by way of conclusion, 'I would like to believe that you are telling the truth.'

> *As one whose mind cannot abide a lie,*
> *Our poor Prévost would much prefer to die*
> *If anything he said was deemed to be*
> *Untrue or lacking in full honesty.*[5]

'As you see, Monsieur de Laleu's library has not been looted in vain by a poor prisoner. I hope I can count on your goodwill.'

Nicolas, still haunted by the past, remembered another desperate prisoner on the eve of his execution, who had also asked for help.[6] It was difficult for him to commit himself.

'Monsieur, rest assured that if the opportunity presents itself, I shan't fail to plead your case.'

'Thank you again. I believe you are a man of your word.'

Nicolas knocked at the heavy door and it was opened for him. In the large room on the ground floor, he again spoke to the governor, who countersigned Lenoir's letter with obvious reluctance. Nicolas reminded him of the necessity for his visit to be kept secret. Monsieur de Rougemont's stubborn, spiteful expression did not augur well for the observation of these instructions.

In his carriage, Nicolas pondered what he had just heard. The man, despite a degree of over-excitement, did not seem to him to have spoken like a madman. When you came down to it, what was held against him? He clearly had not attacked the King, although what he said certainly implied the complicity of the State. Nicolas saw his act as the protest of an honest, even innocent soul faced with an intolerable situation. Woe betide the man who causes a scandal! In fact, what created suspicion, opening the way to the wildest imaginings, was the secrecy jealously maintained by those in power regarding the mechanisms necessary to the trade in grain. In this activity, king's men, ministers, intendants, farmers general, merchants and suppliers were involved without anything being visible. The mystery in which the subject had so long been shrouded merely accentuated the general feeling that the only aim of this secrecy was to conceal corrupt practices. Who could be surprised that a man faced with actual evidence had grasped the crux of the matter and launched into vehement denunciation? Who, in such a situation, was in a position to condemn him without first listening to what he had to say? Of course, it had to be taken into account that there was a great deal that was vague and confusing in the words of a poor wretch crushed by many years of suffering. In his honesty and stubbornness, Le Prévôt de Beaumont had never abandoned an obsession which he took for gospel truth, repeating the same old refrain over and over. Constantly brooding in his hopeless solitude on the terrible injustice done to him, the man saw all kinds of unexpected connections between what had happened and a number of highly placed figures, all supposedly in league with one another.

As a king's man, Nicolas could also understand the reasons for keeping Le Prévôt in solitary confinement. The idea of a famine pact, in which so many subjects of the kingdom believed, could not help but be revived by the release of a man who maintained the idea so firmly and appeared to have little inclination to tone down his urge to denounce. He himself, a commissioner of the King, had been informed in 1774 by his tailor, Master Vachon,[7] of the unfortunate rumours accusing the King of speculating on wheat. Bourdeau, too, had apparently been convinced of it at the time, and had thought his chief quite innocent in the face of so much evidence.

His own conviction led him to suspect that the truth was somewhere in the middle. A system for regulating the trade in grain, clear in its principles, had doubtless given free rein to too many protagonists ready to turn it to their own advantage. The opportunities for abuse had multiplied, remaining unchecked and compromising the reputation of the old monarchical machine. It was among the merchants and all the obscure figures swarming around that essential commodity that the evil had been born, had grown and spread through all levels of the kingdom. In this way, good intentions had given rise to bad actions, and the resulting corruption had created injustice. For reasons of State, the former secretary to the Clergy of France was paying the price for all this.

Nicolas's ruminations were taking him a long way from the urgent concerns of the moment. Even though sadness prevailed in contemplating the tragedy of a man crushed by fate, a fever he knew well, the fever of the hunter on the trail of his prey, soon seized him again. Without any effort on his part, he had discovered the link between the Hénéfiance family and the master baker murdered in Rue Montmartre. That made things more complicated, without doing anything to either incriminate the existing suspects or clear them of suspicion: the two affairs, hitherto separate, might now become hopelessly entangled. Whatever the case, it now became imperative to investigate the precise circumstances of the younger Hénéfiance's disappearance. It was with his mind filled with these new objectives that Nicolas had himself dropped at the entrance to the tranquil Rue du Poirier.

X

URGENCY

Truth, like the sun, cannot move backwards.

BARON D'HOLBACH

Nicolas jumped lightly down from the carriage. Rabouine, having returned from the Châtelet, must surely be at work again beside Tirepot. As for the cobbler, his workshop had been carefully closed up, indicating that he was absent. Nicolas advanced along the street, which was as deserted as ever in the late afternoon. No doubt his spies were concealed in some hidden recess that was not apparent at first sight. He retraced his steps, undecided about what to do and anxious not to miss whatever unusual signal Rabouine chose to show his presence. It might be a bird call, a whistle or a stone suddenly rolling across the ground. But nothing came and Nicolas began to feel worried, imagining all kinds of things that might have happened. One, which ought to have been reassuring, was that the unknown woman had come out again and they had followed her. But that would mean that both Rabouine and Tirepot had embarked on the pursuit and completely abandoned their surveillance of the house. Or else, if Rabouine was absent, detained by some unknown circumstance, Tirepot had set off in pursuit of the woman.

The minutes were passing too slowly and, unable to bear it any longer, he approached the ruined mansion opposite the Hénéfiance house. He noted that there was straw strewn on the ground in front of it. The door yielded to his first push. The layout of the house and its outbuildings was a mirror image of that on the other side of the street. The living quarters were dilapidated, with floorboards that sagged as he cautiously advanced. Suddenly he stopped: he had noticed Tirepot's paraphernalia – the two buckets, the oilcloth and the crossbar – lying on the ground. The fact that they lay in such disorder suggested that some violent act had taken place. His anxiety increased at the sight of Rabouine's tricorn, battered and soiled but still recognisable from its beige colour. What had happened? Where were his two friends? He went through all the rooms, searching feverishly in every nook and cranny. The wood creaked beneath his feet. Everything appeared completely deserted and his search led nowhere.

As he was looking for the way down to the cellar, he heard muffled cries. They came from a heap of rotting and mildewed logs which, when moved aside, revealed the top of a narrow staircase. The cries seemed closer and more distinct. He again used a lighted page from his notebook to illumine a vaulted passageway: a draught immediately extinguished it. As he groped his way forward, he hit something with his foot and, crouching, saw a body lying on the floor. He ran his hand over the face and realised that there was a gag over the mouth. He straightened up, searched in his pocket, took out a thin knife and started cutting through the gag, which finally yielded with a tear, releasing a deep sigh.

'Whoever you are, thank you!' said a familiar voice.

He helped Rabouine to his feet, cut the bonds from his hands and lit another page, vowing to always have a piece of candle in his pocket from now on. Rabouine was holding his head in his hands and swaying so much that Nicolas had to hold him up by the arms.

'Were you alone? Where's Tirepot?'

'Outside, where I left him.'

The pages of the black notebook burnt one after the other. They advanced through the cellar, a kind of vaulted gallery, interspersed here and there with other flights of stairs. They discovered Tirepot lying bound and motionless. At last, after much effort, he was able to speak.

'Once Rabouine had gone inside the house ...'

'Why did you leave the street?' Nicolas asked Rabouine.

'The carriage entrance half opened and someone called my name.'

'Your name?'

'I thought it was you. Who else could it have been? I rushed inside, but there was no one there. I crossed the courtyard, went into the house and there received a massive blow to the head that knocked me out completely.'

'The same thing happened to me,' said Tirepot. 'I saw Rabouine's tricorn being waved in the doorway as if he was signalling to me to come in. I didn't think and, without another glance, I ran to join him. Much good it did me! There was no one in the courtyard and, once I got inside the house, a bang on my head, and then, as if that wasn't enough, a punch in the face and down I went!'

Darkness enveloped them once again. Tirepot took a candle from his waistcoat. In silence they examined the premises. The floor was strewn with wisps of straw. A few yards further on, the gallery ended in a panelled wall. It was only necessary to push it for it to swivel round. Nicolas was astonished to recognise the closed room of the Hénéfiance house on the other side. The moving wall was the same wall that bore the painted inscriptions which had so intrigued him. In the hearth a fire was dying, stifled by a heap of ashes, on which he threw himself. He kicked it onto the floor, helped by Rabouine who had immediately understood what he was doing. The result was disappointing: not a single paper had escaped destruction. Their only harvest was a small piece of brightly coloured cloth with a strange texture, which intrigued them. Why had anyone wanted to get rid of it? Nicolas picked it up, conscious that the slightest clue might help them to identify the mysterious occupant of the house. He would show it to his tailor, Master Vachon, an expert on fashions, cloth and fabric. A close inspection of the rest of the house yielded nothing new. Only the rabbits had disappeared, doubtless transported elsewhere, which explained why there was so much straw on the way from the cellar to the other house. It also meant that a carriage or wagon had been used for the removal.

'I don't think we've left anything to chance. We've seen everything there is to see. I'd wager the place won't be used again.'

'Should we continue the surveillance?' asked Rabouine.

'There's no point. Once an animal has been tracked down, it won't go back to the same lair!'

Out of caution, he decided nevertheless to place seals inside the carriage entrance to the Hénéfiance house. He would do the same at the entrance to the other house. That would tell them if there had been any new visitor. Tirepot recovered his paraphernalia, stating that without being fully equipped, he felt only half a man, and set off on foot for other hunts. Nicolas and Rabouine greeted the cobbler, who was just then returning to his workshop. He was full of gratitude for the welcome he had received in Rue Montmartre, and delighted to have discovered that Catherine was a former canteen-keeper. Nicolas asked him to keep an eye on the two houses and to make sure he was informed if there was any suspicious movement. The *louis* that accompanied this request ensured him the man's devotion and gratitude, if such assurance was still needed.

In the carriage, he dropped Rabouine at the corner of Rue Saint-Honoré, then asked to be driven to Rue Vieille-du-Temple. Without further ado, he wanted to consult Master Vachon on the nature of the piece of material he had saved from the fire. The fact that someone had wanted to destroy it continued to arouse his curiosity. He was pleased to pay another visit to the worthy shop he had so often frequented since his arrival in Paris fifteen years earlier. There was still nothing on the outside to mark it out as a place patronised by so many of the greatest names in the land. Situated at the back of a dark courtyard, this temple to good taste appeared as illumined as a shrine on a feast day. Thin and erect, Master Vachon was holding forth to a group of apprentices sitting cross-legged on the light oak counter.

'Gentlemen, I shouldn't have to repeat this to you. Scissors should never, I repeat never, be passed from hand to hand. One person puts them down, the next picks them up. Otherwise what happens?'

'Misfortune to the house and ruin on its trade,' cried the apprentices in loud voices.

Vachon swivelled round, saw Nicolas and bowed his tall frame. 'Ah, the man of the moment! Everyone's talking about you, Marquis! Greetings!'

Yet again, thought Nicolas, the news reached Vachon's ears with incredible speed: the tailor really was one of the best-informed men in Paris.

'How's business?'

'Excellent, once the flour dust has settled … The forthcoming coronation has meant an increase in orders. Although a great many of the costumes for the ceremony will be produced by Bocquet and Delaistre, respectively painter and tailor to His Majesty's Entertainments, they won't make everything. I can't complain, even though the work has changed a lot. A new reign means new fashions. Elegance, shapeliness, in a word, style, are giving way inexorably to ease, not to say slovenliness. All that matters is licence and fantasy. I shall say no more!'

He had seized his cane and was beating the floor repeatedly. His assistants' heads bent again with admirable unanimity over their tasks, kept in check by their irascible master's frowns.

'Yes, licence,' he went on. 'Now we are in the days of the jacket, the waistcoat – double-breasted, too. How can such a thing be suitable for a man worthy of the name? It's a fashion fit only for young dandies. Just think! The breeches are all crooked, and held in place under the knees with garters! Then you have the trousers, Monsieur, the ratine or twill tailcoat, the black taffeta cravat and the plaited hair embellished by a comb. Velvet winter and summer, thick linen, camelhair and nankeen. Away with embroidery! In the name of simplicity everything is coming apart. It's London that's been setting the fashion since the peace treaty!'

He bowed his head despondently, while his subordinates had a quiet laugh. Then he looked up again, and there was a mocking gleam in his eye.

'As for the ladies, fortunately that's not my business. One of my noble customers described to me the other day what his wife wore to the Opéra: "a flowing dress adorned with superfluous regrets, with a waist of perfect candour. Shoes in the shape of the Queen's hair embroidered with diamonds as acts of treachery and bagatelles of emeralds, curled into elevated sentiments, with a bonnet of assured conquest filled with inconstant feathers. With a fur like a beggar's cloak on the shoulders, behind a Medicis set in decorum, with an opal of despair and a muff of momentary agitation!" A whole sentimental novel in itself! And the madness is spreading. Luxury has ceased to be the vice of the aristocracy. They are not the only ones who need lessons in modesty, the common people are just the same these days!'

Nicolas found that Vachon was exaggerating. Surely he was increasing his income with this unbridled taste? He could not remember it ever diminishing.

'And do you follow this fashion?'

'What else can I do? I follow it and moderate it. I take it and leave it. I preserve what is becoming; the coat, for example, which I provide with a little straight collar, flattening the folds so that they cover the small of the back. Similarly with the sleeves, which no longer flare and whose facing barely shows.'

'Anyway, whatever we say, the common people are still a long way from such nonsense. Look at how restless they are.'

Master Vachon was looking at him with an inscrutable expression. Then he threw an angry and discouraging look at his minions as they sat embroidering and overcasting, took Nicolas by the arm, drew him into a small sitting room adorned with two swing mirrors, and abruptly closed the door behind them.

'Marquis, do you know the reason for all this disturbance, this disorder beating at our walls, and this hullabaloo which is stirring people up from the provinces to Versailles, and from Versailles to Paris?'

'Ever since I've known you, you've always been well informed and an excellent listener. Your talent, nay, your genius, is not limited to cutting and hemming. You are one of those inquisitive minds able to go beyond appearances and get at the underlying causes of events.'

Blissfully, Master Vachon drank in these words, leaning on his cane like a monarch adopting a pose, multiplied to infinity by the two mirrors facing each other. 'Ah, there's some truth in what you say, even though your words are excessively flattering,' he said, in a sanctimonious tone of false modesty. 'If I dared tell you ...'

Nicolas's silence was intended to encourage him, but still he hesitated.

'You know how discreet I am, and why,' said the commissioner. 'I make only one exception ...'

The tailor's face clouded over in an expression of shocked seriousness: the face of an inquisitor confronted with a stubborn heretic falling back into error. 'Monsieur! An exception?'

'Yes, as I was saying only the other day to His Majesty: that good old Monsieur Vachon ...'

'That good old Monsieur Vachon. To His Majesty?'

'Yes, of course. You know in what high esteem and gratitude I have held you since a certain green coat contributed to my gaining favour with the late King and Madame de Pompadour.'

Moved, Master Vachon wiped away a tear. 'How fortunate!' he said quickly. 'Well, what I'm about to tell you may interest the King. You know of course that the highest levels of the nobility frequent my shop?'

'Of course, and with good reason.'

'That some of these powerful nobles – very few, I only accommodate the highest – request my presence in their houses?'

'Certainly.'

'That they have to beg and entreat me for me to consent?'

'Naturally.'

'That only a prince of royal blood has the right to benefit from the privilege of a home visit from me?'

'Obviously.'

'You have always understood me. In short, I was at the Temple, at the house of Monseigneur the Prince de Conti. We had just done the fitting, which showed how perfectly my masterpiece suited him. Magnificent!'

Nicolas, barely able to contain his giggles, almost exploded at these words. 'Yes, and …?'

'You're right, I'm wandering from the point. Well, there I was, folding the costume, making sure the pins did not fall out. The prince had gone into the next room, leaving the door open. Without wanting to, as you can imagine, I overheard the words exchanged … You know how careless the aristocracy can be, not hesitating to talk of secret matters without any heed to who might hear them.'

'What day did this prestigious fitting take place?'

'Why, yesterday, late in the afternoon! My carriage was almost caught up in the disturbances. What an adventure!'

'So the Prince de Conti was talking. To whom?'

'That's still a bit unclear in my head. I was very upset because my box of pins had spilled. When I'm dealing with the aristocracy, they're made of gold, and very expensive. So I was kneeling on the carpet trying to pick them up. From what I could gather, the prince

287

was conversing with an abbé who was talking about his master. The names Rohan, Choiseul and others were mentioned several times, Sartine too. The prince was complaining that Sartine was resisting his advances despite his hatred for the comptroller general. Nothing was going right. He lost his temper. He wasn't interested any more in this famine business, from which he had never expected anything good to come. He himself was suffering the consequences, his estates having seen some disturbances among the peasants. His wish was to see the back of Turgot. The current wave of unrest, badly organised and prepared, was failing. What he wanted was to preserve his income of fifty thousand *livres* from the franchises in the Temple enclosure. If Turgot persevered with his reforms, that lucrative privilege would fall by the wayside. Naturally, I didn't understand a word of this!'

'You know these aristocrats,' said Nicolas, who had understood it all and found it fascinating, although he was certainly not going to say so. 'Was that all?'

'A third man arrived, bringing some unfortunate news. Things had fallen through in Versailles, it was the same in Paris and moreover … This part I really didn't understand.'

'What was it?'

'He said something about a hunting dog that had been running after the prey for too long, a dog they would have to keep an eye on … The prince refused to hear any more, simply saying that it was up to others to deal with the inconvenience and that these trivial details were extremely irksome to him. Then they talked about Choiseul, who was going to see the Queen at Reims and try to speak to the King. The coronation was the last opportunity they would have. But the Prince de Conti said that the future of the former minister was extremely uncertain: time was passing, extinguishing his last hopes, and the King's loathing for him showed no sign of diminishing.'

'What else?'

'That was all. Having picked up my pins, I discreetly left the prince's apartment. All I wanted to do was to make sure they hadn't seen or heard me. I hope you will inform His Majesty. "Good old Monsieur Vachon!" Who would have thought it?' Leaning on his cane, he performed a little entrechat.

'You can depend on me,' said Nicolas. 'His Majesty will appreciate your information and show the greatest interest in it. May I now call on your knowledge regarding another subject of concern to me?'

'Marquis, I am all yours.'

Nicolas took from his pocket the small fragment of fabric saved from the flames in the Hénéfiance house and held it out to Master Vachon. 'Where could this fabric have come from? I've never seen anything quite like it.'

The tailor took it, smelt it, rubbed it between his palms, sniffed it again, and nimbly took out a thread, which he held over the flame of a candle. He looked at it again and then, like an oracle, delivered his judgement.

'Hmm ... An unusual fabric ... from the East ... a weft of cotton and a warp of silk, with gold thread running through it ... Hmm! I've seen it before, on an envoy of the Ottomans. It's from the Indies. Probably the south of India. Or even further, from the Dutch trading posts in Java. I'm positive.'

'I'm grateful to you.'

'Are you going to Reims for the coronation?'

'I'm not sure yet.'

'I'm going to make you a white coat, you'll be amazed! A memento from me. "Good old Monsieur Vachon!" My name mentioned by the King. The King!'

Contrary to the rules of his trade, he supplied his customers with fabrics, assured that his reputation and connections would spare him the problems that anyone else would have faced over such a serious lapse. Nicolas had difficulty extricating himself from the tailor's onslaught of compliments. Much to the amazement of his assistants,

Master Vachon walked him to his carriage, bowing constantly as he did so.

Huddled, as was his habit, in the corner of the upholstered seat, Nicolas stared out absently at the bustle of the streets and tried to draw together the threads of the past few days' events. One thought continued to haunt him: it was clear that a mysterious adversary, informed that the house in Rue du Poirier would be subject to investigation, was taking pleasure in playing cat and mouse with him. How did he know the commissioner's movements in advance? Nicolas had no illusions about La Gourdan's trustworthiness. A sly, dangerous woman to whom betrayal was second nature, she was quite capable of having divulged to a third party the content of her interrogation by the police. Faced with this threat, the unknown party was doing his utmost to distract the commissioner's attention with those painted inscriptions, which were sufficiently obscure to intrigue and sufficiently easy to decipher, thus serving their purpose. Nicolas blamed himself for having facilitated this tactic by not going immediately to the Hénéfiance house. The identification of Master Mourut's body by La Gourdan's maid had delayed the investigation and given the adversary time to stage this diversion and, no doubt, to escape. He had somehow to find a way of drawing this unknown individual into a trap. For the moment, he did not rate very highly Bourdeau's chances of finding the Grand Hiver.

It would serve no purpose to harass La Gourdan: she would not talk twice. It must have cost her a great deal to speak to the commissioner. What clues did he still have with which to get back on the trail? A wretched piece of fabric from the Indies, the mystery of the rabbits and the past history of the Hénéfiance family, not to mention the various suspects at the Mourut bakery. His intuition told him, as did Noblecourt's counsel, to look into the past. He already knew that there was a link between the murdered baker and the younger

Hénéfiance. The past often held the key to the present. He could not think of a single case that had not been illumined by a backwards look. Convinced, too, that the solution often emerged after you had lost interest in the problem, Nicolas decided to think no more about it.

The fact remained that Master Vachon's words cast a new and disturbing light on the matter. For years, the common people had been talking about the famine pact. The current plot, if indeed there was one, depended on the widespread discontent. There were parties who were using it, taking advantage of the situation to advance their secret intrigues. Nicolas carefully thought over the Prince de Conti's words. The freedom of trade in grain was a matter of indifference to the prince, but it was a useful pretext for getting rid of the comptroller general. What Conti feared was, in fact, the continuation of the reforms and, above all, the abolition of the guilds. This measure would ruin the Temple enclosure, a privileged place where various trades and business were conducted freely, much to the prince's advantage. Further reflection indicated that it was important not to confuse those who were merely stoking a fire with those who had lit it in the first place through a concerted effort.

As for the hunting dog, however unpleasant the term, Nicolas could not help but assume that he himself was the person thus referred to by the prince's mysterious interlocutor. Who else, in fact, besides the King, had, since Vienna, been trying to thwart intrigues harmful to the kingdom? As for the abbé mentioned by Vachon, it was highly likely to have been Georgel. His name, along with that of Rohan, who had been mentioned during the conversation, established a connection between what had happened in Austria and events in Versailles and Paris. Even if there was as yet no plot, all the requirements for there to be one had been met. The motley coalition against Turgot might well give rise to a powerful party supported by the Parlements. The only reassuring thing about all this – or so he hoped – was the diversity of the motives driving the various protagonists, which were unlikely to result in general agreement.

There was one thing, however, that overjoyed him. When Sartine's name had first been mentioned, he had felt a certain dismay. He knew Sartine's distaste for Turgot. Yet Conti's disillusioned remarks suggested that Sartine had nevertheless remained his own man and was still loyal to his King.

Outside the Grand Châtelet, a coach was blocking the way. A liveried footman stood by the door of the coach, receiving orders. Nicolas watched from his carriage, with the window down, as the footman approached him. Was he Monsieur Le Floch? If he was, would he please follow him to the coach, as his master wished to speak with him? Nicolas asked who this master was, to be met only with a dispiriting silence. He put Bourdeau's miniature pistol in his pocket. You never knew, and, since Vienna, he had been suspicious of everyone, even though the idea of being abducted at the doors of a building dedicated to the law seemed inconceivable. The coach door opened, pushed by a nervous hand. The commissioner got in and discovered Monsieur de Sartine sitting there in a dapple-grey coat, with a taut expression on his face. The whip cracked and the coach set off.

'So, Monsieur, you force me to run all over Paris to find you. Never where you ought to be. Never available when we need you. I run and you're elsewhere!'

'And never tired of serving you, Monseigneur,' retorted Nicolas, who had heard all this many times before from his former chief.

'And to cap it all, he tries to be clever! For the time being, I demand an explanation from you.'

Nicolas was unsure whether this sour introduction was part of Sartine's usual play-acting or the manifestation of a genuine irritation. 'I am your very humble and obedient servant.'

Sartine slapped his thighs with both hands. 'And what's worse, he mocks me! Humble remains to be seen, obedient perhaps, although you always seem to do exactly as you like. Including enquiring into affairs of State and stirring long-buried memories.'

Here we are, thought Nicolas. He's talking about Vincennes.

'I presume you mean my visit to La Gourdan?' he said innocently.

'La Gourdan! What has she got to do with all this? I'm not talking about brothels, I'm talking, Commissioner, about a visit with neither rhyme nor reason to the royal prison at Vincennes. Using Lord knows what subterfuge, you managed to circumvent Rougemont. What did you imagine? That he would remain silent and conceal your misdeeds?'

Nicolas understood from this that the governor of Vincennes had talked, but had prudently neglected to mention Lenoir's letter.

'I imagined, Monseigneur, that as a good servant, Monsieur de Rougemont would report the matter to his superiors and that, knowing everything as you always do, you would want to have this conversation with me. If the events of the last few days had allowed it, I would certainly have kept you informed of the progress of my enquiries.'

'Who is he trying to fool? Now he doesn't even have time to see me! And besides, what has made you so aware all of a sudden of an affair of State buried deep in a few people's memories for many years? I've asked Lenoir, and he claims not to know anything about it. Well, are you going to answer me?'

So, thought Nicolas, everyone, at this level of power, manages his affairs in his own interests. Whenever these clashed with loyalty, they usually prevailed, in a complex conflict of chance, risk and good faith.

'You seem lost in thought, Monsieur! I await your answer.'

'What can I say, except that when a name cropped up in the course of a criminal investigation, I was led to consult the police archives, which are the best kept in Europe. We can find anything we're looking for. Our search may be laborious, but it's always fruitful. With such information under our belt, we do our best to comprehend the whys and wherefores of a case. We hear, from various sources, that certain people, towards whom our loyalty and gratitude are boundless, are being whispered about, the subject of accusations which their opposition to certain policies might appear to justify. We pursue our investigation, which is linked in a thousand ways to both a domestic crime and a State plot. We also try to help these worthy individuals by paying them the tribute of our modest discoveries, which they are entitled to expect as good and loyal servants of the King.'

On the severe planes of Sartine's face a varied succession of feelings could be seen: astonishment, anger, incredulity, amusement – and even affection.

'It's true that our archives ... Well, there's no need for me to say any more about that. When your principles have prevailed over your excitability, you will reveal your true worth, which is considerable ... But tell me, what did you get from that madman in Vincennes?'

'Oh, not much! A few details about a side issue, which have allowed me to link certain events I could not otherwise explain. And I observed, Monseigneur, that a man who is either mad or just talkative may be unjustly imprisoned without trial, which seems to me to run contrary to what a certain Lieutenant General of Police once taught me.'

'Ah, that old Breton stubbornness! You, more than most, possess an inborn sense of what is just and what unjust. Nevertheless, one had to weigh the consequences. Imagine if this individual were released: he would talk and you are in a better position than many to know what he would say. The newspapers in London, the Hague and Berlin would immediately be full of the story, and pamphlets, lampoons and songs would spread it far and wide. In the salons, the wits would revel in it. Have you even thought about the repercussions for the kingdom? Those who rule often have to choose between two evils, one of which is injustice!' He seemed to hesitate, as if beset by a doubt he could not express. 'Is anything particular being said about me?'

'Someone as strong as you should not be worried about gossip, Monseigneur.'

'More prevarication! I insist.'

'As far as the prisoner in Vincennes is concerned, you can imagine his bitterness towards you ... More generally, it is believed that you still control the police, that Lenoir is merely your underling ...'

'Oh, is that what they say?'

'Also that the unrest in the city was deliberately not suppressed, as part of a pre-arranged plan designed to bring down Turgot, whom you wish to see gone.'

'I don't wish it, I hope for it. Is that all?'

'And others claim that, despite this abhorrence, you have not failed in your duty in any way, and that in exercising this caution, you have weakened the moves intended to chase away the intruder.'

'Oh, they say that, do they? Who exactly says it?'

'My informant mentioned the name of a prince of royal blood.'

'Orléans or Conti, obviously. More likely Conti ... And how do you know what the prince says?'

'I've been in the police force for fifteen years, and I was Monseigneur's pupil.'

'I taught you too well, it seems! What impudence!'

'You also taught me, Monseigneur, that the first rule is that the name of your informant should remain a secret.'

'And you only apply these rules when they suit you.'

'Nevertheless, I'd like you to help me.'

'Ah, now he wants my help! The world has turned upside down! Well, all right, then ...'

'In connection with the case of the prisoner in Vincennes, did you ever hear of a man named Hénéfiance, grain merchant and speculator in Rue du Poirier? You were Criminal Lieutenant at the time.'

'Of course, although I didn't follow the case very closely. It was such a delicate matter that it went all the way up to the comptroller general's office. This man Hénéfiance, if I remember correctly, had been denounced. A public trial was judged unwise, as, given the situation, it might have led to serious unrest. We were still at war … In the interests of the State, the galleys seemed the best solution. I later learnt that, after a year or two at Brest, the man escaped and was never heard from again. He's believed to have drowned. A boat was found drifting.'

'Why would he have escaped by sea?'

'You may not know that it's impossible to escape from Brest over land. The whole area is under close watch and constantly crossed by patrols. Any escape is immediately notified. Every bell tower sounds the alarm. What's more, anyone not speaking Breton would be unlikely to survive.'

It struck Nicolas that, for someone who had supposedly not followed the case closely, Sartine knew a great deal about it. He refrained from making any comment on this, being more than satisfied with what he had obtained from the minister. By now, the coach had found its way back to the Grand Châtelet.

'And how are you getting on with the Chevalier de Lastire?'

'Very well, whenever our paths cross. But events have decided otherwise. I can perfectly well understand that he's been keeping a close eye on the recent unrest and that the Mourut case was of little interest to him. That said, we do sometimes meet and exchange information.'

Sartine seemed lost in thought for a moment, but soon pulled himself together. 'He has in fact been reporting back to me. On the night of Sunday to Monday, for example, he predicted what would happen in Versailles. He has a good nose. Listen to his advice. I shall leave you now. Would you by any chance be on your way to one of those macabre sessions that seem to fascinate you so? Might you have another corpse on your hands?'

'Not at all, Monseigneur,' said Nicolas, jumping out of the coach. 'Just some missing rabbits.'

He watched as the coachman cracked his whip and set the coach in motion, while Sartine stared out at him through the window.

In the duty office, he found Bourdeau and Semacgus deep in conversation.

'How pleased I am to see you both here. I have so much to tell you.'

From the expressions on their faces, he guessed that they were not short of things to tell him either. Without a word, Bourdeau handed him a folded sheet of paper, which Nicolas opened. On it was a question mark crudely drawn in charcoal.

'What's this?'

'After much searching, I found out that the tavern of the Grand Hiver was located in Rue du Faubourg du Temple, near the Courtille. After going in the wrong direction and getting a bit lost, I discovered a charred section of wall and part of a sign, all that remains of an establishment that's been in ruins for fifteen years. But worse was to come. I was looking furiously at the ruin when an errand boy handed me this paper. By the time I looked up, the rascal had already run away, so I wasn't able to ask him who had sent him.'

'It seems to me,' said Nicolas, 'that someone's trying to distract us from something. Our adversary was no doubt hoping to draw me there in order to stop me being somewhere else.'

He looked closely at the paper. Semacgus noticed how interested in it he seemed. 'Does it remind you of something?'

'I do seem to have seen something like it before. The shape is unusual ... I'll have to think about it.'

He told them about his visit to Rue du Poirier and the misadventures that had befallen Rabouine and Tirepot.

'This is really not our day!' cried Bourdeau. 'How are we to lay hands on our man now? The thread is broken and the bird flown!'

'We may find him again. He's searching us out as much as we're pursuing him. Why should he leave us alone now? I have the curious impression it's me he has a grudge against.'

'Gentlemen,' said Semacgus, beaming, 'I have some important news for you. Quite surprising news, too. Nicolas, show me your boots.'

Surprised, the commissioner leant on the table with both hands and raised his right foot. Semacgus crouched, donned his spectacles and, red in the face and breathing in short gasps because of his paunch, carefully extracted some small fragments stuck to the sole. Having got his breath back, he examined them carefully.

'It's just as I thought. You've come back from the same place as the other day, so there's no need to be surprised. The same causes produce the same effects. This fully confirms all my hypotheses.'

'Are you finally going to tell us, Guillaume, the meaning of these strange words of yours?'

'First, I'm going to tell you a story which, as you'll see, will bring us back both to the death of Master Mourut and to Rue du Poirier. A quarter of a century ago, when I had put in at Pondicherry on board the *Villeflix*, a leading merchant from the Isle de France[1] was found dead in the room he occupied in the governor's palace. In the ensuing panic, there was much speculation regarding the cause of death. Some suspected poisoning, so frequent in the Indies. As a merchant ship was proposing to take the body to Port-Louis, the governor asked me to embalm the body. Wanting to set my mind at rest, I decided to perform an autopsy. I discovered disorders identical to those observed in Master Mourut. Soon afterwards, one of the governor's servants died in similar circumstances.'

'And were you unable to come to a conclusion in that case, too?' asked Bourdeau.

'Not at all! There was a witness who stated that the man had been bitten by a hamadryad.'

'What?' cried Nicolas, who had not forgotten his Jesuit education. 'Bitten by a wood nymph?'

Semacgus gave a great laugh. 'Perhaps in the course of a violent bout of lovemaking! No, hamadryad is the scientific term for the Asian king cobra.'

He took from his pocket a lead pencil and a piece of paper and skilfully drew the head of the reptile, which Nicolas looked at closely.

'But what's the connection with Monsieur Mourut? This kind of snake is not common in Rue Montmartre, as far as I know.'

'You're quite right. The fact remains that our man presented all the symptoms of death by snake venom.'

'So he was bitten or stung?'

'Remember my observation about the strange wound to the hand. I didn't want to contradict Sanson in front of you, but that necrotised wound kept reminding me of the one I had once examined. Mind you, this was a cut and not the bites characteristic of a cobra's fangs.'

'Perhaps it wasn't a cobra. Could it have been a viper?'

'I thought about that, but I'm not convinced. The viper's bite isn't necessarily fatal to a human being, even a deep one. Of course it can kill a sparrow, a rabbit, a chicken, even a dog, a very young dog at any rate. I know through Monsieur de Jussieu that a man named Fontana, physicist to the Grand Duke of Tuscany, carried out more than six thousand experiments on the subject.'

'What you say about the wound intrigues me,' said Bourdeau. 'Is it possible that someone introduced the venom into Monsieur Mourut's system through it?'

'That's the hypothesis, if you recall, that I already suggested. Everything points to the probability that we are dealing with a similar situation, in which snake venom replaces the usual kinds of poison!'

'It makes you shudder to think about it,' said the inspector. 'But in order to do that, the murderer would surely have had to have such an animal at his disposal.'

'And to keep it warm, since it's a creature of the Tropics and cannot stand cold.'

'Are there any in the Jardin du Roi?'

'Some stuffed ones, I believe.'

'And in private houses?'

'Not to my knowledge. But it's not impossible. Provided it's kept at the right temperature.'

'Nevertheless,' observed Nicolas, 'your ingenious theory suggests that it's possible to collect the venom, and I don't quite see how.'

'Nothing easier,' said Semacgus. 'I saw it done many times in the Indies. The fakirs and dervishes who handle snakes make them bite into a cloth stretched over a calabash.'

'A calabash?'

'A kind of gourd, actually an emptied and dried marrow.'

'Isn't it risky?'

'Once you hold its head firmly, the snake has no other way of defending itself. You pin it down with a forked stick. That way, you can gather the secretions from its venom gland. You have to be careful, though, when you let it go!'

'So …' said Nicolas, thinking aloud. 'In Rue du Poirier, those rabbits, those castings, that fire in the closed room …'

'And,' said Semacgus triumphantly, waving the fragments he had removed from Nicolas's boots, 'these beige and yellow scales you twice picked up on your boots. Yes, my dear Nicolas, in Rue du Poirier a criminal has been raising a snake whose venom killed Master Mourut!'

This statement was followed by a long silence.

'All things considered,' said Bourdeau, 'this should narrow the field of our enquiries. There is no local trade in this kind of snake, as far as I know.'

'Perhaps *gittani*,[2] who sometimes show snakes at fairs?'

'Highly unlikely. As they're believed to steal children, they're closely watched. If they had cobras, it would certainly be known.'

Nicolas nodded. 'A private individual, then? We're forced back on our unknown adversary. We know there was a snake in Rue du Poirier. Why and how?'

'If I may hazard an opinion,' said Semacgus, 'you're missing the point. Let me explain. Here you are, two wily policemen who have noted the existence of this animal and the consequences of its harmfulness, and have in your possession a piece of fabric coming from the Indies. To me, a mere innocent, it seems obvious that the person who uses such a method must have been a sailor, a soldier, a monk or a merchant, which would explain why such a dangerous living weapon is in his possession. Not that this makes your investigation any easier, but it should at least redirect it on more rational lines, I dare say. I would make a good suspect, for example. I've visited that part of the world, I know about cobras and I'm so devious as to reveal my own stratagem, thus clearing myself of all suspicion.'

'Ah,' said Nicolas with a laugh, 'I fear Guillaume is hoping for another taste of the Bastille.[3] He's right, of course, and we need to prepare our offensive. This is a battle, and the lines are being drawn. Let us review our plans for the days to come.'

He gave them a chronological account of all the phases of the investigation.

'One thing still intrigues me,' said Bourdeau. 'If Hénéfiance was sent to the galleys, his property must have been seized by the crown—'

'Let me stop you there, Pierre,' Nicolas cut in. 'If there was no trial and no official sentence, there are no consequences as to the inheritance.'

'Would that explain why the house remains abandoned?'

'Probably, but not why the furniture disappeared. Many objects must have been moved. Why and by whom? That is the question. Not to mention the mystery of the house opposite. Pierre, I'd like you to look into that. Who does it belong to? Go there, question the neighbours, as well as the local notaries. I sense there's a missing element there that might enlighten us.'

'You would do well,' said Semacgus, 'to also check with the navy. I'm sure Sartine will allow you access to the archives of his department, which is responsible for the penal colony at Brest.'

'Why,' asked Bourdeau, 'do we still talk of being sent to the galleys when these no longer exist?'

'You're right,' said Semacgus in a learned tone, 'that the King's galleys were abolished in 1749, after the death of their last general. Thousands of prisoners remained at the disposal of the navy in Toulon, Brest and Rochefort ...'

'But if there are no more galleys, the prisoners must be idle.'

'Not at all! As you can imagine, nobody wanted to do without such an easily exploitable workforce. I remember passing through Brest in 1755.[4] The convicts were working on the development of the port. With their picks, they were destroying the rocky constrictions on either side of the Penfeld. They were digging, clearing the rock and the silt, pumping, sinking piles, building fortifications and powder magazines. The excavation work was constant and terrifying! That's where we should be looking.'

'The fact remains,' said Bourdeau, 'that however much information we gather, the man from Rue du Poirier keeps slipping through our fingers. It's like searching for a needle in a haystack!'

'We have to reckon with the unexpected. Remember, not so long ago, the consequences of our discovery of traces of pineapple in a victim's stomach.[5] I believe in chance as the obscure manifestation of a will that is somehow beyond us.'

Bourdeau laughed, although it was not clear to Nicolas whether or not he was mocking him.

'All right,' said Nicolas. 'I'll deal with the navy and the French East India Company. Bourdeau will visit the notaries.'

'And what of Caminet?' asked Semacgus suddenly. 'Still nothing? No corpse on which to perform an autopsy?'

'His description has been distributed. The bodies fished out of the river are always carefully examined, as are those found in and outside the city.'

'Good. Then I shall pursue my research into our slippery and venomous murderer among my colleagues at the Jardin du Roi.'

Night was falling by the time they parted company. In his carriage, Nicolas pressed the release of his repeater watch. It struck seven times. He looked at it: it was fifteen minutes past the hour. He felt extremely weary, with a mixture of tiredness and hunger. Nevertheless he felt unalloyed joy at the prospect of dining with Louis and Noblecourt. The thing that brought a pang to his heart, though, was the thought of Aimée d'Arranet. She was apparently determined not to communicate with him. He forced himself not to revive the feelings of anxiety and, although he would not admit it, of jealousy that her silence and absence aroused in him. The ghost of Madame de Lastérieux interposed itself with painful insistence between him and Aimée's charming face, plunging him into a grim inner struggle.

A magnificent coach was parked outside the Noblecourt house. He recognised the arms on the door: the Maréchal de Richelieu was paying a visit to his old friend. His immediate reaction was a certain annoyance: the prospect of a tranquil evening was fading. Going in through the carriage entrance, he felt a genuine sorrow on noting the grim silence that now shrouded Master Mourut's bakery. When would the hot bakehouse smells that usually greeted him return? Life gave and took away. Those tiny everyday moments were precious instants of happiness, but they only appeared that way once they were gone. Now only emptiness bore witness to the place they had once occupied. From the servants' pantry came great roars of laughter among which he recognised those of Louis. He entered and went closer to observe the scene. Catherine, brandishing a ladle, was addressing an attentive and good-humoured audience. Even Poitevin, brush in hand, had broken off from scraping the mud off a shoe to listen. Marion was laughing fit to burst, with tears in her eyes, which she wiped with a corner of her apron. Louis, sitting astride a chair, was shaking with laughter. Cyrus was wagging his tail and barking happily. Only Mouchette, perched on the window sill, watched this incomprehensible human agitation with a kind of impassive contempt.

'Well, now,' Catherine went on, 'this turkey, I serenaded him every morning to get him to eat more. Then the terrible day arrives and, to make the flesh particularly delicate, I cut off his food, for one whole day at least. Then I let him loose in the yard so that he tries to run away and I have to run after him!'

She crouched down and pretended to chase an imaginary bird round the table, to the increased delight of her audience.

'But why all that, my God?' spluttered Marion, choking with laughter.

'It's a way of reducing him to the last degree of exasperation and terror. Because it's in that state of painful excitement that you grab him, tie him up like a criminal, then make him swallow half a glass of vinegar saturated with salt and ginger. He's in agony! Then you strangle him. You leave him hung up for two or three days. After that you pluck him, gut him, and put him first in boiling water, then in cold water. You rub him with salt, pepper and ginger, and put strips of bacon in him. Add cinnamon and cloves and then onto the spit with him.'[6]

In the midst of renewed hilarity, a surprising incident occurred that confirmed Nicolas in his suspicions, if any confirmation was still needed. The first to see Nicolas was Mouchette, who had loved him unconditionally ever since he had found her at the Palais de Cluny. She jumped to the floor and, as usual, came and rubbed her little head against his legs. She was starting to sniff them when suddenly she let out a raucous moan of terror, a shiver went down her spine, her tail swelled like a brush, and she hissed and gave off a musky odour. She was looking at his boots as if they were her sworn enemies. This uncharacteristic display startled the gathering, at last aware that the commissioner had arrived, but he himself was not surprised.

'What's wrong with Mouchette, Father? She's spitting like a demon!'

'Don't pay any attention to her, she caught the smell of an enemy species on my boots.'

'And now she smells just like the maréchal.'

'Nicolas,' said Marion, 'Monsieur is waiting for you. He asked that you go up as soon as you arrive. The maréchal is paying him a visit.'

He took off his tricorn and asked Poitevin to clean his pistol and return it to him discreetly. He had no desire for Louis to handle a weapon whose small size made it all the more dangerous. He went upstairs to see Noblecourt. By the time he was halfway up, he could already hear a high-pitched voice holding forth with great solemnity.

'Imagine, my friend, in Bordeaux those fur-wrapped fools in the Parlement tried shamelessly to oppose me! I'm accustomed to being obeyed without challenge and for everyone to submit to my will. How dare they attack a provincial governor, a marshal and peer of France? They went so far as to try and ban gambling, yes, gambling, in my house! Well, let me tell you, when I went back to Bordeaux to register the abolition of the Parlement, I treated them with the contempt they deserved.'

'You have cause for complaint, then, Monseigneur, that in Paris the revived Parlement is trying to pick a quarrel with you in the unfortunate trial of Madame de Saint-Vincent!

> *'Go back in your shell, Octave, you complain far too much*
> *You want to be spared, yet no one is free of your touch.'*

The maréchal smiled. *'Instead of concealing my troubles, I'm trying to be candid, and I find a secret sweetness in opening my heart to you.'*

'Fine words,' declared Nicolas, entering the room. 'Monseigneur, it is the sage who speaks through your mouth! It is not for nothing that you are one of the forty members of the Académie.'

'Oh, clever fellow. It took a Breton to recognise a quotation from the author of *Gil Blas, Le Diable Boiteux* and *Turcaret*!'

'Le Sage, born in Sarzeau!'

'What was I saying? Oh, yes! It must be acknowledged, above and beyond any resentment on my part, that the abolition of the Parlements was the best thing that could have happened to the kingdom. Otherwise, the magistracy, with the exception of a certain procurator ...'

Half rising from his armchair, Noblecourt bowed.

'... would inevitably have taken over every seat of power, and even the most insignificant bailiff, provided he was shrewd and cunning enough, would have become king in his village or his circle. The King has to reign without constraint and without protest. But who will listen to us now? Well, Marquis, what answer can you give me concerning your son? Shall we make him a page?'

'Maréchal, I am enormously grateful, but we have to ask him.'

'What do you mean, ask him? What a curious idea! What answer could he give to such an exceptional proposition? Let him take his place uncomplainingly in the line of the Ranreuils and we will take him far. Pah! Since when do we consult children about their future? Do they even have a future? No, merely the continuation of the greatness of their house! Fetch him, I'm going to speak to him; I fear the bonny lad is splitting hairs and needs to be told a few home truths.'

What else was there to do but to obey? The maréchal knew that Louis was in the house. This situation troubled Nicolas, who would have preferred to sound out his son first about the proposal. It made him surprisingly sad. He was being deprived of a privilege that was his by nature. He tried to examine more closely what he was feeling. It was obvious that Louis's fate was about to be sealed, and the whole process seemed inexorable. In a flash, he recalled the astronomical clock he had seen and admired in the cathedral at Strasbourg during the journey to Vienna. He thought he could hear the mechanical sound of its gears and, with it, there loomed up an inevitable series of consequences. One day, he himself had been thrust off the common path by a sudden decision of his father, the Marquis de Ranreuil. He had felt unhappy and afraid, but had been unable to resist his destiny. Paris had snatched him up, and Sartine and Lardin had set him on a path he had originally neither wanted nor chosen. On the other hand, there was little doubt that the path opening up before Louis corresponded to his deepest desires. As he went to fetch the boy, he sighed: his own childhood had been stolen from him and now he would have to watch, powerless to intervene, as a crucial decision was made regarding his own son.

The interview went much as he had expected. Richelieu embellished his offer with the most enticing privileges. His caressing tone and the extravagant compliments he lavished on the young Ranreuil, added to what the victor of Mahon must represent in the eyes of a child, would have won over even those less innocent. Without too much effort, he inflamed Louis's imagination and gained his consent to a future that would thrust him into the most brilliant – and most dangerous – of environments: the world of the Court and the aristocracy. In all this, what clearly mattered most to the boy was the prospect of being close to the King and the chance to prepare for the military career for which he yearned.

'Go now,' said Richelieu, graciously dismissing the applicant, 'and do honour to your grandfather and your father …'

He let him withdraw.

'That boy will go far. He bears himself well, he has a handsome face and an alert air. He needs to make a good marriage, to a girl from an important family.' He assumed a ribald air which creased his mummified old face. 'Gentlemen, I am afraid I must leave you. I'm expected in town.'

He waved his hand in a boastful but evasive gesture: he did not need to spell things out. Noblecourt stood up to see his guest out. Nicolas preceded him with a torch to light their descent. The procession thus reached the street in pomp.

'Nicolas, you seem quite sombre,' sighed Noblecourt, walking back upstairs to his apartment, leaning on the commissioner's arm.

'No ... But this has all been so rushed. I fear Louis may have committed himself without much understanding of what he will be obliged to do.'

'Having known you such a long time, I can read your mind. You would have preferred to speak to Louis first. But ask yourself, would the result have been any different? He's more mature than you might imagine. You yourself, when I gave you lessons in law at the request of Lardin, seemed lacking in experience, and yet what force of character was already there! Let him build and strengthen his. Too much earnestness on the part of parents, and fathers in particular, deprives children of their lovable innocence and replaces it with a touch of hypocrisy that makes them odious. Consider his wish to be a good servant to the King. Where do you think this praiseworthy inclination will take him? It comes from the Ranreuils, from you and, I would say, from his mother, an honest woman badly treated by fate. Learn to take it calmly. Don't give your son the impression that you harbour doubts about his choice. On the contrary, support it and give him as much advice as possible, advice which will be indispensable to him in his new situation. I'm convinced it is good to follow one's inclination provided the aim is elevated enough.'

'What do they say,' asked Nicolas, reassured by the former procurator's serene philosophy, 'about the Prince de Conti? You, for whom city and Court hold no secrets, can surely tell me.'

'It's strange that you should speak of him now. Just before you came in, Richelieu, the old fox, was complaining about the prince's collusion with the Parlement. Hence that furious diatribe against the fur-wrapped fools which you caught.'

'He's said to be popular.'

'Pah! He claims to be popular, and many other things, too. He thinks he can lead the Parlement and become a new Duc de Beaufort[7] to the common people. But he's not well thought of by the one and not well known to the other. He's ready for anything and good for nothing. The most handsome and imposing of men, the idol and example of the freethinkers. A manner and style all of his own, quoting Rabelais and sometimes speaking like him. One passage describes him, and it's by his mother: "My son has wit. He has a lot, you see a great expanse of it at first, but he's an obelisk: he gets smaller the more he rises and ends in a point, like a steeple!"'[8]

'Will the maréchal ever stop?'

Noblecourt shook his head sadly. 'There are two ways of being old. One consists of draping oneself in the discomforts of age like a coronation cloak. The other, which Richelieu has chosen, consists of believing and making others believe, through all kinds of expedients, that age doesn't matter at all.

> *'The years of his youth have been very long*
> *So far just eighty and still going strong.'*

'And yours?'

He smiled. 'Why, do you think I'm old? It's entirely up to me if I want to be so. To be honest, I combine the two formulas. I proclaim that I'm not old and sometimes it works. One can at least stop oneself from appearing like an old man: one simply doesn't let oneself go, in body or mind. It's too bad for those who give up. I also tell myself that I don't want to die. I still have too much curiosity ... I don't know how well that will work.'

The murmur of voices and the tinkling of glasses and china could be heard from the library: Marion and Catherine were laying the table. Louis peered in shyly. Nicolas looked at him with pride. It was true that he already bore himself well, much more than he himself had done at his age. He had the same way of holding his head high as his grandfather. Catherine scolded them and pushed them into the library. The soup was eaten in silence.

'Was that affected little man really a great general once, Father?' ventured Louis.

'Ah, the stern judgement of youth!' said Nicolas. 'Louis, never trust appearances. You know the battle of Fontenoy, in which my father took part. Well, did you know that the famous day very nearly ended in terrible disaster? The reason it didn't was all due to that little man. Our troops were being driven from the field, and the officers were in a panic. There was an improvised mounted war council before the late King, who was not sure of the decision to take. Richelieu spoke up. He pointed out that they still had one last resource: a battery that could pound the enemy infantry and cause terrible losses, but which the Maréchal de Saxe had forbidden to be used. "The King is well above the maréchal," cried Richelieu; "he has only to give the order!"'

'And what happened?'

'The King followed his advice, which was the right decision. After two or three volleys, the enemy were weakened and it was at that moment that Richelieu charged with the King's Household and your grandfather, and the enemy were cut to pieces. Thus history is made. Remember that heroic deed, and bear in mind also that the maréchal has always granted me his protection. You will hear much slander about him, for that is the way of the Court. Just remember this: he's a great soldier and a friend to our house and to Monsieur de Noblecourt.'

The latter bowed solemnly.

'Ah, my father, how I would love to have such experiences!'

The enthusiasm of sons, thought Nicolas, increased the anxiety of fathers. He himself had doubtless been a source of concern to the Marquis de Ranreuil ... God knew that in his career there had been no lack of terrible sights. But nothing in his memory could compare with the accounts of the aftermath of battles described by his father with that cold detachment that concealed, as he now realised, the fact that he was haunted by the many horrors he had seen. Images of stripped and heaped bodies crowded into his mind: he tried to dismiss them. Next, Louis questioned his father tirelessly about the functions of a page. His answers were complemented by the advice of Monsieur de Noblecourt, who excelled in drawing useful lessons from the facts. Marion and Catherine had, as always, surpassed themselves. One of the big rabbits that Poitevin raised in a hutch at the bottom of the garden, a practice which obliged him to frequent certain places known to him alone to obtain their food, had been sacrificed and meticulously deboned. Rolled around its own liver and pieces of pig's throat, it had been seasoned with chopped herbs, then wrapped in a caul as fine as hemstitched lace. Thus adorned, the rabbit, lying on a bed of bacon rashers in an earthenware pot, moistened with veal stock and a glass of white wine, had been steamed in the oven. The slices of this delight had been arranged on a bed of sorrel.

'After Juilly, this is Christmas!' cried Louis, who was not easily impressed by food.

'And you haven't seen what comes next,' said Catherine.

There soon appeared a treat, a prodigious stack of omelettes spread with apricot jam, currant jelly and cherry plum compote, covered in sugar and glazed. It was necessary to restrain Noblecourt, who, after sampling the rabbit – his lodger, as he put it – tried to serve himself such a large portion of dessert that it immediately unleashed the censure of the two women, who joined forces to take away his plate, much to his despair.

The evening ended calmly enough, with a discussion of the forthcoming coronation. Louis, his cheeks red with excitement, wondered if he would be able to attend. As yet, there was no answer to the question, but Nicolas promised to take him, as soon as he had time, to see the King's coach, which was on display. More and more people were going every day to gaze at the decorations and paintings on the coach, which were rumoured to be of a richness, finish and beauty to delight the most demanding of connoisseurs. Many were also rushing to Aubert's jewellery shop to see the diamond-encrusted crown, including the Régent and the Sancy, valued at more than eighteen million *livres*. The order of the King's progress and the ceremonies had just been published. His Majesty would leave Versailles in great pomp, with the Queen, the princes, the Court and the ministers. His aunts would remain in the palace with the Comtesse d'Artois, who was pregnant. The monarch would be received in every town through which he passed with a peal of bells, cannon fire and the cheers of the people. These future cheers brought a smile to Noblecourt's face: they struck him as a curious touch, as if they could be ordered up like everything else. Louis announced excitedly that, according to the newspaper, twenty thousand post horses would be constantly running between Paris and Reims. And on this detail, it was time for them to retire to their respective rooms.

'It's quite late,' said Nicolas, glancing at the clock on the mantelpiece.

'Pah!' said Noblecourt. 'That thing's stopped, and they forgot to wind it. Not that it matters, it still shows the exact time twice a day with admirable regularity!'

The night was already far advanced when Nicolas was woken from a deep sleep by a heart-rending cry, apparently coming from Louis's room. He rushed to it and found his son sitting up in bed, wild-eyed, his face dripping with sweat. Nicolas took him in his arms. He was shaking all over.

'Hush now, it was only a nightmare. Calm down, the dinner was too lavish. This is the normal consequence of bad digestion.'

'Father, I saw the Capuchin again.'

'What do you mean? The one from Juilly?'

'Yes, he was trying to drag me away … I resisted … I was going

312

to … Then I woke up.' Calmer now, he seemed lost in thought for a moment. 'Seeing him again in my dream reminded me of a detail that may be of some use to you, Father.'

'Go on, Louis.'

'Do you know how these monks dress?'

'Of course. A pointed hood, a cloak and bare feet …'

'… in leather sandals.'

'And?'

'An image came back into my mind. The Capuchin's ankles looked burnt.'

'Burnt?'

'He had a pinkish scar on each leg.'

'Did you notice anything about his face? Did your dream enlighten you at all?'

'No … At Juilly, he kept his head bowed, with his hood pulled down low. I only saw the top of his beard. Everything was vague, just like in the dream.'

For the second night in a row, Nicolas watched over his son's sleep. After much thought, he too dozed off, and his restless slumber was full of the strange details Louis had just revealed.

XI

ON THE ATTACK

I do not know where we get the confidence
that we can put a stop to this agitation.
If I am not mistaken, such riots have
always preceded revolutions.
LETTER FROM THE BAILLI DE MIRABEAU TO THE DUC DE LA VRILLIÈRE, 1775

Friday 5 May 1775

The next day, Monsieur de La Borde appeared in Rue Montmartre
at dawn. He had been sent on the orders of the Duc de La Vrillière
to fetch Nicolas. The former servant of Louis XV did not know the
reason for this summons. He had received a letter from the Minister
of the King's Household during the night to the effect that he was to
fetch the commissioner as soon as he was out of bed. The old Court
was stirring itself, strengthened by that secret complicity among those
who had been present at Louis XV's death. In the carriage, the two
friends tried at first to make conversation, but it soon petered out.
Nicolas was lost in thought. What could La Vrillière, with whom he
shared a burdensome private secret[1] but who since then had seemed to
keep him at a distance, possibly want with him now?

When they reached the Saint-Florentin mansion, the carriage
stopped in the courtyard. La Borde did not get out and Nicolas climbed
alone to the minister's apartments, not without sadness at the sight of
this place which had been the scene of such horrific events. Provence,
the valet, received him in a friendly manner, like an old acquaintance.
Admitted to the study, where the inner shutters were still closed, he

recognised, in the shadows tempered by the light of the dying fire, the figure of the Duc de La Vrillière, huddled in an armchair, a dressing gown wrapped round his shoulders. Nicolas was struck by the change in him: he was thinner, with drawn features and trembling hands, his eyes sunk deep in their sockets. He threw the visitor an expressionless look, and with a weary gesture motioned him to sit down.

He sighed. 'It seems you're not going to get away now! His Majesty mentioned the Marquis de Ranreuil yesterday at his levee in front of everyone. He was presenting you! Although of course you've long been part of the King's hunt. He added that he would like it if Louis de Ranreuil, your son, was admitted to the pages. That's true recognition!'

Nicolas suddenly understood the reason for Richelieu's insistence. There could be no refusal: the decision had already been taken.

'Monseigneur, I've never at any moment—'

'Do you think I've forgotten how you feel about the title? I remember you expressing your opinion openly to the late King. Madame de Pompadour spoke of it to me a few days before she died. But you must act as if it mattered to you, Monsieur. If only for your son's sake. Especially for your son's sake' – his voice cracked – 'because at least you can show yours!'

Nicolas remained silent, respecting the minister's sorrow.

'Oh, I know how discreet you are. I should have realised that from the start. You are loyal and brave, the late King knew that, and the new King, too, is convinced of it. That's why I wanted to see you. Don't interrupt. I have two or three things to tell you.'

With difficulty, he rose from his chair and moved it closer to Nicolas.

'My days as a minister are numbered. No, no, it's true! I am no longer at Court, even though recent events have drawn me a little closer to the King. But what cause do I have to complain? So many years in power[2] are a source of amazement. Can I not aspire to rest?

Maurepas, my relative, will support me as long as it does not harm him. What we have just witnessed was serious, and could easily have degenerated even further. Despicable posters are stuck to the walls every night, even to the door of the King's study at Versailles! Look, here's last night's harvest.'

He took some crumpled papers lying on a pedestal table.

'Listen to this: "Louis XVI will be crowned on 11 June and slaughtered on 12 June." Or this one: "If bread does not come down, we will exterminate the King and all the Bourbons and set fire to the palace."[3] At least in the old days it was the King's mistress who aroused the anger of the mob.'

He's forgetting the long-standing rumours about the famine pact, thought Nicolas, affected nevertheless by the minister's vehemence. 'Loyal citizens are shocked by such things!'

'Do you understand what's going on? This whole wave of unrest has apparently been organised by leaders who have stayed in the shadows, the whole intention being somehow to threaten the throne. Who do we dare suspect? Those who are above suspicion!'

His voice became almost inaudible.

'Yes, those who are above suspicion. There are plenty of lampoons and pamphlets in circulation, published in England, filled with nonsensical tales and accusing, among others, Madame Adélaïde, Sartine, Lenoir and Abbé Terray. But curiously, the people who are not named are the very ones who could profit from this unrest. Those who are most opposed to royal authority ... One of them, anyway ... His Majesty was particularly anxious about that. "I hope," he said to me, "for the sake of my name, that these are just baseless slanders." That simpleton is obviously the one under suspicion.'

The minister, who was known not to mince his words, had become himself again in his anger. For all his circumlocution in this case, he was clearly pointing the finger at the Prince de Conti. The King's confidential aside was easily explained: he might not like La Vrillière but, in the heat of the situation, the minister nevertheless remained the late King's last confidant, someone to whom he could confide his innermost thoughts.

'The thing is,' La Vrillière went on, 'bread has often been just as expensive and just as mouldy as today without arousing such anger from the people. There have been greater grievances in the past. There is no famine, no shortage, and yet what do we see? People who, in order to get enough to eat, throw in the river all the corn and flour they can find![4] Not to mention the gold lavishly distributed and discovered in the pockets of those arrested!'

'That is in fact the opinion of the Lieutenant General of Police. I mean, of Monsieur Lenoir ...'

'Ah, let's not talk about him! I was highly critical of the way you were disgraced on the death of the King, our late master. I have impressed upon Lenoir's successor Albert that such a thing is not to happen again. For now, and for as long as you are under my protection, and the King's, he will not dare to pick a quarrel with you. You should be aware, though, that he considers you Sartine's creature and won't hesitate, when he think it opportune, to thwart your activities. Changing the subject, who killed Mourut the baker?'

The question caught Nicolas unawares. So the minister was as well informed as ever, almost certainly thanks to Sartine.

'The answer is more complicated than the question and, to be honest, somewhat premature.'

'Just as I thought. Go now, Marquis, and don't weaken! You once taught me never to despair. Remember, if our young King needs our help, we must give it.'

Nicolas withdrew. He had been deeply moved by this interview. The duc was better than his reputation. An expression of real kindness had crossed his haggard face several times, and, as long as he was in power, he would protect Nicolas. When his vices and virtues came to be weighed on the Day of Judgement, his loyalty might well save him.

La Borde was still in his carriage, and apparently in no hurry. He offered to take Nicolas wherever he had to go. The next stop was the office of the French East India Company, located in a former annexe of the Palais Mazarin on the corner of Rue Vivienne and Rue Neuve-des-Petits-Champs. La Borde, who had only recently gone into business, remarked that there was more money in that district than in the whole of the rest of Paris. Bankers and brokers and all those who dealt in money could be seen there, hurrying on their way to the Stock Exchange. He added, with a laugh, that even the harlots were more financial there than anywhere else, and that they could easily spot someone with a lot of money. Nicolas was prepared to take his word for it.

The activities of the Company, a vast commercial empire, had been in abeyance since the loss of most of its possessions in the Indies in 1763. It was no easy task for the commissioner to be admitted to the offices, especially as, not knowing what he was looking for, his request came across as quite vague.

He was passed from arrogant clerks to mistrustful directors. In the end, an usher led him, cane in hand, to the attic, where he was invited to rummage at his leisure through mountains of papers. As he hesitated, unsure where to start, he became aware of a strange noise that grew increasingly distinct as it came nearer. He was immediately on his guard. The noise was a kind of scraping, followed by a rubbing, the whole accompanied by irregular panting. The large room was dimly illumined by the murky daylight falling through window panes grey with dust.

Nicolas put his hand on the grip of the miniature pistol lodged in a wing of his tricorn and gently cocked the hammer. He moved so that he was against the light, at the base of a window protected on either side by large cupboards. Silence had returned, but now he could hear breathing somewhere close. Slowly his eyes came to rest on the corner of a pile of yellowed files. A dark shape had appeared on the floor, which proved to be a huge shoe at the end of a short leg. A misshapen creature followed this strange apparition, dressed in black, hunchbacked, with a huge head on a short torso and disproportionately long arms. Two large, soft black eyes gave a touch of humanity to a bloated face. With a heave, the creature swung his leg and thrust his club foot forward, then straightened up and nodded his head.

'I fear that I scared you, Monsieur,' he said in a solemn voice. 'Please forgive me, that wasn't my intention. God has made me in such a way that my appearance usually creates an unfavourable impression.' He completed this introduction with a slow, complicated bow.

Nicolas took his hand off the grip of his pistol, releasing the hammer, and put it back in the protective wing of his tricorn. 'I am sorry, Monsieur, to have appeared to be on my guard. I am Nicolas Le Floch, police commissioner at the Châtelet. Experience has taught me to be cautious at all times.'

'Justin Belhome,' the man said, with a smile that made his mouth go horribly slack. 'Yes, Monsieur, that's my name. I am the Company's archivist, the lord of the attic. If you have come this far, it means you have been authorised, and so I am your humble servant.'

'Alas, I'm looking for a needle in a haystack! A passenger returning from the Indies. I don't know exactly when he got back to France. Two or three years ago, most likely … It's all a bit vague.'

Suddenly, Belhome clambered onto a cupboard that had no doors. He swung his foot as if to balance himself and, clinging to heaps of files that swayed dangerously, managed to get to the top. With one hand, he seized three bundles of papers, then did an about-turn and slid noisily to the floor until he was once again face to face with Nicolas.

'Let's see,' he said. 'Toulon, 1772, 1773 and 1774. The first thing you need to know is that all you will find here are the lists of ships that touched land, as well as any perils they encountered on the sea.'

Nicolas reflected for a brief moment. 'With these lists, how much can I expect to find?'

'If you have the authority and the means, you'd be able to obtain the passenger lists, too. But for that, you have to consult the offices at Lorient or Port-Louis.'

'How long does it take to look through your lists?'

'Hours … It's all mixed up, Africa and America. I can do it if you like; my other tasks are not especially difficult or time-consuming.'

'Monsieur, I would be embarrassed to burden you with this extra work. But in return, if I can be useful to you in any way …'

'Not at all, Monsieur. If you want to come back tomorrow morning, I'll have finished by then.'

Nicolas left the friendly archivist already absorbed in his registers, following the minute annotations with a ruler. He found La Borde reading and in no way upset at all the time he had been waiting. Nicolas reported the results of his efforts, and informed him that he now had to go to the Department of the Navy in Versailles. La Borde offered to take him there. He seemed so happy to stay with Nicolas that the commissioner agreed. Their conversation led to confidences. Nicolas spoke about Aimée d'Arranet, while La Borde claimed to be very much in love with his young wife. But the difference in age and experience, and perhaps his own demands, had antagonised a spouse who was plagued with illness. Her nervous melancholy firmly resisted all potions and cures. La Borde had come to think that if she had a position at Court, in the Queen's household or in those of the princesses, she would find an outlet that might moderate and gradually dispel this prolonged moral irritation. He begged Nicolas to forgive him for burdening him with his worries, and asked him about Louis.

Learning of his acceptance among the pages of the Grand Stables, he advised his friend to keep an eye on his son, even if only from a distance. It could be the beginning of a brilliant career, but there was much disorder in those circles. It was possible to learn good manners there, yes, but also the worst tone. It was certainly not the place to go for decorum and morality. The young nobles were left very much to their own devices. If a page did not resist the example set by his elders, he could become a thoroughly bad lot.

Once they had crossed the Seine, their conversation centred on the recent events.

'You know our countrymen,' said La Borde. 'The bourgeois and those of private means got a fright, but, as ever, now that calm has been restored, they are starting to blame the government and to excuse the insurrectionists. It is considered quite inappropriate at a time like this for Monsieur Turgot to have committed funds to equipping the troops assembled around Paris. It's all going to cost from thirty to forty million. Now the women of fashion have taken to wearing revolutionary bonnets! There will be songs about it next! A sad first anniversary for the present reign.'

In Versailles, the offices of the navy occupied the same building as Foreign Affairs. Nicolas was about to see if there was a possibility that Sartine would receive him when he saw Admiral d'Arranet coming towards him. He was just back from a mission of inspection and enquired as to what it was that brought Nicolas to the ministry. It seemed to Nicolas that there was a new-found awkwardness between them.

Neither man mentioned Aimée, although she hovered over their words. The admiral led him through the offices and placed him in the hands of a clerk who dealt with the penal colony at Brest. He was bidding farewell to Monsieur d'Arranet when the latter seized him by the hands.

'Do not despair. You brought her back to me once, I'll do the same for you. She's temperamental.'

He muttered a few more indistinct words with a pleasant smile and left Nicolas feeling both happy and perplexed. The clerk admitted him to his office and bent over backwards to please someone who came so highly recommended. He explained in a scholarly fashion what being sentenced to the penal colony meant, and how difficult it was to escape.

'During the day, the convicts are chained to each other by their feet, two by two. At night, they are attached to a wooden table, where they sleep. You also have to remember that it is not easy for them to conceal who they are, as they are branded on the shoulder.'

It was possible, Nicolas thought, that, not having been officially sentenced, Hénéfiance did not have that terrible mark on the shoulder. On the other hand, he remembered Louis's dream and the Capuchin with the scars on his ankles.

'An escapee needs to find other clothes that are less conspicuous than his prison uniform. He has a shaved head. It isn't easy to get out of Brest. The guards are constantly patrolling. The arsenal is surrounded by a perimeter wall, and the city is walled, too. The gates are heavily guarded. As soon as the cannon sounds, the soldiers set off in pursuit. Rewards are offered to anyone helping to recover the fugitive, and the mounted constabulary scour the countryside. You have to remember, Monsieur, that there aren't many ways off the peninsula. The only major road is the one from Morlaix to Rennes. The port of Landerneau is under constant surveillance. If you escaped by sea, you'd have to get to Crozon and from there take the Quimper road. But it's impossible to get around if you don't speak Breton.'

For the information Nicolas wanted, the clerk consulted an archive that rivalled that of the Lieutenancy General of Police. Hénéfiance, who had arrived in Brest with other prisoners in 1768, had disappeared in 1769. Considered intelligent but a bit of a rebel, he had, like many convicts, worked outside the prison. A short note mentioned that while doing so he had learnt Breton. It had not been possible to establish if he had perished in his attempt to escape by sea. There was not even any proof that he had taken the rowing boat that had been found adrift.

As he walked back to where La Borde was waiting, Nicolas wondered if the fugitive had been able to reach a port. Neither Lorient nor Port-Louis was far, and they were natural gateways to the East and the Indies. Speaking Breton would have made it easier to get away by land, the peasants being by nature uncooperative towards the guards from the colony and all the more inclined to help an unfortunate who was able to gain their trust by making himself understood in their language. It was starting to seem likely that the former convict had indeed been a passenger on one of the vessels of the French East India Company. He was therefore expecting a great deal from whatever details Justin Belhome could provide, as well as those that might be gleaned in Lorient. There was a possibility, though, that all these enquiries were in vain: if Hénéfiance had returned to France, it was sure to have been under another name.

He would have to do a great deal of cross-checking in order to sift the essential facts from what was of minor importance.

That would not be enough to find Hénéfiance. An unexpected discovery or event might well be needed to confirm that the ex-convict was indeed his mysterious adversary. Nicolas had not given up hope, trusting in a kind of efficacious grace which often intervened to help him in his investigations.

It was getting late, and La Borde invited Nicolas to dine with him. He could, if he wished, spend the night in the little dwelling his friend had retained in an unassuming street in Versailles after the death of the late King. Nicolas realised that, with the persistence of his wife's illness, the former man about town had not entirely given up on a life of pleasure, and had found an acceptable accommodation with heaven. The evening was a delight, much enlivened by the maid who served them, who was extremely pretty. They talked about opera, travel, cartography and publishing, and evoked emotional memories of Louis XV until late into the night.

Saturday 6 May 1775

Early in the morning, La Borde drove Nicolas back to the Grand Châtelet. Bad news awaited him there. An envoy from the French

East India Company had tried to reach the commissioner at dawn. Justin Belhome had been discovered lying dead amid heaps of fallen files. His skull had been fractured.

The possibility that it might have been an accident had immediately been ruled out. In his fingers, the dead man was clutching fragments from a register that had clearly been torn from his hands. The book itself had disappeared, doubtless after a violent struggle, to which the surrounding disorder bore witness. Bourdeau had rushed straight to the scene and would soon be back. He had asked that the commissioner be kept at the Châtelet if he was to reappear before then.

This wait gave Nicolas the opportunity for some bitter reflections. So, he thought, an innocent man had died because of him. That old fixation of his had returned: Mauval killed in a duel in the dark, an old soldier hanged in his prison cell, Truche de la Chaux executed in the public square ... He recalled Belhome's kindly look as he had unhesitatingly offered his services. Why did he, Nicolas Le Floch, have to be the dark instrument of fate? What demon had led him to the attic of the French East India Company? He felt a sorrow against which reason was powerless, and found it hard to convince himself that he had nothing to do with this death. Canon Le Floch, like Noblecourt but for other reasons, had always said that coincidences were never fortuitous.

The one positive thing he could take away from this tragedy was that it proved his investigation was moving in the right direction. Justin Belhome had died because he had discovered something that was a threat to his killer. What else could it have been but the name of the ship, or even the names of the passengers on it? An emissary had to be urgently dispatched to Lorient with instructions to scour the archives there. Luckily, their search was narrowing. It was, however, to be feared that there might be a long list in which there would be nothing to mark out the adversary. But what else could he do? If the documents kept by the French East India Company in Paris had been innocuous, they would not have led to their destruction and the death of an innocent man. Immediately, he drew up orders for a mission on one of the blank documents signed by the Duc de La Vrillière, which he kept with him permanently and which he used sparingly, and only in urgent cases. This one was extremely urgent. With that document, all doors would open to Rabouine, and even the most stubborn resistance would not stop him finding what he was supposed to find. No sooner had he affixed his seal than Bourdeau appeared.

'We've been looking for you everywhere. The directors of the Company say that you met the victim yesterday.'

'So it was in fact Justin Belhome?'

'Yes. He was working there during the night, the large number of burnt candles bear witness to that. It's a clear case of murder. Scratches, bruises, torn clothes, fractured skull. Ill-equipped physically as he was, the poor man defended himself tooth and nail ...'

Bourdeau took from his pocket some little triangles of crumpled, bloodstained paper and handed them to Nicolas, who examined them carefully.

'You see, Pierre,' he said, 'these are corners of pages marked with the seal of the Company, a crown over a shield with fleurs-de-lis and a Neptune, the whole thing supported by two savages carrying bows. They are what remains of the register he must have been consulting when it was torn from his hands. Do you know why?'

'I don't see what you're getting at.'

'Why do you think he was protecting that register?'

'I have no idea.'

'Because he had no doubt found some information concerning the questions I've been asking myself about Hénéfiance.' He showed him the pieces of paper. 'Look, there are page numbers, 134, 135 and 136, and half of the year 1774. All the same, all he would have found would have been the lists of the ships, and that wouldn't have been enough to tell us what we need to know.'

'So why protect that register in particular?'

'No doubt there was something else in it, something more enlightening perhaps. I'm sending Rabouine to Lorient. There must be a copy of the register there.' He gave him the signed document. 'I want him to leave immediately. Let him take whatever he wants for his expenses. As for me, I'm off to police headquarters to show myself to the new Lieutenant General. That may be useful in the future ... Will we need to perform an autopsy on the poor man?'

'No. There is no doubt about the cause of death. We can rule out an accident. The door of the Company building was closed, but the porter was woken in the middle of the night by knocking. He opened up and didn't see anyone there. It's likely he was still half asleep and didn't notice a thing, that's what he says anyway. In the darkness, the killer may have slipped past him. To get out again would have been child's play; all he needed to do was pull the door from the inside: it wasn't locked, in order to let Belhome out.'

'All of which seems quite likely!'

'And the murderer seems to have had an accomplice, a woman.'

'On what do you base that supposition? Do you have any evidence?'

'Almost. The "owl" witnessed the scene.'

'What? Was Restif there? He always seems to be where you least expect him. Good heavens, his presence could be useful to us.'

'He's here now, if you want to question him.'

When Restif entered the office, his sidling walk reminded Nicolas of the crabs on the seashore of his native Brittany. He did not like the man or the rumours that clung to him, and always felt uneasy in his presence. He was dressed in a greenish greatcoat, and his head was covered by a long hat with raised parallel brims.

'So, Monsieur Restif, still on the lookout?'

'I like to wander amid the shadows of our vast capital. There are so many things to see when all eyes are closed! All secrets interest me, but especially those concerning vice and crime.'

326

'All right, then. Tell me what you saw last night. First of all, what were you doing there?'

'Judge for yourself. The thing was so strange that, as a good citizen, I wanted to tell someone. In the early hours of the morning I went to the guardroom in Rue Vivienne and that was where I saw Inspector Bourdeau.'

'Your words are far from clear. Go back to the beginning.'

'To tell the truth, I was wandering near the Bibliothèque du Roi when suddenly—'

'Let's be more precise. What time was this?'

'Oh, I never bother about the time, but, judging by the moon, it was between eleven o'clock and midnight. Suddenly, as I had almost reached Rue Sainte-Anne, close to the Louvois mansion, I passed a pretty young thing with skirts hitched up high, revealing perfect legs and consequently an exquisite little foot, the kind I idolise passionately. The two often go together! ... In short, I retraced my steps and started following her. I was just about to inform her of the pleasure it gave me to gaze on her when a shadowy figure emerged from a semicircular carriage entrance, approached her, and whispered something in her ear. Gold coins having changed hands, she went off with him. Curious as always about what was going to happen, I remained a few steps behind, hugging the wall in silence. They led me as far as Rue Neuve-des-Petits-Champs. There, there was another exchange of words, which seemed to me a repetition of the first. I was soon to understand the reason for it. The monk—'

'The monk? You didn't mention that before.'

'Forgive me, sometimes I get so carried away by my stories that I leave out details. Yes, a Capuchin monk. Once he had repeated his instructions to the girl, he withdrew into a niche in the wall, out of the light of the street lamps. I soon understood why. The girl knocked at the door of the French East India Company. After a while, the porter appeared. He was either half asleep or drunk, because he was quite unsteady on his feet. The girl drew him a few steps from the door, using the most provocative gestures.'

'For a long time?'

'As long as it took for the monk to slip inside the building. Then the girl pushed the porter away and he fell in the gutter. He got up and went back in, cursing. As for her, she didn't bother to wait for her accomplice. She took her skirts in both hands, and ran off into the night, revealing two delightful ankles in passing. I set off in pursuit and finally, out of breath, caught up with the strumpet in Place des Victoires.'

'Did you question her on her strange conduct?'

'In my own fatherly way …' He rubbed his hands. '"My sweet," I said, "where are you running so fast?" Reassured by my paternal appearance, she had no hesitation in confiding in me. I saw at once that she was fairly new to the profession. Having walked all the way from her village to the big city, and having immediately been taken in hand by a handsome young French Guard, she had since been supplementing his income. The Capuchin who had approached her had fed her a cock-and-bull story to the effect that he was not really a monk but had disguised himself in order to pay a visit that night to a beauty with whom he was in love. All she had to do for him was distract the porter's attention for a few moments. I left Colette, for that was her name, and got back to the French East India Company building just in time to see the lover in question coming out.'

'Was he carrying anything?'

'Now that you mention it, I did in fact have the impression that he was concealing something under his robe. I followed him at a distance as far as Passage de Valois, alongside the Palais-Royal, where, to my surprise, a carriage was waiting for him …'

'And?'

'Alas! It drove off. But I did notice something that I'm sure will be of great interest to you.'

'Out with it!'

'The carriage belonged to a great house, a very great house ...' He winked, which made Nicolas think of the night bird from which the author took his pen name. '... that of the Prince de Conti.'

'Are you sure?' asked Nicolas, startled by the mention of that name, which suddenly linked together other observations he had made in the course of his investigation.

'Very, having seen the coat of arms on the door. Gold with a cross of gules surrounded by sixteen alerions of azure, four in each canton! I should add that a paper had been stuck over it, presumably to conceal it, but the dampness had made it transparent.'

'I see. And would you be able to find this girl again?'

'I'm sure I would, given time. But don't go imagining she'll be able to tell you any more than she told me. She was merely the accidental and innocent instrument of an odious plot.'

'Do you think she'd recognise this monk?'

'Impossible. He had his hood pulled down over his face and always kept well away from the street lamps.'

'You have to find her for us. The day I lay my hands on this man, I will need her to identify him.'

'I will do my best. You know how eager I am to please you.'

'We appreciate your help,' replied Nicolas, although his benevolent nature bridled somewhat at a character about whom he knew so many unsavoury things.

'I remain your obedient servant.'

Once Restif had gone, Nicolas was silent for a while, then resumed his instructions to Bourdeau.

'Don't forget to keep checking on the houses in Rue du Poirier. We now also need surveillance on all carriages bearing the arms of the Prince de Conti. I want to see the Temple enclosure completely surrounded by spies. We mustn't miss a chance to flush out the stranger if he's found refuge in that den of thieves!'

Just as he was setting off back to police headquarters, Rabouine appeared, followed by Tirepot. Red-faced, out of breath and extremely excited, they were both clearly dying to share an important piece of news.

'Something new?' asked the commissioner impassively.

'And very important!'

'Go on.'

'Tirepot first, because it's thanks to him that everything worked out the way it did.'

Tirepot, who was clearly in his element, assumed his wiliest expression. 'Nicolas, my boy, you are being followed and spied on!'

'What do you mean?'

'Exactly what I say. And not by only one man: several have been taking turns to dog your steps.'

'And how do you know that?'

Tirepot gave a smug grin. 'Well, at the request of Rabouine, who's always very concerned about your safety, I've had a whole network of my people protecting you. You know from experience that the person being watched is rarely aware of it. Otherwise, that would be the end of all secret police activity.'

'And?'

'And you have been trailed wherever you have gone.'

'What evidence do you have for that?'

'Yesterday, you went to see Monsieur de Saint-Florentin, I mean the Duc de La Vrillière, in Monsieur de La Borde's carriage. Oh, yes! A cab was following you at a distance. From there, you went to the French East India Company. After that, it was no longer within my province, because you went outside the walls.'

'Actually, I was in Versailles. But today?'

'The same as yesterday. When you got to the Grand Châtelet, Monsieur de La Borde's coach had its counterpart behind it.'

'What are we waiting for to arrest this person?' said Nicolas.

'Ah-ha!'

'I don't understand.'

'We decided to catch him in his own trap, so to speak!'

'Let's stop playing blind man's buff. Enlighten me! But tell me one thing first: how did you spot my pursuer?'

'Ah! We knew you'd come back to the Châtelet sooner or later. We just had to wait. And in fact, a cab was following you.'

'So he's still outside, waiting for me?'

'What do you take us for? We're cleverer than that. We went just that bit too close to the cab in question. Whoever was inside must have been intrigued by our tricks, and the cab immediately left.'

'So you lost it?'

'No,' said Rabouine, taking up the story, 'we deliberately forced it to decamp, the better to have it followed. Tirepot's band are doing their job as we speak, and should be reporting back to us as it moves about.'

'Good,' concluded Nicolas. 'I'll leave you now. Bourdeau will stay here, while I go to police headquarters. Rabouine, try to clear this up before you leave on your mission. Pierre will give you the details.'

Nicolas's visit to Rue Neuve-Saint-Augustin left him feeling bewildered. The new Lieutenant General of Police, a short, impolite man in a reddish wig, received him very briefly, merely ordering him to continue with the cases in progress and report back to him in a few days. These hurriedly uttered words betrayed neither warmth nor mistrust. Nicolas realised that this relatively benign treatment from a man with such an unpleasant reputation was due to the Duc de La Vrillière's recommendation. Now he understood why he had been summoned by Monsieur de La Borde to the Saint-Florentin mansion: the Minister of the King's Household had wanted that audience to be private, so that Monsieur Albert would not hear of it. This visit to police headquarters lost him some precious time, the new Lieutenant

General's unfriendly entourage having kept him waiting for a while. Back at the Grand Châtelet, he found Bourdeau in a darkly humorous mood. The Chevalier de Lastire had just dropped by, bringing some unexpected news: he had found Caminet.

'Where was the body?' asked Nicolas immediately. 'We must summon Sanson and Semacgus.'

'Wait! There's no body. No one has died. The young man, according to your friend, was hiding out in a clandestine gambling den in Rue des Moineaux in the Saint-Roch district.'

'How did the chevalier discover him?'

'He's been frequenting this den as part of what he calls his missions. In the course of a game – they were playing piquet, and you know how easy it is to cheat at piquet – there was an accusation of cheating, which led to a brawl. There were too many high cards in the pack, it seems, and Caminet was careful to cut it in such a way that he always had a high card at the bottom.'

'And even when the advantage is only one card, that's a lot in piquet!'

'Added to which, he was winking at his partner, which gave the game away. Anyway, there was a challenge, and a quarrel. Insults were exchanged and knives were brandished. The owner of the place had to call the watch to break up the fight. In short, the young man is now in the guardroom in Saint-Roch. I was planning to go there, as I assume you want to wait for news of that mysterious cab.'

Left alone, Nicolas was overcome with exhaustion. He sometimes yielded to this impulse, wearied by the agitation that had led him, for so many years, from one place to another like a caged animal. At such times, everything, especially the city he loved so much, appeared sad, dismal and dirty, the grim-faced people around him all seemed to bear the marks of vice and crime, and he would feel a rising disgust at the spectacle offered by this modern Babylon. This would quickly be followed by the temptation to retire. He thought of the Château de Ranreuil, which now belonged to him. Many happy memories from his childhood were connected with the place. Just thinking of it brought the roar of the ocean to his ears. Would he not find there a peace that would distract him more than his own endless activity? And then suddenly a ray of sunshine illumined the gloomy office and revived his energy. It was always thus. Sometimes, out in the street, the grinning mascarons on the fine façade of a new mansion would smile at him and the city would reassert its grip, offering him, yet again, its splendour, its life, its excess. It continued to grow, bursting out of its ancient boundaries, encroaching ever more on its suburbs and their stretches of waste ground. The faces of those he loved brought him gently back to reality, however harsh that reality might be. The face of the young King, for example, whom he so fervently wished to help, out of loyalty to his grandfather and attachment to a principle. His depression was lifting, and he let himself be carried away on a happy wave of certainties, abandoning himself to his fate.

Old Marie drew him from his meditation. A little errand boy had just brought a message from Tirepot. The cab that had followed Nicolas had entered a house in Rue de Vendôme, near the boulevards, next to the Intendance, and opposite the convent of the Filles du Sauveur. Nicolas rummaged in his desk drawer and took out one sheet of the street map. He noted with interest that the house in question was situated near the outbuildings of the Temple enclosure. Deciding to go straight there, he asked Old Marie, who could not conceal his joy at being given these new responsibilities, to collect all incoming information and make sure that the most urgent messages were conveyed to him without delay.

The bells of the chapel at the convent of the Filles du Sauveur were tolling noon when he had himself dropped discreetly at the entrance to Rue de Vendôme. He spotted Rabouine and Tirepot in the shadow of the wall. He approached them and told them to fetch the watch. A group of wagons was blocking the way. The smell seized him by the throat. He immediately realised what it was, and was pleased that this chance occurrence would create a diversion from his approach. The guild of cesspool emptiers was at work. He recognised the widow La Marche, mistress of the guild. This was not the first time he had met her. Some time earlier, Lenoir had sent him to deal with a sordid case. A fetid odour had been rising from a house belonging to a cavalry colonel named Monsieur de Chaugny, who had to be forced to do something about his cesspool, which was clogged with stones. There had been a fierce dispute between the widow La Marche and the old soldier, who, claiming that such negligence was common, had complained about the high cost of the work. It was true that you could easily find casual workers who would offer to do the job at a lower price – even though the noxious vapours they were obliged to breathe in during the course of this filthy, backbreaking labour often killed them.

He noted, in passing, that the widow La Marche was in contravention of the latest edicts. Not only were the stinking contents of the cesspool being poured into barrels with holes in them, which caused a great deal of spillage, but the work should have been carried out between ten at night and dawn, not to mention the fact that they were obliged to wash the soiled ground, which they were not doing. He was too busy at the moment to sanction the widow. All he could do was wag a threatening finger at her, to which she responded with a blown kiss and a wide, toothless smile.

Nicolas found the house easily enough, as it was just opposite the convent. The carriage entrance yielded to his push. It led to a garden and a second carriage entrance through which the carriage the spies had been following must have disappeared. A small door gave access to the living quarters. He approached it cautiously and turned the handle: it opened without any difficulty. Having learnt a lesson from his experience in Rue du Poirier, he was thinking of a way of stopping the door from closing again when he made the mistake of moving forward without noticing the three small steps in front of him. He was sent sprawling to the floor, hurting his knees, while the door slammed shut behind him. He struggled to his feet, climbed back up the steps in total darkness and tried to open the door. Too late, he realised that there was no handle on the inside and that he had been caught in a trap. He did not like being shut in and immediately felt suffocated. Fortunately, benefiting again from the lessons learnt the previous time, he had a candle with him and something to light it with. But just then, there was a sudden light behind him, and he turned and was startled to see a dark figure silhouetted in an open doorway. A monk stood there, his face concealed beneath his hood, threatening him with a pistol. Nicolas would never know by what miracle his immediate thoughts – the words of an old Breton tale he had learnt by heart in his childhood, and which suddenly came back to him – had dictated what he did next.

'Ha yann ha mont ha darch'haouin un taol baʒh houarn gantan diwar e benn, hag e laʒhan hep na reas ʒoken na bramm!' he screamed. ('And Jean hit him on the head with an iron bar, which killed him before he could let out a cry.')

The result was amazing. Assuming that the commissioner was calling to someone behind him, the startled monk turned abruptly, giving Nicolas the seconds he needed to seize the weapon concealed in his tricorn. He fired Bourdeau's little pistol, but missed his target, the monk having again turned before throwing himself backwards and slamming the door. Nicolas found himself once again in silence and darkness. He took a deep breath to calm the beating of his terror-stricken heart. He regretted not having been able to fire a second shot: to do that, he would have had to reload his weapon. With his lighted candle, he began cautiously pacing up and down the narrow space until he discovered a side door which led straight into a vast room filled with an incredible profusion of objects: crates, brightly coloured fabrics spilling from half-torn sacks, pagan idols that stared at him with their dead eyes as he swept the candlelight across them. He became aware of a strange smell, or rather a mixture of animal odours and an unknown scent. Leaning towards one of the crates, he realised that the scent came from the wood of which it was made. In a corner, behind other crates, he discovered a number of hutches filled with terrified rabbits. A detail struck him: blackish stains on the crates suggested that they had originally borne inscriptions – perhaps the name of their owner – which had been burnt off. In another corner, he noticed a pair of thick leather gloves and a pair of big thigh-length boots of the same material.

He saw another door, and opened it, wedging it with his hat so that it could not close again. The room appeared empty apart from a tall wicker basket on a large rug and a porcelain stove that spread a damp heat thanks to a container which let off steam. The temperature here was different from that in the other rooms. As he approached the basket, he noticed – and he could not believe his eyes – that the rug seemed to be undulating of its own accord. Suddenly, the fringe of the rug lifted and a shape sprang out, casting a huge shadow on the wall because of the candlelight. Frozen in horror, Nicolas knew that he had before him the hamadryad whose presence in this case Guillaume Semacgus had long since suspected. He recognised every detail from the drawing his friend had made. The cobra, its eyes gleaming in the light, was staring at him, its hood spread open, its body totally still. A soft repeated hissing could be heard. In a flash, Nicolas analysed the situation. He was unarmed and some distance from the door: impossible to escape. The slightest movement risked provoking the snake to attack. Would the candlelight keep the animal spellbound? He absolutely had to protect the flame, which would not last much longer. He realised at that moment what the gloves and boots were for: they presumably helped the mysterious occupant of the house to handle the reptile without danger to himself. But they were too far away for him to be able to use them.

The cobra had started moving, bringing the rest of its long, savagely beautiful body out from under the rug. Its white and beige scales glimmered in the light. 'Your name is legion,' Nicolas thought. Should he keep still? The adversary had come closer, arching its body. It seemed ready to strike. Nicolas felt overcome with despair. He would have liked to cry out, and had to stop himself doing so. He began praying. The snake's mouth was opening when, suddenly, a hand was placed over Nicolas's mouth and, at the same time, he heard the beginnings of a strange, savage chant. Before his eyes, a taut brown hand appeared, the fingers pointing straight at the beast. The chant continued, the voice becoming deeper. The cobra seemed to be relaxing, its head swaying to the rhythm of the voice. Gradually, it lowered its body until it lay stretched out on the floor, as if dead. Nicolas was pushed abruptly aside. The person who had been chanting gently took hold of the snake's triangular head, lifted it to his mouth and breathed on it. The cobra's body went limp. It was thrown nimbly into the basket and the lid immediately closed.

Nicolas's saviour turned. Nicolas picked up the dying candle and lifted it. In astonishment, he recognised the tattooed face of his friend Naganda. They embraced.

'By what miracle, my dear Naganda, do you spring up like this and save my skin?'

'Let's not talk of that, I owe you so much more. At the Châtelet, where I had hoped to find you, Old Marie told me you had just left for Rue de Vendôme. I jumped in a cab and, on arriving here, met Monsieur Rabouine, who added to what I already knew. He was upset to be going away, fearing that you were in danger.'

'He was not mistaken.'

'I hurried to the house he pointed out to me. From a distance I heard the sound of a gunshot.'

'Alas, I only had one bullet. I missed my attacker and had to face that beast unarmed!'

'And here I am, happy to have been of service to you.'

In the fading candlelight, the terrifying face of the Micmac chief grew soft with emotion. He was wearing a dark-blue coat of military cut, and a tricorn concealed his long hair, which was tied with a bow at the back. He crouched to adjust the wooden peg that kept the wicker basket closed.

'Better to be safe than sorry. I don't know this specimen. It's quite big, and probably poisonous. Where I come from, the most dangerous kind is the marsh snake which we call in our language the *makassin*.[5] Its bite is fatal.'

'Does it obey you,' asked Nicolas with a smile, 'as this king cobra or Asian hamadryad has done? Although, coming from you, nothing would surprise me!'

Naganda placed his hand on his friend's shoulder and looked into his eyes with his own dark eyes. 'My people are familiar with many secrets of nature. As you know I am not only their chief, but more than that.'

This enigmatic reply reminded Nicolas of certain incomprehensible manifestations which had marked his first encounter with the Indian from New France.[6] Thanks to the commissioner, he had been cleared of a charge of murder, and had been chosen by the late King to keep an eye on English intrigues on the borders of the colonies of New England and Canada.

'To what do I owe the joy of seeing you again?'

'Because of all this unrest, the young King wishes to hear my reports at first hand. He remembers our previous encounters, and has invited me to represent my people at his coronation in Reims.'

'I'm delighted to hear it. Where are you staying?'

'With Dr Semacgus ... We wanted to surprise you, but you are impossible to get hold of! In fact, the reason I set off to look for you is that Kluskabe, our frog hero, sent me a vision: the son of stone was in danger! I immediately leapt into action. Incidentally, I brought our friend some plants and grains from home. I think this …'

'Cobra.'

'… will make him very happy. He will be able to donate it to his colleagues at the Jardin du Roi.'

As briefly as he could, Nicolas told Naganda all about the case. They searched the house. It was clear that nobody lived there. Having forced the door, they noticed that a paved path led to a third carriage entrance, which opened onto the grounds of the Temple enclosure. They went back inside and examined more closely a heap of carpets, statues, strange objects, elaborate silver dishes, copper and ivory caskets: a whole miscellany from the Indies.

'We shall have all this confiscated and inventoried. The monk has flown the nest, and he won't be back. We are blocking off his lairs one by one and forcing him to flee.'

They heard a noise, snuffed out the candle and hid in the shadows. After a few minutes, Rabouine appeared, accompanied by men of the watch.

'I was really worried about you. It was only knowing that Monsieur Naganda was with you that reassured me somewhat.'

Nicolas told him what had happened. Rabouine shook hands with Naganda, then turned back to Nicolas. 'But I have something else interesting to tell you.'

'As usual!'

'As we were coming back to Rue de Vendôme with reinforcements, a carriage stopped and a man got out. I wasn't sure who he was at first, because he had a handkerchief over his mouth because of the smell. He headed straight for the house. Suddenly, he recognised the uniforms of the watch and immediately turned tail, and although he was in everyday clothes I recognised him from a distance.'

'Who was it, then?'

'Our abbé from Vienna. Georgel.'

This revelation came as a surprise to Nicolas. But it strengthened his belief that what had happened in Austria was closely linked to events in Paris. What was taking shape opened such alarming prospects that the mind was sent whirling helplessly, like a bird that has lost its way. Nicolas advised Rabouine to immediately prepare his departure for Lorient. The mail coach was too slow and subject to the vagaries of the road. He should use his mission orders to obtain the fastest horses from the post houses.

Nicolas and Naganda went back to the Grand Châtelet. Soon afterwards, Bourdeau appeared, pushing before him a surly-looking young man in a yellowish wig and smoked glasses, with his hands tied and his head bowed.

'Here is the prey we've been hunting,' announced the inspector solemnly.

Nicolas recognised Caminet. He had only ever seen him before now dressed as a baker. The features of the face were prematurely withered by debauchery and base thoughts, suggesting a degree of corruption rare in one so young. Nicolas drew Bourdeau aside and whispered in his ear. He was going to try to bring the suspect round to confess the truth, by throwing out almost casual statements designed to throw him off balance. For that reason, he would not proceed directly to the main subject, the tragedy in Rue Montmartre. Caminet was staring at the commissioner as if expecting salvation from him: having known him for years, he might well be hoping for leniency.

'What is this that we learn? You have embarked on a truly calamitous path. Is that what an honest apprentice baker should be doing, going to earth in a place of ill repute populated by fallen women and inveterate cheats?'

As if to underline these words, Bourdeau threw on the table several packs of cards of mismatched sizes. Nicolas spread them out.

'What have we here? A rogue's paraphernalia that'll lead you straight to the end of a rope. Blood has already flowed, I gather?'

'It was self-defence,' the young man said in a pitiful voice. His wig had slipped, uncovering an unruly lock of brown hair.

'You were wise to defend yourself,' said Bourdeau. 'You stole twenty *pistoles* from an innocent wretch who was playing in good faith.'

'But ... I just can't lose.'

'Now that's a good excuse! How could you lose with this?' The inspector picked up an eight and a king. 'With the high cards being bigger than the low ones, you can easily feel them when you cut the cards! We know you cheated, and we know you used violence, hitting your opponent over the head with a stool, which might well have killed him. Thank heaven and luck that you only knocked him unconscious.'

Caminet seemed relieved. 'I'll make amends, Monsieur Nicolas.'

'It wouldn't be before time. What I'd rather hear is why you fled Master Mourut's house.'

The apprentice's expression turned shifty and inscrutable. 'I don't like the work. The master's always breathing down my neck.' He made a gesture with his hand. 'I've had it up to here with flour and ovens.'

'Your workmates bear the life well enough.'

'Oh, them!' he said with a knowing smile.

'They seem praiseworthy to me,' said Nicolas. 'Always punctual, hard-working, pleasant to the customers.'

'Much good it does them!'

'You don't seem to think much of them. You'd do well to model your attitude on theirs.'

'On that ...'

'That what? Out with it! Who are you referring to? Mademoiselle Friope?'

Misunderstanding Nicolas's words, Caminet lost his temper. 'More of a mademoiselle than you think, that trollop!'

341

'Oh, we know she's a girl, and we also know that you were blackmailing her and her friend.'

The blow had struck home. The apprentice was sweating, clearly unsettled by the fact that they were now talking about something quite other than the reasons for which he had been arrested.

'That was nothing. It's normal for workmates to tease one another.'

'I'm sure it is. But it's another matter when we have two suspects imprisoned and threatened with the full weight of the law. Two unfortunate creatures who have no alibi, in other words, whose whereabouts at the critical moment are unknown.'

'The critical moment?'

'But they are not the only suspects,' Nicolas went on. 'And—'

'I don't know what you are talking about.'

'I doubt that. Madame Mourut has told us everything.'

'What kind of thing?'

He would have to tell a lie to get at the truth. 'That you wanted to get rid of her husband and run away with her.'

Caminet started laughing uncontrollably. 'What does she imagine? That I'm still interested in that dried-up old thing? Look at me and then look at her.'

'We are looking at you,' said Nicolas gravely, 'and we see a criminal on whom suspicion is falling ever more heavily.'

'But I'm the victim!' Caminet burst out. 'Me, me! He kept nagging at me with his advice! Always lecturing me! He never stopped!'

'The victim of what, of whom?'

'Of … of … He hit me.'

'Who? Mourut? Tell me about that.'

'I was in an inn with the madwoman.'

'Why do you spend time with her, if she's mad? Such gallantry is beyond me!'

'For her money. She could never refuse me anything. Anyway, I was in this inn.'

'A strange inn, I think.'

Caminet looked at him, aghast. Did the commissioner really know all that?

'I went downstairs to get some wine, and that was when I saw Mourut with a lot of other people. He recognised me. I immediately realised how I could turn the situation to my advantage. I'd long wanted to break away and leave Rue Montmartre. I informed Céleste, without telling her what I was really thinking. I went down again and out into Rue des Deux-Ponts-Saint-Sauveur. He was waiting for me, of course! I told him what I really thought of him. He didn't want me to go, I don't know why. He hit me. I fell to the ground, unconscious. Then it started raining, and that revived me. I got up and ran away. I'm the victim.'

'Quite a story! So now that you were free, with not a care in the world, you immediately chose lodgings in a place of debauchery.'

'I'd been there before.'

'Wrong!' said Bourdeau. 'A witness who has no reason to lie to us will testify that he'd never seen you before you showed up after three in the morning on Monday 1 May, holding a paper with the address of his house.'

'He's lying. He'll pay for this!'

'It will be a long time before you can settle any scores, believe me!' said Nicolas.

'And another thing,' said Bourdeau, with a wink at the commissioner. 'What funds did you have at your disposal?'

'My savings.'

'Really? It's said that you are excessively spendthrift and that Master Mourut, apparently so strict with you in other respects, gave you everything you needed in the way of money. Not that he got much in return!' Bourdeau put a thick leather purse down on the table, the metal inside clinking as he did so. 'Found in a cupboard in Rue des Moineaux, Commissioner. It still contains nine hundred gold *livres*. Impressive for the savings of an apprentice! I should add that, according to my information, this gentleman has lost more than he's won despite his cheating at cards since he's been living in Rue des Moineaux. Either he's not very good, or the girls relieved him of some of it. It seems he had two thousand *livres* when he arrived.'

'Well, now!' said Nicolas. 'That is indeed quite a sum! I await your explanation. Where did the money come from?'

'From Madame Mourut.'

Bourdeau took a ring, some pendants and a necklace from his pocket. 'No, it didn't. Here are the jewels she gave him. He didn't even sell them.'

Something suddenly occurred to Nicolas, and he decided to try his luck. 'The dispenser of so much favour was obviously the Capuchin, wasn't it?'

Caminet's reaction was all that the commissioner could have hoped for. He turned his head right and left as if looking for a way out, wrung his hands, then bent over and burst into sobs.

'I think it's time to tell us the truth,' said Nicolas.

'This monk ... stopped me in the street.'

'Where and when?'

'A few days before I ran away, outside Saint-Eustache. He made me a proposition. I was supposed to arrange to meet Céleste at La Gourdan's house on Sunday night. At a given moment, I would be told when to come downstairs so that Mourut could see me. I told the monk I wanted to leave my mistress and lead my own life. He gave me a purse, this very same one, or rather, he showed it to me and promised I would have it if everything went as he wished.'

'I don't think that's all.'

'No, I was to be abusive to the master, push him to the point where he would hit me. Then I had to fall heavily on the cobbles and pretend to be dead. Which I did. I heard Mourut being led away, then someone coming back and bending over me. In fact, the man, who I didn't see,

I swear, touched me as if checking how I was, and took advantage of that to slip the purse into my coat, and a paper with the address in Rue des Moineaux.'

'All right,' said Nicolas. 'Why did you get to your destination so late?'

'I lost my way. It was raining and I was scared.'

'That will need to be checked. We know what time your master was killed. Going by what you've told us, you would have been able to get back to Rue Montmartre, get into the bakehouse with the key in your possession and, there, kill your master with means which the Capuchin or someone else could have provided you with. That's the real ending of the story, isn't it? You knew, didn't you, that you would inherit if he died, that Mourut was not only your master, but also your father?'

Caminet looked at Nicolas, apparently uncomprehendingly. 'My father?'

'Yes, your father.'

For a long time, the old fortress echoed to his screams as he was led to the dungeons.

'Culprit, accomplice or victim?' said Nicolas, pensively. 'We will know soon enough.'

XII

THE VICE

After having badly managed one's career,
one does not easily take another path.

MASSILLON

From Sunday 7 May to Friday 12 May 1775
On Sunday, the whole household of Rue Montmartre, Monsieur de
Noblecourt radiant at its head, attended high mass at Saint-Eustache.
Louis had the honour of holding the purse for the collection. The
presence of Naganda, whose upbringing led him to believe that all
theological controversy was vain and who happily reconciled his faith
and the beliefs of his people, at first scared the congregation, then
distracted it, and finally impressed it. For his sermon, the officiating
priest read the extraordinary address which Louis XVI had sent to all
the bishops about the recent events in the kingdom. His voice rang
out beneath the high vaults: 'You are all aware of the unprecedented
banditry which has affected stocks of wheat all around the capital,
and almost before my eyes in Versailles, and which seems to threaten
several provinces of the kingdom. If this movement should approach
your diocese or even enter it, I have no doubt that you will oppose it
with all the obstacles which your zeal, your attachment to my person,
and even more so the Holy Religion of which you are the minister,
will suggest to you. The maintenance of public order is a law of the
gospel, as it is a law of the State, and anything which disturbs it is
equally criminal before God and men.'

'That is of a higher standard than the address to all the parish priests in the kingdom,' murmured Noblecourt in Nicolas's ear. 'I was given the text to read. It was awkward, verbose and full of sophistry. A lame defence of the comptroller general, though I fear it is more likely to provide weapons against him.'

In honour of Naganda, an excursion was planned. When they left the church, they found cabs waiting for them. In one of them was Semacgus who, like the sage of Ferney, respected the Lord but did not spend much time in His company. Gaily, they headed towards the tollgates, in the direction of the Basse Courtille des Porcherons. Their destination was the Tambour Royal, the tavern kept by the famous Ramponneau, the idea being to show the Micmac chief the simple pleasures of Parisian life.

Once past the sign, they walked down three steps into a vast rectangular room, with the kitchens off to the right. The monumental hearth, gigantic ovens and glittering brass fountains made Marion and Catherine envious. At the many tables and benches sat a good-natured crowd. At times, the noise they made reached an unbearable level. The host, a fat, squat, ruddy-faced man with a neck like Silenus,[1] received them with good humour and led them to a well-positioned, slightly raised table, offering a panoramic view of the gathering. He had recognised Nicolas, having had dealings with him on several occasions. Louis amused himself deciphering the inscriptions on the wall: *Pleasure is everything, Good humour, Credit is dead, Bonum vinum laetificat cor hominis: good wine gladdens the heart, Gallus cantavit: the cock has crowed.* Their joy reached its height on discovering a mural painting of Ramponneau himself sitting astride a barrel.

The food and wine, simple as they were, were highly regarded. Courtiers were not averse to mixing with the riff-raff here – incognito, of course. Semacgus ordered the meal, with the help of Awa, who had also been invited to this feast. They gorged themselves on fried fish, spit-roasted poultry and fricassee of rabbit in wine, accompanied by a chicory salad in which neither garlic nor hard-boiled eggs nor sliced bacon had been spared, and in which there was also an abundance of chives and chervil. Semacgus was pleased that the fricassee had been made as it should: it included, along with the pieces of rabbit, the indispensable pieces of young eel previously fried in butter with mushrooms and small onions. It was important to be quick with the fish in order not to break it. As for the rabbit, it had to simmer in a suitable mixture of white wine and stock until reduced to a third of the whole. An unpretentious little Suresnes wine accompanied this feast. They finished with plates of cakes and biscuits, coffee and a digestive ratafia flavoured with angelica. Outside the establishment, the crowd were bustling to the sound of shrill violins. Monsieur de Noblecourt, who had been given permission by Semacgus to try everything, felt young again and borrowed an instrument. Beating time with his foot, he began a Neapolitan tune which delighted the crowd and set it dancing. This set off the traditional *course*, a kind of farandole involving between a hundred and three hundred people which habitually ended dinner at Ramponneau's. The public went wild, running and jumping with all its might around the room, crushing underfoot those who had the misfortune to fall.

During the following days, the investigation threw up a number of discoveries. On the one hand, Bourdeau's search among the notaries bore fruit. He informed Nicolas that, by court order, the Hénéfiance residence in Rue du Poirier had been put up for public auction after the presumed death of the convict at Brest. A man named Matisset had announced his intention to purchase it. What made this all the more interesting was that Matisset was a well-known former grain merchant. The same person had bought the house opposite. Nicolas jumped at the mention of the name and consulted his notes. Not only had Lenoir mentioned Matisset as being at the centre of rumours about the famine pact, but Le Prévôt de Beaumont had denounced his actions, describing him as the organiser of a vast network of corruption. Further questions about the man were raised when Bourdeau added that these purchases, as the notary had admitted after a little pressure, had been carried out in secret on behalf of a famous person – although he obstinately refused to name him.

Nicolas immediately sent out his spies and informers.

In the next two days, Matisset was spotted, followed and reported to have met several times with Abbé Georgel. On the other hand, he seemed to have been turned away from the Temple. It appeared that, given the turn taken by events, the Prince de Conti was less inclined to continue with certain relationships. Clearly, he did not want to be connected with any of those involved behind the scenes in the unrest.

Long walks in the Tuileries would allow Nicolas to put some order into his thoughts. If Hénéfiance had not died in escaping, he thought, he must be alive. Where had he made his appearance? Obviously he had wanted to take revenge on Mourut, the man who had denounced him. And as for the latter, why was a traitor still so highly regarded by the brotherhood as to participate in its secret meetings? Was it easier to keep an eye on him that way? Had not his decision not to lower the price of bread resulted in threats? What to make of these contradictory observations? The lessons of his Jesuit masters came back to him and also those of Descartes, their pupil at La Flèche: 'The human mind manages to be mistaken in two ways, either by taking more than it is given to determine a question, or, on the contrary, by forgetting something.' He vowed to go over everything he knew of the apparently linked cases.

With this in view, the commissioner resumed his investigations in order to confirm Caminet's statements. One thing intrigued him, about which he reflected methodically. It now seemed clear that the mysterious Capuchin, who could be anyone, was heavily involved in all aspects of the case. He had made contact with the baker's apprentice, had corrupted him to the extent of getting him to agree to a deception of whose tragic outcome he was unaware – or was he? The fact remained that this individual, whoever he was, must, previous to the scene at La Gourdan's brothel, have discovered all there was to know about the Mourut household, including its hidden, shadowy aspects. The only thing of which they were certain was that the baker had attended the secret meeting. But then the Capuchin had also to be the man bending over Caminet's body, as seen by Friope and Parnaux. Whatever the man did seemed to leave Nicolas on shaky ground.

How did the Capuchin know the secrets of the baker and his entourage? Who could have informed him? The two baker's boys? Nicolas thought it unlikely. Madame Mourut? That was a possibility. Caminet? The monk already knew everything when he had approached the apprentice. He thought suddenly of La Babine, that embittered gossip who knew everything about her masters' private lives. He went at once to see her. Reluctant as she was to say anything at first, he wore her down to such an extent that in the end, almost foaming at the mouth with anger, she spat out the truth. Yes, a man had approached her as she was doing her shopping at the Rue Montorgueil market. No, she could not remember the exact date. Yes, he had asked her a lot of probing questions. Yes, she had given him the information he asked for. The sum offered had been a large one, and what she had earned from Mourut over the years would not allow her to support herself in her old age. She did not want to be reduced to the poorhouse, eating soup full of leftovers. And now that the baker was dead, she knew she had been right. Besides, how could she have refused a man she had known for so long? Many years earlier, Master Mourut had been in business with him. She had told this Monsieur Matisset everything about the various people in the household, so carried away by the demon of her tongue that she had gone into the most sordid details, without wondering why she was being asked all these things. Thus, little by little, the pieces of the puzzle were falling into place. The more Nicolas thought about it, the more he saw this whole affair as being one of interlocking plots.

During the following days, while waiting impatiently for Rabouine to return from Lorient, Nicolas devoted himself to Louis and Naganda. He learnt that his friend had married and now had a son. These were precious moments of happiness, when time seemed to stand still. They haunted the promenades of Paris, and attended games of pall-mall at the Arsenal where, in an avenue of trees marked out with planks, young people skilfully knocked wooden balls through small iron hoops stuck in the ground. From the terrace of the Tuileries, they admired the view of the Palais-Bourbon and the Cours-la-Reine, and hurried to Chaillot to watch a promising young female artist painting the portraits of Cardinal Fleury and La Bruyère intended for the Académie Française. The artist's name was Louise Élisabeth Vigée. Fascinated by Naganda's face, she did a quick gouache portrait of him and gave it to him, much to his delight. They went to see the coaches and equipages for Reims, as well as the jewels, the diamond crown, a gold chapel offered by Cardinal de Richelieu in 1636, and a coronation cabinet commissioned long ago by François I, covered in embroidery and paintings based on drawings by Raphael. Last but not least, they busied themselves with getting Louis fitted out by the best suppliers for his debut with the pages.

On 11 May, the century reasserted its hold on Nicolas once more. Late in the morning, a summons arrived in Rue Montmartre, brought by one of those ageless clerks who haunted police headquarters. It informed Commissioner Le Floch, on the orders of Monsieur Albert, that he would have to attend, wearing his magistrate's robe and wig and carrying his ivory rod in his hand – he recognised the pernickety character of his new chief in these detailed instructions – the execution of those arrested and sentenced to death after the riots of 3 May. As Nicolas got ready, he questioned the envoy about the condemned men. Only two death sentences had been pronounced: one on Jean Desportes, a wigmaker, and the other on Jean-Charles

Lesguille, an unemployed worker and known criminal, arrested in the act of looting. Nicolas was sure that this was an attempt to reassure the bourgeois and artisans who had been thrown into a panic by the riots, and was chilled to realise that their execution had been arranged before the ink on their sentences had even dried.

Outside, he was struck by the massive deployment of troops. The closer he got to Place de Grève, the greater the numbers. Bayonets glittered and mounted dragoons patrolled the streets. In front of the old town hall stood two unusually high gallows – deliberately built that way, the clerk explained solemnly, because the Lieutenant General of Police wanted the execution to be seen from as far away as possible, in order to discourage any attempt to repeat such unacceptable unrest. Mounted troops and foot soldiers were spread out along the route of the procession. Two rows of soldiers surrounded Place de Grève, some turned towards the perimeter, the others towards the gallows.

Nicolas got out of his carriage, lifting the tails of his robe to join the group of magistrates present. Sanson, in his great red executioner's uniform, greeted him from a distance with a grim, almost imperceptible smile. Nicolas realised that this would be the first time he would see him perform his official duties. He felt a profound sadness at this, as if faced with a mystery he would have preferred to know nothing about. The condemned men arrived, accompanied by a muted clamour which could have been an expression of pity or a cry for vengeance. The two men yelled that this was a denial of justice and called on the people to riot: it was for the people, they claimed, that they were dying. Right up to the steps of the scaffold, they proclaimed their innocence, after which everything went very quickly.

Nicolas closed his eyes, and felt in his own flesh the dull thud of two bodies falling and the brief convulsions that followed. A great silence fell over the gathering. Little by little, without a cry, grim and silent, the crowd dispersed. On the way back, he heard many words exchanged. In general, the people felt sorry for the executed men, who had been sacrificed to public order and so that the true culprits, 'who of course would get away with it', could sleep easily in their beds. It seemed to him that these accusations, although well founded, nevertheless omitted other responsible parties whose secret intrigues had steered the rioters' actions. Late that evening, in Versailles, he gave an account of the day to the Duc de La Vrillière, who this time poured out his feelings openly. Before retiring, the King, the minister told Nicolas, had condemned the executions and ordered Monsieur Turgot to 'spare those persons who had merely been led on and to discover the leaders of this whole movement'.

Friday 12 May 1775

Exhausted, covered in mud and his horse's lather, Rabouine appeared in Rue Montmartre early in the morning. He immediately took a crumpled piece of paper from his shirt front and handed it over. Nicolas read it, sent for a carriage, and set off with Rabouine for the Grand Châtelet. Louis was given the task of feeding and watering the horse before taking it back to the stables of the Messageries. Bourdeau was immediately summoned to the duty office at the Châtelet. After a brief exchange, he set out on a number of specific errands, while the commissioner took a carriage for Versailles, where he arrived late in the morning.

Ignoring orders, he interrupted an audience by Vergennes, intercepting Sartine who was about to go back to Paris and almost forcing him to accompany him to see La Vrillière. He informed them that he had some serious revelations to make and that a council should be called as soon as possible to examine them. The timely arrival of a message from Vergennes backed up his request.

Back in Paris by early evening, he met Lenoir, who invited him to dinner at his home. He in turn invited Lenoir to attend the council planned for the following day at the Saint-Florentin mansion in the presence of Sartine. The Chevalier de Lastire was also summoned, given the crucial role he had played in the investigation by tracking down Caminet in Rue des Moineaux. Flattered to be included, Lenoir asked what role his successor would play in the proceedings. On the orders of the Duc de La Vrillière, the new Lieutenant General of Police would be left out of a case most of which had not taken place under his mandate. Lenoir smiled at this elegant excuse for preventing that muddle-headed fellow, thought of as Turgot's creature, from interfering in such an unusual affair, in which the security of the State and the throne combined with private considerations.

Saturday 13 May 1775

Bourdeau appeared in Rue Montmartre very early. He went up to Nicolas's apartment to give a detailed account of his mission. In return, he received instructions. He immediately set off again, laden with recommendations, especially to organise the transportation of certain suspects to the Saint-Florentin mansion as and when they were required.

It was agreed that the inspector would come to the meeting place at exactly eleven o'clock. Nicolas exchanged some pleasantries with his son, who was waiting for Naganda and Semacgus in order to visit the Jardin du Roi and see the famous cobra, then walked to Place Louis XV by way of Rue Saint-Honoré. Anyone observing him would have noted that his lips were moving as if he was reciting to himself a lesson learnt or the text of a role in a play. In fact, stimulated by the rhythm of his walk, he was putting together arguments that he would have to develop in front of a cautious audience. There were still a few pieces missing: he hoped that they would appear in the course of the debate to which his words would be sure to give rise.

Provence, surprised by an event that disturbed the calm of the mansion, greeted the commissioner with the deference due to a man who had cleared his master of a terrible accusation.[2] As Nicolas climbed the grand staircase, it seemed to him that the figures in the great painting *Prudence and Strength* were looking at him ironically. Was fate cocking a snook at him? Today, he would need those two qualities more than ever. He entered the minister's study.

As so often, the room was plunged in semi-darkness and there was a raging fire in the great marble hearth. The Duc de La Vrillière, Sartine and Lenoir were conversing in low voices. He bowed to them ceremoniously, then approached the master of the house and whispered in his ear, while Sartine looked on inquisitively, not at all pleased. The minister nodded.

Nicolas rang for Provence and gave him his instructions. A few seconds before eleven, the Chevalier de Lastire appeared, in his lieutenant-colonel's uniform, bewigged and without a bandage. Sartine greeted him in a friendly manner and introduced him to the duc and Lenoir.

'Here is one of the best elements of the bureau I created, whose objective you know.'

'All right,' said La Vrillière, 'we can start. Marquis, you may proceed.'

Could there have been a more elegant indication that this session was secret, almost private, and that the minister held the commissioner in great esteem? That at least was how Nicolas took this introduction.

'Gentlemen, you entrusted me with a mission to Vienna, the pretext for which was to deliver the bust of the Queen to her august mother, and the hidden purpose to try and elucidate the circumstances in which Austria had been able to penetrate the King's secret networks. I could not have imagined that it would lead to Paris, thanks to a domestic crime which I can now prove is linked to the events we have just lived through.'

'The link being flour, I assume?' asked Sartine, with that irony he rarely managed to abandon.

'Come now!' grunted La Vrillière. 'If we interrupt the beginning, we'll never get to the end! Please go on.'

'The unrest in the kingdom, the apparent nature of the riots and the contradictions that can be detected in them all lead one to suspect, if not a conspiracy, at least a secret mastermind who used the disorder for his own ends. Any other hypothesis, apart from the fact that it would open some alarming prospects, would imply a perverse desire to attack the throne, which reason as well as sentiment refuses to allow.'

'This takes us a long way from Vienna,' observed La Vrillière, breaking his own instructions.

'On the contrary, Monseigneur, it takes us back there. Several things have become clear to me. On the one hand, out of either arrogance or naivety, Abbé Georgel ...'

'Abbé Georgel, naive?' said Sartine. 'Are you expecting us to believe that?'

'... secretary to Prince Louis, the King's ambassador, served as an instrument of the Austrians, both as a way of letting us know that they knew our secrets, and in order to pass us documents which were either false or innocuous. The abbé went along with this, because it suited his own interests and those of his friends in Paris, even though it gravely compromised the position of the kingdom. Then there was an attempt on my life, which I was only able to escape thanks to the intervention of the Chevalier de Lastire ...'

Lastire bowed.

'... and the discovery of the remains of Georgel's political correspondence, containing some quite disturbing predictions of the near future. I believe I can state categorically that there was collusion, whether voluntary or involuntary, between the Austrians and a group of plotters who were doing everything possible, with the help of Georgel, to kill me, or at the least, to keep me as long as possible in Vienna. What had I discovered? Only, doubtless, the truth! Now I must talk about my return to Paris and an incredible sequence of events which I claim were all connected, for one convincing reason.'

He stood up and began pacing slowly up and down the room, without taking his eyes off his three interlocutors.

'No sooner had I passed the tollgates and entered Paris than I learnt that my son had vanished, led astray by an unknown Capuchin bearing a letter from me, which was in fact a complete forgery. Only a fortunate combination of circumstances stopped the boy from trying to get to London. That would have sent me off in pursuit of him ... Then came the death of Master Mourut, a baker and a tenant in Rue Montmartre of Monsieur de Noblecourt, with whom I myself live. The causes of his death in his bakehouse are the source of so many troubling details that we can only conclude it was a murder. The murder weapon appears to be poison, but the method by which the poison was administered, through a wound in the hand, is unusually intriguing. I concentrated above all on this investigation, to the detriment of keeping an eye on the mounting unrest, although I had been vociferous in insisting how serious it was.'

He looked Sartine in the eyes, but his former chief did not flinch. Lenoir had his head bowed. La Vrillière, who did not miss a thing, was looking at both of them.

'I will spare you the ins and outs.'

'Oh, please do,' said Sartine, 'or we might think ourselves in some kind of Arabian Nights tale.'

'It is, however, necessary to look in some detail at the personality of the victim. A baker, yes, but above all a speculator in grain. Suspected of being part of a secret circle of merchants ...'

Lenoir coughed.

'The person in charge of this circle, Matisset, is rumoured to have organised the famine pact. You all know the man, so I shan't say more about him.'

'A cruel and atrocious slander,' muttered La Vrillière.

'The aforementioned Mourut once denounced one of his colleagues

357

whose interests clashed with his. This person, whose name was Hénéfiance, was sent to the penal colony at Brest, from where he escaped. It was believed that in doing so he died at sea, although there was no proof. Either because he was acting in accordance with the intentions of his brotherhood, or for some other reason, Mourut did not suffer in any way from this affair. The fact remains that recently he was able to stand in the way of the brotherhood's plans by hesitating to raise the price of bread. He may have been responding to threats he had received, or he may have been more inclined to wait until there was a real shortage which would have justified an increase. To complete the picture, he had a hidden son whose apprenticeship he pretended to pay, whose spendthrift ways he overlooked, and whom he named in his will. In Rue Montmartre, there is no lack of suspects who might have wished for the baker's death!'

'Does the association to which he belonged gain from his demise?' asked Lenoir.

'Certainly, in so far as he was defying them by refusing to contribute to the common chest and acting on his own account. His death might have served as an example to anyone thinking of doing the same.'

'Are you really suggesting,' cried Sartine, 'that this powerful secret society couldn't find other means than murder to force a poor baker to submit to its rules? I observe that we are talking at great length about something which hasn't even been established!'

'I've never suggested, Monseigneur, that this society is responsible for a death which everything leads us to believe is of a criminal nature. I was merely answering Monsieur Lenoir, and I will finish what I have to say: yes, this death does serve the interests of the society.'

'We really are getting off the point. Please continue.'

'Let us consider Mourut's wife,' resumed Nicolas. 'The thing that most drives her is bitterness, and the feeling that she married beneath her. Did she want to start a new life with a younger man? The idea of getting rid of her husband must have occurred to her. Was she an accessory? Are we to believe in her innocence, when on the night of Mourut's death she was in the arms of Caminet, the apprentice and Mourut's hidden son?'

'You haven't told us about him yet!' cried Lenoir.

'He's a young rogue. Did he know his parentage? Did he know that there was a will making him the sole heir? Others knew it or suspected it, and they might have informed him. A denizen of brothels, a gambler, a card cheat, spending money like water. Everything about him arouses suspicion. Was he the culprit? Or an accessory? Who knows? Let us come to the two baker's boys, Parnaux and Friope. The latter is in disguise and turns out to be a girl, and what's more, pregnant by the former. Caminet discovers their secret and blackmails them. Their position is precarious. If Caminet denounces them, Mourut will throw them out and they will be on the streets without resources. Which may have led them to wish secretly for the death of their master. As for the maid, La Babine, her hatred of her mistress is so great that she would do anything to destroy her, even accuse her of a capital crime.'

'But you, Marquis,' said La Vrillière, 'what is your opinion of this case?'

'I must reveal to you a crucial fact. The way in which the baker was murdered implies such preparation that none of those I have mentioned could have been the sole culprits. I'm not saying that they're not guilty, but I assert that, in order to be so, they must have had help.'

'Another of those strange instruments that appear in your investigations?' said Sartine, in a decidedly acrimonious tone.

It seemed to Nicolas that Lenoir's disgrace and Turgot's accusations had cut Sartine to the quick and that his mood reflected this. The Duc de La Vrillière was nervously stroking his silver hand, a vital piece of evidence in a previous tragedy.[3]

'Not at all, Monseigneur. This time, we are dealing with a

hamadryad, a king cobra, a snake much feared for its speed and fatal venom.'

His interlocutors looked at each other in alarm.

'So it was an accident, then?' said Sartine, the first to recover his composure.

'No, it was a murder, a diabolical murder! Let me explain. All one has to do is collect the venom of the animal and, through a deliberately produced wound, introduce it into the victim's blood, thus reproducing nature. Thanks to the sagacity of Dr Semacgus, the autopsy revealed a wound in the hand. The rest is pure mechanics. Taking the necessary precautions, wearing thick leather boots and gloves, you seize the snake's head and force it to bite the edge of a bowl with cloth stretched across it. The venom flows out and you collect it. The next part is child's play, a handful is enough, a gloved hand of course. A small phial of glass filled with the fatal liquid which breaks, the flesh is gashed and the venom penetrates …'

'Where is this glass?' asked Sartine, in surprise.

'It cracked under my feet on the floor of the bakehouse and I picked up the pieces. It took me a long time to understand its meaning. It's only in the last few days that I made a connection with Semacgus's hypothesis.'

'And where is the snake?' asked Sartine.

'You can take a look at it at the Jardin du Roi, where our surgeon has had it put for study purposes.'

'All right,' said La Vrillière. 'I assume that this discovery led you to the murderer?'

'Of course,' replied Nicolas, beaming, 'after many difficulties. The rabbits helped a lot!'

Sartine stood up and began pacing up and down the room, as was his habit. 'Commissioner, are you trying to mock us?'

'If only you would let him continue,' said Lenoir softly. 'Just let him explain, that's what he's here for.'

'The use of such an unusual animal suggests a murderer of remarkable perversity, who premeditated his act for a long time. It implies that he acquired an example of this kind of snake where he lives. I will add other details: it is necessary to keep this dangerous specimen alive at a temperature which suits it and which matches the climate of its home region. Finally, gentlemen, the cobra has the characteristic of only feeding on live prey, hence the presence of rabbits.'

'How horrible!' cried the Chevalier de Lastire. 'And how did you track him down?'

'It's a strange story which combines intuition and chance. I shall try to explain it to you as briefly and precisely as possible. We must go back in time, so that the events will appear to you with greater clarity. Hénéfiance, the man denounced by Mourut, is sent to the galleys, that is, to the penal colony at Brest. There is no public trial, no sentence. He disappears secretly, like so many others ...'

For the second time, Monsieur Lenoir coughed.

'In fact, we have no idea of the true nature of Mourut's accusations against him, although important interests must have been in play for the reaction to be so severe. At Brest, we know that he is considered something of a rebel and that he learns Breton. That is the necessary condition for organising his escape. I don't believe in the hypothesis that he escaped by sea. The boat that was found was merely a deception to make it seem as if he had died. I assume that he went across country, got to Lorient or Port-Louis, and from there set sail for the East Indies. Where did he land? What became of him? For the moment, we have no idea. On the other hand, we are certain that he returned to France: the existence of the cobra proves it. On his return, either because he manages to justify himself, or because his denunciation no longer threatens the interests of the society, he resumes relations with it.'

'But what identity has he assumed?' asked Lenoir.

Nicolas closed his eyes and fell silent for some time. 'That is indeed the question! My wager is that he was often hidden in the cowl of a Capuchin monk ... He knows his enemy's address, he wants to punish him and take his revenge. He uses Matisset to gain information about the Mourut household. The baker's maid, La Babine, plays a major role in this. We come to the night of 30 April to 1 May. At the house of La Gourdan in Rue des Deux-Ponts-Saint-Sauveur, Mourut, his wife, Caminet and a third man who must have been Hénéfiance ...'

'It isn't with suppositions,' cried Sartine, 'that we—'

'Let's just get to the point!'

'Caminet, corrupted by Hénéfiance, presents himself conspicuously to the baker as he is leaving. The baker waits for him at the door. Caminet appears, there is an altercation, they come to blows, and the apprentice pretends to fall on a boundary stone. The third man appears, and says that the victim is dead. He takes Mourut into his carriage, and drives him back to Rue Montmartre. Once in the bakehouse, he murders the baker. I can hear your objections: couldn't he have used a more traditional weapon? My answer is that the killer wanted to make it seem as though the baker had died of a fit of apoplexy, or that, in despair at having killed his own son, he decided to use a mysterious poison. We are lucky that Dr Semacgus lived in those regions ...'

'Wait a second, Nicolas,' said Sartine. 'Did you actually witness any of these scenes you describe so cheerfully?'

'My descriptions are based on the statements of several witnesses: La Gourdan's maid Colette, and Friope and Parnaux, who were both present and were suspects for some time.'

'Are you sure Mourut left in a carriage?'

'A witness heard the noise of wheels. What I find more convincing is that the corpse was wearing clean shoes. Immediately after the scene in Rue des Deux-Ponts-Saint-Sauveur, it started raining, and you know how muddy Paris can get.'

'One last point,' said Sartine. 'Why didn't Mourut recognise Hénéfiance?'

'I asked myself that question, Monseigneur, and I think I've found the answer. If the man was indeed Hénéfiance, as I fear, I'm not at all sure that he was known to Mourut, who mostly had dealings with his father. I'm almost certain that he didn't know his face. I would add that, even if he did, ten years of exile, first in a penal colony and then the Indies, can change a man.'

'That's all well and good, but does not tell us how you got onto the trail of the man with the cobra.'

'During a visit to La Gourdan's house, we found a paper with Hénéfiance's name on it, which led us to Rue du Poirier. Doubtless warned by the brothel-keeper, the occupant has been playing with us, slowing us down, sending us off on mysterious errands. Nevertheless, I found some strange clues on the scene. A snake's scale stuck to my boot, and the reaction of my cat confirmed Dr Semacgus's intuition. Unfortunately, the occupant had fled and there was a great risk of losing him. He then made his first mistake: he followed me. Our spies, who are the best in Europe, spotted him.'

For the first time, Sartine smiled.

'They in their turn followed him. Alas, in the meantime, alerted by my interest in the archives of the French East India Company, he mercilessly killed the man who was looking, on my behalf, for information on the movements of ships coming from the east. In doing so, he fell into a trap by snatching from the hands of Belhome, the victim, a register relating to the years with which we are concerned. Our spies followed him to a house in Rue de Vendôme, adjoining the Temple enclosure ...'

For the third time, Lenoir coughed, and La Vrillière shifted in his chair.

'Now I know I'm on the right track. A Capuchin threatens me, I fire, I miss him, and he escapes. Searching the premises, I am attacked by the cobra, and only Naganda's intervention saves me from a terrible death.'

'Naganda?' said La Vrillière. 'The Algonquin so greatly appreciated by our late King? Is he back?'

'Indeed he is, Monseigneur, and invited by His Majesty to the coronation in Reims.'

'We should be full of admiration for the work of a peerless policeman,' cried Sartine, 'not to mention the risks he has run. But a crucial element is still missing. Who is this Capuchin? We all understand that he may be Hénéfiance, but under what name is he acting? Have you found him? He should be arrested.'

'There we come to the great unknown. If you'll allow me, I'd like to admit Bourdeau, who may have some enlightening documents for me.'

Without waiting for a reply from La Vrillière, he rang.

The inspector entered, handed him a bundle of papers tied with a blue ribbon, and disappeared. All eyes were on Nicolas.

'On 1 July 1774, the vessel *La Bourbonnaise*, of the French East India Company, landed at Lorient with, on board, some soldiers, some merchants and a few priests from the foreign missions. I have here–' he waved a document – 'the passenger list and a description of the effects, including crates and trunks. The log book indicates that on 30 April of the same year, a ship's boy of fifteen years old, Jacques Le Gurun, was buried at sea after a religious service. He had died in mysterious circumstances without anyone being able to determine the cause. The case was so strange that the ship's doctor recorded the details. They suggest, on reflection, that the boy may have been bitten by a cobra which was present on board. One name on the passenger list caught my attention. It was the name of an officer. I therefore visited the offices of the Ministry of War in Rue Saint-Dominique …'

'And?' asked Sartine.

Nicolas consulted a paper. 'What do we learn of this officer? That since 1770 he had been in the service of Haider Ali.'

'And who on earth is that?'

'Haider Ali, Monseigneur, was the general of the Rajah of Mysore, whose power he usurped. With the help of French officers, he organised a confederation of the Maratha chieftains against the English. Our officer was finally caught in an ambush. All his companions fell, he alone escaped. He remained a prisoner for several years before escaping and reappearing in our trading post at Pondicherry. Nobody had seen him before and consequently nobody was in a position to identify him. He returned to France where his family had all died. I was able to find a medallion that shows him as a young man. And now, I am going to tell you another story.'

'What? Will it take us just as far?'

'It will take us to France. One man passes himself off as another, assuming his name and his rank. And the worst thing about this affair is that he manages to obtain support from a group hatching plots in the shadow of the throne, taking advantage of the King's youth, the return of the Parlements and long-repressed ambitions. A group who are, rightly or wrongly, infuriated by the comptroller general's reforms. Their connections allow this group to find a place for this person in the service of a minister, what's more, in a bureau recently created to counter the intrigues of powers hostile to France. When they learn of my mission to Vienna, they realise that they'll be able to keep a close watch and thwart my enquiries. A document found in Abbé Georgel's room proves that he began a secret correspondence with these people and that he was in league with the very officer who had been asked to protect me!'

Sartine rose to his feet. 'You have often gone too far, Monsieur, but this time your effrontery is quite unacceptable. I can hardly believe my ears! So I deliberately placed the Chevalier de Lastire—'

'Whoever said that, Monseigneur? Unpleasant as it may be to admit it, you were as much a victim as I.'

'Monsieur,' said La Vrillière, turning to Lastire, 'have you heard the serious accusations made against you? What do you say?'

The chevalier shrugged his shoulders. 'What can I say to such absurd allegations? Monsieur Le Floch ought to remember that he owes me his life.'

'That's right!' cried Sartine. 'You were thanking him a few minutes ago.'

'The truth, alas, is quite otherwise. I have reflected a great deal about that episode. I think the chevalier saved me because the staging of the attack required that ending to be fully believable.'

'Where is the evidence for any of this?'

'My suspicions first. The evidence will follow. Let us go back in time once again. During the journey from Paris to Vienna, the supposed chevalier talked about his military campaigns. Did he ever mention the Indies? All he talked about were battles he had fought in Germany. But in the heat of a conversation, as he was trying to calculate the exchange rate for various currencies in the Empire, he spoke about *anas*, which are copper and silver coins from the Indies. He told me, as I remember extremely well, that he had once before worn a turban. At the time, I assumed he had been on a mission to the Ottomans. Finally, there is this medallion, which I found in that heap of crates in the house in Rue de Vendôme. What do all these discoveries mean if Lastire isn't Hénéfiance? And there is better yet …'

'All smoke and mirrors!' muttered the chevalier.

'You have just used the correct word! On three occasions, an identical smell of tobacco struck me. In the hotel in Vienna where you smoked your pipe, in Master Mourut's bakehouse, and in Rue du Poirier. The same unusual odour with which you filled our carriage. No doubt your hidden presence while the Austrian police were searching our baggage was also smoke and mirrors? Yesterday, Rabouine, after much hesitation, fearing that he had made a mistake, revealed to me that he had seen you. In fact, you were following us, and informing our pursuers. And was that forged letter in my name to my son smoke, too? He recognised the handwriting, and with good reason! I had given you the task of delivering my mail, which gave you the opportunity to imitate my handwriting, or have it imitated by someone else.'

'Are you casting doubt on my wound?' cried Lastire. 'Didn't you see my bandage?'

'Yes, a false turban found again in Rue de Vendôme! That wound was a story cooked up to explain your delay in getting back to Paris. A false bandage, a false wound, a false Capuchin, and the true murderer of Mourut, Belhome – and Nicolas Le Floch if fate had not decided otherwise!'

'A single word and this whole house of cards comes crashing down. Clearly, someone who resembles me is using my name. I'll give you the proof immediately. Here it is: at the time the baker was being murdered, I was with Monsieur de Sartine, bringing him news of the latest unrest. And last but not least, who, yes, who brought you Caminet? Is that the behaviour of a guilty man? I am quite confounded …'

'Indeed you are!'

'… by your attitude, Monsieur. It is worse than an insult, and I demand satisfaction!'

'I am at your disposal – if that is, the King allows me to cross swords with a murderer!'

'Gentlemen,' interrupted La Vrillière, 'let us continue. Could the chevalier tell us how he can be so certain at what time the murder took place?'

'It was I myself who told him,' said Nicolas, 'given that I trusted him.'

'I see. So you were with Monsieur de Sartine?'

'That's true,' said Sartine himself. 'I was woken and received him. I think I told you about it. It was on the night of 30 April to 1 May, at half past midnight: the clock in my study had just struck. At what hour do you place the crime?'

'The murderer could not have been at your house before two o'clock in the morning.'

Nicolas was thinking. He remembered something that Monsieur de Noblecourt had said: a stopped clock shows the exact time twice a day.

'Who admitted Lastire?'

'My old valet. You know him.'

'Was your visitor waiting for you in the study?'

'Yes, but I don't see—'

'So he may have had access to your clock?'

'Of course!'

'Does it strike the half-hour?'

'Yes, but I still don't understand where—'

'I understand perfectly well! I observe that at that time of night, one stroke may mean half past midnight, one o'clock, or half past one. We may never know if a perfidious finger slowed down the movement. Or rather we will just have to question whichever of your servants has the task of rewinding it. I am sure of the answer.'

Sartine seemed petrified. Nicolas took the medallion from his pocket. It was hanging from a chain, and he swung it to and fro. Then everything started moving quickly. Lastire leapt to his feet, strode up to Nicolas, struck him in the face with one hand, tore the medallion from him with the other, stamped on it, then picked it up and threw it in the fire. All this happened in such a short period of time that the stunned onlookers were unable to intervene. The first to rise was Sartine, but no sooner had he done so than the chevalier took a pistol from his shirt front, waved it threateningly at them, retreated towards the door, flung it open and rushed out.

'Don't move!' screamed Nicolas, who was getting to his feet, blood pouring from his nose. 'My men are well prepared. He won't get away!'

Muted sounds reached them, then a great silence, followed by confused bursts of voices and two almost simultaneous shots, and again silence. Finally, the door slowly opened and Bourdeau came in, hesitantly, a trickle of blood running down the side of his forehead. He had to sit down. The commissioner rushed to him.

'He tried to jump out of the window. I made to stop him and he threatened me with his weapon. We fired almost simultaneously. He missed me … or rather, a bullet just grazed the edge of my skull. Mine on the other hand did its work, and he fell backwards into the courtyard. He was a tough character!'

'Truly,' said La Vrillière, 'this house is cursed.'

Everyone was silent while Nicolas took off his coat, tore a sleeve of his shirt and began bandaging the head of the inspector who, although touched by his concern, pushed him away gently. Monsieur de La Vrillière ran to a drinks cabinet and filled two glasses with a greenish liquid which he handed to them.

Everyone resumed his place.

'One question, my dear Nicolas,' said Lenoir. 'What about the medallion? I assume that was a trap set for Lastire, I mean Hénéfiance?'

'You are correct, Monseigneur. In fact, what he did not know was that this object, supposedly discovered in the crates belonging to the real Chevalier de Lastire, did not exist. There was a copper and glass box that contained nothing. I can imagine what was going through his mind: had he overlooked the medallion when he went through Lastire's effects, which had doubtless been left in storage in Pondicherry when the latter set off on his mission to Haider Ali in Mysore?'

'He might have assumed that the medallion was not in the luggage.'

'I think he sensed a trap. After all, I might have discovered this evidence in France.'

'But … but …' stammered La Vrillière, 'in that case, he ought not to have reacted at all. That merely proved he was indeed the person he was claiming to be.'

'No, because, as the ultimate argument, I had in my possession—'

he took from the pocket of his coat a small oval snuffbox with a pastel miniature on the lid – 'a genuine portrait of the chevalier found with some jewels deposited with his notary before his departure for the Indies. I think you will agree ...' He held it out to them.

'... that Lastire didn't look anything like Hénéfiance!' cried Lenoir.

'That's why he stuck desperately to his assertions, convinced he would get away with it. What I said about the clock was not evidence. Whereas, faced with this object, the truth was unavoidable: if he wasn't Lastire, whose portrait we had, he could only be Hénéfiance. Just one thing remains to be determined. How did he manage to outwit the Minister of the Navy?'

Nicolas was enjoying his little revenge for Sartine's blindness.

'That remains a mystery,' he went on. 'He must have had a particularly powerful guarantor to impress a magistrate as wise as you, Monseigneur! I can't imagine who.'

'There's no point in asking the question, this enigma will not be solved,' said Sartine, watched closely by a pensive La Vrillière. 'I admit that I was deceived. I didn't even ask for his service record. But others would have been deceived, too. Anyway, all that is now happily resolved. I am glad I was able to help with this delicate investigation. The talent of my men can easily be seen in your actions.'

Nicolas said nothing. If you enjoyed the pleasure of Sartine's company, this bad faith of his was something you just had to accept. Only the President of the Parlement, de Saujac, could rival him in this practice.

'Very well, then,' grunted La Vrillière. 'What are we to do with Caminet? The culprit is dead, so there need be no legal proceedings. We shall have to keep the whole thing secret, because, from whichever end we approach this case, starting with Sartine being deceived and finishing with the guilty party being discovered in Rue de Vendôme, near ... No need to say more, or we shall have to mention some formidable names ... I propose that, as far as the apprentice is concerned, we charge him with cheating and brawling and let the law take its course. We shall give our Criminal Lieutenant, Testard du Lys, instructions to bring everything to a swift conclusion. After all, the young fellow is very lucky not to be charged with complicity in murder.'

'Nicolas,' asked Lenoir, 'what are your last thoughts on Hénéfiance?'

'I think, Monseigneur, that misfortune and injustice can plunge a man into the darkest despair, which can lead to a hard heart and a desire for revenge. Hénéfiance was both victim and executioner. What might he have accomplished if he had used his shrewd brain in the service of good? May God grant him forgiveness. That's all I can say.'

'One last question. Those boots and gloves of a leather so thick as to withstand a cobra's bite, where were they from?'

'From the Indies. I showed them to Dr Semacgus, who examined them carefully. He recognised elephant hide.'

'That completes the collection,' growled Sartine. 'Rabbits, a cobra and now an elephant!'

EPILOGUE

From 5 June to 19 June 1775

Now that the unrest was over, the time for the coronation had come. On 5 June, the Court moved to Compiègne, where, for the first time, Louis de Ranreuil attended a boar hunt as a page and had the joy of supplying his father with a horse. Nicolas had been given the task by the Duc de La Vrillière of ensuring security during the various moves and ceremonies. On the evening after the hunt, the King summoned him to his apartments to take delivery of his report on the circumstances surrounding May's events. He sat down and, spectacles in his hand, went through the document with tense concentration. He sat motionless for a long time after this reading, then looked a little to the side of Nicolas and addressed him.

'I thank you, Monsieur. This is most enlightening. But I have no desire for my reign to open with an act of severity. Those wretches from 11 May are enough … There are balances it is better not to upset …' He threw the papers in the hearth and watched them burn. 'Continue serving me well, you and your son. I saw him this afternoon. And always tell me the truth, whatever the cost to you, or to me … You may go, Monsieur.'

Nicolas bowed and kissed the hand the King held out.

The royal procession traditionally went through the estates of the first Merovingian kings: Villers-Cotterêts, Fismes and Soissons. The Queen and her entourage took the Chemin des Dames. Nicolas, on horseback, galloped close to the King's carriage, and the King sometimes leant out of the window to chat to him. As for Louis, he was travelling with his fellow pages in the Maréchal de Richelieu's suite. The weather was gorgeous and the road unrecognisable, having been swept, sanded and decked with flowers by peasants performing statute labour: they would be the last, as Turgot was preparing to abolish the practice. Nicolas noted in passing that the price of bread was still very high everywhere, but was glad to see that the unrest had petered out. The Bercheny Hussars, commanded by Monsieur de Viomesnil, were patrolling, prepared for any eventuality. The fact that the coronation had to be protected by these troops caused much murmuring.

On Friday 9 June, the King entered Reims in his ceremonial coach at the head of an endless procession of carriages and horsemen of the King's Household in full dress uniform. Fanfares sounded, soon joined by the great bell of the cathedral. Welcomed on the square before the cathedral by the archbishop, Monseigneur de la Roche-Aymon, and the clergy, the King entered the shrine to hear the first prayers.

The next day, Nicolas paid his respects to the Queen, who was receiving in her excessively small apartment in the archbishop's palace. She was so charming and engaging that she reminded him of her mother Maria Theresa. The crush of visitors was overwhelming in the first heat of summer. The Comte d'Artois, who was present, was joking in a carefree tone and whispering in the ears of the ladies, while his brother Provence looked on disapprovingly.

The same day, Nicolas had time to take Louis to a park in the city to see a female elephant that was drawing the crowds with her graceful tricks. She uncorked and drank from a bottle, demonstrating both skill and intelligence. Louis's joy and enthusiasm reminded him that his son was still little more than a child. The King attended the coronation vespers and heard the sermon given by the Bishop of Aix, in which he stated that France could only perish through her failings, and that if she stayed as she ought to be, she would be the arbiter of the world and bring it happiness.

Late that night, Nicolas was summoned by the First Groom of the King's Bedchamber, Monsieur Thierry. He dressed in haste in the poky little room he had been assigned near the royal apartment. He found the monarch in the company of the captain of the guards. Together, they drove to the basilica of Saint-Rémi, where the King, who was dressed simply in a brown coat and a round hat, wished to pray on the eve of his coronation. He was silent on the journey. The basilica was humming with the chants of monks. The King knelt and spent the next two hours in prayer. When he stood up again, he appeared transfigured. He looked at Nicolas, who had emerged from the shadows to follow him, as if seeing him for the first time. He held out his hand.

'Monsieur, I shall never forget that you are beside me this evening. You were my grandfather's, now be entirely mine.'

The following day, 11 June, Trinity Sunday, the bishops of Laon and Soissons knocked at the door of the King's bedchamber. Twice they called him and twice the answer came: 'The King is asleep.' The third request was different: 'We ask for Louis, whom God gave us as our king,' and the door opened. In a long silver lace jacket, and supported by the two prelates, he was conducted to the cathedral and sat down in an armchair beneath a canopy decorated with fleurs-de-lis that hung from the vaulted ceiling. Nicolas took his place beside the Epistle in a magnificent white coat, a masterpiece by Master Vachon. He was awe-struck by the spectacle before him: the Queen's carved and gilded rostrum, the rows of benches and the spaces between the columns filled to the brim with ladies glittering with diamonds, the throne, mounted on a false gallery, where the King would take his place. The finest tapestries from the royal depository had been draped over the walls, completing the pomp and splendour of the decoration.

After the *Veni Creator*, the King, with his hands on the Gospels, took the three traditional oaths. The archbishop buckled the sword of Charlemagne on him and the Comte de Provence attached his spurs. The prior of Saint-Rémi opened the Holy Ampulla and handed it to the archbishop who, with a gold needle, took from it a drop the size of a grain of wheat, which he mixed with holy oil. The King lay down flat on the ground, the archbishop beside him despite his age. Then he got up on his knees to receive the six unctions on the flesh, his jacket and camisole having been opened. The ring was blessed and put on. The King received his sceptre and the hand of justice, and the archbishop took the crown and held it over his head, crying, 'May God crown you with this crown of glory and justice.' He then lowered it onto the King's head, and the twelve peers, both lay and ecclesiastical, laid their hands on it, as if forming the spokes of a symbolic wheel.

Now that Louis XVI had been crowned, the moment had come for the enthronement. He was clothed in the royal cloak, adorned with an ermine sash strewn with fleurs-de-lis, with a long tail under which he wore a tunic and a dalmatic. With his crown on his head, and holding the sceptre and the hand of justice, he was led ceremoniously to the throne overlooking the audience. The great doors were opened, the people entered, the trumpets sounded, doves were released, salvoes echoed outside, and the bells pealed out. Cheers from countless voices rose in jubilation, carrying up to the vault the acclamation of 'Long live the King!' The archbishop joined his cry to that of the crowd and began the *Te Deum*.

Once again, the King appeared to Nicolas transfigured, borne aloft by an unalloyed joy. There emanated from his whole person a new authority and gravity. The Queen burst into sobs. Tears overwhelmed Nicolas. The memory of the sad evening when the body of Louis XV had been transferred to Saint-Denis was fading. The coronation seemed to bring the time of misfortune to an end. The monarchy to which he had devoted his life was continuing. Down there, at the foot of the throne, he saw his son, face flushed with pride, in the livery of the King's Household and, further on, among the ambassadors, Naganda in a long multicoloured cloak of feathers and pearls, standing in a hieratic pose and gazing in wonderment at the scene. Suddenly a hand came to rest on his shoulder. He turned and saw Aimée d'Arranet in a great Court cloak. With a smile, she bent her head tenderly towards him. The sky was clearing and his heart felt free. It seemed to him that a new life was beginning for him, and he suddenly believed in the possibility of happiness.

Ivry – Glane – Rome – La Bretesche
March 2004 – May 2005

NOTES

CHAPTER I

1. Querelle: both the name and the case are genuine.
2. See *The Nicolas Le Floch Affair*.
3. At the time, French was considered the universal language for respectable people in Europe.
4. Kaunitz: chancellor of the Austrian empire.

CHAPTER II

1. Duke of Rifferda (1690–1737): a Dutchman in the service of the King of Spain. Disgraced in 1726.
2. Mesdames: the daughters of Louis XV.

CHAPTER III

1. Phalanx: see *The Saint-Florentin Murders*, Chapter VIII.
2. *Flee, star...*: a chorus from Rameau's opera-ballet *Les Indes Galantes*.
3. Huascar, etc.: characters from *Les Indes Galantes*.
4. Magistrato Camerale: president of the Chamber of Finances in Lombardy under Austrian rule.
5. See *The Châtelet Apprentice*.
6. This incident is based on real events that took place near Auxonne, Burgundy, in 1775.
7. See *The Nicolas Le Floch Affair*.

CHAPTER IV

1. Seventy-two *livres*: about fifty-four euros.

2. Art objects: the Bibliothèque Nationale in Paris still has some of these. Bertin's natural history cabinet is now part of the Queen of England's collection.

3. Usual informant: regular readers of this series will recognise the Duc de Richelieu, an old friend of Monsieur de Noblecourt's.

4. Abbé Galiani (1728–87): man of letters, the author of dialogues about the grain trade in which he attacked the economists.

5. Antiquarian: at the time, an expert on the Ancient World and an interpreter of inscriptions.

6. See *The Phantom of Rue Royale*.

CHAPTER V

1. See *The Nicolas Le Floch Affair*.

2. The image is borrowed from the writer Louis-Antoine Caraccioli (1721–1803).

3. A melody by Albinoni: the reader may recall that Monsieur de Sartine owned a musical wig library.

4. Giulio Alberoni (1664–1752): Italian cardinal and prime minister to Philip V of Spain.

CHAPTER VI

1. *Grandig*: in a bad mood. A provincial Austrian term known to have been used by Marie Antoinette. The word used today would be *grantig*.

2. Monsieur de Vaucanson: see *The Saint-Florentin Murders*.

3. 'The Louvre': the last fenced enclosure of the palace.

4. This is a translation of the actual text of the King's letter.

CHAPTER VII

1. See *The Châtelet Apprentice*.

2. The good lady of Choisy: Madame de Pompadour.

3. Married women: anything concerning the sacred institution of

marriage was considered extremely serious.

CHAPTER VIII

1. The hermit of Ferney: Voltaire.
2. De Gévigland: see *The Saint-Florentin Murders*.

CHAPTER IX

1. It was not until 1784 that the school for pages and their accommodation were installed in premises belonging to the royal stables.
2. This is a translation of the actual text of Louis XVI's letter to Lenoir.
3. Mirlavaud: see *The Nicolas Le Floch Affair*.
4. Le Prévôt de Beaumont: both the character and his story are authentic. He was finally freed on 5 September 1789, after the fall of the Bastille, having spent twenty-one years in prison. He wrote about his experiences in a book entitled *Le Prisonnier d'État*.
5. This is a quotation from Racine's play *Athalie* (Act III, Scene 4) with Le Prévôt's name substituted for that of the character Josabet.
6. See *The Man with the Lead Stomach*.
7. See *The Nicolas Le Floch Affair*.

CHAPTER X

1. Isle de France: Mauritius.
2. *Gittani*: gypsies, who were believed at the time to come from Egypt.
3. Bastille: see *The Châtelet Apprentice*.
4. I am indebted to Philippe Jarnoux and his fine work *Survivre au bagne de Brest* (2003) for these details.
5. Pineapples: see *The Saint-Florentin Murders*.
6. This recipe is taken from the book *L'Ancienne Alsace* (1877) by Charles Gérard.
7. Duc de Beaufort: François de Bourbon, grandson of Henri IV, dubbed 'the king of the markets' during the rebellion known as the

Fronde.

8. See the Memoirs of the Prince de Ligne.

CHAPTER XI

1. See *The Saint-Florentin Murders*.
2. The Comte de Saint-Florentin, Duc de La Vrillière, was a minister for fifty years.
3. Translations of genuine texts from 1775.
4. These remarks were in fact made by Voltaire.
5. Makassin: the moccasin, a poisonous snake from North America.
6. See *The Phantom of Rue Royale*.

CHAPTER XII

1. Silenus: a forest deity, the foster-father of Dionysus.
2. See *The Saint-Florentin Murders*.
3. See *The Saint-Florentin Murders*.

ACKNOWLEDGEMENTS

First, I wish to express my gratitude, as always, to Isabelle Tujague for devoting such care, and so much of her free time, to preparing the final version of the text. I am also grateful to Monique Constant, Conservateur Général du Patrimoine, for her encouragement over a long period, to Maurice Roisse, for his tireless checking of my manuscripts, and to my publisher and his colleagues for their friendship, loyalty and support.